GORGEOUS AS *Sin*

SUSAN JOHNSON

BERKLEY SENSATION, NEW YORK

THE BERKLEY PUBLISHING GROUP
Published by the Penguin Group
Penguin Group (USA) Inc.
375 Hudson Street, New York, New York 10014, USA

Penguin Group (Canada), 90 Eglinton Avenue East, Suite 700, Toronto, Ontario M4P 2Y3, Canada
(a division of Pearson Penguin Canada Inc.)
Penguin Books Ltd., 80 Strand, London WC2R 0RL, England
Penguin Group Ireland, 25 St. Stephen's Green, Dublin 2, Ireland (a division of Penguin Books Ltd.)
Penguin Group (Australia), 250 Camberwell Road, Camberwell, Victoria 3124, Australia
(a division of Pearson Australia Group Pty. Ltd.)
Penguin Books India Pvt. Ltd., 11 Community Centre, Panchsheel Park, New Delhi—110 017, India
Penguin Group (NZ), 67 Apollo Drive, Rosedale, North Shore 0632, New Zealand
(a division of Pearson New Zealand Ltd.)
Penguin Books (South Africa) (Pty.) Ltd., 24 Sturdee Avenue, Rosebank, Johannesburg 2196,
South Africa

Penguin Books Ltd., Registered Offices: 80 Strand, London WC2R 0RL, England

This is a work of fiction. Names, characters, places, and incidents either are the product of the author's imagination or are used fictitiously, and any resemblance to actual persons, living or dead, business establishments, events, or locales is entirely coincidental. The publisher does not have any control over and does not assume any responsibility for author or third-party websites or their content.

GORGEOUS AS SIN

A Berkley Sensation Book / published by arrangement with the author

PRINTING HISTORY
Berkley Sensation mass-market edition / March 2009

Copyright © 2009 by Susan Johnson.
Excerpt from *Sexy as Hell* copyright © 2009 by Susan Johnson.
Cover art by Aleta Rafton.
Cover design by Diana Kolsky.
Interior text design by Laura K. Corless.

ISBN: 978-0-425-22681-0

BERKLEY® SENSATION
Berkley Sensation Books are published by The Berkley Publishing Group,
a division of Penguin Group (USA) Inc.,
375 Hudson Street, New York, New York 10014.
BERKLEY® SENSATION and the "B" design are trademarks of Penguin Group (USA) Inc.

PRINTED IN THE UNITED STATES OF AMERICA

10 9 8 7 6 5 4 3

CHAPTER 1

London, August 1891

PROSPER HUTCHINSON, THE barrister of choice for London's wealthy, rose from his chair to greet the tall, handsome aristocrat walking through his door. "At last, Your Grace." He'd sent the duke a message five days ago.

"I was in the country." The Duke of Groveland stripped off his tan riding gloves as he crossed the sumptuous Axminster carpet custom-made for the imposing corner office overlooking Piccadilly Square.

"Yes, I know." The duke was entertaining his newest paramour while her husband was shooting in Scotland. Everyone knew.

An easy smile graced the duke's fine features. "Don't glower so, Hutchinson. I eventually arrived, and admit it— your messages *always* smack of crisis."

"*This* crisis could cost you a fortune."

"How much of a fortune?" George Montagu Fitz-Robbins Monckton calmly asked, tossing his gloves on Hutchinson's large, ornate desk and taking a seat across from his barrister.

"Ninety thousand." The portly barrister dropped into his chair with a grimace.

The duke arrested his slide into a lounging pose, his dark brows rising faintly. "That much."

"Perhaps more should your plans for Monckton Row come to naught because Mrs. St. Vincent won't sell."

"Mrs. St. Vincent? A theatrical name or"—a smile quirked his lips—"a female of a certain profession?" Apparently over his initial surprise at the sum quoted by his barrister, the duke unbuttoned his fawn-colored silk tweed jacket, stretched out his jodhpur-clad legs, and rested his head against the tufted green leather some decorator had chosen for Hutchinson's office chairs.

"She is rather a lady of a certain *obstinacy*, Your Grace," Prosper Hutchinson grumbled, rapping his fingertips on his desktop to emphasize his displeasure. "All the other properties east of Berkeley Square have been purchased, but with Mrs. St. Vincent standing in your way, your ninety thousand is at risk. The very mulish lady has asserted that she has no intention of *ever* selling. She told me your grace may go to Hades for all she cares."

"She did, did she? You spoke to her?" As a rule, Hutchinson didn't take part in purchase negotiations. He employed twenty barristers to take care of such matters.

"I had to." Hutchinson leaned forward over his paunch to underscore his vexation. "The troublesome female had flatly refused five of our offers. And I'd sent my very best men." The barrister picked up a gold filigreed letter opener, held it between his fingertips, and gazed at it for a moment, pursed lipped. Then he looked up, met the duke's languid gaze, and said ruefully, "You might as well hear it from me first, Your Grace. Apparently Mrs. St. Vincent disapproves of—I believe her words were 'Odious, prodigal scoundrels who think their titles and wealth give them carte blanche in the world.'"

The duke looked amused. "It seems the lady is of a socialist bent."

"I rather think her remark was of a more personal

nature." Groveland's reputation for prodigality and dissipation was well known.

"She isn't the first woman to disapprove of me," the duke casually returned, his indifference to censure a marked trait. "But a female who's not susceptible to your bank drafts"—a note of drollery colored his words—"now that's a first, isn't it, Hutchinson?"

"Yes, Your Grace." Groveland's female entanglements occasionally required the barrister's intercession to amiably end an affair. And to date, bank drafts had always proved effective.

"So what now?" A soft, unruffled query. In the duke's experience, the world generally bent to his will. It wasn't hubris, just a recognition of reality. He was illustriously titled, the bearer of an enormous fortune, and for what it was worth—in matters of seduction more than anything—blessed with the Montagu dark good looks.

"We are at an impasse unless you wish to increase your offer substantially. I didn't feel I had the authority to do so without speaking to you and explaining the unfortunate situation."

The twenty-third Duke of Groveland pursed his lips. "Substantially you say."

"I'm afraid so, Your Grace. The woman is obstinate to a fare-thee-well and in my estimation outrageously so for someone in her circumstances."

Groveland's grey gaze turned razor sharp. "What circumstances?"

"Her husband left her all but destitute when he died. From all appearances she is eking out a living. She resides above the bookstore, which is a saving, of course, but really, she should be exceedingly grateful for your generous offer rather than refusing it out of hand." Leaning back in his chair, Hutchinson softly sighed. "Women, Your Grace. Quite irrational creatures."

Now the duke knew women better than most. In fact he had outstripped all previous records apropos the number of females who had fallen prey to his charms. And gentlemen's clubs were partial to keeping such scores. Seduction was a major amusement for Groveland—some said...his avocation. It was only natural he would say, "Why don't you leave her to me, Hutchinson. I have had some luck with convincing women to, ah...accommodate me."

Forgetting his consequence for a moment, Hutchinson exhaled loudly and blurted out, "I was hoping you might take a hand. The lady is beyond my capabilities, and I'll admit, I haven't felt such frustration in a decade or more. I never lose, sir—you know that. It's intensely disconcerting to acknowledge defeat."

"Nonsense, Hutchinson. You have no reason to feel defeated. Haven't you masterfully acquired every piece of property I've ever wanted? Of course you have. This woman may be irrational or addled in some way—particularly," he added with a faint smile, "if she's a socialist. Her personal biases are certainly not your fault. Let me talk to her, and then we'll see where we stand."

"Since her shop is on the corner, it's a pivotal piece in the architect's plan," the barrister pointed out, his shaggy brows knotting in a scowl.

"Perhaps Mrs. St. Vincent knows as much. She may have spoken to some of the other property owners who sold to us. She may feel she now holds the winning hand."

Another grim scowl. "If so, I wish you well, Your Grace."

"Come, enough long faces." The duke nodded at the liquor trolley behind Hutchinson's desk; a Scotsman was never far from his drink. "Pour me a whiskey and tell me what you know about the properties you've already acquired."

Since he'd cajoled Clarissa into leaving Green Grove and seen her comfortably settled at Frances Knolly's country house party, the duke was currently free of encumbrances. And frankly, after a fortnight with Clarissa, no matter how heated and exotic the sex, he'd been ready to transfer her into someone else's care. His capacity for boredom was slight, a defect no doubt of a life free of restraints. He'd been indulged from the cradle save for by his father, and when the former duke had had the good grace to drink himself to death before George could kill him, the title had devolved to the young heir. Despite his youth, the twenty-third Duke of Groveland had found the larger world equally amenable to his wishes.

Although no one but his mother dared call him George. Since he loved her unconditionally and she him, he even allowed her to call him Georgie on occasion. To the world, however, he was Groveland or Your Grace; to his friends he was Fitz or The Monk, while his lovers generally called him *darling* with great enthusiasm and affection.

Surely he could charm one woman into accepting his offer—particularly a destitute female. Accepting his glass from Hutchinson, he listened while the barrister explained in some detail the entire litany of recent property purchased for what would soon become Monckton Row—God willing and Groveland's cultivated charm gainfully applied.

When Hutchinson's recitation came to an end, the duke held out his glass for a refill. "Now, tell me what to expect from this curious woman. If she's a widow, she must not be in her first blush. And I gather she isn't a lady of the night or an actress. Would she be predisposed to some small gift—flowers, candy, a bit of jewelry perhaps? You're certain, too, she knows who I am."

"I assume so, Your Grace," Hutchinson replied, pouring a goodly bumper of whiskey into the outstretched glass. "She cited you by name as she consigned you to Hades. As to her age, she's not young, but she's not old; she has reddish hair and is above-average height, I believe," the barrister explained like a man without an ounce of the Lothario in his soul—a man incapable of describing his wife or daughters without a photograph in hand. "In terms of a gift, I confess, sir, you might know about that better than I." Groveland was not called The Monk without express and explicit irony.

"Is there anything about her deceased husband or her background that might be useful for me to know? The bookshop is a relatively recent addition to the neighborhood if I'm not mistaken." He often walked by it en route to Bond Street.

"It's been there almost seven years, Your Grace. Edward St. Vincent was a poet of some small fame thanks to the Queen's interest in his work, but apparently he was a gamester as well and not a very good one. There were rumors about his death—that he may have taken a hand in ending his life, but it's impossible to know, of course. Not that losses at cards aren't often a precursor to self-destruction. We all know such instances.

"As for the widow herself, she is of respectable birth. She enjoys the title, the Honorable Rosalind Pitt-Riverston, but her family is without fortune. Her father, Baron Pitt-Riverston, dabbles in the natural sciences I've been told. In some remote area of Yorkshire, I believe."

"So she is not a working-class female."

"No. On the contrary. She exudes an air of hauteur."

Groveland's eyes narrowed slightly. "You don't say." He lifted the glass to his mouth and drank down the whiskey as if it might better clarify his thoughts.

"Indeed, I do," Hutchinson retorted with a decided sniff. "I was sent on my way with the most high-handed arrogance."

"Hmm. Audacious *and* difficult."

Hutchinson grunted. "A vast understatement, Your Grace."

The duke held out his empty glass. "One more of your fine whiskeys and then I will take myself off to reconnoiter the formidable opposition."

But as it turned out, when the duke exited Hutchinson's faux-Renaissance office block, he ran into Viscount Islay.

"Hi-ho, Fitz!" the viscount cried. "I hear you're rid of Clarissa. What say you to a game at Brooks's?"

"Christ, gossip travels fast." He'd just left Clarissa three hours ago.

"Margot Beaton stopped by to see my sister as I was leaving home. She was just down from Knolly's country house party. She despises Clarissa by the way."

"Most women do," the duke replied drily.

"And most men don't."

Groveland raised his dark brows in sportive rejoinder. "But then Clarissa exerts herself to please men."

"How much did she exert herself for you?" the viscount quipped.

"She wore me out, hence my rustication in the city. And I'd be more than happy to take some of your money at Brooks's," the duke said with a smile, uninterested in discussing Clarissa after a fortnight in her company.

Freddie Mackenzie grinned. "You can try, you mean."

"But not very hard as I recall?"

Freddie was sober, however, so he paid attention to his cards and taking his money required a degree more concentration than normal for Fitz. But the duke was as lucky at cards as he was with women and ultimately he prospered for having met the viscount.

In the course of their play, the men met several other of their friends, one thing led to another, and it was well after midnight when Fitz stood under Brooks's portico, inhaling the tepid night air and debating his options. There were numerous ladies more than willing to welcome him to their beds despite the hour, but after only recently escaping Clarissa he wasn't particularly in the mood to play amorous games. Clarissa could suck the life out of a twenty-year-old stud, not to mention her propensity for banal conversation took away one's taste—at least temporarily—for vapid female company.

Her acrobatic abilities aside, he should have sent her home a week ago.

Had he been less polite perhaps he wouldn't now be beset by ennui and indecision.

He abruptly shrugged, having long ago decided that regret was a useless commodity. Bidding a friendly goodnight to Crawford, the seemingly immortal doorman, he took the stairs in a leap and strolled away toward Berkeley Square and home.

Tomorrow he would meet with the intractable Mrs. St. Vincent.

He much preferred tomorrows to yesterdays in any event—his life predicated on the maxim *Never look back*. A reaction perhaps to a complicated, chaotic childhood.

And truth be told, he was looking forward to the confrontation—discussion, negotiation . . . whatever his encounter with Mrs. St. Vincent entailed.

He was rather of the mind that he would win the day, though.

Didn't he always?

CHAPTER 2

WHILE THE DUKE of Groveland was making his way home through the gaslit streets of Mayfair, Rosalind St. Vincent was seated at her writing table, nibbling at her penholder, trying to dredge up a synonym for *penis* that she hadn't already used a million times. Not that she had the leisure to deliberate for long when the next installment of *Lady Blessington's Harem Adventure* was scheduled for the printer in the morning and she still had ten pages to write.

Why not the eunuch's *golden horn*? The story took place in Constantinople, after all; she rather liked the play on words. And the eunuch wasn't really a eunuch—a nice little plot twist if she said so herself.

But not half as nice as the lucrative erotica market that her well-mannered, cultivated husband had discovered. Not that she had known about Edward's alternate writing career until after his death when she'd discovered the manuscripts in his armoire. In the course of searching for something suitable in which to bury him, she'd found the neatly tied volumes hidden behind his coats, each cover page bearing a notation of the sum realized for the work.

She'd been shocked, both by the discovery *and* the substantial proceeds such stories commanded. Erotica appeared to be considerably more profitable than poetry.

While Edward had been lauded and feted when his first poems had been published and he'd savored his celebrity, it had soon become apparent that fame was fleeting and the earnings from his verse would not long sustain a household.

Of course, Edward's unfortunate addiction to gaming had also contributed to their financial problems. As did his unfortunate lack of initiative. *And* his guileless propensity to befriend unsavory characters. He was gulled by swindlers and artful dodges on more occasions than she wished to recall—always by men he'd perceived as bosom compatriots.

She'd always forgiven him, though. He was so sweet and naive.

Perhaps they both had been at one time.

But someone had had to overcome youthful innocence and see the world with clarity. That task, by default, had fallen to her, and she'd mustered the wherewithal to face their challenges. She'd managed to garner enough from Edward's successful second edition of *Yorkshire Memories* to purchase the bookstore and in doing so had kept them solvent.

Immediately setting about to learn the trade, she'd asked questions and took advice from any successful merchant who was willing to respond to her queries. She'd also studied the prosperous bookstores in the city, noting which business practices, displays, and public readings drew the most customers. Very quickly—since their funds were limited—she'd mastered the necessary aspects of bookselling and merchandising. To those tried and true principles, she'd added particular elements of interest to her: a free library for the working poor, a small gallery where women artists could show their work, a Saturday evening reading group open to all. She also kept a steaming samovar on a table near the doorway so customers could help themselves to tea when they walked in.

The bookstore had granted them a modest living. But coming as they did from families of moderate means, they were well acquainted with living simply. While Rosalind had concentrated on managing the bookstore, Edward had written and published poems and, unbeknownst to her, authored the auxiliary works that had rendered him funds for gambling.

There had been times during the years of their marriage when she'd felt overwhelmed. Their financial resources were always stretched thin. But she'd never long succumbed to desolation—a testament perhaps to her father's hearty spirits and her mother's optimistic nature, which she'd inherited. Her mother had served as helpmate and inspiration to her father, who had spent a life engaged in scientific research. Eschewing fame and monetary recompense, he'd been intent on the pure joy of discovery.

So she'd fully understood Edward's passion for poetry; she'd even sympathized with his fascination for gambling. She had only wished he might have been luckier at the tables. And slightly less moody. Stronger.

But they had both been so young when they married. Young and full of dreams.

She'd wondered more than once if he'd accidently fallen into the Thames that stormy night or whether he'd jumped from Westminster Bridge.

Her unconscious sigh shattered the silence, jerking her back to reality and her fast-approaching deadline.

She glanced at the clock. Two fifteen.

She put pen to paper, the nib fairly flying over the page. She didn't have time for maudlin introspection or reflection on what might have been. She had to finish ten pages by eight in the morning. And that was that.

She was paid by the page.

It was piecework, pure and simple—like a seamstress who was compensated for the number of garments she completed in a day.

Rosalind smiled.

This was easier.

She'd never learned to sew despite her mother's best efforts to make her a genteel young lady who could embroider her husband's slippers or sew a fine seam. Fortunately her father had taken her side and she'd studied his favorite subjects instead: botany, anthropology, history, Latin, and Greek.

Even more fortunately, she'd quite by accident forged a new market for her steamy novels. Her publisher was ecstatic—his delight measured in increased fortune for her and less agreeably in persistent demands that she write faster.

Her stories ran counter to the accepted male narrative of domination bolstered by various fantastic devices with which to restrain female characters. Not that she was averse to an occasional bondage scene. After all, their bookstore had always sold books by Anonymous that were kept behind a screen in a back room. The risqué books and magazines bound in innocuous bindings had generated excellent sales.

But when she'd first undertaken the task of continuing Edward's secret work, she'd instinctively penned tales appealing to her feminine sensibilities. Almost instantly, word of mouth had translated into a tidal wave of eager customers. Women readers, a major component of the bookstore's customer base as well, had quickly heard of her writing—not that they knew it was *hers*—and had taken to indulging themselves in sexual fantasies tailored to female imaginations and passions.

Not that her male customers were averse to purchasing the weekly magazines that published her books in serial chapters. Mr. Edding's *Facts and Fantasy* was a typical example of the cheap serial fiction that boomed after the abolition of the Newspaper Stamp Tax in 1855. But what increased the volume of her readership so remarkably was the additional female audience.

Perhaps it shouldn't have been so surprising. It was, after all, an era of sweeping social changes, many of them specifically directed toward women's rights. There was increasing ferment for women's suffrage, and reforms in marriage, divorce, and inheritance laws had over the past fifty years broadened the scope of female self-determination. Women could now sue for divorce, gain custody of their children, retain control over their own property—not easily, but it could be done. Women were, on the whole, leading much more complex and productive lives.

Female artists were coming to prominence as well in exhibitions previously closed to them. Sexual issues, unrelated to chauvinist bias, were being researched for the first time, and the studies were being published in the burgeoning field of psychology both in England and on the Continent. Radicals, socialists, and feminists had come together in the Men and Women's Club to debate, dispute, converse, and expound upon the sexual issues of the day even while the vast public barely noticed. The government's policies directed at mass education had given rise to unprecedented numbers of readers hungry for knowledge and entertainment. And with the advent of the typewriter, more and more women were entering the workforce, domestic service no longer the sole occupation open to females of lesser rank. Also, universities had begun enrolling women, albeit in limited numbers, and those pioneering females were unprecedentedly taking firsts at Oxford and Cambridge.

In some small measure, her stories ran parallel to contemporary women's pursuit of liberty and freedom in all areas of life. Not that women were free from their corseted, high-collared, straitlaced world of patriarchy, puritanism, and prejudice, but critical change was in the air.

And with it, a crisis of masculinity had begun.

Enough, enough! She had no time for musing.

Her piecework had to be finished.

She smiled. If her stories continued to sell well, someday she might actually *visit* Constantinople.

She wiggled her toes in her slippers, shoved a heavy fall of auburn hair from her forehead, and bent to her task.

Should Lady Blessington sigh or scream in orgasmic ecstasy?

The erstwhile eunuch was very well endowed—*very* well, indeed.

She rather thought Lady Blessington might scream, she decided, her pen once again racing over the page.

Rosalind didn't look up again until the last page was complete, the newest chapter conveniently coming to an orgasmic conclusion. Then she checked the time, smiled, and stretched leisurely.

Six. She had a sufficient interval in which to bathe, dress, and breakfast before carrying her manuscript to Bond Street and turning it over to Mr. Edding. His stationery shop was *tres* fashionable; only the best clientele ordered their monogrammed writing materials from him. And he looked so very unlike a publisher of bawdy literature that her anxiety about having her secret occupation exposed was minimal.

MR. EDDING LITERALLY rubbed his hands in delight when she walked through the doorway of his shop at eight. "What a pleasure to see you, Mrs. St. Vincent!" he exclaimed. "We are *most* anxious for your new chapter. You'll be pleased to hear that the circulation has increased to six thousand copies! I hope you may find the time to increase your production. Perhaps add another serial for our little periodical." He put up his hand. "I know, I know, your business requires attention as well. But, my dear lady, if you would be amenable to an increase in your wages— say double the amount—you could hire someone to oversee your shop and satisfy your readers in the process."

"Why don't I see what I can do, Mr. Edding." Rosalind refrained from showing her excitement as she handed him her manuscript. *Double! Good Lord!* Perhaps she might be free of debt soon if she could write faster. Not only did the bookstore require constant funds to maintain its inventory, but her free library and Saturday reading group that offered tea and sandwiches for those less fortunate were also substantial expenses.

In addition, there remained a balance due on Edward's funeral. It had cost dearly, but she'd wanted her husband buried in a fashionable cemetery with an elegant, tasteful headstone to mark his grave, and such tangibles had come at no small price. "Your generous offer is welcome, of course," she blandly murmured as if she were generally indifferent to finances when, in fact, she was dancing with delight in her imagination.

"Good. Might I have another chapter of *Lady Blessington's Harem Adventure* in a week and perhaps the first chapter of a second series as well?"

She repressed a gasp, and her voice indicated only the veriest agitation when she spoke. "I would need more time I think, Mr. Edding."

"Very well. But think about hiring a shopgirl." The clandestine publisher smiled. "You have a rare talent, my lady. Quite, quite rare. I'd like very much to see you devote more time to your writing." Sliding the package under the counter, he opened the cash register, withdrew an envelope, and handed it to her. "Cash as you prefer, my lady. And may I say how much I appreciate the quality of your work." Glancing over her shoulder, he waved his hand as though shooing someone away.

Rosalind stiffened but kept her back to the door. She deliberately came to Mr. Edding's shop before it opened in order to avoid being seen.

"It was some passerby, my dear, who apparently can't read the hours painted on the door. He's gone. You're quite safe." He understood her fear of exposure; if it were revealed that she was a writer of erotica, her reputation not to mention her livelihood would be at risk. The scandal could ruin her.

A moment later, Rosalind bid good-by to Mr. Edding, left the shop, and walked home through the quiet streets. Only after she entered her apartment above the store did she allow herself to give in to fatigue. Not that she was unfamiliar with weariness after so many nights with little sleep.

Fortunately today was Tuesday—normally not a busy day, particularly in August with the beau monde having deserted London. Even the bourgeois were at the seashore with their families. She didn't expect many customers.

She would rest for a brief time; the store didn't open until ten.

Then fortified by another cup of tea—several actually—she would survive another day with limited sleep. But tonight, she would allow herself a rare treat and go to bed by midnight.

CHAPTER 3

GROVELAND ARRIVED AT Bruton Street Books shortly before ten.

An early riser, he'd already spent some hours with his new secretary, Stanley. All his correspondence, which had been left in abeyance during his absence, was now in order, and young Stanley was much relieved. The duke's casual disregard for his mail was unfathomable to the meticulous lad, but then Stanley was still young and idealistic—neither of which characterized the duke. The duke was thirty-five. And *his* youth had been marked by tumult and violence when his father was in his cups—not an atmosphere likely to foster idealism.

Fitz had explained—again—that Stanley could do what he liked with the billets-doux; they were of no interest to him. As for his business correspondence, if Stanley had questions and couldn't reach him, he could speak to Hutchinson. The remaining mail could be dealt with in whatever manner Stanley chose. He'd tried to be diplomatic for the young man was doing his best to shoulder his new responsibilities. "The point is," he'd finally said, "I don't want to deal with most of this. You understand?"

Now in terms of further diplomacy…

Fitz surveyed the bookshop's bow windows filled with
colorful volumes, then the glass-paned, canary yellow door
with the hours clearly noted thereon. He slipped his watch
from his waistcoat pocket and checked the time. Ten. He
tried the door once again. Apparently, Mrs. St. Vincent
wasn't the punctual type.

Ah, there, a woman was coming toward him from the
back of the store.

Mrs. St. Vincent it appeared from Hutchinson's brief
description—her hair color and height identifying factors.
But as Fitz's connoisseur gaze swiftly took her measure, he
wondered if Hutchinson could have been wrong about her
background. This woman had the look of an actress: star-
tlingly beautiful, tall, and shapely, her heavy auburn hair
piled casually atop her head à la Pre-Raphaelite portraits.
Or maybe it was that particular shade of hair that called to
mind their work.

Although she also affected the aesthetic mode in her
attire: elements of Japanese motifs embroidered on her
blouse, the fabric of her moss green linen skirt handwoven
from all appearances, her splendid form visibly without
corsets. Having spent enough time in artists' studios buying artwork or in pursuit of some lovely model, he recognized the avant-garde style.

Women in his world preferred French couture, opulent
silks and satins, velvets and lace rather than hand-loomed
wools and linens, and corsets were as de rigueur as a hand-
span waist. And no lady he knew would appear in public
with her hair as casually arranged as Mrs. St. Vincent's.

She wasn't working class, but she had definitely moved
beyond the conventional world of her birth. For instance,
she wasn't wearing mourning, although her husband could
have been dead for some time; he'd have to ask Hutchinson. Certainly in style and dress she appeared very much
the modern woman. Not that he paid much attention to the
controversial battle for women's rights. In the insulated
world in which he moved, the subject was, if not anath-

ema, generally ignored. The ladies of his acquaintance were more concerned with gossip, the most stylish gown, or their newest lover.

Speaking of lovers, Mrs. St. Vincent definitely piqued his interest.

She was quite lovely.

Rosalind, meanwhile, in the process of mulling over a possible speaker for her Saturday reading group, didn't notice the duke until she reached the door and looked up to unlock it. Her eyes flared wide and her first thought was: *My Lord, Groveland is tall!* Her second thought, thoroughly uncalled for and quickly suppressed was: *He is as handsome as sin—gloriously so . . . like a Leighton depiction of some Greek god or Roman gladiator—all overwhelming strength and chiseled beauty.*

He was a favorite of the scandal sheet gossip mongers. And whether at the races, some hunt, or a fancy dress ball, a woman was always clinging to his arm.

Not that his looks or his scandalous life should concern her in the least, Rosalind sternly reminded herself; she was well aware of why he'd come.

Groveland was here because he wished to acquire her store—and with it, her livelihood and all that was positive in her life. Not that he wasn't offering her generous compensation. But she didn't wish to sell for any number of reasons. Of prime importance, perhaps, was the fact that she'd fashioned a busy, satisfying, and increasingly lucrative life for herself since Edward's death.

And she saw no cause or reason to relinquish it.

Yes, yes, she understood it might be possible to reconstruct such an existence elsewhere. But why must she disrupt her life and business simply because Groveland was wealthy, titled, and insistent?

She *liked* that her free library was frequented by so many of the laboring poor; she took great pleasure in knowing that her Saturday reading group was filled to overflowing because she offered speakers and books addressing the pertinent issues of the day. And while her small art gallery in the back of her store had originated by chance, the women artists who exhibited there were drawing increasing critical acclaim.

Furthermore, soon she would be free of debt *without* the duke's offer.

But perhaps what may have ultimately sealed her decision was her fundamental dislike of men like Groveland—idle, leisured aristocrats who lived only for their amusements. Noble lords who had never wanted for anything, who expected immediate compliance, who resented challenge or contradiction. Who lived off the income generated by ill-paid retainers.

Good Lord, I've become a bona fide radical!

Whether it was Groveland's rapping on the window pane or the shock of her latent radicalism jarring her back to reality, she quickly slipped the latch free and opened the door.

"A pleasant good morning." The duke bowed faintly. "Mrs. St. Vincent, I presume. I'm Groveland."

"Good morning, Your Grace. Are you in the market for some reading material?" Rosalind sardonically inquired. That he looked every inch the exquisite noble from the top of his deliberately ruffled hair to his biscuit-colored summer shoes inexplicably annoyed her.

She is *a bitch*, he thought. But adept at humoring women, at the top of his game according to Brooks's betting books, Fitz offered a practiced smile. "Actually, I came to speak with you about your bookstore," he said, smooth as silk. "I was hoping you would allow me a few moments of your time."

She found his suave charm and easy smile insufferable, his expectation that she would succumb to it even more irksome. After a deliberately long pause, she said, "I suppose I could give you a few minutes. Come in and say what you have to say." She waved him in with a flick of her hand. "Not that it will do you any more good than the ten others who came here to do your bidding."

He flexed his fingers against an urge to throttle her, her

tone, her stance, the chill in her emerald eyes, like a gauntlet thrown.

Hutchinson was right. She was audacious.

His mind racing with options other than that of throttling her, he moved past her into the store. Was it possible his architect could redraw the plans and work around her damned corner property? Could Williams design a new entrance to Monckton Row and the luxury townhomes planned for the site. Could he tell this shrewish bitch to go to hell?

The sound of the door closing behind him brought him back to his senses. Marginally. He understood that responding to her insolence in kind would hardly serve his mission, that tact and diplomacy would more likely win the day. But Groveland rarely met a quarrelsome woman; in fact, he never did, the women in his life universally disposed to please him. So he reined in his temper with effort. "We can trade insults if you wish." He smiled tightly. "I'm more than willing and better at it than you I expect. Or you can do me the courtesy of listening to my proposal. I promise to be brief."

Rosalind blew out a small breath; he was asking for little. She could at least hear him out. "I apologize. I was unnecessarily rude. I didn't sleep much last night." She smiled faintly. "At least I have an excuse for my incivility."

Fitz couldn't help but smile in return, although he hadn't intended to. No more than he'd intended to say in a lazy drawl, "For all you know, I may not have slept much last night either."

"But then no one would expect a man of your proclivities to have spent your night sleeping, would they?"

The little vixen was a flirt. "What could you possibly know of my proclivities?" he murmured, back on familiar ground, seduction his particular metier.

"The whole world knows, Your Grace. You're infamous."

"Should I apologize?" His voice was low and velvet soft, his gaze explicitly carnal.

It was unconscionable that a tremor of desire should

immediately spike through her senses. That his deep, husky voice and heated gaze should prompt her cheeks to flush rosy pink. That for the briefest moment she'd fall prey to his tantalizing allure.

But she was a woman of resolve, even more so since her widowhood, so she resisted the heady temptation. "No need to apologize, Groveland." She offered him a bland look and a blander smile. "May I offer you tea?" Clearly, a moment of respite was in order. She understood now why he was the byword for amorous play. He was quite impossible to resist—a wholly inexplicable phenomena to date in her life, but shockingly real.

She really could use a cup of tea if for no other reason than to put some distance between herself and Groveland's disconcerting sexuality.

"Yes, thank you," he murmured with a polished bow. He could drink tea if he had to, although cognizant of Mrs. St. Vincent's tantalizing response, he would have much preferred a taste of the lovely widow's heated passions.

At his graceful bow, Rosalind immediately pictured him on a ballroom floor, bowing to some woman, poised and elegant in full evening rig. *Good God, I've been writing fiction too long.*

"I heated the samovar earlier," she quickly remarked, finding the sudden silence disturbing, feeling the need to fill the hush. "I keep tea at the ready for my customers and myself. I'm addicted I'm afraid, and customers like it as well...especially when the weather turns cooler—not that it's cool today, of course," she added, chiding herself for sounding like some dithering young miss just out of the schoolroom. "Please, over there," she restively finished, gesturing to two chairs near the window.

After a cup of tea, she'd politely refuse his offer and send him on his way. She was no innocent maid whose head could be turned by a handsome face and a captivating smile. *Truly, seriously*, she silently admonished herself.

The lady's contemptuous hauteur had vanished, Fitz reflected, following her, along with her abrasiveness, and in their place was this lovely, sweet tremulousness. His next thought was bluntly male and hackneyed: *What she needs is a good, hard orgasm to calm her nerves.*

His third thought was perhaps even more of a cliche considering his reputation for licentious pleasures: *Might she be available for a bit of dalliance this morning?* He was fresh and rested after a good night's sleep. Although he fully understood that his lustful desires had more to do with the lady's fascinating sensuality than a bracing night of repose.

Taking a seat in a worn leather club chair while she busied herself pouring tea, he slid down into a comfortable slouch and observed her from under his lashes. He had only to pull out a few pins and her heavy, silken hair would tumble down her back. His fingers unconsciously flexed in pleasant anticipation. Her blouse buttoned down the front. Convenient. She wore a minimum of petticoats under her simple skirt, too. Really—it was as if fate was taking a hand, he thought, contemplating the ease with which he could disrobe her. He shifted slightly as his erection grew, the image of Mrs. St. Vincent nude vastly arousing.

He shot a glance toward the door, as if he might curtail impending customers by will alone.

"Sugar?"

It took him a second to reply, distracted as he was by his imagination racing full tilt. "Yes, please," he said, crossing his legs to conceal his erection. "Four."

Her brows rose in surprise, but she only said, "Milk?" rather than what she was thinking.

"Half milk, please, if it's not too late."

She glanced at him and smiled. "You don't actually drink tea, do you?"

He smiled back. "I do on occasion."

"When you're trying to please some woman."

He grinned. "Yes, mostly then."

"I could find you some liquor, I suppose." But even as she spoke, she realized how she'd compromised herself and quickly added, "Actually, I can't."

"Tea's fine," he murmured, as if he hadn't noticed her brief moment of unintentional goodwill.

She tried not to be overly mindful of how he casually lounged in her chair as if he sat there often, nor how splendid he looked in his beige linen suit—powerful, virile male outfitted in gentlemen's finery. And yet the brute animal remained beneath the veneer, London's best tailors unable to trivialize the underlying brawn and muscle. In contrast—strangely perhaps, given his reputation for vice—he had the look of some troubadour of old as well with his dark, ruffled hair curling over his collar, his grey eyes revealing a hint of soulfulness, his sensual mouth eminently kissable.

She had to admit he was incredibly attractive.

She had forgotten what it felt like to be enticed.

But she knew better than to succumb to Groveland's much-heralded seductive skills, and when she carried over two teacups and handed him his, she was careful not to meet his gaze.

Infamous he might be, but she was not, she noted in cautionary restraint, sitting down across from him and taking a sip of tea.

"When I first saw you, you reminded me of a Pre-Raphaelite portrait." Fitz smiled over the rim of his teacup. "You hear that often, I expect."

"I admit, I do. It's my hair, I think."

"And your eyes and nose. I own several of their paintings—Rossetti and Millais in particular. The similarities between you and their models are quite remarkable."

"You own Rossetti and Millais?" She couldn't quite keep the shock from her voice. She'd not expected him to be a patron of the arts—other than for paintings of nudes, perhaps. And nudes were not either artist's speciality.

"You sound surprised."

"Your reputation is for other things."

"That's because gossip is by definition about *other things*," he noted with a faint smile. "Scandal attracts more interest than cultural endeavors."

"And you're engaged in cultural endeavors?"

He laughed. "I'm pleased to see you're not carping by nature. I know women who could seriously outrival that arch look of yours."

"From all reports you know women who can do most anything."

"While you're a country mouse, bereft of feminine artifice," he sardonically countered.

"Feminine artifice *is* beyond my scope. As for the country mouse, once perhaps I was," she returned with a rueful smile. "But life and untoward circumstances intervene and alter one's character whether one likes it or not."

"Your husband's gambling, for instance."

She frowned. "You overstep, Groveland."

"My apologies. So you became a managing woman," he noted with a lifted brow.

She knew what he meant; she also knew *a managing woman* was not a charitable term. "Maybe I did," she said, though because she had neither the inclination nor the resources to take on the idle role of society belle. "By necessity in the beginning and now by choice." She smiled. "I'm not of your world, Groveland, nor do I aspire to that life."

"You endorse socialist principles?" He didn't care, but he enjoyed watching her, and to that purpose, he asked questions.

"I endorse helping those less fortunate. Call it what you like."

"We all help those less fortunate."

"If by *we* you mean those of your class, I beg to differ with you. There are nobles who have run their tenants off their land without a qualm, and others who live off the labor of their crofters without offering them a living wage." She lifted her brows. "Do you want me to go on? The disparities between rich and poor are comprehensive and deplorable."

"My tenants are well cared for and well paid."

"Good for you."

Her gaze had turned heated and not in a way that would advance either his business or personal desires. "Tell me what books your customers favor most. I expect there are certain subjects that sell better than others."

How incredibly urbane he was, shifting facilely from the contentious issue of the poor to an innocuous topic without so much as a flicker of a pause. Understanding that she wasn't going to humanize the aristocratic class with a few pithy comments to Groveland, she replied with equal civility. "Travel books are most popular, I suppose." She dared not tell him the truth: erotica sold best.

"If you allowed me to purchase your store, you could travel wherever you liked."

"My bookstore is earning a good return. I may soon travel without your money."

"Soon?"

Good Lord, he was quick-witted. "My profits are increasing nicely."

"I, on the other hand, could make you financially independent immediately. Twenty thousand would give you considerable independence."

Good God! Twenty thousand! That's three times his barrister's last offer! Clearly, he is serious! She drew in a small sustaining breath, then set down her teacup, conscious that his cool gaze was scrutinizing her closely. "Your Grace, I don't wish to lead you on," she said, knowing she was perhaps being illogical, but allowing her heart to rule. "As I've already informed your many surrogates, I have no wish to sell. The bookstore is more than a profitable business; it's my home and my passion—particularly with reference to my small charities. Helping others offers me enormous pleasure and a sense of fulfillment I'm not sure you'd understand. I'm sorry to be a hindrance to your plans, but I'm quite determined to stay here."

"You only paid three thousand for the store," Fitz pointed out, logical when she was not. "With twenty thousand, you could buy another store, do more charitable works, indulge your interest in travel. And in all candor," he gently noted, setting down his teacup, "your property stands in the way of my project."

A flush of anger instantly colored her cheeks. "Your project? What about mine?"

He frowned. "You're being unreasonable."

"I could say the same of you."

"Do you realize you're obstructing a major urban enterprise?"

"*Your* enterprise, you mean."

"Of course that's what I mean," he irritably replied. "This little bookstore of yours could be anywhere; it doesn't have to be on this particular corner."

"I happen to *like* this particular corner." Her voice had taken on the same contentious tone as his. "This is my *home*, Groveland. What if I asked you to sell Groveland House? Would you mind?"

"That's different," he brusquely retorted.

"Because it's yours, you mean, and you're rich as Croesus and you always get what you want!" Her voice had taken on a strident tone.

"I don't," he gruffly returned. "You're quite wrong." *If I always got whatever I wanted, I would have had a different father and a different childhood. A normal one.*

"Then you won't find it so unusual when you don't get my store!"

"It's incomprehensible that you'd cut off your nose to spite your face," he coldly rebuked. "I'm offering you twenty thousand for a store that's worth three."

"We disagree on what it's worth," she answered as coldly.

"You want *more*?" he said very, very softly. The woman had the instincts of a highwayman.

"Everything *isn't* about money, Groveland!" How dare he speak to her in that accusing tone. "In fact, the things that truly matter are *never* about money! Not that someone like you could possibly understand! Now, do me a favor! Get out and leave me alone! Permanently!"

He was surprised at the degree of anger her tirade generated. Every muscle in his body was taut with rage. "There's nothing I can say to change your mind?" Twenty thousand was a goddamned fortune and she knew it.

"Not a thing!" Hot, bellicose words.

He was utterly still save for a muscle that twitched over his stark cheekbone. "I could make your life exceedingly difficult," he said, his voice soft with menace.

She sat back in shock. "Are you threatening me?"

Pushing himself upright in his chair, he leaned forward slightly, the devil glowing in his eyes. "I am."

Her spine went rigid. "Do what you will," she snapped, furious at his arrogance. "I'm *not* selling!"

He came to his feet in a powerful surge. "You don't know who you're dealing with," he growled, towering over her.

"On the contrary," she rebuked, looking up at him, her gaze flame hot, "I know very well who I'm dealing with! A spoiled, self-indulgent debauchee who's never worked a day in his life or cared about anyone but himself! But I am not intimidated by your wealth and power! I'm here and I'm staying!" As if empowered by her heated words, she rose to her feet in a flash and jabbed her finger into the fine silk jacquard of his waistcoat. "Now, get out!"

He grabbed her wrist in a viselike grip. "You unmitigated bitch."

She gasped in pain.

His fingers tightened for a flashing moment, then he abruptly released her and bending down so their eyes were level, whispered, fierce and low, "They say your husband jumped. Now I know why."

She slapped him so hard, a stabbing pain shot down her arm.

He almost slapped her back but caught himself just short of her face. "This isn't over," he snarled, letting his hand drop. Turning, he strode away, nearly knocking over a rotund, middle-aged woman coming through the door.

"My goodness!" Mrs. Beecham murmured as soon as the duke slammed shut the shop door. "Was that the celebrated Duke of Groveland?"

"Yes." With considerable effort Rosalind overcame the fury in her voice, the single word escaping in a sibilant hiss.

Mrs. Beecham was staring out the window at Groveland's swiftly retreating form. "Can you imagine a man of his consequence coming into your little store?" she exclaimed in wonder. "Do you think he might return? I do so wish he might. He is quite the eligible party, my dear. I do hope you were on your best behavior with such a superior person."

"Indeed, Mrs. Beecham. He is *most* unusual," Rosalind said, curbing her inclination to describe his character in vile, graphic detail.

"Isn't he just! Rich, handsome, with a distinguished, ancient title—and single, my dear. Even dukes marry beneath them on occasion. Did he seem taken with you? Perhaps even the slightest bit?" she queried, breathlessly.

"I didn't detect that sort of interest, Mrs. Beecham," Rosalind muttered.

Rosalind's sarcasm wasted on her, Mrs. Beecham said with an insinuating little wink, "Well, if he returns, I'd suggest you put yourself out to please him. You have to think of your future, my dear. You're out of mourning now, and you're not getting any younger."

"I'm sure Groveland is quite busy with the revels of fashionable society. I have no expectations, Mrs. Beecham—none at all. Now, let me show you the new novels that arrived yesterday. Mrs. Thornhill has written a most delightful story and I know she's one of your favorites."

After Groveland's spiteful threats the last person she wished to discuss was his eminence, the most odious, hateful man in England!

CHAPTER 4

WHILE GUIDING MRS. Beecham to the new novels, Rosalind only half listened to the woman's chatter, planning instead how best to defend herself against Groveland's attack—which would surely come.

He'd turned out to be the exact spoiled, arrogant aristocrat she'd expected. Quick-tempered when rebuffed, indifferent to all but his own wishes, intent on riding roughshod over anyone who stood in his way.

But she would not be intimidated.

She owned her building; he could not dislodge her.

No matter what.

STRIDING SWIFTLY DOWN Bond Street toward Piccadilly, Fitz was currently focused on that *what*. And the mood he was in, the Monckton Row project wasn't even a consideration.

Retaliation was foremost in his mind.

And winning against the insufferable Mrs. St. Vincent! He cautioned himself to calm as he quickly made his way toward Hutchinson's office, but with his temper in high dudgeon, issues of reason and restraint were largely nullified. All he could think about was triumphing over the hot-tempered, unreasonable, *defiant* bitch.

Good God, he'd never before felt like striking a woman. Never.

That she was the most perverse and bold-as-brass female he'd ever met was no doubt cause for his aberrant behavior.

As for the circumstances of her husband's death, after bearing the brunt of Mrs. St. Vincent's sharp tongue, he thought it rather likely that she *had* driven the poor man to jump.

Crossing Piccadilly Square, Groveland entered the grand Italianate palazzo that bespoke Hutchinson's repute as a jurist. Passing through the resplendent marble-columned foyer, he took the stairs at a run and barged into Hutchinson's office suite like a bull in a china shop. "I'll see myself in," he crisply asserted, striding past the law clerks who served as assistants, errand boys, and in this case, gatekeepers.

One of the young men jumped up and courageously blocked Fitz's path. "I'm sorry, Your Grace, but Mr. Hutchinson is with a client."

"Then get rid of him."

The young man's bravery faltered before the duke's blunt, gimlet-eyed order, but only for a moment. "I'm sorry, sir, I can't do that."

Fitz gave the young man credit for nerve. "I see. Then could you tell me who Hutchinson is with?" A flicker of amusement gleamed in Groveland's eyes. "Or would that be too much to ask?"

"No, sir, of course not, sir. Mr. Hutchinson is with the Earl of Somerset."

Fitz smiled. "Charlie won't mind if I intrude." Smoothly sidestepping the young clerk, he strode toward Hutchinson's office. "I'll make sure to tell your employer you did your best to stop me," he tossed back over his shoulder.

Seconds later, he closed the door behind him and smiled

at the two men who had turned at his entrance. "Your boy tried to stop me, Hutchinson. Don't sack him. Morning, Charlie. I'm in a helluva temper and even more of a rush. I need a few moments of Hutchinson's time."

Charlie Melville grinned. "Some woman after your skin?"

"On the contrary, some woman needs to be put in her place."

"Hell, Fitz, I thought you knew how to do that better than anyone. In bed and under you. Ain't that your way?"

"Unfortunately, this woman is proving difficult. Have a drink Charlie," Fitz suggested, nodding at Hutchinson's drink trolley, the earl known to often drink his breakfast. "This won't take long. If I could speak with you, Prosper," he added, indicating a grouping of chairs across the room with a wave of his hand.

As the men took their seats a moment later, Hutchinson said, "I gather Mrs. St. Vincent wasn't cooperative."

"She is unspeakably ill-natured and blind to all reason," Fitz brusquely retorted. "I want her crushed." Holding up a finger, he smiled thinly. "Let me rephrase that. I want her gone. I don't care how you do it."

The barrister suppressed his astonishment; Groveland was not a vindictive man. "While I understand your exasperation," he cautioned, "as your barrister, I have to remind you that certain legalities must be observed."

"Yes, yes, I understand," Fitz murmured, dismissing Hutchinson's reservations. "Naturally, she must be dealt with lawfully. But you know as well as I that legalities are, shall we say, flexible."

"To a point, Your Grace. Only to a point."

Fitz's dark brows rose. "That definitive point is what I pay you for, Hutchinson. I expect you to calibrate the boundaries to a nicety." He blew out a breath. "I'm not unreasonable. I just want it done."

"I understand. Naturally, I'm at your disposal."

Hutchinson always had the capacity to calm; maybe it was his voice. Or his steadiness and lack of alarm. Fitz sighed and smiled faintly. "Imperturbable as usual, Hutchinson. What would I do without you?"

Since Groveland was his best client and a decent man as well, the barrister said with utter sincerity, "I could say the same, Your Grace. You have been a most generous patron."

"This particular problem will tax your ingenuity as well as your patience, I'm afraid. Not that I'm advocating all out war mind you—for now at least." His gaze narrowed faintly. "It might be helpful to investigate Mrs. St. Vincent's personal life with an eye to gaining some leverage. Does she have debts, for instance, and if so, who holds the paper? Does she engage in dalliance? Might we unearth some scandal in that regard? Is it possible her family might be useful in persuading her to accept our offer? I'll leave it to you to find some means to change her mind."

"Consider it done, sir."

"I knew I could count on you," Fitz warmly noted. "In the meantime, I'll attempt some personal persuasion with regard to Mrs. St. Vincent. I'll offer her an abject apology for my impetuous temper." He smiled. "I mentioned her husband's death in uncivil terms for which I'll eat humble pie and do penance. Then I'll ply her with the usual bibelots women fancy and attempt to win her over with my"—he smiled again—"largesse. We shall employ *your* sticks and *my* carrots to a, hopefully, successful conclusion. By the way, I offered her twenty thousand."

Hutchinson wasn't prone to gasp, but twenty thousand drew a rare gasp from him. "She turned it down?" His barrister's mind wished complete clarity on such breathtaking moral rectitude.

"Emphatically. And caustically, I might add." Fitz stood. "I won't intrude further on your time. Keep me informed of whatever information you unearth. I'm off to speak with Williams now. He might be able to redesign that corner or at least postpone construction as it relates to her bookstore until we acquire it." Turning, he waved at Somerset. "Thanks, Charlie! Are you hunting at Arlie's next month?"

"Would I miss it?"

"Then I'll see you there."

His mood much improved, the duke leisurely strolled toward St. James's. Hutchinson's staff would be fully engaged in obtaining pertinent details on Mrs. St. Vincent's personal life that could prove useful. She, like everyone, had skeletons in her closet—the husband's gambling activities, for one. And with a woman of Mrs. St. Vincent's arresting beauty, he doubted she lived a chaste life.

While he personally ignored society's strictures when it came to morals, a woman, particularly one of lesser rank, could not so easily disregard them. Scandal accrued to females of middling rank who engaged in fornication outside the marriage bed. And as he understood it, the husband had been deceased for some time. Surely, in her widowhood, the beautiful, voluptuous Mrs. St. Vincent had been tempted to indulge her passions on occasion.

In fact, had he not detected a moment of prurient interest—however quickly suppressed—this morning over tea?

The thought of which was intriguing. Nor could he completely discount the satisfaction he would experience—beyond the obvious sexual gratification—if he were successful in bringing the lovely Mrs. St. Vincent to bed in the course of his *persuasion* campaign.

Was she a screamer?

He smiled.

He rather thought she might be.

CHAPTER 5

At the same time Groveland was contemplating making love to his adversary, the object of his musing was seated across from her friend, Sofia Eastleigh, and explaining in a voice of contained fury, "You can't imagine the high-handed, barefaced gall of the man! His Grace, the *esteemed* duke of every profligacy on the face of the earth, said to me with shameless arrogance, 'Your property stands in the way of my project,' as if I should instantly capitulate because my bookstore happens to be in his way and *his* wish is my command! Ha! Never!"

Sofia grinned. "I expect he was angry when he left."

"Not as angry as I, believe me! If Mrs. Beecham hadn't come in as he was leaving I would have screamed the heaven's down around his insolent head! I am so completely disgusted with rich nobles who think they can have anything they want simply because they want it! It's outrageous! And wrong!"

Sofia had lived too long on her own resources to look askance at wealth of any kind, but she kindly said, "You see the world through your social consciousness, darling. I confess I don't. Not that I don't understand policy reforms would offer better lives for the poor. But consider, Groveland is offering to buy you out for a considerable sum."

"I'm doing very well on my own," Rosalind said with a contemptuous sniff, reaching for another slice of poppy cake in her frustration.

"You just don't like men of his ilk. Admit it."

"Of course I don't," Rosalind said through a mouthful of cake. "Why should I when"—she swallowed—"men like Groveland do nothing but make love, gamble, and hunt? What a useless life!"

"Useless he may be in some respects," Sofia murmured, "but I thought him very charming when I met him at Leighton's last year." Unlike Rosalind, Sofia viewed men as utilitarian adjuncts to her life: as lovers, payers of rent, amusing companions over dinner, race track associates when she was flush.

Rosalind scowled. "I suppose he can be altogether charming when he doesn't want anything of yours!"

"Or anything other than a roll in the hay. Which is his speciality as everyone knows—not precisely hay, of course; I'm sure he prefers more civilized venues for making love."

"From all accounts he's not so scrupulous," Rosalind said haughtily.

"That could be. He was flirting with Flora, Leighton's model, that day I met him, and everyone knows she's not averse to offering herself standing up in a corner if a suitor comes bearing gifts or is handsome enough." Sofia lifted her pale brows. "And you must concede, Groveland is extremely handsome."

"I don't care if he's the handsomest man in the world! Nor do I care if he and Leighton's model had relations in the middle of Leighton's studio! *His Grace*," Rosalind wrathfully articulated, "is rude, overbearing, brazenly autocratic, and he's *not* getting my bookstore!" She reached for another slice of cake.

"Then you win and he loses. And you needn't spend

another second infuriated with him. Nor," Sofia pointed out with a smile, "eat the entire cake because you're in a rage."

Rosalind sighed. "You're right." She looked at the slice of cake in her hand, then at the few remaining pieces on the cake plate, and grimaced. "If I keep this up, I'll look like a horse."

"Hardly, darling. I could only hope to have your voluptuous curves."

"Then you might think about eating occasionally. One of these days you're going to simply float away. While I shall waddle away," Rosalind said with a grin, putting down the slice of cake. "As for Groveland and his kind, they don't deserve another moment of my time." She sat up straighter. "There. I am calm. Calm and in control. My life is agreeable in every way." She smiled. "I apologize for my rant. You've been a dear to listen so patiently."

"Why shouldn't I? You're always willing to hear my laments about Luke and the evils of the Academy?"

"How is he by the way?"

Sofia wrinkled her delicate nose. "As bad as ever."

"You really must find someone else," Rosalind insisted with the objective clarity of an uninvolved party.

Sofia smiled ruefully. "Like you found someone other than Edward?"

"He couldn't help his gambling addiction," Rosalind murmured.

"He didn't even try."

Rosalind made a moue. "I know."

"And of course you wouldn't think of divorce."

"No." She and Sofia had gone over this ground before. Who would have taken care of Edward had she divorced him? And more to the point, who would have paid for the divorce? "But do consider finding someone who treats you well, darling. You're so enormously talented. Luke will never be a brilliant painter like you, and he resents your artistic gifts."

"I wish I could argue the point." Sofia shrugged. "At

least the world is slowly changing. Just think, before long, women might win a place in the greater scheme of things."

Rosalind smiled. "First we need the vote."

"True, and yet," Sofia softly replied, "we have more options than our mothers did."

"Indeed. My mother has given up her entire life to care for my father. She doesn't begrudge her role, but I find myself unwilling to play the mute, compliant wife."

"As if you ever did," her friend drolly noted.

"Someone had to deal with the day-to-day living. It was not Edward's strong suit."

"Maybe it's time you think about playing the merry widow," her friend suggested with a sly smile. "You work too hard. You don't have enough fun." Sofia winked. "Carnal amusements can be a very satisfying diversion. And while I'm not advocating for Groveland, if you were in the market for a diversion, he'd be certainly high on anyone's list. His reputation is well deserved according to my friend Annie. She spent Ascot week with him and they never actually saw a race."

Rosalind grimaced. "That's exactly why Groveland holds no interest for me; he's a complete libertine. Even if I chose to divert myself as you put it, I'd prefer my partner remember my name. I'm sure the women in Groveland's life are no more than a nameless blur."

"Who cares if he remembers your name if the sex is memorable. It's not about conversation, darling, but about pleasure. But I'll say no more. I just think you should consider adding sexual satisfaction to your life. Widowhood isn't healthy."

Rosalind smiled. "So we're speaking about my health now?"

Sofia pouted prettily. "Fine, ridicule me if you wish, but I'd rather get my exercise from orgasms than a walk in Hyde Park."

"Amorous entertainments are quite wonderful I don't doubt. But I'm perfectly satisfied with my life. And I'm too busy anyway."

"You really should think about taking a holiday." Sofia smiled. "Maybe you'd meet someone at the seashore."

Rosalind laughed. "You're certainly persistent, but who would take care of my store? The fairies? And you should talk. I haven't seen you on holiday lately."

"Touché. Perhaps we're both obsessed. Now that my work is selling, I want to paint even more. I have money for supplies for the first time in my life, for canvas and brushes, good ones. And for the best paints."

"Success couldn't come to a more deserving person," Rosalind said with a warm smile. Sofia had first approached her about showing her work two years ago, and together the women had contrived to bring not only Sofia's work but also that of several other female artists into the public arena. Eventually, even the critics—who generally supported conservative rather than progressive trends—began to review their shows. "And I guarantee your new landscapes will all sell within the week. They're absolutely gorgeous." Coming to her feet, Rosalind picked up Sofia's newest painting. "Let's put this in a place of honor on the back wall so everyone will see it first on entering the gallery."

"It is rather nice if I do say so myself; it's Augustus's backyard," Sofia remarked, following Rosalind as she made her way toward the back of the store, and temporarily abandoning the subject of Rosalind's overlong celibacy. It was a long-standing topic of conversation between them anyway. "The man is the most glorious gardener."

"I agree; your impression of his delphiniums is particularly lush. The color fairly dazzles the eye."

"And so we shall dazzle the critics tonight," Sofia playfully declared, moving on to innocuous matters. "I sent notices to all the papers last week."

Rosalind glanced back over her shoulder. "Perhaps that handsome young art critic from the *Times* will be here tonight. He seemed to appreciate not only your work but *you* as well the last time he reviewed our show."

"We'll see." A pretty model before she took up painting, Sofia was familiar with fawning swains. "After Luke's sullenness of late, I'm not sure I'm inclined to be pleasant to a man."

"You'll be in a better mood once all your paintings are sold and you're a good deal richer."

Sofia grinned. "Oh yes, money definitely raises my spirits."

WHILE THE WOMEN were hanging Sofia's painting, Fitz met with his architect, Ian Williams. Williams was disappointed at the delay in their schedule, but cooperative. Naturally, he would redesign the entrance to the secluded mews he said, but he made it clear to the duke that the character of the private street lined with elegant townhomes would be sadly marred should the bookshop continue to occupy its present site.

"I expect the shop will soon be mine," Fitz replied soothingly. "But should an alternative be required, I'd like to be prepared."

"I understand," Williams said grudgingly, the idea of having to alter his plan disconcerting to his artistic temperament. "Would it help if I showed the lady my designs, Your Grace? If she understood the critical position her store occupies, she might more readily agree to sell."

"I rather doubt it, but thank you for offering," Fitz replied. "An optional plan is only a precaution. I fully anticipate being back on schedule within a fortnight."

"That's a relief, sir." The fashionable young architect smiled for the first time since Groveland had entered his office.

"Hutchinson and I are both dealing with the lady. We expect all to be resolved very soon. In the meantime, I'll rely on your creativity to provide an auxiliary concept— something to distract the eye from the bookstore perhaps. Or shield it in some way. She owns the building but not the pavement. I believe that is mine according to the legal documents."

Williams grinned. "I could barricade her as it were."

"Indeed you could." *A ten-foot wall perhaps.* "We are agreed then," the duke more gracefully remarked as he came to his feet.

"Yes, sir."

"Then I'll wish you a good day. Send my secretary a note when the new plans are finished."

After leaving Williams's office, Fitz returned home and searched out Stanley. He found him cataloguing recent additions to the library.

Entering the large, well-lit room that had been built by one of his Georgian ancestors and added to by each subsequent generation, and which was now considered one of the finest libraries in England, Fitz approached the desk where Stanley was working. "I have a commission for you," he crisply said. "I'd like you to go round to Grey's directly and speak to a Mr. Montgomery." He paused in his instructions while Stanley reached for a paper and pen. "Tell him I need several little fripperies," he continued once his secretary's pen was poised over the paper. "He'll know what I mean. A few modern pieces, too. The lady's taste is avant-garde. I'll give you some inscriptions to bring along. Montgomery will know what to do with those as well." Having reached the desk, Groveland bent forward, pulled a sheet of paper toward him, took the offered pen, and quickly scribbled several lines. "That should do." He handed the sheet to Stanley and took a step back. "I'm in the process of wooing Mrs. St. Vincent away from her current address," he said, smiling faintly.

"For the Monckton Row project."

Fitz nodded. "She's the last holdout, as you know. I intend to apologize to her tomorrow, so see that I have the baubles by this evening. The store opens at ten in the morning." He held up crossed fingers. "You may wish me luck."

"Good luck, sir. By the way, have you read her late husband's poetry?"

Having turned to leave, the duke swung back. "No, have you?"

"Yes."

He met Stanley's gaze. "And?"

"It's of a rather maudlin nature, sir. I hear the Queen enjoyed it, which may indicate the audience for that particular style of verse."

"Old ladies, you mean."

"And also those of a sensitive nature," Stanley added with a raised brow.

Fitz's eyes flared wide for a second. "Don't say the man was—"

"No, no, sir, I meant a certain tender aesthetic imbues the poetry that perhaps touches a similar delicate vein in those who admire it."

"Still," Fitz softly murmured, contemplating another ripe avenue of investigation, "it might not hurt to look into the late Mr. St. Vincent's amusements."

"To all accounts, sir, he was the best of husbands."

"Discounting his gambling habit. You've already looked into this?"

"Just a little, sir. I happen to know Marcus Dodd, who was a poet friend of the late Mr. St. Vincent. We were at Eton together."

"Find out everything you can about St. Vincent. Scandals preferably. We need some means of exerting pressure on the lady. Now, the jewelry in my hands by evening. Understood?"

"Yes, sir, I'll go to Grey's immediately."

"Do you have a particular lady friend?"

The young man blushed. "I'm hopeful, sir."

"Well, get the young lady some trinket in recompense for all your hard work."

"You already pay me handsomely, sir."

"But not handsomely enough to buy jewelry at Grey's," Fitz said with a grin. "So buy her something with my blessing, and I'd suggest you add some pretty inscription. Women like flowery sentiments I've found."

CHAPTER 6

FITZ SPENT THE afternoon at Tattersalls buying new bloodstock, followed by drinks and cards at Brooks's with those of his friends still in town. And despite his activities—all quite normal and unexceptional—images of Mrs. St. Vincent kept looping through his mind. Erotic images of the most lascivious nature that persisted despite every effort to dismiss them.

He should ignore her attraction and his carnal urges. At base, it was probably more about their skirmish over the property—about winning and losing—than anything else.

Women never offered him challenge. That he wished to subdue her was perhaps male instinct at the most primordial level—sex, the ultimate submission. Or primal motive aside, he might simply be reverting to type. Mrs. St. Vincent was beautiful and tantalizing; why wouldn't he want to fuck her?

The large amount of brandy he'd imbibed may also have contributed to his salacious and urgent desires.

Although, he wasn't drunk.

He didn't get drunk.

But that he was increasingly fixated on whether or not the lady was a screamer could not be denied.

About to raise on a winning hand, he abruptly gave into his impulses and set down his cards. "I'm out."

"Why? It's still early." Lord Bedford waved toward the mauve twilight visible through the windows. "The ladies at Madame Rivera's are barely out of bed. Might as well stay."

"You can't leave now, dammit," Avon muttered. "There's no one else can match me drink for drink."

Fitz handed his markers to a flunkey who had materialized at his side. "I have a meeting to attend."

Everyone at the table stared at him dumbfounded.

"What? Is that so unheard of?"

"It is at this time of day," Freddie said with a jaundiced glance. "So who's the lady?"

"No one you know," Fitz replied, rising to his feet. "I wish you a pleasant evening."

"Dammit, Monk, tell us her name," Freddie insisted while a buzz of queries erupted around him: "At least give us a hint, Fitz. She must be bourgeois; everyone is gone from town. Does she have friends? Of course she has friends. Don't keep the ladies for your eyes only. It's not fair. Don't we always share?"

Reticent to his friends' lively inquisition, Fitz only said, "Fair or not, this lady is for *my* eyes only." His brows flickered briefly. "She's a rare challenge, gentlemen. Need I say more?"

As Fitz walked away, a flurry of conversation echoed in his wake. The Monk always had been more than willing to share his lady loves, his exhibitionist tendencies not only well known but also much admired. In the insulated club world in which the privileged nobles of Fitz's acquaintance had been raised, making love was often perceived as male sport. And spectators were part of the amusement.

As for a challenge, the rank heresy made them speculate that this female was either illicitly young or some wife locked away by a jealous husband. They couldn't conceive of any other circumstances that would challenge The Monk's seductive skills.

Naturally, bets were made as to which was the case.

Immune to his friends' speculations, intent only on personal gratification, Fitz made his way home. After bathing, he partook of another brandy while his valet helped him dress for the evening.

"The dowager duchess will be in town tomorrow, sir," Darby said, holding out a fine cambric shirt. "On the eleven o'clock train."

Fitz shot a look over his shoulder. "Are you sure? I thought she was in Paris." Setting down his glass, he slid his arms through the sleeves and slipped the shirt over his head.

"According to Stanley, Her Grace tired of Lady Montrose's company. As anyone would, I expect, sir."

"Agreed. Thank you for the warning," Fitz noted, sliding the pearl studs into place down his shirtfront. "I'll make sure to be home for lunch. See that we have those strawberries Mother likes."

"All is in order, sir." Darby held out a white silk waistcoat and waited for the duke to tuck his shirt into his trousers. "The cook is busy making the sweets the dowager fancies, the blue suite is being aired, and the dog bed is in place under the windows."

Fitz buttoned up his trousers. "And little Pansy will run all our lives once again."

"Indeed, sir," Darby grumbled as he slipped the waistcoat over Fitz's shoulders. "It's more a mop than a dog if you ask me."

"But Mother's dear mop," Fitz said with a grin, fastening the self-covered buttons down the front of his waistcoat. "So we shall do our duty, eh, Darby?"

"Yes, sir." He held out Fitz's evening coat.

"How long is Mother staying?"

"Stanley didn't know."

"Hmm…" Fitz regarded himself briefly in the cheval glass before taking the ironed bills Darby held out to him and shoving them into his trouser pocket. "Then I must be on my best behavior for an unknown period of time."

"Just make sure you're home by the time the dowager duchess arrives," Darby sardonically replied, realistic about the duke's style of entertainments.

Picking up the glass of brandy, Fitz quickly drained it, handed it to Darby, and said, "Don't wait up for me."

"Would you care to leave an address should I have to fetch you?"

"Don't worry. I'll be back before Mother arrives."

"Just don't forget."

"I'm warned, Darby. But I'm only off for an evening stroll. There's a possibility I may return shortly."

"Care to make a wager on that, sir?" the valet drily said.

Fitz grinned. Darby had been his valet since childhood. "Excellent. I hope you're right. I am facing a veritable minefield of distrust tonight."

"I expect you'll find your way through, sir."

"Your confidence inspires me," Fitz waggishly replied.

"Don't forget the jewelry, sir." Darby nodded at the sparkling objects on a nearby table. "I expect those baubles will clear your path right quick."

"Ah, yes…thanks for the reminder." Fitz slipped the items in his coat pockets, patted them lightly, and grinned. "I suddenly feel a run of good luck."

"Lady Luck generally comes through when you get that feeling, sir."

Fitz gave Darby a considering look. "You're right. Say, why don't you take one of these in honor of the fortuitous occasion? We'll have the inscription changed for Sarah. Here, take this one." He pulled out a glittering slither of rubies. "She'll like it."

"No, sir." His valet held a palm up. "Really, it's not necessary."

"Take it. I insist. Rubies aren't really right for Mrs. St. Vincent's coloring anyway. She has reddish hair." Fitz held the bracelet up to the light and shook his head. "Actually, they're completely wrong." He stuffed the bracelet into Darby's jacket pocket. "And remember to go to sleep early tonight. You know how busy tomorrow will be with Mother in residence."

A moment later, Darby was alone, only the duke's retreating tread audible as he made his way toward the main staircase. Pulling the bracelet from his pocket, Darby studied the sparkling jewels. Another item to add to his wife Sarah's collection. With the duke's liberal generosity over the years, he and his wife could have retired long since.

But the boy needed taking care of; he had from the first.

His pa had been the devil incarnate and his ma had been busy with her society friends, so Darby and Sarah had taken a hand. And if he said so himself, Darby thought, the young scamp had turned out right well.

And so he said to his wife when he went below stairs a short time later. The magnificent bracelet had been put away and they were having a cup of tea in their cozy quarters.

"Now if only the boy could find some woman to love, and I don't mean that kind o' love," his wife muttered, stirring her tea furiously as if in rebuke. "He's been alone too long. It ain't good for him."

"We can't *make* him fall in love," Darby pointed out.

"Not to mention all them society belles are scatterbrained, misbehaving females," Sarah grumbled. "It ain't gonna help him any to marry someone what will jump from bed to bed like him."

"He's got his ma. They're good friends. He's not alone."

"But he needs a wife." Sarah sent her husband a sharp look. "Where's he off to tonight?"

"To see that bookstore lady who's givin' him trouble. His pockets are full o' jewelry Stanley picked up for him this afternoon."

"What does she look like? Tall, short? How old is she? Is she married? I hope not, although she at least works for a living, which is more than I can say for all the fine ladies he knows. And the not-so-fine ladies he knows who make a living on their backsides. Well, tell me about her," his wife finished, brows raised and waiting for answers.

"Stanley says she's a widow. Beautiful as Venus, he says. He went lookin' in case the duke needed his help. But she's bein' real difficult, Stanley says."

"There ain't a woman who can turn down the kind o' jewels Fitzie gives away. She'll come around," Sarah pronounced. "They always do."

"I'm not so sure this time. And taking gifts don't mean nothin'. It don't mean she'll sell her place, and it don't mean she likes him neither. Stanley seems to think she's different somehow."

"Like how?"

"Respectable, he said. Not the usual kind. A woman who stayed with her husband who didn't do much of anything to support her. He wrote poesy verse."

"Then she might like a man what is a man who can do anything. You know, Fitizie. There's nothing he can't do," Sarah proudly declared. "He'd make the right woman a right fine husband."

"Now don't start," her husband warned, recognizing the matchmaking look in his wife's eyes. "You ain't been lucky so far."

"Then my chances are improving. Right?"

Darby gave his wife a lowering look. "Wrong."

CHAPTER 7

SHORTLY BEFORE NINE, Fitz was strolling toward Bruton Street, drawn to Mrs. St. Vincent's bookstore for reasons other than business.

Boredom perhaps.

Lust certainly.

A curiosity beyond the sexual nudged his sensibilities as well, although that unknown factor was quickly suppressed.

Regardless his motivations, fate appeared to be taking a hand in his undertaking for as he approached the lighted store he saw that Mrs. St. Vincent was entertaining. Or rather hosting an event. He recognized the young art critic from the *Times*; they often met at artists' studios. He also observed the correspondent for the women's pages in *Country Life*. He and Miss Baldwin had shared a heated rendezvous at Countess Dalton's costume ball last year. So even if Mrs. St. Vincent demurred, he mused with a small smile, there was a good chance he wouldn't be without a bed partner tonight.

Apropos Mrs. St. Vincent, however, the circumstances

couldn't have been more opportune. Rather than having to privately approach the lady who had angrily dismissed him that morning, he could simply become another guest admiring the art at a public exhibition.

She wouldn't dare throw him out. Think how awkward such a contretemps would be with reporters in full view.

He smiled. Darby was right: Lady Luck was definitely on his side, or perhaps, he reflected, offering up a prayer of thanksgiving, some sympathetic deity had intervened. Eros maybe.

Whatever the manner of auspicious fate, he was feeling a rare excitement.

Vastly uncommon of late.

And he knew it wasn't Miss Baldwin arousing his senses. Not that she could be faulted for either her fair beauty or sexual enthusiasm.

Rather, it was the stunning Mrs. St. Vincent inspiring his sensibilities. The possibility she might yield to him brought another smile to his lips. A night of shared passion not only would be a personal victory but might also lead to a successful business transaction.

She was particularly breathtaking tonight in cream charmeuse and very little else unless his eyes deceived him. Her gown was quite daring.

Which further piqued his interest.

Would she be equally daring in bed?

ROSALIND SAW HIM the moment he walked in, her reaction enough to cause Sofia, who was standing beside her, to follow her gaze.

"We are singularly graced with the aristocracy tonight," Sofia said softly; the avant-garde exhibits were generally outside the purview of the upper classes. They preferred the vetted Royal Academy shows.

"He's here for no good," Rosalind muttered.

"Or he could be interested in the exhibit. Remember, he *is* a collector."

"I doubt his motives are benign. Make sure you stay by my side." Rosalind ordered, feeling herself tense as the duke walked toward them. Then inexplicably, a flaring excitement raced through her senses and furious at both Groveland's magnetic appeal and her shameless response, she greeted him with an unmistakably snappish tone. "To what do we owe this pleasure, Your Grace?"

"Am I intruding? I thought this was a public exhibition." His voice, in contrast, was softly urbane.

"Indeed it is," Sofia quickly interposed, sending Rosalind a quelling glance. "Everyone's most welcome."

"Forgive me. You're welcome of course," Rosalind murmured, understanding that her personal feelings were immaterial; selling paintings was the prime object of the evening. "Your Grace, allow me to present Sofia Eastleigh, one of the artists whose work is on display. Sofia, Groveland."

"We've met before." Fitz smiled at Sofia. "And I recognize your work." He nodded at her delphinium painting visible in the distance. "Although, I haven't seen you at Leighton's of late."

"My leisure time is limited now that my art is actually selling. The more I paint, the more I sell," Sofia explained with a grin.

"Congratulations. Although anyone with your talent was sure to meet with success."

"Thank you. According to Leighton you're no mean draftsman yourself."

"Leighton is being generous," Fitz replied with well-bred grace. "I'm the most amateur of dabblers."

"Didn't you have two drawings in the last Academy show?"

Fitz lifted one brow. "Sir Joffrey had partisan motives. He likes to fish at my Scottish property."

"You're much too modest. They were excellent."

Just as Rosalind was beginning to feel like a third wheel, Fitz turned to her and said with a disarming smile and a singularly intimate gaze, "Might I impose on you to show me around your gallery, Mrs. St. Vincent?"

Rosalind suddenly felt as though she were alone with him in the midst of the crowd, his intense grey gaze mesmerizing. Then out of the blue, a flame-hot jolt of desire spiked downward, shocking her senses, inciting wholly unacceptable passionate cravings.

She faintly heard Sofia say, "Go," but only when she felt the pressure of Sofia's hand on her back did she regain a modicum of self-possession.

"If you please, Groveland," she said, her words still faintly breathy. Warning herself to get hold of her senses, she dipped her head in his direction and added more lucidly, "Do follow me."

Tantalized by her shapely form on display beneath the simplicity of her clinging gown, captivated by the heated moment when their eyes had met, only too aware of her jasmine scent in his nostrils, Fitz was in the mood to follow her anywhere at all.

Which meant his plans for the evening were falling nicely into place.

She was willing even if she didn't know it.

The point was, he did.

Her slender, curvaceous figure was equally enticing from the rear, her gliding walk, the gentle sway of her hips pure temptation. The radical chic of her gown offered the merest sop to convention. She might as well have been naked beneath the sleek medieval-style dress reminiscent of Rossetti's paintings.

Hopefully she soon would be.

He glanced at his wristwatch. Merde. He'd have to play the gentleman for some time yet.

And so he did, listening politely as she guided him around the exhibit, making the appropriate responses to the work shown him, never overstepping the bounds of politesse. In short, presenting a completely different persona than he had earlier that day. However, he liked that she blushed if he held her glance a moment too long, and he also liked that her manner toward him softened as they wandered the exhibit.

The space was relatively small, though, so afterward, when he took time to speak to the various artists either in Rosalind's company or alone, he was never far from the object of his pursuit. Including the time Miss Baldwin cornered him and commenced pressing her suit with vigor. Pressing her substantial bosom against his chest as well with complete disregard for their audience.

"People are looking, sweetheart," he murmured, keeping his hands to himself, not wishing to openly push her away for fear of embarrassing her.

"I don't care," she purred, rubbing against him, the lace ruffle on her low decolletage suddenly catching on one of his pearl studs.

"Ah, but you should care, dearest," he added under his breath, trying to detach the lace without tearing it. Oh, Christ—Mrs. St. Vincent had glanced his way and frowned. "Why don't we plan on spending some time together tomorrow instead?" he suggested, needing to quickly extricate himself from Miss Baldwin's clutches and lace ruffles.

Her upturned gaze was suddenly sharp. "When tomorrow?"

"Anytime." He stepped back. *There, finally.*

"Are you busy tonight?" A small pettish query at both his excuse and the fact that he'd backed away from her.

"Actually, my mother is coming in on the midnight train," he lied.

"Your mother?" Her sky blue eyes were skeptical.

"Yes, upon my word." *All's fair in love and war.*

She paused briefly in consideration, then looking at him from under her lashes, coquettishly said, "Very well. The Savoy at four."

He smiled. "Excellent. Do you like roses?"

"Of course, darling." She reached out and ran her fingers down the fine silk of his waistcoat in a proprietary gesture. "Red roses," she murmured in a sultry contralto.

Watching Miss Baldwin walk away, it took him a moment to collect himself, having only narrowly averted a scene. And he well knew she was not a woman who gave up gracefully. After Charlotte's costume ball, she'd relentlessly pursued him, going so far as to call at his home. Fortunately, the race season had begun at the time and he was rarely in London. As for the Savoy engagement, time enough to deal with that tomorrow. Right now, he had more pleasant prospects in mind.

For the remaining hours of the exhibit, he avoided Miss Baldwin and unostentatiously pursued Mrs. St. Vincent. Rather than offering posies and charming phrases in the usual seduction, Fitz cultivated the lady's good will instead by purchasing a dozen paintings.

Rosalind was naturally delighted. She was further enchanted by his amiable rapport with her artist friends; she had not thought a peer of Groveland's consequence could be so unaffected. Particularly after his high-handed arrogance that morning.

But he turned out to be enormously gracious and engaging, even so kind as to send for champagne from his cellar for her guests. Rosalind couldn't help but be gratified. She found herself reconsidering her previous judgment, viewing him now in a much more favorable light.

After all, the show was a huge success thanks in part to Groveland's largesse. The women artists she sponsored were considerably more prosperous—again, thanks to the duke.

Sofia, apparently, was in accord when it came to Groveland's benevolence for she spoke up for him sometime later as they were refilling trays of sweets in Rosalind's kitchen. "You might want to change your mind about Groveland, darling. Not only is he a generous patron of the arts, he's really quite lovely in any number of ways. As you may have noticed."

Rosalind gave her friend an arch look. "I wouldn't expect anything less from him. Is he not known for his cultivated graces?"

"I'd say his manner is particularly affable to you."

"Please," Rosalind said. "He has ulterior motives as you well know."

"Of course he does, and if I were you, I'd seriously consider taking him up on his offer."

"Sell my store!" Rosalind tossed a mutinous look her friend's way. "Never!"

"I *meant*, darling," Sofia soothingly replied, "why not spend the night with him and let him gratify your senses? He is in great demand for all the right reasons—very *large* reasons, I've heard."

"For heaven's sake, Sofia!"

"Some say he posed for Zeus in Noland's *Rape of Danae*," Sofia went on undeterred, Rosalind's rosy flush indicating interest—whether she realized it or not. "Have you seen the painting?" Sofia's pale brows rose in signal hyperbole. "*Very* impressive male anatomy."

"I rather think the correspondent from *Country Life* will be taking advantage of Groveland's impressive anatomy tonight," Rosalind said with a little sniff.

Sofia looked up from the petit fours she was placing in neat rows on a tray. "I think it bothers you that she might."

"It certainly does not!"

"Please, I've know you too long. Be honest—it does."

"Well if it does, it shouldn't," Rosalind crisply retorted.

"Yorkshire rules? Come, darling, you're in London now. There aren't any rules when it comes to passion. Here it's strictly about self-indulgence or better yet," she added with a wink, "overindulgence."

"I'm not interested in passion or indulgence of any kind," Rosalind firmly said, as if a resolute delivery would translate to an equal decisiveness in her mind.

"Of course you are," Sofia calmly returned. "Despite your protests. So why not indulge in the breathless joys of passion? And who better than Groveland to offer you those pleasures?"

Rosalind smiled tolerantly at her friend; how many times had they covered this subject in the course of her widowhood? "While you may embrace such breathless sensibilities, my life is about customers and sales, book orders and events like this. But should the time ever come when I'm in the grip of your thrilling emotions, you can be sure I'll consider gratifying them."

"Perhaps later tonight," Sofia slyly murmured.

"No, not tonight." Rosalind placed the last strawberry tart in place and picked up the tray. "Now enough nonsense. Let's see if we can sell another painting."

As a matter of fact, several more paintings were eventually sold, and by eleven the gallery guests were departing, the tarts and petit fours were all eaten, the champagne drunk, and a sense of an evening well spent pervaded the air.

Groveland was standing beside Rosalind as the clock struck the hour.

Taking note of the time, he said, "It's getting late. Thank you for a lovely evening." His smile was practiced, but Mrs. St. Vincent was quite inexplicably redefining his casual regard for the women in his life. She inspired a rare predatory instinct; he disliked the feeling. "I'll send my men in the morning to collect my paintings." It had been a mistake to come.

No, don't go! Rosalind impulsively thought, only to instantly equivocate. *Just say goodnight; do not become involved with the much too charming Duke of Groveland.*

Who, unfortunately, wanted her store.

It may have been gypsy fate that Sofia walked over at that moment, or random chance or kismet. Or perhaps scheming design. She was clinging to the arm of the *Times* art critic, who in turn was holding up a bottle of Fitz's champagne. "If we open this last bottle, will you two have a drink with us?" Sofia brightly inquired. "Since we seem to be the only ones left."

"I wouldn't mind a glass," Fitz heard himself say. So much for reason in the presence of a hot-spur libido.

"I don't know," Rosalind objected politely, *her* voice of reason still operating. "It *is* late."

"How long will it take to drink one glass?" Sofia coaxed, intent on Rosalind taking advantage of Groveland's obvious interest when her dearest friend had been celibate too long. "One little drink, darling," she cajoled, "to celebrate the success of the show and my increased fortune."

Since Sofia's good fortune was due to Groveland's numerous purchases, Rosalind relented. Or told herself she did because of that. "Very well. One drink."

The die was cast.

Not that Rosalind knew until later.

But Sofia did.

And Fitz did.

In fact, he knew with such certainty that he literally checked his watch as if marking the time when he'd carried the day. Or night as it were. As for his obsession with Mrs. St. Vincent, by morning he'd have had his fill of her and he could get on with his life.

Retiring to the back of the store, the two couples found seats on worn sofas Rosalind kept there for customers of her free library who needed a bed for the night. The couches' frayed frieze upholstery and scuffed mahogany trim, the stacks of books littering the floor, the night sounds of the city drifting in through the open window were all irrelevant to the cozy group drinking champagne and exchanging postmortem comments on the show.

Rosalind was surprised at Groveland's comprehensive understanding of the newest trends in modern art. She felt quite out of her element as the three others discussed the Paris and London art shows of recent years: the artists of note, those on the rise, the avant-garde styles most likely to endure. She realized that Groveland had a life beyond his scandalous reputation; she understood, too, that Sofia might have been right. Perhaps she was pleased after all that the *Country Life* siren had not taken Groveland away.

But as quickly as she acknowledged his sexual attraction, she recognized how out of character it would be to yield to her impulses. She was not a free spirit like Sofia. Furthermore, she reflected, ticking off additional reasons to reject the infamous Groveland, her capitulation would mean less than nothing to a man who, according to rumor, had slept with untold women.

Is he really that good?

The unspeakable thought stunned and electrified her senses.

Sent a shiver up her spine.

He noticed and turning to her, murmured solicitously, "Would you like my jacket?"

"No, no…I'm fine…really," Rosalind stammered, quickly looking away from the tantalizing query in his gaze.

"You're sure."

He knows, she thought. *He can tell*. She forced a smile and said in a scrupulously neutral tone, "It must have been a draft from the window."

Fortunately, at that moment Sofia asked him a question about the Royal Academy that initiated a lengthy conversation. And by the time Sofia had fully vented her myriad resentments on the stupid old men controlling the annual judging, Rosalind had composed her restive emotions.

Before long, the champagne exhausted, Sofia rose, took her partner's hand, and pulled him to his feet. "I don't know about you," she said with a wink for Rosalind and Fitz, "but we have better things to do. Right?" Rising on tiptoe, she brushed Arthur Godwin's cheek with a kiss.

"Absolutely." He grinned. "You don't know how long I've been waiting."

"Since last year at Michaelmas when I met you in Chelsea," Sofia matter-of-factly declared.

"Before," he softly returned. He was slender and fine-featured, handsome in the style of the first Duke of Buckingham.

Sofia's eyes widened. "Where?"

"Three years ago. You were in a box at Covent Garden."

"You'll have to tell me all about it," Sofia said, smiling. "Ciao, darlings," she cheerfully proclaimed, and waving to Rosalind and Fitz, she pulled her admirer from the room.

An awkward silence fell.

Skilled at putting women at ease, Fitz spoke first. "Miss Eastleigh is vastly talented." He smiled faintly. "She's also somewhat of a modern woman."

Rosalind blushed. "Very much so."

Another small silence ensued.

"I should go." A politesse; perhaps not. Nothing was as it should be tonight.

There was the veriest pause and then, resisting what were clearly perilous desires, Rosalind said, "Yes, it's quite late." She came to her feet. "Thank you again for your patronage."

He hadn't been rebuffed by a woman since... actually, never. But Mrs. St. Vincent was standing very straight, her hands clenched at her sides, and even knowing she was suppressing her desires, he had no intention of forcing himself on her. He'd never forced himself on a woman, nor was he about to begin. Particularly when he wasn't even sure he should be here.

Equivocation scented the air; it had all evening.

Rising from the couch, he sketched her an elegant bow. "Thank you for your hospitality. My men will come round in the morning for the paintings." Turning, he walked away, the evening not completely wasted; he'd added some splendid paintings to his collection. More important, Mrs. St. Vincent had been restored to her rightful place in his life. Someone at cross purposes with him in business and nothing more.

Halfway through the store, the front door in sight, he heard her. Or had he? The sound was so faint he may have imagined her voice. *Be sensible*, he said to himself. But he turned back—like a dog in heat, he thought, thin-skinned and moody.

She was standing well distant in the gallery, the colorful paintings at her back, her hands still clenched at her sides. But she said, "Stay," this time clearly enough that there was no misunderstanding.

Her breathing was rapid, her lush breasts rising and falling in the most flaunting display; her skin was flushed, and even across the breadth of the store it was obvious she was sexually aroused.

He suddenly felt as if he were being offered a rare prize—this from a man indisposed to flights of fancy, a man who'd always considered undue emotion a weakness. Had he drunk too much? But even as he considered the possibility, he was closing the distance between them. And whatever impulse drove him, when he stopped before her and saw the tremulous desire shining in her eyes, he understood that he was a very lucky man.

That and nothing more.

No thoughts of property negotiations or winning entered his mind. No further nebulous uncertainties about subversive emotion clouded his thinking. Not even a scintilla of sexual triumph registered in his brain. All he felt was an exaggerated sense of pleasure.

"Thank you for calling me back." His smile was very close, urbanity stripped from his voice. "I'm extremely happy and I don't exactly know why."

"I know less why I called to you," she answered so softly he had to lean in to hear her.

"It doesn't matter. I'm glad you did." Simple words simply spoken, a sense of inevitability so sweet he could taste it.

She was agitated, uncertain.

He knew better than to make a sudden move and frighten her.

Then she swayed forward an infinitesimal distance; to anyone not involved in the fevered encounter, the movement would have gone unnoticed. "I'm very pleased you came tonight," she whispered.

"Then we both are." A velvet soft utterance freely given, knotty issues dismissed.

She knew he wasn't alluding to the art show or the paintings he'd purchased, and drawing in a small breath, she wondered how long it had been since she'd lain with a man. Or more to the point, a man of unparalleled physical perfection and immoderate charm, a man for whom she felt a fierce, wild passion unlike anything she'd ever known.

"Perhaps kismet actually exists," he offered with a smile.

Her eyes flared wide. "Do you think so?"

He was about to say no, but she looked so genuinely art-less, he didn't have the heart. "I do."

"You're not just saying that."

"No." A kindness not a lie. "People more clever than I subscribe to the theory. And consider how many thousands of years the concept has shaped people's destiny."

"So you're saying destiny is involved tonight."

By any standard her smile was flirtatious, her uncer-tainty suddenly replaced by a playful drollery. "All I know is there's no place I'd rather be," he said very softly, aston-ished at the pleasure he felt quite apart from lust.

"Well put, although I suspect you're better acquainted with these situations than I."

"Not this particular one." His brows rose. "I have no explanation."

She smiled. "How sweet—and generally effective, I expect."

"On the contrary, I'm quite sincere." He had no idea why he felt compelled to such frankness when prevarica-tion had always rendered better service in circumstances such as this.

She held his gaze for a second, weighing her precon-ceived notions against Groveland's candor. Quickly decid-ing that truth or pretense mattered little when their desires were so clearly aligned. "I suppose," she said, perhaps just a trifle briskly for the world of dalliance, "we shouldn't just stand here."

A teasing light instantly warmed his eyes. "I know I'd rather not." He couldn't accuse her of coyness. She was so obviously unfamiliar with the game, it was going to be like deflowering a virgin.

Not that he had personal knowledge, having always avoided virgins. But Mrs. St. Vincent was definitely an innocent when it came to amorous play. Of that he was certain.

"Should we go upstairs?"

But she'd balled her fists again when speaking as though

facing the hangman instead of a night of pleasure, so he decided kisses might be in order first for the widow. "In a minute," he murmured, and dipping his head, he kissed her gently in reassurance and even more gently placed his hands on her shoulders and slowly drew her close.

Allowing her ample time to change her mind should she wish to.

But when her soft, warm breasts first came in contact with his chest, she didn't pull away, and as his erection immediately sprang to life, surged upward, and pressed into her stomach, she didn't flinch.

Instead, she gasped—in astonishment and wonder. Had he known...

But he didn't. And he debated how long he would be obliged to play the modest lover and restrict himself to kisses. Sweet as they were, he thought with an equivalent astonishment.

But suddenly, she threw her arms around his neck, melted into his body, and breathed against the warmth of his mouth, "Forgive me for being so brazen, but you make me feel *ever* so good..."

"I'm glad," he whispered, sliding his hands downward, cupping her bottom, holding her hard against his cock.

Another little gasp, and she breathed whisper soft, "You're...*enormous*!"

Suppressing his impulse to say, "The better to fuck you with," he kissed her less sweetly, with the novel urgency Mrs. St. Vincent inspired even as he searched for the door to her upstairs apartment. Finally—*there*—stairs were visible through a half-opened door in the far corner. Quickly lifting his head, he swept her up in his arms and said with a smile, "I'm taking you upstairs. Feel free to stop me at any time." A politesse only; God himself couldn't have stopped him.

"I won't," she whispered, clinging to his neck, her words excusing him from possible sacrilege. "I want you too much."

"I want you more," he said with an easy smile.

"Impossible."

"I doubt it." The lady smiling up at him was a restorative to his jaded soul, tremulous and needy, dew fresh and beautiful.

Her brows rose. "Care to make a wager?"

He almost took her right there, the possibility of dueling lechery racheting up his libido another ten notches. "Anything you like, darling," he said, controlling his lust with effort.

"Do you feel lucky?"

He laughed. "Damned right."

"Me, too." Tonight was serendipity, pure and simple, she thought, reveling in the blissful illogic. After a lifetime devoted to undeviating steadiness, she was experiencing a degree of covetousness beyond the perimeters of memory.

The rapturous feel of his hard, muscled body against hers, the intoxicating, soul-stirring passion warming her body and soul were unutterably joyous. Perhaps Sofia was right; perhaps it was time she began to live again or *finally* live or *flamboyantly* live. *Or resist such base urges*, a muted voice of reason obstinately submitted.

But muted voices were easily brushed aside when under the spell of high-flying lust and fevered desire. And who better than Groveland to satisfy her salacious urges—a man who was a byword for vice?

And while she'd not yet experienced the full extent of his sexual renown, the hard, splendid length of his erection against her thigh suggested satisfaction on a grand scale.

CHAPTER 8

I CAN PERFECTLY well walk upstairs," Rosalind said as Fitz began mounting the stairs.

"But why should you?"

Her first thought shouldn't have been that Edward never could have carried her up the stairs so effortlessly. Or at all. He wasn't tall and powerful like Groveland, nor corded with muscle. Shameful thought; why was she comparing her husband to Groveland? And then, as if the devil were whispering in her ear, she heard Mrs. Beecham's voice saying, *You're not getting any younger*, and she found herself thinking, *I deserve this*.

"Penny for your thoughts," Fitz murmured, aware of the lady's reflective silence.

"Do you think I'm old? Oh Lord, pretend I didn't say that," she quickly declared, blushing furiously.

In the dim stairwell lit by a single electric light sconce at the top of the stairs, he glanced down and was charmed to see the most fetching, rosy-cheeked mortification. Mrs. St. Vincent was a rare delight; no aristocratic lady he knew would have called attention to her age. "I think you're absolutely gorgeous," he murmured, smiling, "and what—eighteen or so?"

She laughed, a bright silvery sound. "You're a darling."

"Wait," he said with a grin. "It gets better."

"So I've heard. Sofia tells me you're celebrated for your expertise."

"Hardly," he modestly replied. "But I'll contrive to amuse you in whatever fashion you prefer."

"Is this about amusement?"

Uncertain of her tone, he gracefully replied, "It's about whatever you want."

"Because you're versatile."

There was that trifling pettishness again. "No, because I very much wish to please you. You're quite exceptional; this evening is exceptional. Nothing about *this*—*us*—is about versatility or amusement. I apologize for my choice of words. You've been a constant in my thoughts today."

Her expression turned guarded. "Because you want my store."

"No." He didn't even take issue with her comment. "Because I find you fascinating."

"And you want what you want."

"Good God, don't fight with me." He smiled. "You don't know how much I'm out of my element."

She drew in a small shaky breath. "We both are."

"Then we'll navigate this unknown terrain together. You lead and I'll follow."

She couldn't help but smile at his flattering candor. "It might be wiser if you lead and I follow."

Since he rarely contradicted a lady when it came to making love, he whispered, "Whatever you say." Although, he rather thought she was right. Having reached the top of the stairs, he crossed the small landing, walked through the open door into a parlor illuminated by another simple light fixture, and halted. "Which way? Over there?" He nodded toward a closed door on the far side of the sparsely furnished room.

"Oh dear."

Looking down, Fitz met her wide-eyed gaze. "Is something wrong?" There was no mistaking the doubt in her voice.

"I don't know—maybe...probably. Oh Lord, now I'm not sure."

Faced with such tremulous reluctance, he debated his course of action. Toying with a squeamish woman could turn out to be a disaster. Sophisticated females with a flair for the game were more his style—like Miss Baldwin. She'd been more than willing.

And yet, there was no question it was Mrs. St. Vincent he wanted.

Notoriously self-indulgent, and highly motivated, he decided the lady's uncertainties were open to interpretation. She clearly hadn't ordered him to *put me down this instant and leave*. A good sign.

So, attuned as he was to the nuances of female acquiescence, he carried her toward what looked to be a bedroom door. Crossing the small parlor in a few strides, he shoved open the door with his shoulder and stepped over the threshold.

Rosalind shivered—in anticipation at this point, Groveland's celebrated reputation was one of excess.

"Are you cold?" he gently asked, coming to a halt, although he knew better. Aroused women were not without precedence in his life.

"No, quite the opposite."

"I'm delighted to hear it," he said.

A brief flash of amusement shone in her eyes. "I'm hoping you delight *me* as well."

He laughed. "I shall strive to fulfill your hopes."

"Do you ever get complaints?"

His look of surprise was quickly shuttered. "Not about this," he said.

She shouldn't ask personal questions. Even unfamiliar as she was with dalliance, she knew better. But she found herself intrigued by the man behind the prodigal reputation. "What complaints do you get?" she impetuously asked, the words coming out in a rush.

He looked at her so oddly, she immediately said, "Forgive my curiosity, but you're a constant subject of the scandal sheets."

"Does that interest you?" His voice had taken on a cynical edge. Was her innocence a pose? Was she looking for something out of the ordinary tonight, like the others?

His gaze was cool. "I apologize again," she quickly said. "I'm new to this."

Illogically, he felt a sense of relief. Maybe he was turning into a romantic. Or maybe Mrs. St. Vincent was as lush a female as he'd ever had the good fortune to bed and he should stop overintellectualizing her motives and his. "New is good," he smoothly observed, and began walking toward the bed.

As he moved, the solid length of his erection nudged her right hip and bottom, sending a heated shimmer of excitement racing along every impatient little nerve ending in her body. She'd been aroused for some time—if she was honest with herself, since he'd walked into the exhibition. Without so much as a word or gesture from him, she'd immediately turned dewy wet in readiness. It was astonishing how he could tempt her to such madness with so little effort—with none. Her wanting him was a kind of extravagant delirium. "No, no, not there," she blurted out, wrenched from her musing as he stopped by her bed.

Since at this stage of their acquaintance, politesse was required, he swiftly surveyed the small room, searching for some other piece of furniture or surface capable of holding them both. In the light from the open doorway, the shadowed interior revealed a flimsy dressing table, a too-high chest of drawers, a narrow fragment of carpet before the hearth, the shabby interior provoking a sudden, inexplicable resentment toward Edward St. Vincent. How could he gamble away his money and force his wife to live like this?

"The chair perhaps."

Her voice intruded into his rancor, and casting aside his irrational concern, he said with a smile, "The chair will do nicely." Or at least until such a time as he could coax Mrs. St. Vincent into her former marriage bed.

Another first for a man who was more familiar than many aristocratic husbands with their marriage beds.

But then tonight was alive with firsts. Most significant, his outrageous interest in a woman who had been, at best, inhospitable to him only a few hours ago. Perhaps the challenge of overcoming Mrs. St. Vincent's initial distaste fueled his lust.

Or maybe the lady's ripe opulence struck some primal nerve.

Or maybe the whys didn't matter when it came right down to it—only the fucking.

While Fitz was engaged in a novel introspective, Rosalind's troublesome voice of reason had inconveniently resurfaced and was taking issue with her having sex with the man who was out to steal her property.

What are you doing? He's your enemy.

Wait, wait, her fevered passions swiftly intervened, bargaining frantically. *Couldn't tonight be in the way of a research exercise?*

Of course. There. All was quickly reconciled. Lust triumphant.

With her voice of reason appeased, Groveland's enormous erection featuring largely in her swift decision, she looked forward to a night of sumptuous carpe diem pleasure. Sofia was right; she'd been celibate too long. "I feel I should apologize again—about the bed this time," she murmured. "I'm just not ready to—"

"No need to explain," Fitz interposed, averse to hearing some explanation about her husband. Not that anything—including dead husbands—was likely to dissuade his aching cock from its target goal. "We'll sit in the chair instead," he pleasantly said, dropping into the wing-back chair, disposing her on his lap, and shifting to plan B.

The hard imprint of his erection instantly made contact with her throbbing vulva in the most delectable fashion, and Rosalind shifted her bottom slightly to better absorb the wildly intoxicating rapture. "You—this . . . makes me feel"—she smiled up at him—"decidedly wanton."

Lounging back in the chair, Fitz's mouth twitched. "Naturally, that pleases me."

His cool equanimity was perversely sexual, as if he had but to wait and women always came to him. "Such insouciance, Groveland," she said, a small heat in her eyes. "It almost makes me angry."

"But not quite, I'd wager."

"Nor could you get up and leave, *I'd* wager," she countered, not as cooly as he, but as pointed.

"No." Not so cool that time, an edginess in his voice.

They were both restive under their baffling urges, not entirely sure why they were here, why they were doing what they were doing, why they couldn't just walk away.

Then less practiced at the game, less jaded, or rather, not jaded at all, Rosalind capitulated first. "I don't know why I'm taking issue with your expertise when look"—she held out her quivering hand—"I'm trembling for want of you."

"Why don't I take care of that."

His careless offer of orgasmic pleasure smacked of arrogance. But it also incited piquant little vibrations in every seething, palpitating secret recess of her body. "Naturally, that pleases me," she murmured, oversweet and smiling.

"Bitch," he said, but he was smiling, too.

"*In heat*, thanks to you. How do you do it?"

In the usual way, he could have said, seduction a well-rehearsed, predictable game. "Why don't we find out?" he said, husky and low, slipping his hand under the soft silk of her skirt, gently easing her thighs apart to offer the lady a short prelude as it were to the coming drama. Her muscles tensed as he brushed aside the slight barrier of her drawers, although some charitable foreplay was obviously needed after a flinch like hers. "Shut your eyes and think of England, darling," he whispered, his voice gently teasing.

"Sorry, it's been a *very* long time . . ."

He couldn't possibly relate, this man who'd been standing stud since adolescence. But he was right about the wooing required to see that the lady's body and sensibilities were eased into the night's play. "Should I talk you through the first time, ply you with kisses, recite Ovid," he sportively offered.

She was about to ask him if he was ever serious, but he'd slipped his fingers into her silken flesh and suddenly she was having trouble thinking about anything other than degrees of pleasure. Her head dropped onto his shoulder, her eyes closed, and she understood that whatever reservations she might have had about Groveland paled to insignificance against his deft skill. The man was a virtuoso—touching her exactly where she wished to be touched, deeply, deeply, with the lightest of strokes, as if he could read her mind, her body, her nerve endings, her most rarified fantasies. He was incredibly gentle as well, something she wouldn't have expected from so large a man. Most important, he somehow knew that she liked the rosebud of her clitoris be given a good measure of attention—and he did.

Perhaps a libertine had his advantages, she thought, floating on her blissful cloud. He was much better at this than she.

He was so much better in fact that she was beginning to believe in bewitchment or if not that fanciful illusion, the ravishing hysteria engulfing her entire body in a steamy, rapturous exultation might be closer to heaven on Earth. Or perhaps something even better, she decided a few moments later as her orgasm began to slowly swell into a small seething rampage, assaulting her senses with increasing fury, spreading with unchecked speed—quickly, too quickly. She whimpered, helpless against the climactic momentum, wanting the exquisite rapture to last. Then she cried out as the storm and fury overwhelmed and ravished her, as the feel of his fingers buried deep inside her triggered voluptuous, overdrawn waves of pleasure, as he transported her to a paradise of his making for long, long, euphoric moments.

He didn't move while she was in the throes of orgasm.

He knew better.

When at last her body stilled and her eyelids fluttered opened, even then he waited until she smiled at him and whispered in languid content, "Thank you. I really needed that."

He couldn't help but laugh, although her hard nipples and plump breasts pressing against the fine charmeuse of her gown, her luscious bottom warming his cock, and her even more luscious cunt warming his fingers gave him potent reason to believe that she'd be needing more.

Fortunately, he was here to help her.

And himself. Withdrawing his fingers, he wiped them on his pant leg. "It takes the edge off doesn't it?" he drawled, well versed in degrees of lust.

"It did considerably more than that. You're *very* good."

"In contrast to?" Why it mattered he had no idea. But then nothing about his response to Mrs. St. Vincent made sense.

"To nothing. You just made me feel ... incredibly wonderful."

Her frankness constantly confounded him. In the brittle world in which he moved, frankness was considered a parvenue gaucherie. But he responded with an easy grace. "My pleasure," he said.

Hers more than his, Rosalind pleasantly decided, since he fulfilled her every erotic fantasy ... any woman's, she didn't doubt. He was a splendid male animal, physically powerful, handsome, with a huge erection that was impossible to ignore and yet he somehow did. Another virtuoso skill perhaps—which notion immediately evoked a host of licentious images starring the Duke of Groveland. "What if I were to say I was looking for adventure tonight?" she inquired, driven by rash impulse, her newly awakened libido, and the very real possibility she'd not have this opportunity again.

Fitz didn't move a muscle—no blink, no indication of surprise, not so much as a twitch of his cock at the good news. "I'd say tell me what you want."

"I don't suppose you know anything about harems?"

"I'm afraid not." His friend Lady Melville did, so he in turn did, but she was into hashish and bondage, which wasn't on his agenda tonight. "We'll think of something else."

"Good, because you inspire the most intense desire in me," she artlessly declared, having been recently exposed to an exorbitant standard of orgasmic pleasure formerly unknown to her and finding herself greedy for more. "Now I fully understand why you're so much in demand," she added, wrapping her arms around his neck, smiling at him from very close range, allowing pure emotion to reign supreme. "Really, I'm happier than I've been in ages."

"Then we both are ... happy," Fitz murmured, liking the feel of her clinging to him, actually meaning what he said when he never did at times like this.

"How sweet, but then you know what to say, don't you?" she lightly replied, and tightening her grip on his neck, she offered him a dazzling smile. "There's pleasure sure, in being mad." Dryden understood this sweet insanity.

Fitz laughed, recognizing the phrase if not the author. "I must brush up on my literature."

"You needn't do anything at all; I am quite, quite content!" she cheerfully proclaimed.

It took him a moment to assess such an utterly guileless sentiment in the context of her need for adventure. Wild sex and poetry perhaps. Although his contentment was predicated rather more on just fucking her for hours. Not that such bluntness would serve. Instead, he said, "Whenever you're ready, I could offer you additional contentment."

She flushed. "Oh dear, how selfish of me. Of course, you must have satisfaction, too."

He suppressed his smile with effort, her mea culpa charming. Although when it came to selfishness, she didn't know she was dealing with a man born and bred to the principle. "There's plenty of time," he said.

"I don't want to use my bed," she quickly declared.

"Fine. We won't."

"I mean it."

"I understand." He was intent on being agreeable until such a time as his cock was buried in her warm, soft body— at which point he would become even more agreeable.

"Why do I get the feeling you'll say anything?"

Because that's what people do in situations like this. "No bed." He smiled. "I promise."

"And *he* must behave," Rosalind murmured, unable to resist shifting her hips ever so slightly in order to feel his gloriously large erection.

His brows rose, on guard. "Meaning?"

"You mustn't climax in me."

"Agreed." That was easy. Begetting a bastard was no part of his plans.

"So sure?" Dare she ask if he was lying?

Fitz smiled. "He does as he's told."

Her brows lifted slightly. "Such control."

"I'm a practical man." Her raised brows told Fitz that Edward St. Vincent hadn't been fully in control. Common enough—and one of the reasons he was so much in demand with the ladies. "It's all about mutual pleasure, darling, not a game of chance." A quick smile. "Since we're about to become closer friends, do you have a given name?"

She grinned. "Is this about friendship?"

"Of course."

"Are you friends with all the ladies in your life?"

"I am."

"You astonish me." She stretched lazily, still marginally basking in a postcoital glow.

"I haven't even begun to astonish you," he roguishly declared, his gaze on her rising breasts, mentally ticking off the length of time he had to fuck her before morning. "If you don't want to tell me your name—"

"Rosalind. And yours?"

"I'm called Fitz."

There was that restraint she'd heard before in his voice. "You don't like your given name?"

"No."

His curt response effectively curtailed her next question.

"Then allow me to say"—with her desires clearly on the rise once again, she was selfishly avoiding any offense—"I look forward to getting to know you better, Fitz."

"Who made your gown?" His given name—his father's name—rife with discord, he deliberately changed the subject.

"One of Sofia's friends designed it. Would you like it off?"

She continued to surprise him. "Yes, I would," he replied with equal frankness. "Let me help you."

Sliding off his lap, she rose to her feet, her earlier equivocation long since taken flight. "Unbutton the back for me."

As she turned her back to him, his mouth curved in a smile. The lady no longer required wooing.

He was back on familiar ground.

Spreading his legs, he pulled her between his thighs and reached for the silk covered buttons at the neck of her gown.

CHAPTER 9

FIVE MINUTES LATER, she was standing nude before him, her dress draped on the back of his chair, her chemise, drawers, and petticoat in a pile on a nearby table. She was clearly restless and impatient, her nipples taut, her skin pinked in arousal, her hips undulating faintly as if she could barely wait until he was undressed and inside her.

To that end, Fitz was swiftly disrobing, dropping his clothes on the floor with malc disregard for subtleties. His jacket, waistcoat, shirt, and tie were off, as were his shoes and socks. He was unbuttoning his trousers when she whispered, "Let me do that."

He looked up, the wistful longing in her voice instantly bringing his erection to full mast. *Is this real or play?* Then he let his hands drop to his sides and said, "Be my guest," because it didn't really matter which it was.

She reminded him of an innocent maid, so tentative were her actions, her hands shaking as she unfastened a button. Or maybe just an impatient widow, he thought, although the style of woman mattered little to his libido. Only with effort did he resist pushing her head down and

shoving his cock into her mouth. It took even more constraint not to pick her up, carry her to the bed, and plunge
into her lush body.

Rosalind wasn't similarly motivated by constraint, having dispatched the former practicalities of her life in favor
of extravagant, feverish, liberating desire. And if she'd not
already decided to thoroughly enjoy Groveland's legendary
talents, the sight of his massive, upthrust penis freed now
from his trousers would have been reason enough.

She couldn't help but stare as he casually stripped away
the last of his clothing. He was much larger than she'd
expected, his size intimidating, although he was relaxed,
familiar with women looking at him unclothed.

"I won't hurt you," he said, aware of her tremulous
gaze.

"I wasn't thinking about that." She looked up, rosy
cheeked and breathless. "May I?"

It had been a long day enlivened by too many erotic
fantasies in which Mrs. St. Vincent played a starring role.
More to the point, his amorous activities rarely involved
wooing a lady, the reverse usually the case. And he'd been
drinking for hours and any number of other excuses may
have motivated his novel impatience. "You may." Reaching out, he cupped her head in one hand, pressed it downward, guided his erection into place with his other hand,
and watched his cock slide into her mouth.

He smiled faintly as the lovely widow instantly took to
her task.

No innocent maid at least in terms of enthusiasm.

Although her ineptitude would require some tutoring;
her fingernails were cutting into his penis she was gripping
it so tightly. Not that her impassioned earnestness wasn't
more than making up for that slight pain. With a mind to
mitigating his discomfort and enhancing the pleasure, he
loosened her grip with his fingers and whispered, "I'm not
going anywhere."

Instantly contrite, she lifted her gaze, her face pale in
the shadowed light and framed by heavy waves of hair,

her mouth filled with half his cock, and said in muffled accents, "I'm sorry."

The sight was enough to bring a monk to climax.

Or a real one at least.

The Monk of London restrained himself with well-practiced skill.

He had his sights on the lady's cunt.

Until such a time, however, he wasn't averse to enjoying what the lady was enjoying. Not that she wouldn't improve with a little training. Not that he wouldn't like to train her—a curious reflection from a man who abhorred clumsy sex. And if he'd been in a rational frame of mind, he might have noticed the heresy.

What he noticed instead was her little whimpers, the familiar sound evidence of the young widow's ravenous desire. Her hips were swaying in feverish adjunct to her breathy exhalations, her thighs were pressed tightly together as though to contain the fire within, and he briefly debated where and how he wished to climax.

A very brief debate.

Slipping a finger into her mouth, he eased his erection free, lifted her into his arms, carried her the few steps to the chair, and sitting, disposed her with effortless strength so she was facing him on her knees, his upthrust cock nudging her hot little pussy.

"I can't wait," he said, this man who generally made love with careless dispassion.

"Oh, good," she panted, in artless confession. "I'm vastly impatient to feel you inside me."

There was something about her innocent candor that touched him beyond the obvious anticipatory pleasure her words evoked. But after a lifetime of eschewing undue emotion, he quickly dismissed the singular feeling. "I almost tumbled you this morning," he said with a small smile, "so welcome to the world of impatience."

"Now, if you please." A brisk command, a wiggle of her hips and a green steady gaze.

"And if I don't take orders?" A lazy drawl in contrast.

"Allow me to change your mind." In her new unconstrained mood, she sank down his rigid length like a catapult, and resting on his thighs a second later, impaled and content, she smiled up at him. "I almost *let* you tumble me this morning."

He laughed.

She felt his laugh in delicious compensatory flutters deep inside her and gently rocked her bottom to savor the flaunting enchantment. "So you see, we are both after the same thing."

"This?" Flexing his legs, he thrust upward and was gratified at her soft, rapturous moan. Gently grasping her hips, he held her securely. "And this?"

Another blissful groan before her lashes lifted marginally, and holding his gaze, she whispered, "And this as well," as she began slowly rising to her knees.

The delectable friction of skin on skin, the tingling nerve endings sliding one against the other, the exquisitely tight pressure of his erection stretching her pulsing tissue brought new meaning to the word *stimulation*, the degree of tactile sensation lurid.

Stopping midway on her leisurely ascent, she said, breathy and astonished, "Do you feel that?"

He smiled. "Everywhere you can possibly feel anything." He placed his hands lightly on her hips.

"I know. I think I'll keep you," she teased.

"I might let you." *Christ, where did that come from?* As if to nullify his startling reply, he planted his feet firmly on the floor, tightened his grip on Mrs. St. Vincent's hips, and exerted a hard, forceful downward pressure with his hands.

He didn't hear her breathy squeal as he plumbed the depths of her glossy, silken warmth, or if he did, the sound didn't register with his brain in the grip of a cataclysmic upheaval. Although, shortly after, as he caught his breath, he noticed with the tunnel vision of heated sexual congress that she was shifting her hips, asking for more.

How fucking convenient.

In the following highly impressionable interval, he operated on instinct, lifting her up and forcing her back down until she assumed the rhythm with an impetuous frenzy he was more than willing to accommodate. She climaxed quickly again, whether by nature or due to her recent celibacy, it didn't really matter. He only waited for her last little sigh to echo in his ears before gently moving inside her again.

"No, don't—please," she whispered into his shoulder, collapsed on his chest.

"Just a bit more, darling. There, see"—her vaginal muscles were stirring—"it feels good, doesn't it?"

How does he know? But suddenly the reason why was irrelevant, for a warm delicious glow began spreading through her senses again and languishing desire revived with an acute, raw intensity. As if each time was better than the last. A glorious thought.

After waiting all day to be engulfed in Mrs. St. Vincent's hot cunt, Fitz *knew* each time was better than the last.

He also knew this chair wasn't going to suit for long.

To that purpose, he concentrated on bringing the voluptuous woman warming his cock to fever pitch again. Not a difficult task; she was highly receptive, her vagina slick with desire, her neediness and sexual appetite charming. And very soon, his talents being what they were, she was once again overwrought and panting.

Now, he decided. Sliding his hands under her bottom, holding her firmly impaled, he surged to his feet. She squealed in a rapturous little sound that suggested his cock had stood with equally bracing force.

"Tell me I won't die of pleasure," she whispered, clinging to his neck, her legs wrapped around his waist, her gaze half-lidded and feverish.

"Not yet." His voice was soft as silk. "Soon."

The explicit promise in his words streaked through her body like liquid flame, his long-legged gait jostled pleasure receptors up and down her vagina, and she desperately hoped soon was measured in seconds. "Is it always like this with you?"

He didn't immediately reply as he approached the bed. Then, ignoring the dangers in sincerity, he said, "No, never."

"Oh good, although I don't know why it should matter; what are you *doing*?" she cried as he came to a halt.

"Seeing that you die of pleasure," he said with a smile, smoothly easing them both down on the small bed without dislodging himself from her silken warmth. "Don't argue."

As if she could, Rosalind understood, every nerve in her body poised, taut, quivering for surcease. As if she could do anything at all but wait breathlessly for the fierce convulsive ecstasy brought to her by the good graces, deft skill, and prodigious physical endowments of the Duke of Groveland. Like that...oh, God, oh God, she was completely gorged; she couldn't take any more. "No, no, I can't..."

"Just a little more, darling—see...you can do it..."

Whispered force majeure, velvet soft, and so excruciatingly fine she felt herself melt around him as if he held the key to her carnal soul.

"There...see, you *can* take it all. If you were in my harem you'd have to take this and more, darling. You'd have to conform to my every wish. I could keep you naked by my side day and night. Would you like that?" He began to slowly withdraw.

"No, no...I mean, yes, yes, of course," she quickly corrected, fearful he would leave her.

"That's better. I like compliance from my houris." He held himself arrested, midstroke. "Do you understand?"

"Yes, yes, perfectly. Don't leave me, please."

"So you'll do anything if I stay."

"Yes, yes, anything."

Blood surged through his penis at such unconditional surrender, his libido enticed by her carte blanche permission. "I'll be fucking you all night," he said. "Is that a problem?"

"No, no...not at all." She was trembling on the brink; she would have promised him anything.

No novice, he recognized preorgasmic delirium, but inexplicably, he wanted more. "You won't be allowed to refuse me. Is that clear?"

She hesitated.

He drove into her yielding flesh a fraction more to encourage her answer.

She gasped as the infinitesimal movement jolted every eager, covetous nerve in her body like a hammer blow. "Yes, it's clear," she breathed.

It shouldn't have mattered. Women had been saying yes to him his entire adult life. But Mrs. St. Vincent's small breathless reply was flagrantly erotic. Neither unctuous nor flattering as was normally the case, but explicitly reluctant, as if he were trespassing into forbidden territory.

And he'd finally been given access.

Slipping his hand under her thigh, he lifted her leg to allow himself deeper penetration and drove into her succulent warmth. It had been a long day and a longer evening of waiting for this; there was a point where even a worldly man was no longer impervious to hot-spur passion.

"Finally," she whispered, as though reading his mind, and when he laughed, she wrapped her legs tightly around his waist, smiled into his amused gaze and purred, "Welcome my lord, Sultan."

"I'm very glad I purchased you," he whispered, adjusting his downstroke to her rising hips. At her immediate, hotly contentious stare, he grinned. "It's only play, darling—here in the harem."

"It better be."

"I'll let you know when it isn't," he softly said, biting back the reply that came to his lips. Allusions to her store were counterproductive at the moment.

"Meaning?"

"Are you really going to fight with me now?" he drawled, flexing his legs to deepen his thrusting downstroke.

She softly moaned, her legs gripped his back more tightly, and she whispered, "Later."

Equally headstrong and in a better position to exert his

autocratic impulses, he made her wait that time, taking her to the edge over and over again, always withdrawing just short of her climax. Making it clear at least in this instance, that the advantage was his.

Until she abruptly grabbed his hair, tugged hard, and with her hot gaze only inches away from his, hissed, "I'm climaxing this time with or without you."

"Fine. You do that." She exasperated him more than any woman he'd ever met.

"I will!" Shoving him away—or rather, he allowed her that drama—she rolled over, jerked open the drawer on the bedside table, and pulled out a slender glass bottle, empty of its contents.

He shouldn't have cared what she did. With anyone else he would have watched, calmly waiting his turn, or gotten up and left. Instead, he snatched the bottle from her fingers, tossed it aside, pushed her onto her back, spread her legs with a quick, rough brush of his hands, dropped between her thighs, and hot-tempered, rammed his cock into her so hard he felt the impact clear up his spine.

She should beat him away, scream her dissent, do anything other than die of pleasure, Rosalind seethed, wondering how it was possible to feel this ravenous craving while bristling with rage. But rational thought failed to function with the haze of passion beginning to vaporize her consciousness, and as her body yielded to his onslaught with wanton acquiescence, she knew she could no more refuse him than she could curtail the hysteria beginning to overwhelm her senses.

Raising her arms, she twined them around his neck, lifted her hips into his downstroke, held on tightly, and surrendered to desire.

He kissed her then, smiling against her mouth, his anger, too, overwhelmed by sensation so magical he was inclined to consider the lady of Pre-Raphaelite splendor as a gift from the gods. She was turning out to be insatiable in her appetites—a charming attribute he'd half suspected but was nevertheless grateful to confirm. There had been something about her that morning, beyond her voluptuous beauty—perhaps her hot-tempered resistance or the brief glimpse of passion he'd seen in her eyes. And now he was here reaping the benefits of his earlier presumption and her highly charged libido.

As though in response, he felt her first little preorgasmic ripples slide up his cock, and recognizing her soft, suffocated groan, benevolent once again, he buried himself deep inside her in readiness for the approaching onslaught.

Half a heartbeat later, her climax detonated with full-scale violence and her high-pitched cry exploded like a shrapnel burst into the shadowed room.

Her voice resonated in her ears as though from a distance.

Less overwrought, Fitz heard it clearly and from very close range.

Her screams persisted, a fierce, seething climax convulsing her senses, spilling into every palpitating crevice in her body, dispersing flame-hot, soul-stirring ecstasy in rapturous profusion for seemingly endless moments.

At the last, as her grip relaxed on his shoulders and her cries died to whimpers, Fitz unwrapped her legs from his waist, withdrew, and came on her stomach in one of the more prolonged, tempestuous ejaculations of his life.

Afterward, she didn't open her eyes for so long he began to worry; she hadn't even moved when he wiped his semen from her stomach.

When she finally lifted her lashes, she looked up to find him propped on his elbow beside her, watching her with concern.

"What?"

"Nothing. How are you feeling?"

"Deeply satisfied," she murmured, sleepy eyed and blissfully content.

Relieved, he grinned. "Friends?"

"Oh yes, very much so. How do you do it, Your Grace?" Her voice was playful. "My toes are still curled, and my toes *never* curl."

Years of practice. "You're easy to please," he said instead.

She smiled. "I suspect it has more to do with you than me. I must say, I feel deliciously and sumptuously ravished. Like all those languishing Danaes male artists love to paint." At his lifted brows, she translated, "You know a woman in the grip of an orgasm is a male favorite."

He grinned. "And there's something wrong with that?"

She laughed. "Touché. I'm definitely not in the mood to complain."

"So, if I were to keep you orgasmic, you'd be disinclined to complain?"

"You say the *nicest* things," she murmured, lazily stretching, arching her back, reveling in the sweet afterglow.

"It's pure selfishness, darling."

Her green gaze was sportive. "Am I your darling?"

"Without a doubt." They were by chance or happenstance or the aimlessness of fate physically matched—as in a perfect fit. And he should know.

"I rather like the idea," she whispered, reaching out and sliding her finger up his only marginally diminished erection. "And him, of course, and his very credible talents."

There was something electrifying about the lush Mrs. St. Vincent, he decided, drawing in a small breath, sumptuous pleasure still pulsing through his penis and gonads—albeit in lesser measure. "We thank you for your inspiration," he murmured, leaning forward slightly to kiss her, a politesse learned at his French governess's knee. Literally.

"How nice you are. Thank you, too." Rosalind smiled at the conventional courtesies. "Did we just finish a waltz?"

"In a manner of speaking." He grinned. "You're a very good dancer."

"And you've done this once or twice before."

"Yes, once or twice," he said, not sure where she was going with her remark.

"I should be grateful, I suppose."

What had she expected? That he was some saint? "I certainly am grateful for your participation." His voice

was urbane, his smile charming. "You're quite amazing."
Women were prone to talk about their feelings after sex.
Why should Mrs. St. Vincent be the exception?

"So your reputation remains intact, does it not?"

"Are you complaining?" For a woman who'd just climaxed three times, he rather thought he'd done her a favor.

She had the good grace to blush. "No."

"Good," he softly said, slipping a finger under her chin
and holding her gaze. "Because we're not anywhere near
finished."

As if on cue, she saw his erection begin to swell, and
quite removed from reason or intellect, an answering ripple of arousal shimmered through her vagina.

"This is sheer madness," she said much too softly.

Her equivocation in word and tone was a flashing sema-
phore to an experienced cocksman like Fitz. "Probably," he
said as softly. "Because I'm thinking about taking you into
the country for a month."

Her eyes flared wide. "You wouldn't!" But even as she
protested, the pulsing between her legs accelerated, her
nipples stiffened, and a wild lustful flame burned through
her body.

"I would," he said, pointed and deliberate.

"You can't."

"I can do anything I want."

He was a duke and rich. She understood rules didn't
apply to him. "You have no compunction about coercing
a woman?"

"Until now I would have said yes." He suddenly smiled.
"You affect me differently."

Gratified to see his teasing smile, she said, "It's only
lust. You'll get over it."

"I hope so. Now then, you were looking for adventure.
What did I do with my tie?" Rolling off the bed, he walked
toward the pile of his discarded clothing. "Maybe we'll
play harem after all."

He didn't ask her permission; there was something provocative in his assumption of authority. Was he her eunuch come

to life? Or was he the master of the harem, or simply Groveland in the flesh? Or didn't it matter who he was after he'd said
What did I do with my tie? because her body had instantly
responded to the lascivious suggestion in those words?

"Here we go." Holding the strip of white silk aloft, he
returned to the bed. "I've only heard about slave markets,
so we'll have to improvise." Leaning over, he lifted her to
her feet, drew her hands together before her, and bound
them with a loose slipknot. "What is it that appeals to you
about harems? Stand there." He indicated a point near the
bed with his finger.

"The exotic atmosphere, I suppose," she said, moving
the few steps. "Where women are—"

"Sexual objects, receptacles for a man's pleasure?" His
brows rose. "How does that appeal to a woman of your
independence?"

She shrugged. "The departure from the norm or the bla-
tant sexual content or—"

"Being tamed and mastered and forced to have sex?"

She took a small breath to contain the prurient rush of
lust flaring through her senses, felt a need as well to meet
the challenge in his soft query. "I'm not sure," she said,
holding his gaze. "Does it matter?"

He smiled. "Not to me. You're the one on the auction
block. I'm just here to make a purchase. Should I find you
pleasing."

"Then I must do my best to please you."

This time it was he who required a small inhalation to
suppress the ruttish surge bringing his penis fully erect,
Mrs. St. Vincent's whispered reply shocking in its impact.
He didn't particularly like the feeling, the lack of control
she provoked. Perhaps taming her wouldn't be exclusively
a game. "Where do you come from?" His voice was crisp.
"Circassia with your auburn hair?"

"Tripoli," she said, smiling faintly, liking that she'd rattled his cool nonchalance. "And I can cook, my lord."

"I have a cook."

"I can also sew."

His mouth slowly curved into a smile; the lady had an imagination. "If only I was looking for a seamstress."

"Perhaps you need someone to warm your bed."

"I have a large harem."

She bit back the comment that came to her lips, his statement much too true. "I could give you fine sons, my lord."

"What if I have enough sons?"

She held his gaze. "You don't have mine."

Nor did he intend to. "Open your mouth," he brusquely said, changing the subject. When she did, he ran his finger over her teeth as if checking a horse for its age. "Adequate," he murmured. "Turn around."

Astonished at the fierce passion aroused by his soft commands, she hastened to comply.

He swept his hands over her shoulders, down her back and legs with a brisk efficiency. "You must not have been in the harem long; you still have muscle tone. Face me again."

She swivelled around so quickly, her breasts quivered with the motion.

Ignoring the provocative tremor, he cupped her large breasts in his hands and cooly said, "These are serviceable. You haven't suckled a babe, I gather."

"No, my lord."

"You could be barren then."

"My late master was old and impotent."

"And his sons didn't want you?"

"They did, but the chief wife didn't. She sent me away to be sold."

"So you're relatively untried." He lifted her breasts slightly, weighing them in his hands. "Were you beaten?"

She wasn't sure how to answer; a certain ambiguity echoed in his voice. "Very little, my lord."

"For what infractions?"

"Speaking out of turn."

He laughed, let his hands drop away from her breasts, and said, "I'm not surprised. Perhaps I could teach you obedience."

"Perhaps you could."

"Are you being impertinent?"

"No, my lord. On the contrary I'd find obedience to you most interesting."

"Why don't we find out. Turn around, bend over. Brace your hands on the bed. Let's see if you're worth buying." His instructions were gently put, a mildness in his voice as if he were ordering a cup of tea.

But an underlying command echoed beneath his words, and her senses instantly responded to that unspoken presumption, as if knowing how delectable the compensation. Quickly moving into position, she suddenly understood the true meaning of unslaked lust, the concept directly related to Groveland—or rather, his highly rewarding cock, she decided with a frenzied little shiver.

Walking up behind her, he surveyed the pale expanse of opulent female flesh with rich satisfaction. That Mrs. St. Vincent offered him the ultimate submission was gratifying after her parting words this morning. That he was pleasantly anticipating having sex with her an even better feeling after experiencing a surfeit of ennui of late. "Are you ready to show me your usefulness?" he mildly inquired, even as his penis swelled larger at the prospect.

"Yes, yes." Flushed and feverish, ravenous for him when she'd only written of the feeling before but never felt it, she breathlessly added with a quick look over her shoulder, "If it please my lord."

"That depends. Show me what you can do." He didn't touch her, not so much as a steadying hand on her hips before he entered her in a swift, hard thrust and buried his erection deep inside her.

With his huge cock straining every frenzied sexual receptor in her pulsing vagina, motivated by inexorable orgasmic pressures, she quickly obeyed, swinging her hips in a swift, rocking rhythm, back and forth, side to side, undulating her bottom with hot-spur urgency. Shuddering at each thrilling, exquisitely tight downstroke, drawing in a sustaining breath at each slow withdrawal, subject to a pleasure beyond her wildest dreams, Rosalind had crossed the impressionable boundary into the untrammeled world of Lady Blessington.

By ordering Mrs. St. Vincent to service him, Fitz sought to gain control over his unnerving cravings, restore normalcy to this sexual encounter, persuade himself that her submission acquitted *him* of involvement.

But his involvement couldn't be long denied, no more than Rosalind could pretend that it was someone else and not Groveland who aroused her every pleasure center and made her greedy for what he offered.

"Faster," he murmured, thinking selfishness would absolve him of entanglement.

Shameless in her need, she complied, her lower body pumping like a piston, every swinging back stroke eliciting a little ecstatic gasp from her parted lips.

"Roll, spin...that's it, that's better—just like that," he directed, gently guiding her plump bottom with his fingertips. "Good. Perfect. You follow instructions well."

It was clearly Groveland's voice she heard—no fantasy lord or sultan.

If his resplendent cock wasn't sliding in and out of her, ramming and cramming her full, if she wasn't so near to orgasm she could see nirvana through a rosy haze, she might have disputed his gross absolutism. Or ignored the flame-hot spasms of lust spiking through her body.

"Don't you dare climax," he growled. But leaning forward as he spoke, he freed her hands with a tug on the slip-knot, slid his palm over her belly, and delicately caressed her clit.

Whether it was his rough threat or his tender touch, she felt as though he'd pressed some orgasmic button, and with a skittish, suffocated cry, she came.

Just as he knew she would.

With scarcely less restraint, he waited only until her first orgasmic frenzy had swept over her before he jerked out and climaxed in a violent, unruly trajectory. "Sorry about...that," he murmured, breathing hard. *Christ. What a mess. Although better than coming inside her.* "Where are . . . your towels?"

She'd collapsed facedown on the bed so her reply was muffled.

Finding his underwear on the floor, he wiped himself off, used a portion of the sheet to do what he could to clean up his semen, and went in search of a bathroom and towels.

A short time later, he returned with towels, two peaches, and a half-empty bottle of champagne to find her sitting on the side of the bed, dressed in a robe, her back ramrod straight, her hands clasped in her lap. A determined look on her face.

"Forgive me for making a mess," he said, coming to a halt near the bed. "I'm usually not so juvenile."

"You're forgiven, but I'd like you to go now. I dislike feeling so dependent on that"—she pointed at his crotch—"particularly with a man like you." His penis even in repose was impressive, she grudgingly noted.

"Whatever you say. Would you like one?" He held out the peaches cupped in one palm.

"No. Now please go," she firmly said before she could change her mind. He was the most beautiful man she'd ever seen. An assessment quickly seconded by her libido that was beginning to divorce itself from her pragmatic resolve.

"I actually know someone who's been in a harem," Fitz observed, dropping the towels on the bed and sitting beside her. "If you're interested. Champagne?" He offered her the bottle.

She shook her head.

A taut, restrained gesture, he decided. One open to equivocation, he also decided, since she'd not repeated her dismissal notice. "A lady I know accompanied her family on a diplomatic mission to Constantinople." He didn't say *her husband* in the event Mrs. St. Vincent had become prudish about fidelity as well as making love. "She became friends with several of the sultan's concubines. The harem is a world unto itself apparently—very luxurious if not for its lack of freedom, of course. Many of the women were quite content, though, Sally said." He set the bottle on the floor, one peach on the bedside table, and took a bite out of the other. "Your peaches on the kitchen table reminded me of her stories," he said a moment later. "Apparently, peaches are favorites in the harem."

"Was she actually inside a harem?"

Ah, that first nibble of curiosity. Gratifying. "Her family was at the court of the sultan for three years. Very eventful years for Sally." He smiled faintly. "She became very fond of hashish as well as peaches."

"She smoked hashish?"

He was delighted to hear a modicum of excitement in Mrs. St. Vincent's voice. "Everyone does, I'm told. It helps with the tedium of the harem."

"Does it enhance sensation as rumored?"

"She says it does. I could have brought some if I'd known you'd like to try it."

"Oh, no, no . . . That is, stories tell of a heightened imagination under the influence of the drug."

"There's hashish dens enough in London. Wales likes to end his evenings there—or he did when he was younger. It's another amusement for the haute monde. If you'd like to try it sometime, let me know."

"No, thank you. I was wondering though"—an impetuousness in her voice again—"did she tell you anything about eunuchs?"

"Let me think. She did mention two. One was a very large Ethiopian, the other a Greek, I believe. Both were favorites in the harem."

"Do you know why?" Avid interest in her query.

He told her all he'd learned from Sally, racking his brain for details that might intrigue her, remaining scrupulously polite during his recital, although he was pleased later when she agreed to several sips of champagne. And in time, when he moved to sit back against the headboard and said, "Come sit with me and I'll describe all the costumes Sally brought back from Constantinople," she didn't resist. Fortunately, Sally had modeled several of the harem designs for him so his descriptions were detailed.

"I've read many travel accounts of Constantinople, but to hear firsthand from someone actually having seen a harem and returning with all those wonderful clothes"— she gave him a small smile—"is quite wonderful."

"Diplomatic credentials open doors otherwise closed to visitors, not to mention, England's influence is considerable at the sultan's court." Fitz offered her another drink of champagne. "It's still moderately cold."

While they finished the champagne, Fitz answered more questions about harems. All with cultivated grace and scrupulous self-restraint, taking care not to so much as touch her as she sat beside him.

"You're extremely informative," Rosalind commented, when at last she'd run out of queries. "And restful as well"—she made a small moue—"when you're not making me feverish with lust."

"It's always a good idea to take a break. It makes it better the next time."

"There shouldn't be a next time."

"Why not? It makes you feel good."

There was no reasonable answer to his simple statement. "I suppose I shouldn't bring up moral arguments."

"You could if you like."

With an agreeable contentment warming her senses, she said with a soft sigh, "Maybe later."

In the interest of curtailing such an event, Fitz said, "There's something else I heard about the harem. If you'd like to try it."

The sudden silence was pregnant with possibility.

"You'll like it." His voice was velvet soft.

She hesitated, bit her bottom lip.

"I was told it can be very arousing," he lied, thinking Sally wouldn't mind sharing one of her favorite treats.

"How do you know all this?" She turned to meet his gaze.

"Sally talks a lot." He smiled as he perjured himself; he and Sally did more than talk. "Really," he added at Rosalind's skeptical look. "We've known each other for years. She grew up near me; we spent summers together when we were young."

Rosalind wasn't sure she could picture him young, this elegant, polished seducer. "How old were you?"

"When Sally and I roamed the countryside?"

She nodded.

"I suppose we were eleven or twelve. What did you do during your childhood summers?"

"Searched the countryside for fossils and plants. It wasn't work," she said to his pained expression. "I enjoyed it."

"And yet here you are in the city."

Rosalind shrugged. "One never knows. Have you planned your life?"

Fitz chuckled. "Hell no. Things happen, I've discovered."

"Like this."

"Yes." She was right, despite his ulterior motives. "Like this."

"So then?"

He turned to her, enticement in her innocuous phrase.

"Since we seem to be engaged in a serendipitous adventure." Her voice was very soft. "And I'm experiencing a curious sense of addiction..."

"I must not be derelict," he softly drawled.

She smiled her agreement. "Opportunities like this don't come my way everyday, you know."

"Nor to me." Strangely, despite his prodigal life, he meant it. "Are we ready then for whatever unplanned events transpire?"

"I believe I've been ready since you walked in tonight." An admission long in coming.

"How nice." Not that a woman wanting him was unusual, but that it mattered to him, was. "I admit I may not have come for the paintings alone," he said with a boyish grin.

With her libido seriously focused on harem adventures, equally aware that an amorous situation such as this might not befall her again, Rosalind held his gaze. "Compliments aside, darling, must I ask again?"

"God no." Her impatience was charming, as was her appetite for sex. Sitting on the edge of the bed, he helped her off with her robe. "There now," he said a moment later, reaching up to hang her robe on the bedpost. "Lie back against the pillows just a little." He arranged the pillows behind her so she was half reclining. Then he gently spread her thighs wide, bent her knees, and crossed her feet at the ankles. Her sex was now prominently displayed. "Does that stretch your muscles too much?"

Glancing up, he saw her watching him intently.

"Are you taking notes?" he teased. "Would you like me to go more slowly?"

Her eyes flared wide for a second before she smiled. "I'm just curious. I haven't the advantage of your considerable knowledge in this area."

"In that case, ask questions if you wish. Apparently, diversions such as this were not uncommon in the harem. The sultan had four hundred concubines at the time Sally was visiting."

"Four hundred?" Rosalind breathed. "I hope the sultan was young and virile."

"Alas, he wasn't. Consequently, these little pastimes were habitually practiced to whet his jaded appetite and also bring relief as it were to the ladies—like your bottle." He nodded in the direction he'd tossed the makeshift dildo. "You should have something better than that."

"At the moment, I do," Rosalind sweetly replied.

"Not yet."

"I can wait. Actually, you've been a darling already. I've never climaxed so many times in my life."

Such artless innocence was a powerful aphrodisiac. "Hush, darling, or I'll forget about being unselfish."

"On the contrary, you're the most unselfish man I know."

He'd been complimented by women for years, and yet knowing he pleased her was curiously gratifying. Her husband may not have, he decided, and that, too, was pleasing. And lunatic. He deliberately shut down so bizarre a thought. "Allow me to serve you again, my lady," he playfully offered instead, preferring the familiarity of boudoir sport. "Consider me the harem eunuch here for your edification and pleasure."

Startled, she drew in a breath—her fantasy come to life.

"Don't be frightened," he said, misreading her inhalation. "I'll make sure you're ready for the sultan's pleasure before I go on. I'll kiss you here"—he rained soft kisses on her eyes, nose, chin—"and here"—a trail of kisses followed the curve of her throat. "And then we'll kiss your pert nipples until you're wet enough to take what I have for you."

She'd never realized how effectively words could arouse; he had but to promise her carnal delights and her body opened in welcome, twitched and danced with excitement, sent a lurid message to her brain with quicksilver speed. And when his mouth closed on her nipple, the additional stimulation sent a lascivious jolt through her nervous system.

Mrs. St. Vincent was unconstrained in her desires—as usual, Fitz reflected, increasing the pressure of his mouth, sucking harder on her ripe nipple. She was already squirming, softly moaning, searching for surcease. Like the proverbial nymphet of every male fantasy.

But he took his time and saw that both her nipples were thoroughly worked into hard, peaked crests, that she was visibly panting and pinked with passion before he raised his head and whispered, "Let's see if you're wet enough now."

She nodded, unable to speak, seething inside, trembling, every instinct feverishly focused on consummation.

Slipping a finger inside her vagina, he withdrew it and held it up. "Look. Do you think you're ready?"

It took considerable effort to lever her eyes open, distracted as she was with the fierce throbbing in her cunt, the overpowering ache of desire.

"See all that white, pearly liquid? You have the most succulent little cunt."

"I need you," she breathed.

"If only I could," he gently replied. "I'm a eunuch."

"No you're not," she whispered, alluring as Eve. "Please?"

"If you satisfactorily discharge your harem duties, we'll see if we can find someone who hasn't been castrated to service you later. One of the guards perhaps. But first you must oblige the sultan. Do you understand?"

Restive, she made a fretful face.

"Decide," he softly said.

She squirmed and fidgeted, wrinkled her nose. "You'll find me a guard afterward?"

"If you please the sultan."

She shuddered as a violent tremor spiked through her vagina. "Do I have a choice?"

He smiled faintly. "Of course."

"Damn you," she hissed.

"One learns obedience here, my lady."

She nodded.

The imperious bitch he'd first seen that morning surfaced in her condescending nod, but there was no question who was in charge, so his voice was temperate when he said, "The sultan has these fruits"—he lifted the small peach from the bedside table—"specially grown for his harem. This particular size is much coveted by the outside world and by the harem ladies. Why don't we see if you like them as well." Leaning forward, he eased open her labia wide enough to gently wedge a portion of the golden fruit into her soft flesh.

She softly moaned as pressure was exerted on her clitoris.

"The sultan may wish you served up to him later. He has a penchant for such displays. Can you feel that?"

An unnecessary question as she shuddered under his hand.

"You must take more." Spreading the inner lips of her labia, he slid his finger around the sleek flesh, stretching it enough to force the peach in slightly deeper. "There, now we can see this little bud again," he murmured, grazing the sensitive tip of her clitoris with his finger, smiling as she softly groaned. "You have to accept more or the sultan won't approve. He has definite preferences. Are you ready?"

With every impressionable, gushing sensory response screaming its assent, nearly delirious with need, she took a deep breath and whispered, "Yes."

Fitz was very careful at this stage, intent on keeping the fruit intact, planning on seeing how many times the lady could come when he ate it later. Known for his good hands—part natural talent, part acquired skill—he deftly inserted the peach, stretching her pink flesh little by little until the peach was firmly lodged between her taut vulva lips, the portion of fruit still visible, protruding slightly, golden and tantalizing. "There. I think the sultan will approve. You've accommodated it nicely."

Trembling on the brink, she breathed, "Please, please . . . I need you."

"Patience, my pet. The sultan dislikes assertive females. I suggest you learn to hold your tongue." He smiled as she shut her mouth firmly in an effort to please—in hopes of a quick orgasm, he assumed. "That's better," he whispered, gently smoothing her stretched flesh, his long, slender fingers delicate as he stroked her glossy tissue and the portion of the golden sphere still visible. "The sultan will be pleased."

Sitting back, he admired his handiwork, the vision lushly erotic, the voluptuous reclining female, thighs spread wide, was offering up her fruit-filled cunt for his pleasure. And he thanked whatever random act of fate had brought him here tonight, Mrs. St. Vincent one of the more delectable morsels he'd seen in a very long time. She was flushed in arousal, her eyes shut, her mouth slightly open, her fevered moans softly audible.

Would she come if he touched her?

Or how soon would she come if he touched her?

He proceeded to find out.

With extreme delicacy, he ran his finger over the strained membrane of her labia, pressing gently against the soft fruit imbedded in her cunt, bending low to draw one nipple into his mouth as he caressed her ripe sex.

Whimpering, tormented by the sweet ache throbbing between her legs, her body gorged, her sense of self disappearing in the torrid heat of an all-consuming sexual hysteria, she wondered if he was right after all. That she wanted taming at some primal level, wished to be an object of lust. Like this—like now, offering her breasts to be suckled, lavishly filled to overflowing, bursting at the seams, receptive and submissive, enslaved to the passion he evoked.

Attuned to female arousal, recognizing the rising pitch of her whimpers, his fingers sliding more easily over her drenched slit, the peach inside, slick with pearly fluid, he lifted his mouth from her nipple. "The sultan will be watching now, so be on your best behavior."

She only half heard him, overwrought, so near to orgasm his voice came from a great distance. But instinctively, selfishly, nearly wild with longing, she breathed, "I'll be good," because she knew that's what he wanted to hear.

There was no reason to feel such gloating satisfaction at her blanket submission; he immediately chided himself for such vanity. And then because he was adored for his kindness in the boudoir and not his physical splendor alone, he set about furnishing the lady with a richly deserved climax. Uncrossing her ankles, he made room for himself between her legs, drew her engorged clit into his mouth and licked and sucked with exquisite restraint, with unstinting competence, with a crucial sense of place. With a flare for timing.

She screamed much louder that time, he thought, but then she'd waited longer than usual.

As her breathing returned to normal, he gently soothed her, running his hands slowly down her arms, over her breasts, delicately brushing her eyebrows, skimming her flushed cheeks with his fingertips, tracing the smooth curve of her belly with his warm palm. And after a time, moving his hand lower.

She jerked awake as he exerted pressure on the peach. "No, no...no more."

He gazed up at her from between her legs. "Hush, darling, you always want more. Trust me."

She had no way of knowing he was right until afterward. She never did. But having stood stud to a good many women in London, he did. And after her third climax, he ate the peach in situ, not spilling so much as a drop of juice, bringing the lady to a shrieking orgasm once again. He wondered if Mrs. St. Vincent and Sally would enjoy each other's company, similarly inclined as they were to delight in peaches.

Moments later, as Rosalind lay in a deeply sated torpor, Fitz came up on his knees and entered her very, very gently, barely moving until she opened her eyes, smiled up at him, and whispered, "Don't ever go."

"Not likely," he said with an answering smile, in full agreement about the merits of carnal sensation. "How are you feeling?"

"Sexy," she purred. "Very, very sexy."

"Then there's no need for me to say, 'Ignore me, this won't take long,'" he observed with a grin.

"Since I seem to be addicted, no. Take all the time you want."

He did, and they both entered a new realm of sensation, one where sentiment intruded into sensual pleasure and tenderness pervaded even the most self-indulgent, prurient play.

Very late that night as they lay postcoital, panting side by side, he turned his head and said with a smile, "I'd be more than willing to shower you with gold...my darling Danae of Bruton Street. Just say the word. I'm totally bewitched."

"Speaking of bewitchment," she murmured, wallowing in bliss, "I'm going to need...just a little more of him." Reaching over in a lazy drift of her arm, she ran her fingertip down his rampant erection. "You have the most phenomenal cock. He's indefatigable and most charitable. Thank you, Your Grace," she teasingly purred.

Since she'd been effusive in her thanks, he already knew she was appreciative. The question was whether he could keep up with her. So far so good. But he was well aware that tonight would be a record of sorts for him; that from a man who already held all the confirmed records in the world of amour. "Give me a minute," he said, good-humored and obliging. "I'll be right with you."

On the other hand, the thought of fucking himself to death with the hot-blooded Mrs. St. Vincent was not without its novel appeal.

CHAPTER 10

IT WAS SHORTLY after nine, the air already heavy with heat, the muslin curtains hanging limp at the open windows of Rosalind's bedroom. Fitz was almost finished dressing. He was debating wearing a coat when he was already sweating. But his shirt looked like it had been walked on...more than once. Which may have been the case. Not that his coat and trousers weren't the worse for wear as well. Oh, what the hell; he slipped on his swallowtail. It wasn't as though this was the first time he'd come home in rumpled evening rig.

Nor was it likely the last.

As for the lovely Rosalind—all sweet tenderness this morning—he was definitely inclined to call on her again.

They'd previously exchanged all the courtesies, each thanking the other in turn, he with suave practiced grace, she more impetuous in her sentiments. But then she'd been pleasured beyond her wildest dreams. It was only natural.

He bent to pick up his watch that had been discarded on the floor the previous night. Sliding the leather band around his wrist, he clasped the gold buckle as Rosalind

offered up another appreciative compliment on his kindness—a curious word, he thought. But as he smiled and
answered her in kind, he found himself thinking this might
be an opportune moment to bring up buying her store. She
appeared to view him with considerable affection.

So he did. Ask.

Lounging in bed, Rosalind looked at him with mild surprise. "Was last night just a way of negotiating with me?"

"No, and yet I can't say I wouldn't like you to recon-
sider," he pleasantly replied.

"Sorry, darling. But thank you nonetheless for a night
of unbelievable pleasure." She smiled. "Although I expect
you hear that often."

He didn't like her blasé tone; he particularly didn't like
to think of her lying nude in bed like that speaking to some
other man with such casualness. Not that it was any of his
business, he quickly reminded himself. Reaching into the
pocket of his evening coat, he pulled out the jewelry from
Grey's and set it on the bedside table.

"What are you doing?" A decided umbrage rang through
her query.

"Leaving a few small gifts." In the light of day, habitual
custom held sway, the heated passions of the previous night
appeased.

"Are you *paying* me for sex?" Frost in every syllable.

"God no. It's nothing of the kind."

"Then take them back!" Rolling over on her side, she
reached out, grabbed the glittering pile, and gimlet-eyed and
wrathful, held the jewels out to him. "Here, take them!"

"I don't want them. They're engraved with your name in
any event, so they won't do me much good." He was moving toward the bedroom door as he spoke, feeling equally
sulky and resentful. Why the hell was *she* indignant? Any
other woman would have offered profuse, heartfelt thanks!
But then she was the same obstinate woman who was
standing in the way of Monckton Row!

Half turning as he reached the doorway, he cooly measured her with his gaze, as though calibrating her enter-

tainment value. "Thank you for your hospitality and"—he paused in his drawling delivery just long enough to let the insult drop into the silence—"gratifying enthusiasm." Then he turned and walked out, pulling the door shut behind him.

He heard the jewelry hit the door.

Bitch, he thought.

A damnably sexy bitch, he had to admit—one who'd kept his prick primed and ready for action all night long. Unfortunately, she was also a major thorn in his side. And that defiance trumped even world-class sex.

As soon as he'd paid his compliments to his mother, he'd call on Hutchinson. Perhaps his barrister's agents had discovered some unfavorable information about the St. Vincents since yesterday. Hopefully, something he could use to destroy the irritating cunt who stood in the way of his development project.

Or if not precisely *destroy*—perhaps that was too malevolent a verb after Mrs. St. Vincent's excessive receptivity last night—at least convince her to sell.

LYING IN BED, Rosalind silently fumed as she listened to the swift echo of Groveland's footsteps descend the stairs. Only when the back door slammed and silence reigned did she finally give vent to her feelings. Swearing like a trooper, yelling at the top of her lungs, she conjured up every derogatory expletive she'd ever heard and pithily and comprehensively bestowed them on Groveland's reprehensible person. And with an older brother to ape, she'd acquired a large and colorful repertoire.

When both her breath and invective had run its course, she lay panting. In that small lull, she found herself peevishly contemplating her blackened and besmirched reputation. And allocating blame where blame was due.

To the dissolute Groveland, naturally.

At present, logic and reason were truant with hell-hath-no-fury in charge.

How dare he view her as some whore or doxy who could

be bought off with a few sparkling bits of jewelry! And prior to that, she hotly contended, how dare he invite himself upstairs! And prior to *that*, why did he present himself as some benevolent noble interested in buying all the art on display! Fraud and charlatan! He was nothing but a scurrilous rogue as everyone well knew, and she had mistakenly forgotten after several glasses of champagne! She softly groaned—not only galled at her blunder but also concerned that she might have hurt her vocal cords while tantrumishly screaming. Damn—it hurt when she swallowed. Reaching for the bottle of champagne left on the bedside table, she thought to remedy her sore throat with a soothing draught.

As she rolled over, the scattered jewelry laying at the base of the door suddenly hove into view. And there were considerably more than a few sparkling bits.

Not that it mattered one whit that Groveland could afford piles of jewelry, she rancorously thought, putting the bottle to her mouth and swallowing some overly warm wine. He was no doubt in the habit of dispensing lavish gratuities to all his lovers.

Oh hell. She flushed red-hot. Now *she* was one of that ignoble rank.

Damn his seductive allure, she lamented. Damn his dark beauty and his magnificent—she stopped in midthought, refusing both the image and coarse word that had leaped into her mind. And yet, she silently wailed, how could she have succumbed like some shameless hussy to his...his...virility.

How could she have so forgotten herself?

Not that remorse was likely to nullify either her shame or her fall from grace, she sensibly decided. And rather than dwell on regret—Edward's gambling habit having caused her to be mindful of its uselessness—she devoted herself instead to the more profitable exercise of devising various vile and devious schemes of retaliation.

Revenge is sweet had been coined for just such occasions.

She considered accosting Groveland in numerous ways or mortifying him in some other yet to be deter-

mined fashion—cutting him down to size, as it were—
preferably before an audience. Not necessarily achievable,
she acknowledged, since she lived outside his fashionable world, and was not likely to receive any invitations
from those in the beau monde. She also doubted that he'd
respond with favor should she call on him at home. In fact,
she'd probably be turned away if she appeared at his door.
Nor could she challenge him to a duel, even if she could
afford passage to Calais where duels took place now that
they'd been outlawed in England. She wasn't a good shot.

She swore, more softly this time, thinking, *What a pity.*

So, in any real sense, retribution was futile. Save for one
instance alone, she reflected with a cool, slightly sinister
smile.

And she'd see him rot in hell before she'd ever sell him
her bookstore.

Marginally and perhaps ungenerously mollified by her
power over the duke in that single area at least, she allowed
herself a small moment of triumph.

As if penalized for her transgression, she was precipitously jerked from her victorious fantasy by the ring of
church bells announcing the hour.

Glancing at the clock, she let out a yelp of surprise, leaped
from her bed, and was stopped in her tracks by a stabbing
pain. Hardly daring to breath should she accidently move in
the process, she realized that engaging in sex for an entire
night apparently left its mark. Good Lord, she was sore.

How fitting.

Groveland's departure had left her disenchanted in more
ways than one. Her next thought—thoroughly unwanted and
also unseemly—took center stage in her brain: was Groveland
as sore or did he have callouses after so many years at stud?

She literally shouted, "Stop!" because she didn't wish
to pursue such a debauched train of thought. In fact, she
would not, under any circumstances, spend another minute
thinking about the vile scoundrel. She would not!

Concentrating on her own affliction instead, she slowly
made her way to her minuscule bathroom, taking very small

steps to lessen the pain. Filling up the tub with steamy hot water, she lay back, soaked her tender parts, and half dozed. Only when the church bells rang the quarter hour, did she reluctantly set about readying herself for the day.

The decision to go without drawers was simple. Any chafing no matter how rudimentary would have been insupportable in her present condition. Slipping on a chemise, she chose a simple printed linen frock from her limited wardrobe and dressed without so much as looking in the mirror. Today would essentially be a matter of counting the hours until she could close the store and go to sleep. She was exhausted. And sore.

After tying her damp hair back with a bow at the nape of her neck, she ate three large pieces of bread and jam. That she was outrageously hungry did not bear close scrutiny when she had vowed to *not* think about Groveland.

By the time she left her apartment and slowly made her way down the stairs, it was past ten.

She would have given anything had it not been Mrs. Beecham waiting at her door. But she was being punished for her sins, she suspected.

"Tsk, tsk," Mrs. Beecham chided as Rosalind unlocked the door. "Keeping a customer cooling their heels is not good business, my dear. My heavens!" Wide-eyed, Mrs. Beecham surveyed Rosalind from head to toe. "You look like you haven't slept a wink. Are you ill?" She quickly took a step back. "I dearly hope not since my frail constitution leaves me quite defenseless against the smallest malady."

"Rest easy, Mrs. Beecham. I am quite well, although I admit the heat last night interrupted my sleep," Rosalind lied. *And your corpulent form, Mrs. Beecham, looks anything but frail.*

"Ah, yes, this sweltering August weather. My sleep suffers as well." Mrs. Beecham smiled. "Which accounts for my early arrival, my dear. I am quite addicted to Mrs. Thornhill's works, but I've read them all. Might you have something comparable for me to read?"

CHAPTER II

Fitz saw the luggage piled in the front hall as he entered the house and silently groaned. Not that his mother's schedule was ever certain. She did very much as she pleased when she pleased.

As a footman approached him, he handed over his hat and gloves. "Where's the dowager duchess?"

"In the breakfast room, Your Grace." Not so much as a glance for his master's disheveled appearance.

"Has she been here long?" Although it couldn't have been long or her luggage would have been carried upstairs.

"No more than twenty minutes, Your Grace."

"Did she say why she arrived early?"

"I believe she told Mallory she missed London."

A platitude. "So what's the ever popular Pansy having for breakfast?" Fitz muttered, running his palms down the front of his wrinkled waistcoat.

The young man's lips twitched. "Fresh beefsteak, Your Grace. Cooked three minutes on a side."

Fitz rolled his eyes. "I should have known. I'll announce myself, Norton. Bring me a brandy."

A few moments later, he shoved open the double doors to the breakfast room at the back of the house and entered the sun-filled chamber.

"You darling boy!" A slender, elegant, russet-haired woman whose youthful beauty was still much in evidence, gazed up from the breakfast table and opened her arms wide. "Come give your adoring mother a kiss!"

Ignoring Pansy, who was racing at him, yapping like a banshee, Fitz smiled. "You're early."

"I couldn't wait to see you, so I took an earlier packet. You haven't slept much from the look of things," Julia Montagu sweetly said, surveying her son's rumpled evening clothes and lack of tie with a twinkle in her eyes. "Pansy, be good now. Hush. Don't growl like that. You know Georgie."

"I expect the truth was you were bored," Fitz lightly countered, thinking how satisfying it would be to launch the pesky lapdog across the room. "And you needed a change of scene." Bending down, he held his hand out to be inspected by the odious little animal.

"Perhaps," the dowager duchess said with a coquettish smile. "But you're always the main reason I come home."

He glanced up from under a wave of black hair as Pansy licked his fingers. "Is Kemal in town?"

"We traveled together from Paris."

That answered all his questions: his mother's sudden change in plans, her ostensible annoyance with Lady Montrose, her early arrival. Kemal must have some urgent business in the city. Picking up the dog after it had decided Fitz smelled familiar after all, he carried it to the table, handed it to his mother, and kissed her cheek. "Are you staying long?" Taking a chair beside her, he held out his hand for the brandy Norton was carrying his way.

She smiled. "Some people would think that an insensitive question."

"You know very well it's not." He smiled back. "You're my only love. I was simply wondering whether we have any common social engagements in store, whether you're on your way to Green Grove or planning on settling in."

His mother waved her slender hand in a fluttery little gesture. "I have no plans."

"You're waiting on Kemal, you mean."

"Only partly. I wanted to spend some time with you, darling."

Fitz drank down half the brandy in one swallow. Not that he didn't adore his mother, but she had no compunction interfering in his life. Which always required he give the appearance he had nothing of interest for her to meddle in.

"I hear you've been unable to charm some young lady into selling you her bookstore. I thought your seductive charms were quite unrivaled."

He almost choked on his brandy. "Good God, mother," he said, swallowing to clear his throat. "You don't believe that rubbish."

"Of course I do. Everyone does. And why shouldn't they? It's no secret you're much in demand with the ladies. So tell me, what does this young lady not like about you?"

Not very much, he decided, recalling last night with an unexpected jolt of pleasure. "It's not about me," he said, taking pains to show no emotion. "She doesn't want to sell her store."

"You haven't offered her enough."

"Yes, Mother, I have. Apparently, it's not about money."

The dowager duchess's brows rose. "You don't say. The cardinal virtues are not yet dead," she sardonically noted. "I expect she's holding out for more," she cooly added.

"If you don't mind, Mother, Hutchinson is very capable of taking charge of the situation. You and I need not bother ourselves."

"I heard you may lose ninety thousand if your development has to be suspended."

"You've heard a great deal it seems."

"You needn't be grouchy. I'm simply concerned. I'm your mother. I want you to be happy."

"I am happy. Rest easy in that regard. As for this bookstore, all will be resolved in good time," he gruffly said.

Julia Montagu smiled sweetly. She knew better than to continue to press her son when he spoke in that tone. "Were you with anyone I know last night?" she pleasantly inquired. "Clarissa perhaps?" She reconsidered. "Of course not—her husband's back in town, and he does have his rules, doesn't he? What a strange little man. But then he's in biscuits or something, isn't he?"

"Soap," Fitz corrected.

"You don't say."

"I do. It's very good soap according to all reports," he mildly noted. Clarissa, the fourth daughter of an impecunious earl, had married one of the new multimillionaires recently brought into the peerage thanks to the Prince of Wales's penchant for gambling. Wales liked to surround himself with arrivistes who didn't mind lending him money—never to be repaid, of course.

But unlike the aristocracy who had learned long ago to discreetly look the other way when it came to the little peccadilloes of marriage, Lord Buckley insisted Clarissa keep him company when he was in town.

"So," the dowager persisted in honeyed accents, "if not Clarissa, was she anyone I know? And you needn't look at me like that. I'm sure the news is circulating below stairs as we speak and the whole town will know by teatime."

"For heaven's sake, Mother. Since when have you become a voyeur?"

"Don't tell me then," she soothingly replied, recognizing whomever he'd been with was not someone of her acquaintance. As aware as she that gossip traveled at lightening speed, Fitz normally would in some minimum fashion at least tell her who he'd been with since inevitably everyone in society would soon know anyway.

Musical beds was not only common but also habitual in the aristocracy. Once a wife had done her duty by providing her husband an heir, she was allowed her pleasures. And while everyone knew who was sleeping with whom, as long as wives and husbands discreetly ignored the details as it pertained to them, conjugal harmony was maintained.

"I'll be out this afternoon," Fitz declared, fending off further questions by changing the subject. "Hutchinson might have some new information for me as it relates to this bookstore. Are you dining at home tonight or are you going out?"

"We've been invited to Bunny's."

He didn't have to ask who she meant by *we*. "In that case, I'll see you at breakfast tomorrow. Have you met my new secretary Stanley?"

"I have indeed. A most lovely young man. Do you like him?"

He smiled. "How could I not since you arranged for him to enter my employ."

"Dear Abigail is in such straits I knew you wouldn't mind helping her son. A shame she has a husband so bloody poor at cards."

Fitz instantly thought of Edward St. Vincent and his wife—particularly his wife—when he shouldn't. It took him a fleeting moment to shake off Rosalind's image, and when he spoke his voice was unexpectedly husky. "Don't worry about Stanley." Quickly clearing his throat, he went on in a normal tone. "I'll see that he is well compensated, and if the boy wishes to move on to larger endeavors at some point I promise to see him properly placed."

"Thank you. You're a darling. You're *my* darling," she softly said, wondering who he'd been thinking of a moment ago when his voice had gone soft. Her son was not a man of sentiment, other than in their relationship, where he was most tender. She'd have to speak to Sarah. Darby never gave up a clue when it came to her son, but she and Sarah had been close for years. Hadn't they both been mother to Fitz? "Have you eaten, sweetheart?" she politely asked, intent on putting her son at ease, purposely not commenting as he held his empty glass out for a refill. "I believe all your favorites are on the sideboard."

"I'll eat later." He handed a flunkey his glass and said, "To the rim." He was finding it difficult to ignore the images of Rosalind that had come to mind when his mother had unfortunately mentioned gambling. The kaleidoscope of graphic, sexually explicit scenes was deeply unwelcome. Swivelling around, he searched for the flunkey. Where the fuck was his drink?

Julia wasn't particularly concerned that Fitz was drinking his breakfast. That wasn't uncommon for men of his class. But she'd not seen that shuttered look in his eyes in years. Having survived all the bad times with the former duke, she and Fitz were extremely close. She knew when he was unsettled. "Tell me about the design of your new development, darling," she interposed, hoping to assuage his moodiness with something of interest to him. As one of the largest property owners in Mayfair, Fitz usually enjoyed discussing his urban projects.

"Later, Mother. Once things are resolved." And having received his brandy, he lifted the glass to his mouth and drained it.

"Did you get my letters from Antibes?" she brightly queried. "You must come with us sometime. You'd love the sailing, and the weather is lovely beyond words even in the summer." Antibes was fashionable in the spring.

"Yes, thank you, your letters came. Kemal's villa sounds very . . . like those on the Bosporus," Fitz finished in lieu of the phrase *a benighted pile of gilded domes and flamboyant ornament* that had come to mind.

"I know it looks like a frosted wedding cake," Julia noted, recognizing her son's tactfulness, "but it represents the comforts of home to Kemal."

Does it remind him of his many wives as well? While Fitz liked Kemal, he was protective of his mother.

"I will *never* marry again," she flatly said, "so you needn't scowl at me like that. I don't require your protection."

"I know, Mother. It's a reflex."

"Furthermore, you're not in a position to even think of chiding me about nuptial ties when you're the third party in any number of marriages," she crisply noted.

"You're quite right, Mother. I stand corrected. And I

like Kemal. Who wouldn't? He's intelligent, affable, and damned good at baccarat."

Julia held her son's gaze for a telling moment, then smiled. "Forgive my temper. I just don't need you to take on the role of knight errant for me."

Fitz laughed. "You're years too late. Knight-errant types have peach fuzz on their cheeks and a rosy optimism. I'm a cynic."

"You certainly are not."

"I am. But there's advantages in seeing the world with unclouded eyes. You needn't worry, Mother. I'm quite content."

"You don't look content."

"I'm just tired."

"Then be sensible. Go upstairs to bed."

"I might." Suddenly, a wave of exhaustion washed over him. All for a good cause, though, he decided, no longer even trying to dismiss the carnal memories of the lovely Mrs. St. Vincent that were racing through his brain. "Wake me if you need anything," he politely remarked as he came to his feet. "It's nice to have you back, Mother," he added with a warm smile. "The house seems lived in again."

The dowager duchess watched her son as he walked away, a faint frown on her face. Something was amiss. It might just be the Monckton Row project that was in peril, although she rather thought it was another matter. Fitz didn't as a rule concern himself overmuch with business affairs. While he kept abreast of his various pursuits, by and large, Hutchinson took care of the day-to-day issues.

As the doors shut behind her son, she said, "Come, Pansy, let's find Sarah. She'll know what's bothering Georgie."

Pansy wagged her tail, and barked *yip, yip* as if she understood.

And maybe she did.

CHAPTER 12

WHILE FITZ WAS leaving a trail of clothes behind him and Darby was busy closing the bedroom drapes, the dowager duchess was making her way toward Sarah's apartment.

Due to their special position in the household, Sarah and Darby had their own cozy apartment overlooking the kitchen garden. They had accompanied Julia from home on her marriage, and their loyalties were unequivocal and unwavering. At Fitz's birth, Julia had placed her son under their care, confident they would protect him as if he were their own.

As a duke's daughter, Julia's world had changed little with marriage other than having to contend with a husband who was a monster. Not that other aristocratic marriages were necessarily ideal. She was not alone.

So she coped as did so many other beautiful young ladies married off by their families for reasons other than love. She avoided her husband whenever possible and filled her days with the amusements the beau monde substituted for happiness. While the fashionable set never changed, the locales for their amusements did: London in the Season, Scotland for fishing, the hunt country or Paris in winter, Monte Carlo or Biarritz in early spring, and then back to London again.

Within this whirlwind of travel and entertainments, Sarah and Darby saw that Fitz's life was relatively tranquil and unafflicted. When the duke was in residence, however, particularly when he was drinking, tranquility was beyond the capabilities of mere mortals. Complete anarchy ruled; the duke's temper was an explosive force, unaided by judgment, to paraphrase Horace. In those violent times, Sarah and Darby had orders to keep Fitz out of sight of his father if possible.

And it wasn't always possible.

Since the women were old, dear friends, the moment Julia walked into Sarah's kitchen, Sarah said, "Sit. I'll get us tea. I expect you're wondering about that woman."

"Is that why Fitz is drinking this morning?"

Sarah turned from the stove where the kettle was steaming. "I don't know for certain about the drinking, but I know he come from her place this morning."

Julia's brows lifted. "I thought it might be a woman." Taking a seat at the table, she settled Pansy in her lap. "He's come trailing into breakfast in his evening clothes before, but he was different today."

"Young Stanley's the one what seen her first, and he says she's a real beauty. A Venus, he says. The bookstore lady," Sarah added at Julia's questioning look. "That's where he were last night."

"Ah. That's why he didn't want to tell me where he'd been. Interesting," Julia murmured. "Now I know why he didn't want to talk about the bookstore. I asked him about it just to make conversation and he cut me off."

"Trouble in paradise," Sarah pronounced, spooning tea into the pot. "That bookstore lady's been tellin' him no, and he don't take to no real well like."

"Indeed," his mother concurred. "I blame myself for being too indulgent."

"It ain't your fault," Sarah replied. "The boy's always wanted what he's wanted and that's that." She could have said *like you*, but she didn't.

"Tell me everything you know about this woman. Although, I expect she's a bold little piece planning on lining her pockets with Fitz's help," Julia added with a little sniff of disapproval. "He says she won't sell even though she's been offered a considerable sum."

Carrying over two cups of tea, Sarah set them on the table. "First off, I don't know naught about the lady other than she's a looker. As if that ain't enough for Fitz," she sardonically added, taking a seat across from the duchess. "Anyways, I sent Darby after the boy, thinkin' we'd best know where he was spendin' the night efen' we had to drag him home what with you arrivin'."

Julia smiled. "He'd be incensed if he knew."

"Well, he don't and he won't. If you hadn't been comin' into town, he could've slept with the devil for all I cared. But you were comin'. A mite early as it turned out," Sarah noted with a dip of her head. "James had orders to fetch Fitz at half past ten."

"Still," Julia mused, "how is it possible for this woman, no matter how Venus-like, to have such an effect on him? He was moody at breakfast. Are you sure he hasn't been ruining himself at cards? Or losing at the races?"

"Does the boy ever lose at cards or the races for that matter with his stable of prime bloodstock?" Sarah shrugged. "Could be he's jes a mite tired and we're makin' a whole lot outta nothin'."

"You could be right. Yes, I'm sure you are." Julia preferred to ignore problems. If they couldn't be ignored, she generally handed them over to someone else to solve—a not untypical reaction of those in her privileged class who had been waited on from the cradle. "On the other hand," Julia murmured, her motherly instincts overcoming even her own creature comforts, "maybe it wouldn't hurt for us to pay a little visit to this bookstore and see this woman for ourselves."

Sarah grinned. "I thought you'd never ask."

The two women exchanged a look of understanding.

"I ain't goin' to mention it to Darby," Sarah noted.

"I certainly don't plan on telling Fitz," Julia cheerfully returned. "When shall we go?"

"You decide," Sarah said, already knowing the answer.

"Fitz is sleeping," Julia offered with a conspiratorial wink.

"Perfect."

Julia came to her feet. "Meet me in the entrance hall in ten minutes. I just have to fetch my bonnet."

CHAPTER 13

ROSALIND FELT THE hairs on the back of her neck rise when the two women walked into the store. One was obviously a servant or companion, the other vaguely familiar. She tried to place the face of the woman in the yellow silk muslin couturier gown who occasioned such a feeling of unease. But whatever was prompting her disquiet remained locked away.

The store happened to be busy at the time, so a lengthy interval lapsed before Rosalind took notice of the women again. Or rather her attention was dramatically directed to them at the entrance of Lady Tweedsdale. "Hail and welcome, Julia, my love!" she trilled in a high falsetto. "You're back! I saw Groveland yesterday and the rascal didn't say a word!"

A chill ran down Rosalind's spine. Were these women Groveland's spies? What was he up to? Not that it mattered, she reflected, shock quickly supplanted by anger. She would not be harassed *or* spied on. Just as soon as Lady Tweedsdale left, she'd send the two women on their way!

Lady Tweedsdale was too good a customer to offend,

nor could Rosalind afford any whiff of scandal in the event Groveland's name come up. The fact that these women were here so early in the morning gave her pause on that score.

She couldn't help but overhear their conversation, especially Lady Tweedsdale, who spoke in a tone more appropriate to the back benches of Parliament. Discoursing at great length, she described her social schedule in detail, the litany of her entertainments at various country house parties prodigious. She particularly bemoaned her fate in having suffered a week in the Highlands with her husband, who was shooting grouse. "Not to mention we were obliged to pay our addresses to Wales's newest hussy," she finished with a disparaging sniff.

During Lady Tweedsdale's lengthy recital, Rosalind had perhaps too much time to contemplate the well-dressed lady's possible relationship to Groveland. Which, inevitably, turned her thoughts to Groveland himself—and more pertinently resurrected heated memories from last night. Titillating, sensual memories that provoked a fierce, explosive rush of pleasure into every impressionable nerve ending in her body. Even those still somewhat tender.

Instantly repressing her wayward senses, she sternly reminded herself that she was not lost to all reason. *Especially now that Groveland is out of reach*, a little voice inside her head drolly noted. *And if you really don't care*, the pesky little voice went on, *don't listen to what Lady Tweedsdale is saying now.*

"Groveland has tired of Clarissa, I hear. She was quite left in the lurch," Lady Tweedsdale colorfully noted. "Margaret had all the tiresome details from Clarissa, who is quite resolved to cut your son cold next she sees him."

"If only Fitz cared," Julia sardonically returned.

But Rosalind didn't notice her reply with the words *your son* ringing in her ears and her body responding like a tuning fork to the mere mention of the notorious rogue. Half-breathless with a tremor of longing shimmering deep inside her, she wondered if it was possible to become addicted to sex overnight. Or had Groveland woven some spell over her?

She knew the answer even as she asked the question.

Anyone even remotely familiar with the scandal sheets knew what he was and where his skills lay. It wasn't addiction she was feeling so much as craving the pleasures Groveland so casually dispensed—*casual*, unfortunately, the operative word. The reason as well that she would firmly and emphatically curb her desires.

Thank God, Lady Tweedsdale was coming her way. Salvation.

In a very few minutes, she could dispatch Groveland's spies and with them her dangerous and shameless cravings.

"I wish to order more of Lady Oliphant's work," Lady Tweedsdale briskly pronounced. "As quickly as you may," she imperiously added. "How soon may I expect them?" She always spoke to Rosalind in her lady-of-the-manor voice, making it clear who was inferior to whom.

"If I order them today, I should have them tomorrow." If she took issue with every customer who treated her like a servant, she'd not sell many books.

"Send them round the moment they arrive." With a dismissive nod, Lady Tweedsdale turned away, called out good-bys to Julia and Sarah, and exited the store.

Now was her opportunity to send the women away, Rosalind resolved. With their departure, she could dismiss Groveland from her thoughts and return to the safety and orderliness of her life. Walking toward the two women with a determined tread, she rehearsed her presentation. She must be firm and resolute in telling them that she wouldn't allow herself to become the object of Groveland's harassment and insist that they leave.

Before she could speak, however, Julia looked up as she approached and pleasantly asked, "Would you happen to have any books on Turkey?"

Her smile was familiar, the cadence of her voice echoing her son's, and suddenly Rosalind's thoughts were in tumult—vacillating between fascination and affront, interest and umbrage as various replies raced through her mind.

But she finally said, "You don't actually want a book on Turkey, do you?" because, ultimately, she saw no advantage in befriending Groveland's mother. Not when Groveland had infuriated her in numerous ways—most prominently by seducing her purely for personal gain.

"But I do if that's all right with you," Julia calmly replied, thinking this young lady must have led Fitz on a merry chase last night. She was different from his usual inamoratas who fawned and flattered him. She had an edge.

"I doubt I'd have anything you're interested in," Rosalind said, thin-skinned and peevish.

Julia smiled. "I see why Fitz has had such difficulty negotiating with you."

"Then you'll also understand why I'm not interested in any further conversation. He's already sent over a dozen people with offers, all of which I've refused."

"I don't want your store," Julia said bluntly.

"Allow me to be skeptical. You're here because your son sent you."

"He doesn't know I'm here, and," Julia added with a smile as charming as her son's, "I'd appreciate it if you didn't tell him. He doesn't like when I meddle in his affairs."

"Rest assured, I won't be telling him," Rosalind testily replied, "because I won't be seeing him again."

"You're angry with Fitz."

"A mild word for what I'm feeling," Rosalind cooly retorted.

"If it's any consolation," Julia offered, not sure why she was confiding in this woman but heeding her motherly instincts, "Fitz drank his breakfast today—I'm assuming because of you."

"He's just displeased because I turned down another of his offers. But then, I'm not silly enough to be blinded by his amorous charms." There was no point in beating around the bush. They both knew where he'd spent the night, and living as she did outside the beau monde, she didn't have to worry over much about its censure. Not that Groveland's lady loves endured condemnation by the fashionable world. According to the gossip sheets, they were, in fact, envied.

"I see you're a woman of principle. Quite uncommon, my dear, as you no doubt know," Julia observed. "Over and above Fitz's business, though, I really *would* like some books on Turkey. I have a friend who would enjoy them. And rest assured, I have no ulterior motive for coming here other than wanting to see the woman who has put my son out of sorts. He's normally quite indifferent to the women in his life, so you understand my curiosity."

Rosalind was momentarily taken aback by such candor. The dowager duchess certainly couldn't be accused of prevarication. Quickly deciding that refusing such a civil request would give her the appearance of a petulant child, she said, "This way if you please," as if their conversation had never occurred. "I have a very nice section on Turkey."

As she guided the women to the back of the store, the duchess's remark about Fitz drinking his breakfast looped through her brain.

And warmed her heart when it shouldn't.

She cautioned herself not to interpret so innocuous a comment as anything more than it was—a simple statement of fact.

She also warned herself against feeling anything at all for a disreputable rogue who did little but play at love. She would only be hurt.

There. Reason had come to the fore.

Moments later, as the duchess began perusing books, Rosalind realized she was being offered an excellent opportunity to send back Fitz's jewelry. She'd already wrapped it, intending to have it delivered to Groveland House. But how much better to entrust the expensive items to his mother.

"If you'll excuse me a moment," she murmured as the duchess leafed through a book, "I have something I'd like you to bring back to the duke."

Julia looked up and without so much as a scintilla of query in her gaze, said, "Certainly, my dear. I'd be delighted."

At least two of them would be delighted, Rosalind decided, as she made her way upstairs. She wasn't so sure about Groveland.

Taking the stairs with considerably more speed than she'd descended them that morning, she was pleased to no longer be wincing in pain. She felt almost normal again, and once she'd disposed of Fitz's jewelry, she'd feel even better. Both the gift and the casualness with which it had been bestowed offended her.

She disliked being bought and paid for.

She disliked even more being classified as simply another of Groveland's apparently numberless lady loves.

Returning downstairs a few minutes later with the small parcel, she set it on the counter and waited for the duchess and her companion to select their books.

"I will see that Fitz gets this," the duchess said, picking up the silk-wrapped bundle when they were ready to leave. "And thank you for your help with the books. My friend will be delighted."

Everything turned out quite well after all, Rosalind reflected as the two women walked away with their purchases. Fitz's mother seemed pleasant enough, she apparently had no reason other than curiosity for coming to the shop, and now Fitz's jewelry was being returned by the very safest means.

In addition, she was feeling quite recovered from the excesses of last night.

She glanced at the clock. Now if only the hours would fly by so she could climb into bed and get some much-needed sleep.

WELL," SARAH POINTEDLY said as they retraced their steps to Groveland House, "what do you think of Mrs. St. Vincent?"

"You know very well what I think. The same thing you do."

Sarah grinned. "Not only stunning but out of the ordinary. A novelty for the boy."

"And hardly likely to play the coquette. I see why he's intrigued."

"Don't forget, she said she's done with him," Sarah cautioned.

Julia flashed a sideways glance at her friend. "I rather think Fitz might change the lady's mind."

"I ain't so sure," Sarah muttered. "If she were the kind to have her head turned, you wouldn't be carryin' them jewels back home."

Julia shrugged. "She has principles. That in itself should entice him."

"I dunno," Sarah murmured thoughtfully. "He might not get his way with this'un."

"Naturally, that's for Mrs. St. Vincent to decide," Julia serenely replied.

CHAPTER 14

SHORTLY AFTER ONE, barefoot and half-dressed in trousers and an open-neck shirt, Fitz walked into his mother's sitting room. Clearly confrontational from his pugnacious stance to his fierce scowl, he held Rosalind's package aloft. "What the hell is this?"

Julia set her book beside her on the settee. "You needn't swear."

His nostrils flared. "Very well, Mother. I would *appreciate*," he said with deliberate courtesy, "if you'd tell me where this came from."

"Mrs. St. Vincent."

"She was *here*?"

"Not exactly."

He groaned. "Don't tell me you went to see her."

"I just wanted a little peek," Julia returned, unruffled. "She seems quite nice by the way."

"She *is* nice, Mother. She's also an incredible nuisance." Each word was measured and controlled; he was clearly tamping down his temper. "In the future, though, I would be grateful if you stayed out of my affairs."

"You seemed out of sorts this morning. I was curious."

"I was perfectly fine this morning," he said, cool and clipped.

"No you weren't."

He silently counted to ten. "I was tired, Mother."

"I see." She smiled sweetly. "Are you feeling better now after your nap?"

"You're not getting off that easily," he growled. "I'm bloody irritated. You shouldn't have interfered."

"I'm sorry, darling," she amiably replied, ignoring his growl and glowering look. "But you needn't be angry. I bought some wonderful books for Kemal. Mrs. St. Vincent's stock is quite extensive."

Fitz blew out a long-suffering breath. He might as well be tilting at windmills, and it wasn't as though he hadn't expected her to meddle. She always did. Extending his arm, he nodded at the package on his open palm. "I suppose you looked in here."

"No, I didn't. But it's obviously jewelry. Mrs. St. Vincent is an unusual woman, darling, you must admit. When have any of your lady friends ever returned any of your lavish gifts?"

"Bloody right she's unusual," he grumbled, dropping his arm. "She's likely to cost me ninety thousand if I can't get her to move."

"Do you think perhaps you haven't approached her properly, my dear." Julia spoke with the patience and forbearance one would use addressing an unenlightened child. "She seemed quite reasonable to me."

He rather thought he'd approached her every which way, diligently and repeatedly last night. "On the contrary, Mother, she is entirely unreasonable," he brusquely said, not about to enter into a discussion with his mother on negotiation techniques. He half lifted the package. "Would you like these? I have no use for them."

"Leave them if you wish, sweetheart. I'm sure I can find some purpose for them." *There is always the possibility the lady will want them back at some point.* "Will you be home for tea?"

"No. I'm about to go out." After having his jewelry sent back, he had even more reason to see Hutchinson. He wanted this impasse resolved.

CHAPTER 15

IN A BETTER temper than he'd been on his previous visit, Fitz waited his turn in Hutchinson's elegantly appointed reception room. Offered his choice of beverages by a solicitous clerk, he'd barely had time to finish his brandy when Hutchinson appeared in the doorway.

"A pleasure to see you again, Your Grace, and opportune. One of our agents just sent in some interesting information."

"Excellent." Fitz came to his feet. "Because Mrs. St. Vincent remains as obstinate as ever."

"You've spoken to her again?" Hutchinson inquired.

"Yes." He didn't say when. As the men walked from the room, he said instead, "She's determined to stay."

"Women are less rational in their decision making. An observation based on considerable experience," the barrister added with a lifted brow. "Very few women are motivated exclusively by money."

Fitz smiled. "In contrast to men."

"Indeed. After you, Your Grace." Hutchinson waved Fitz into his office.

While Fitz took a seat, Hutchinson flipped through a mass of papers on his desk. "Ah, here it is," he said, dropping into his chair. "Pernell's report." Sitting down, he quickly perused it. "Yes, there it is—Dilmore Jones. He's an unsavory fellow, a gambling cohort of Edward St. Vincent." Hutchinson looked up. "Men of Jones's stamp are always willing to disclose what they know if the right sum of money is involved."

Fitz leaned forward slightly, "What exactly does he know?"

"It seems Edward St. Vincent supplemented his poetry income with something less inspirational. He wrote erotica."

Fitz smiled. "You don't say—a favorite poet of the Queen's writing risqué stories. Is there proof? More important, did his wife know about his sub-rosa activities?"

"As a matter of fact, we do have proof. Jones *sold* Pernell three of St. Vincent's books. As for his wife being complicitous, we don't yet know."

"The publishers might know. With the books in hand you have their names or at least a clue to their identities." Publishers of erotica were often fly-by-night operations with transient names and addresses that allowed them to stay one step ahead of the law. It was an era of boundless vices, public virtue, and epic hypocrisy.

Hutchinson nodded. "The publishers were obviously using pseudonyms, but the addresses were real—for sales reasons, I presume. Pernell already interviewed a Mr. Edding, who naturally denies any knowledge of either St. Vincent or his work."

"So now what?"

"We keep the man under surveillance. As you might know, the obscenity laws are an indiscriminate hodgepodge, sometimes enforced, generally ignored. But occasionally—in extenuating circumstances—raids are made on such publishers . . . for the public good."

"What if it were suspected that St. Vincent's work was being harbored—say, at his former residence." Fitz smiled faintly. "Might a raid be arranged."

After a moment of consideration, Hutchinson said, "After

talking to the right people, calling in a few favors, it could be done." He raised a finger. "A word of warning, however. We would need to know whether such books exist before authorizing a raid. There is danger of incurring a lawsuit for defamation or breaking and entering should nothing be found."

"Then her premises must be searched first. You have people who could do that?"

"Certainly. In her absence, of course. We can't afford witnesses."

Fitz frowned. "That could be a problem. She lives above the store."

"Surely she goes out on occasion."

"She must—yes, I'm sure she does," Fitz replied, thinking of Rosalind's friendship with Sofia. "As far as I know she doesn't have hired help, so her socializing would be confined to the evenings."

"We'll put the store under surveillance and wait for an opportunity. We'll also monitor the publisher. The threat of a prison term makes people like him vulnerable to pressure," Hutchinson noted. "By the by, I sent one of my barristers north to speak to Mrs. St. Vincent's parents. I thought if her family understood the sum she'd realize by selling the shop, they might influence her decision."

Fitz rested back in his chair and smiled. "You are ever efficient."

"The matter's well in hand, Your Grace. Knowing what we know about St. Vincent's supplementary activities strengthens our hand immeasurably. Should his erotica writings come to light, his wife's options will be severely limited. England is not like the Continent, Your Grace. Our obscenity laws are not as lax."

"If all goes well, perhaps we could start building in a fortnight," Fitz murmured, eminently satisfied with the state of the investigation.

Hutchinson relaxed against his chair back as well, confident and at ease. "I can almost guarantee it, sir. Would you like a fresh brandy? I might have a wee dram myself to celebrate."

CHAPTER 16

WHILE THE MEN were planning Rosalind's denoue-
ment in Hutchinson's office, she and Sofia were having
tea—with lemonade in deference to the heat of the day.
The air was still and sultry, customers were at home behind
drawn shades, and the ladies were quite alone in the quiet
of the gallery. The windows overlooking Rosalind's sketchy
patch of garden were open wide in the hope of some wayward breeze.

Sofia was lounging on a cast-off wicker sofa Rosalind
had salvaged and recushioned, her spirits high, her conversation limited to one of two subjects: Arthur Godwin's
incredible prowess in bed or his gratifying promise to pub-
lish a glowing review of her work in the *Times*. "I know
he means it, too," she enthused. "I could tell by the way he
raved about my talent"—she grinned—"my artistic talent,
darling. As for the other, he's sooo much better than Luke,
I couldn't begin to explain."

"Nor need you do so," Rosalind quickly interposed,
more fastidious than Sofia when it came to detailing sexual
intimacies. "He sounds as though he's very nice, though."

"*Nice!* I should say so." Feigning a dramatic swoon, Sofia looked up and grinned. "Guess how many orgasms I had last night?"

Rosalind smiled. "I'm sure you'll tell me."

"Ten. *Ten!* Can you believe it! The man's a veritable dynamo."

"I'm pleased for you. You seem happier than you've been for some time."

"I am…truly, truly. And considerably richer, too, which also inspires my good cheer." She grinned for the umpteenth time. "Thanks to Groveland, of course. Did he stay, by the way?"

Rosalind's face flushed with color.

"Obviously he did," Sofia murmured, sliding up against the sofa-back cushions again. "I won't ask you for an in-depth account because you're blushing like a schoolgirl. But everyone knows Groveland's the gold standard in bed; I expect you enjoyed yourself. I hear he can be indifferent in the cold light of dawn, though. Did you find him likeable?"

"He seemed pleasant enough," Rosalind replied neutrally.

Sofia smiled. "Really—just pleasant? Have you been keeping something from me—a lewd, libertine past of some kind," she drawled, "that allows you to answer so blandly? Most women would give Groveland higher grades than just *pleasant*."

Rosalind hesitated, then with obvious reluctance said, "He was highly skilled, imaginative, indefatigable, and gratifying in every way. Satisfied?"

"At least *that* sounds like Groveland."

"Which is the problem," Rosalind acidly noted. "He's too familiar with the game, too practiced. I doubt he can distinguish one woman from another or remember who he's been with from night to night."

"Are you angry with him?"

"Of course not."

"It sounds like you are."

Rosalind didn't immediately answer. She pouted fretfully and looked away for a moment before offering a limited accounting. "I discovered that he only slept with me in the hope I'd change my mind and sell the store. How's that for the height of vanity, or is it venality? Or cold calculation?" She grimaced. "So, yes, I suppose I am angry. Mostly, that I was stupid enough to be duped by a smooth-talking, seductive rogue."

"Relax, sweetie," Sofia soothed. "Obviously you didn't sell the store, so you weren't, as you say, duped. You also had what you described as a night of gratifying sex with a man reputed to be a phenomenon in bed. Personally, I think you won all round."

Sofia's logical reasoning did much to mollify Rosalind's vexation. "When you explain it like that..."

"It's God's own truth," Sofia pointed out. "You're just not thinking objectively because you're focusing on Groveland's mercenary motives. In contrast, his actual performance was superlative in every way you said. And that's a more vital priority, it seems to me, than *why* he was in your bed." She smiled slyly. "Which begs the question: How many times did *you* climax?"

"For heaven's sake, Sofia!"

"You're red as a beet so it must have been more than once. How many more?"

"I have no intention of telling you," Rosalind muttered, shifting in her chair as a disquieting tremor of delectable recall stirred through her senses.

"Fine, don't. But look, darling, you have some glorious memories if nothing else," Sofia softly observed. "That's not all bad."

"I suppose you're right," Rosalind grudgingly conceded.

"And you've been celibate for ages. You absolutely needed some wild, passionate sex."

"Sofia, good gracious, stop!"

"What if he comes back?" Sofia drawled, pale and ethereal against the cabbage rose chintz cushions. "Are you going to sleep with him again?"

"He's not coming back, believe me. He left in a huff."

"Did he now," Sofia murmured, her pale brows lifting into delicate arcs. "A huff? I'm surprised. Groveland is known for his nonchalance."

"He was in a rage over the store," Rosalind explained. "It had nothing to do with me."

"He has been relentless in his pursuit of your property. Just think, you may be the only person who has ever said no to him."

"Then it's about time the great and mighty Duke of Groveland realizes that he can't have everything he wants in life," Rosalind crisply declared. "The rest of us learned that stark truth long ago."

"But, consider, darling, he *is* a duke—and a very wealthy one," Sofia waggishly noted. "He's always gotten everything he's wanted."

Rosalind smiled for the first time since their discussion had turned on Groveland. "I confess, the thought of having dealt him perhaps his first defeat in a life of endless privilege is gratifying."

"As gratifying as sex with him?"

Rosalind looked amused. "Let's just call it a draw."

Sofia laughed. "So he's that good."

"Yes, indeed." Only a Jesuit could have argued the point.

"Then why not use him again?" Sofia saw men as means to various ends; she was a modern woman in every sense of the generally disparaging term. Not that she noticed or cared.

"Like a gigolo, you mean?"

"Except in this case you don't have to pay him. He'll probably pay you."

Rosalind looked startled. "What do you mean by that?"

"I mean he always dispenses lavish gifts. Leighton's model Flora said he sent her a very expensive ruby bracelet the next day. If he didn't leave you anything, he'll probably send you something today."

"I should hope not! I'm not one of his doxies!"

Sofia shook her head in bemusement. "You're soo old-fashioned, darling, and too decorous by half. Having sex with someone doesn't make you a tart. All the society ladies sleep with everyone, and they certainly don't regard themselves as hussies. They expect gifts, believe me."

"Well *I* certainly have no intention of taking gifts from Groveland!"

"My God! He gave you something!" Sofia sat up straight and fixed Rosalind with a sharp look. "Don't lie; you're blushing clear down to your toes. *Tell me!* What did he give you?"

"I already sent them back." Rosalind didn't say with whom, wishing to avoid the grilling that would ensue.

"Sent them back? Not just *one* item? He must have had a really good time," she teased. "Now, I *really* want all the details."

Understanding an answer was required or Sofia would continue badgering, Rosalind said crisply, "He left some expensive jewelry, several things; I didn't count them."

"Oh Lord," Sofia softly exclaimed. "You're such a complete innocent. But a very sweet one," she added with a smile. "Groveland must be absolutely flummoxed. I doubt anyone's ever returned his pricey trinkets." Sofia gave her friend a long, assessing look. "If you ask me, he's going to be even more intrigued now."

Pursed lipped, Rosalind shook her head. "He's not intrigued, nor am I. We're both *very much* not intrigued. We are, in fact, archenemies."

"Whatever you say," Sofia murmured, although she was thinking that the lady doth protest too much. Very interesting, Sofia reflected: the pure-in-heart Rosalind and the prodigal rake.

"Then what I say is *enough* about Groveland," Rosalind firmly declared. "I'm finished discussing him. His servants came for his paintings a few hours ago, which means I will not have to see or think about the despicable man again!"

"Very well. No more talk of Groveland," Sofia tactfully agreed. "Did I tell you Arthur is taking me to an exhibit at the National Gallery tonight?" The drama of Rosalind and

Groveland would unfold all in good time, Sofia decided. She had but to sit back and wait for the curtain to rise.

"How nice. Which exhibit?"

"The Turner watercolors. You should come with us since you're forever drooling over Turner's work."

Rosalind thought for a moment. "Maybe I will."

"So you say, but you never actually do," Sofia retorted. "Why not come this time? We're going to visit some friend of Arthur's afterward. He's an up-and-coming architect with a new house in Holland Park. Modest, but in the newest style, Arthur says. You might even meet some nice man there. Someone exactly opposite of Groveland."

When in the past Rosalind would have refused the invitation, she suddenly felt the need for some alternative to the potent memories of last night still roiling her brain. Despite her repudiation, she was finding it difficult to forget Groveland and the pleasure he so charmingly dispensed. "I *will* go with you this time," she said decisively. "What are you wearing?"

"One of Glynis's gowns. Wear the saffron silk she made for you. It's wonderful with your hair." Sofia smiled. "I'm glad you're coming with us. Should Arthur bring an escort for you?"

"No, no, please," Rosalind quickly replied, putting up her hand as further deterrent. "I just want to enjoy the show. I'm not in the mood to be entertaining."

But all the talk of Groveland had set her creative juices flowing, and after Sofia left, she sat in a comfortable chair near the window and quickly filled fifteen pages of her notebook with the opening scene of a new series.

In her excitement over the new story that was practically writing itself, Rosalind closed the store for ten minutes during a lull in the afternoon and ran the first chapter over to Mr. Edding.

After nervously waiting for a customer to leave his shop, she dropped her pages on the counter and said with a degree of agitation, "I can't wait. I locked up my shop to dash over here. It's the first chapter of my new series, *The Duke's Doxy.*"

"Capital! We go to press tonight so it's very opportune! Wait, wait, let me pay you," he quickly added as Rosalind made for the door. Swiftly counting out the bills, Mr. Edding slipped them into an envelope and slid it across the counter.

A moment later, he watched Mrs. St. Vincent rush away and began mentally estimating the profits he'd realize from a second series by his very popular new author.

The moment the store closed for the day, Mr. Edding saw that Rosalind's first chapter was delivered to the printer in the East End.

It would be hot off the presses and on sale in the morning.

CHAPTER 17

YOU'RE FINALLY BACK," Julia said, walking into Fitz's dressing room without knocking shortly after seven. "I need you to change your plans, darling. Kemal has deserted me."

"You *could* knock, Mother," Fitz drawled, taking his shirt from Darby and waving him out.

"Pshaw! As if I haven't seen you half-naked before." Dropping into a chair in a swish of green silk skirts, the duchess smiled at her son, dressed only in trousers. "I won't require your escort for long, darling. An hour or so early in the evening. Kemal had promised to take me to the Turner exhibit, but then some tiresome diplomatic crisis came up." She waved her hand dismissively. "In any case, I'm off to Bunny's dinner afterward—don't scowl...I'm not asking you to accompany me to that event. So you see it's nothing more than a little slice of your time this evening. That won't be so bad, will it?" she cheerfully finished.

"It won't be bad at all," Fitz said, sliding one arm into a shirtsleeve. "I'm going anyway."

"With whom? Do I know her?" Julia rightly assumed he was escorting a woman.

"No. She's one of Leighton's models." Slipping the shirt over his head, he began fastening the studs on the shirtfront.

"Well, I shan't ruin her evening for long."

Fitz smiled. "You won't ruin her evening at all, Mother. She'll be thrilled to be seen in your company."

"How sweet." The duchess raised her brows. "Does she speak the Queen's English?"

"Yes, Mother. She speaks very well and has excellent manners. Her father is a notable surgeon."

"And yet she takes her clothes off for Leighton."

"For art, Mother. There's a difference, I'm told," he drolly added.

"Come to think of it, Constance Radford has taken her clothes off in public for much less reason."

"On more than one occasion," Fitz sardonically noted.

"Indeed," Julia agreed. "And you needn't worry, I shall be ever so polite to your little model."

"I wasn't worried." He began tucking his shirt into his trousers.

"Because I'm always cordial to your lady friends," Julia said with a twinkle in her eye.

He looked up. "As I am to Kemal, Mother."

She came to her feet, not about to rehash a discussion they had agreed to disagree on long ago. "What time is the carriage coming round?"

"Half past seven. Flora wanted to see the watercolors in natural light."

"Then I must hurry," Julia declared, moving toward the door.

"If you like, we could come back for you."

"No, no, I can dress in a flash." She opened the door. "I'll be downstairs at half past."

Darby reentered the room as the duchess exited and took Fitz's coat from the armoire. "I expect we'll see you in the mornin'," he said, waiting while Fitz slid his white, embroidered suspenders over his shoulders.

"I assume so."

"Some of your Turners are on display tonight as I recall."

"Three or four. The Swiss landscapes."

"It looks to be a right fine evenin' to be out. Positively balmy it is."

"A perfect night for a carriage ride with the top down."

"Would you be wantin' some champagne to take along?"

"Flora has friends coming over to her place in Chelsea. I think she already ordered what she needed."

"Lady Buckley rung up this afternoon, Stanley said. Did you hear?"

"He told me." After which Fitz had given Stanley instructions to have a note and a small gift delivered, with his regrets, to Miss Baldwin at the Savoy.

Darby didn't inquire further; he'd done his duty. From Fitz's reply it appeared he wasn't planning on responding to Clarissa's call. During the remaining time it took for Fitz to dress for the evening, the men spoke instead of their upcoming hunting trip.

At seven twenty-five Fitz descended the main staircase. He was waiting in the entrance hall when his mother arrived breathless and flushed fifteen minutes later.

"Sorry, darling. Clara had trouble with my hair."

"It's not a problem." He smiled as he held out his arm for his mother. "We haven't gone out together for months. I'm looking forward to the evening."

She patted his arm. "You're such a sweet boy."

"It must be because I take after you," he said with a grin.

She chuckled. "I'm sure that's the case."

ROSALIND WAS HARRIED as well in her dressing, but not because her maid was having trouble with her hair.

First, she didn't have a maid, and second, her hair was piled on top of her head in its usual casual disarray. What *had* disrupted her schedule was a customer arriving as the store was closing.

Mrs. Greening was an excellent client so Rosalind couldn't simply shoo her away much as she would have liked to. Instead, she'd been obliged to cater to the dithering woman's many whims until she'd finally selected the books she wanted for her trip to the seashore.

Then when she'd arrived upstairs, she'd been faced with a bedroom awash in soiled towels, not to mention the tie and underwear Fitz had left behind. The towels had gone in the laundry basket, the tie and underwear in the trash, although she hadn't had time to change the sheets on the bed. Now she'd have to look at the scene of her trist on her return when she would have much preferred forgetting everything that had happened last night.

Fortunately, Rosalind's saffron silk was a Grecian-style silk muslin that was simple to don. She had but to drape it around her body, fasten the shoulders with the pretty little enameled brooches Glynis had made, tie the sumptuous purple silk sash around her waist, and her toilette was complete.

But she kept one eye on the time as she dressed, fretting at the fast-moving minute hand. Sofia and Arthur were coming to fetch her at seven and she didn't want to be tardy.

The clock was striking seven when she heard Sofia's hallo drift up the stairs.

"I'm ready!" she cried out, slipping her feet into gold leather Grecian sandals Glynnis had sent over along with the gown. Glynnis was both a friend and an artist who displayed her handmade designs in Rosalind's gallery; the gown and slippers had been a thank-you gift.

Catching sight of her flushed face in a mirror as she dashed through the parlor, Rosalind vowed to sit quietly in the hansom cab on the way to the exhibit and hopefully appear less like a day laborer in from the fields by the time they reached the National Gallery.

CHAPTER 18

FITZ WAS FACING away from the door so he didn't see Rosalind when she walked into the exhibit. Julia did, but knowing Fitz wouldn't appreciate her interference, she turned her attention back to her companions. Inspired by Turner's glowing watercolors of Venice, Flora had been going on at some length on the topic of her family's recent visit there.

The Turner exhibit was mounted in the West Room of the National Gallery where many of Turner's paintings were permanently on display. It was a modest-size space, and crowded. In fact, it was a crush.

Under the circumstances, there was every possibility that Fitz and Rosalind wouldn't encounter each other. Had not some young actress swooned—whether genuinely or for publicity—*and* had not the throng opened up around her, their eyes would not have met across the room.

Rosalind immediately turned away.

Fitz's nostrils flared. *Infuriating woman.* But as Rosalind disappeared into the crowd, he smoothly replied to a query Flora had just posed. "The first time I saw Turner's work was in Bristol. Remember, Mother, Paget was selling his uncle's estate? That small Thames River scene was my first major purchase as a youth."

"As if you're old now, darling," Flora purred, smiling up at him. "You're in your absolute prime..."

"Indeed, Fitz, darling," his mother agreed, looking amused. "You can't be old because then I'd be old."

"And you aren't at all, Your Grace," Flora gushed. "You don't look a day over forty."

Julia repressed a smile. "Thank you, my dear. How very sweet of you. Isn't Miss Nesbit the dearest girl?" She shot Fitz a look of complete innocence.

"She certainly is," he agreed, hoping his mother would behave.

Having been praised for her beauty from the cradle, Flora accepted the compliments not only as accurate and credible but also as her due. "And you're the most *wonderful* man I know," she said, fawning and fulsome, squeezing Fitz's arm. Turning to Julia, she added with a sugary smile, "Fitz is a credit to your motherly gifts, Your Grace."

"Would anyone like a glass of sherry?" Fitz interposed, hoping to curtail the unctuous flattery. "I know I would."

Julia met her son's gaze. "I don't suppose they have brandy."

"I'm sure they do." He dipped his head to Flora. "And you, Miss Nesbit?"

"A sherry would be excellent."

"Fitz! Fitz! Over here! Over *here*!"

Fitz inwardly groaned, the voice familiar. Glancing in the direction of the cry, he spotted Clarissa pushing her way through the crowd.

Flora scowled.

The duchess smiled faintly. Two aggressive females in pursuit of one man *along with* a curious audience. It should be an interesting evening.

Moments later Clarissa arrived, flushed and smiling. Ignoring the women, she smiled at Fitz and breathlessly exclaimed, "How absolutely *delicious* to find you, darling, because I'm quite *alone* tonight!" Her emphasis on the word *alone* was accompanied by a flirtatious wink. "Lord Buckley is off again on some dreadful hunting trip. I declare, men are never content unless they're shooting something." Having made her availability abundantly clear, she uttered a soft little sigh and added fervently, "Don't you just *adore* Turner's work? I wouldn't have missed this exhibit for the world."

Such gross insincerity elicited a moment of stunned silence.

Flora was looking daggers at her rival.

Fitz was wondering how best to negotiate the dangerous waters.

Knowing full well her duty as a mother, Julia stepped into the breach. "Fitz, darling, why don't you get us those sherries? I'll entertain the ladies while you're gone."

Fitz shot his mother a grateful look.

"Now don't forget my brandy," she directed and waved him off. Having lived her entire life in the modish world where insincerity was an art form, Julia overlooked the palpable animus between the two women and offered Clarissa a gracious smile. "My dear Clarissa, you must hear about Miss Nesbit's delightful family trip to Venice." The duchess turned her bright smile on Flora. "My dear, explain to Lady Buckley how your father happened to acquire his amazing collection of medical instruments in that little shop near the Rialto."

If not for the din from the crowd, it might have been possible to hear the ladies gnash their teeth.

"Now, I forget," Julia prompted. "Did your father discover the origin of that very curious ancient scalpel was Arabia or Egypt?"

"Egypt," Flora muttered, clearly not in the mood for conversation.

"Such an exotic locale!" Julia said enthusiastically. "The pyramids at twilight are quite breathtaking. Everyone says it of course, but it's absolutely true! Weren't you with Bunny's party in Egypt last year, Clarissa dear?"

While his mother was offering him momentary deliverance from what could turn into a battle royal, Fitz escaped downstairs where a bar was always available at events such as this. In no great hurry to return to the volatile situation upstairs—Clarissa a loose canon under the best of conditions, the current ones clearly challenging—he ordered two large brandies.

Anesthesia, as it were, for the coming battle.

And perhaps to numb his brain as well. He was thinking too much about his brief glimpse of Mrs. St. Vincent. Which was profoundly useless.

So it was only natural he would have preferred not seeing Arthur Godwin come up to the bar a few minutes later. He was trying to forget last night, not be reminded of the lady's tempestuous passions.

After exchanging greetings and a few polite words about the exhibit, Godwin ordered drinks—two sherries and a whiskey. Fitz shouldn't have been mindful of the order, nor should he have turned and watched Godwin walk away. It was simple curiosity, he rationalized, nothing more.

Certainly, there was no earthly reason to follow the art critic.

There was even less reason for his pulse to spike when he saw to whom Godwin brought the sherries. There she was. He could see her through the doorway of the basement study room where Turner sketches were stored. Sofia was with her, and both women smiled as Godwin offered them the drinks.

He should have taken serious warning at the jolt of raw lust jarring his nerve endings. Instead, he was contemplating how easily he could undress Mrs. St. Vincent. All he had to do was unclasp the brooches at her shoulders, unwind the sash at her waist, and her gown would drop away.

She didn't wear corsets, the fact obvious for all to see.

It would take less than a minute to divest her of her underclothes, and voila! She'd be available. And after last night, her willingness was not in question.

Not that reason didn't immediately argue its case. *How can you even think about fucking her when you're arranging her destruction? Have you no decency? No scruple or conscience?*

Libidinous urges quickly countered. *She can say no if she doesn't want sex. Consider, too, the ninety thousand you might lose. If you keep her away from her store tonight, Hutchinson's men will have time to search the premises.*

Moral issues aside, he was beset by a chafing resentment that the mere sight of her gave rise to an ungovernable need to mount her. He begrudged his urgent compulsion; in the past women had always been a pleasure but never an obsession.

And now Mrs. St. Vincent was threatening his laissez-faire existence.

A sensible man would forget he'd seen her, get the drinks for the women, and go back upstairs, his voice of reason advised. Furthermore, only a brute and a bounder would dally with a lady while in the act of ruining her.

A practical man at heart, Fitz ultimately came to his senses, turned away, and retraced his steps to the bar. Moments later, he was ascending the stairs, a flunkey following behind with a tray of drinks.

For the next half hour, Fitz parried the barbs flying fast and furious between Flora and Clarissa—a common enough situation for a man much sought after by women. In fact, by dint of considerable experience, his skills at accommodating overwrought females were finely honed. It also helped that he drank several more brandies—the flunkey had orders to keep his glass filled. When his mother decided to leave and join her friends, he was able to casually wave her off compliments of considerable brandy.

At this point, with the liquor warming his blood, he was pondering the merits of a ménage à trois since neither woman seemed willing to cede the field to her rival. He was actually making such an offer when Rosalind walked back into his line of vision and his voice died away.

The subdued lighting or perhaps the dark paneled walls exaggerated the gleaming copper of her hair and the brilliant saffron of her gown. Her voluptuous form beneath the draped silk brought to mind paintings of a mythical Arcadia with enchantresses disposed in various provocative poses. Not that Rosalind was posing at the moment; rather, she was moving cautiously through the crowd, trying to keep her sherry from being jostled. And damned if Harry Moore wasn't following in her wake—eyeing her like the lecher he was. "If you'll excuse me," Fitz murmured, hot with jealousy, every man she passed turning to stare as well. "I'll be back in a minute."

"Where are you going?" Flora sharply quizzed.

"I'll go with you," Clarissa said, more practiced and cunning.

"No, don't." Blunt as a hammer.

His curt retort gave even Clarissa pause.

Indifferent to the ladies' sullen gazes, he strode away.

Scanning the crowd in the direction Rosalind had taken, Fitz searched for a glimmer of her auburn hair or Harry's blond locks. Not that he was entirely sure what he'd do after he found her or Harry. The room was awash with other friends and acquaintances as well, not to mention his mother. Mrs. St. Vincent would likely discourage his advances. Numerous difficulties existed to complicate the situation.

None of which halted his swift advance.

Ah, there. He spied the group in a far corner. Fortunately, they were well away from Flora and Clarissa. Although, driven by brute impulse, he wouldn't have cared if they weren't.

He smiled faintly.

Christ, he might have been a grass green youth so irrational was his behavior. Or more like a barbarian, he decided, recognizing what he was about to do. Fuck Harry—he was going to drag her off whether she liked it or not.

His manner was smoothly urbane when he greeted the

small group. "Good evening." He bowed gracefully. "Are you enjoying the show?"

"Yes, indeed." Sofia smiled. "What a pleasant surprise."

Arthur Godwin nodded. "Good evening again, Your Grace."

Rosalind shot a look at Arthur, then dipped her head in Fitz's direction, her expression chill.

"You're a long way from the racetrack, Harry," Fitz drawled.

"Didn't know you were an art lover, Fitz."

"I'm here with my mother, but I seem to have lost her," Fitz blandly noted, his gaze turning to Rosalind.

He knows about his mother's visit to my shop. She refused to rise to the bait, especially after having watched him being fawned over by two beautiful blonde women who could have been a matched pair. *Just like him*, she pettishly thought. *Pretty, flighty blondes without a thought in their heads beyond vying for his favors.*

"Turner's work is magnificent, isn't it?" Sofia interposed, hoping to avoid a brawl between the two men or possibly between Fitz and Rosalind, who was scowling grimly. "The colors, the atmosphere, the sheer technical proficiency. It quite takes your breath away."

"Lot of messy paint if you ask me; can't make out whether it's a tree or boat over there. But the company more than makes up for the rubbishy art," Harry murmured, smiling at Rosalind.

"The man's a genius, Harry," Fitz muttered.

"Not in my book. Stubbs—now there's a genius. Could paint a horse so real you could touch it."

"Don't you have somewhere to go?" Fitz's blunt, contentious words matched the scowl on his face.

"Lord Moore is entitled to his opinion, Groveland. Art is perception; no more, no less," Rosalind said, offering Harry a charming smile.

"The lady agrees with me, Fitz," Harry gloated, still rankled over having lost Clarissa to Fitz not long ago. "Don't you think your mother's missing you?"

"She isn't, but I left Clarissa by the stairs. Buckley's shooting again," he cooly added.

"Is that a fact."

"Yes it is. She's with Flora. You remember her, don't you?" Flora had come to a masquerade as Springtime several months ago and her costume had left little to the imagination.

"If you'll excuse me, ladies, gentlemen." Harry made his bows. "I believe I see my brother in the crowd."

"Are you pimping now?" Rosalind snapped as Harry made a hasty exit.

"Rosalind, for heaven's sake!" Sofia exclaimed.

"You would have found Harry a boor," Fitz softly said, as if Sofia hadn't spoken, his gaze for Rosalind alone.

"That's not for you to decide," Rosalind testily replied.

"Forgive me. Would you like me to call him back?"

"And if I said yes?"

A muscle in his jaw clenched, his gaze drifted from her eyes to her lush cleavage on display in the deep vee of her gown, and he said, silky smooth, "If that were the case, naturally I'd be happy to *accommodate* you in any way whatsoever."

"For God's sake, Groveland," Rosalind snapped, her temper cracking under his brazen stare and the insinuation in his words that had nothing to do with Harry Moore. "You'd think you'd never seen breasts before!" How dare he strip her with his eyes in full view of the world; how dare he send Moore away!

Fitz looked up, his smile insolent. "I was admiring your gown."

She glared at him. "Libertine."

"Do forgive me, Mrs. St. Vincent"—he held her gaze for an overlong moment—"for offending your sense of propriety. I didn't realize you had such a fastidious sense of decorum." The mockery in his voice was only thinly veiled.

"You bastard," she muttered. "Go to bloody hell." Without regard for Sofia and Arthur's shocked looks, nor for others in the vicinity who were raptly listening, Rosalind spun around and stalked off.

"It was a pleasure to see you again," Fitz murmured, following Rosalind with his gaze. "Don't worry about Mrs. St. Vincent. I'll see that she gets home."

Trailing Rosalind's haughty retreat, he caught sight of his mother as he was nearing the door and nodded to her in passing.

Having seen Mrs. St. Vincent stalk by only seconds before, Julia understood that she would have to find a hansom cab for herself and Flora. Unless the young lady found another escort to see her home—which was not at all unlikely.

Wishing to avoid a skirmish in the gallery, Fitz chose not to overtake Rosalind until she reached the outside portico. When she paused at the top of the stairs, he quickly closed the distance between them and seized her wrist—a trifle roughly perhaps. But awareness of his overharsh grip didn't in the end move him to moderate it.

"Unhand me, you beast!" Rosalind hissed, trying to pull free without attracting the notice of visitors streaming past.

"I just want to talk to you," he returned, keeping his voice low.

"Go talk to your two little blondes," she caustically returned, skewering him with her flame-hot gaze. "They looked more than interested. I'm not!"

"If I wanted to talk to them, I'd be talking to them," he muttered, beginning to move down the stairs, annoyed that she was annoyed. Annoyed that she wasn't being reasonable. Refusing to address his rash actions in driving Harry off or the fact that only Mrs. St. Vincent would do tonight when he'd never been particular before. Sex had always just been about sex. Damn her.

"For God's sake, Groveland...what do you think you're doing? Stop this insanity!" Rosalind tried to dig in her heels, but the soles of her sandals were slipping on the marble stairs polished smooth over decades of use. "Stop! Do you hear? Stop this instant!" She might have been talking to herself for all the good it did. Fitz neither responded nor looked back on his full-tilt downward progress.

People on their way up stared or cast furtive glances their way, but on meeting the duke's basilisk gaze, they quickly looked away.

"Damn you, I'll scream! I'll scream to high heaven!" Rosalind panted, stumbling in an effort to keep up with his headlong pace.

"Scream all you want."

The indifference in his voice was stunning. In the midst of a crowd, she thought, he didn't care what anyone thought. Including her. Before she could further contemplate his iniquities, they reached the bottom of the stairs and in an additional act of madness, he swept her up in his arms and strode like a man possessed toward the line of carriages parked at the curb.

Embarrassed at the tawdry spectacle, she buried her face in his shoulder, hoping no one she knew had seen her, praying most that they'd soon be away from all the curious eyes.

The drivers lounging beside the carriages stared openmouthed as Fitz strode past, aware that they were witnessing a bona fide abduction—a highly unusual event in the modern era. Not that anyone intervened.

Fitz came to an abrupt stop when he reached his carriage. "Put the top up, Ogilvy, then Mertenside." Tossing Rosalind over the side of the landau with precise aim if not courtesy, he jerked open the half door, climbed in, and dropped into the seat opposite her.

"You won't get away with this flagrant abuse," Rosalind sputtered angrily, bristling as she struggled into a seated position. "I'll have you arrested for kidnapping," she threatened, jerking her skirts down over her legs, straightening her decolletage, trying to distance herself within the narrow confines of the carriage. She briefly wondered if there was a chance of outrunning him, but quickly realized there wasn't. Even if she could escape the carriage, which was doubtful with Groveland only a few feet away, she could no more outrun him than she could outdistance a racehorse. "I could have you arrested for rape," she muttered, sulky and bitter.

Fitz shot her a startled look, then turned to help Ogilvy secure the leather carriage top. Only when the last snap and buckle was fastened and the carriage was moving did he sit back and address her. "You and I both know it wasn't rape," he said.

She had the good grace to blush. "It could have been."

He smiled. "Perhaps, if you hadn't kept saying, *Please, just once more*."

She sniffed. "I don't want to talk about it."

"As you like," he calmly replied, sliding into a lounging pose, stretching out his legs, content now that he had what he wanted. "I *would* like to talk to you about something else, though." Experience had taught Fitz that women liked to talk more than they liked flattery and kisses; conversation was always effective as foreplay.

"Right. And I'm the Queen of Sheba."

"Maybe not Sheba," he said with a raking glance and a wicked smile. "But Venus certainly. You wear the most amazing gowns. Who's your dressmaker?"

"I'm poor, Groveland," she crisply retorted. "People like me don't have dressmakers."

"Nevertheless, someone made that frock. It's quite lovely. Not that the body underneath isn't even more lovely."

She gave him a flinty look. "Save your suave charm for your doxies. I'm not interested."

"You seemed interested last night."

"Everyone makes mistakes from time to time. You were mine."

His lazy smile warmed his eyes. "Perhaps I could change your mind."

"I'm not selling my store," she firmly declared, sitting up straighter as though good posture was defense against a charming smile. "So I suggest you save your seductive skills for someone more susceptible."

"What if I said this isn't about your store?"

"Then I'd say you're a bloody liar."

He grinned. "I'd still try to talk you into bed."

"So subtle, Groveland. It makes me quite giddy."

"Fitz."

"Groveland."

He smiled. "You really do fascinate me."

"While you simply irritate me," she briskly replied, not exactly truthfully, but opting for prudence in this unpromising relationship. "Kindly have your man take me home."

"In due time," he calmly said.

"What the hell does that mean?"

"It means I'll take you home later."

"For your information, it's 1891, not the Dark Ages when abductions were just another adjunct to male dominance. Women have rights now, we are no longer chattel, we are equals," she hotly contended even though she knew better. She was making a point. "What you're doing is completely outrageous and you know it!"

"You're quite safe." His voice in contrast was mild.

"From sex with you?" she shot back. "I doubt it. And for the record, I'm refusing your rude advances."

"Just talk to me then."

"About what pray tell? We have nothing in common."

He smiled. "Allow me to disagree."

"Sex is sex. It's not conversation."

"But pleasant nonetheless."

"I'm sure there are any number of women who would be more than willing to pleasure you. Acquit me, Groveland, from such endeavors. Now, are you taking me home?"

"No. Tell me, what do you think of Mother?"

She stared at him, the waning light of the sun shining through the carriage windows casting flickering shadows over his stark features. "Are you drunk?" Both his blunt refusal and his abrupt conversational shift were disconcerting.

"No. I'm perfectly sober. Be frank. About Mother," he said as if they were dinner table companions sharing a bit of common gossip.

"Good God," she retorted, agitatedly touching one of the brooches fastening her gown as she recalled the duchess's morning visit and the motive for it. "What do you want me to say?"

"Say anything you like." Although it took more than a modicum of restraint to answer blandly when he was mentally unclasping that brooch.

"Very well. Is it normal for your mother to inspect your…" She paused, unsure of what to call herself.

He looked amused. "Lovers? No, not ordinarily."

She hesitated, not sure she wished to be interrogated, even less sure that she should speak her mind about his mother.

"Tell me what Mother said?" he prompted, wanting her to relax, enjoying the sight and sound of her, and ultimately, of course, waiting to fuck her.

Rosalind sighed. "If you must know, your mother said you were sullen at breakfast and she thought I might have had something to do with it."

His brows rose. "Perceptive of her. I was pissed."

"Don't even start with the reason why. I have no intention of selling my store to you."

He thought of the men probably searching her apartment even as they spoke. He should have felt some guilt. Instead, he felt only lust. "I won't say another word about your store," he offered. First things first. After he was done fucking her, time enough to consider business matters. "I feel, too, I should apologize for Mother. She interferes in my life on occasion."

"Are you an only child?"

He nodded. "And you?"

"I have an older brother."

"Here?"

"No, in Yorkshire. He's a solicitor."

So her family wasn't averse to trade. There were those in the gentry that were, no matter their poverty. "Is he married?"

She gave him a narrowed look. "Why do you ask?"

"No reason. I was just making conversation."

"While you're in the act of abducting me," she sardonically remarked, pointing at the open window. "I see we've left the city."

"I thought you might enjoy my villa on the Thames. It's not far."

"I have no intention of enjoying your villa on the Thames."

The faintest of smiles graced his fine mouth. "I wonder if it's your outspokenness that appeals to me most."

"Please, Groveland, the only thing that appeals to you is sex."

"How do you know after only one night?"

"Let's just say I'm a fast learner."

"You are."

"Am I supposed to say thank you?"

"On the contrary, I should thank you."

"This might be an opportune time to mention I'm not in the mood for sex tonight. I was quite sore this morning."

"I'm sorry."

"It's not entirely your fault. I could have said no. But there you have it, so you might as well tell your driver to turn around. I'm sure you don't want to waste your time."

While her disclosure somewhat altered his plans, he still preferred she not return to her store until later in the evening. *And keep in mind*, the lustful voice inside his head asserted, *she may yet change her mind about having sex.* "It's not dark yet. We can sit by the river and watch the sun go down. Have some champagne. You can tell me about your family."

"Call me suspicious, but why would you care about my family?"

He shrugged. "To be perfectly honest, I don't. But I like the sound of your voice. I like to look at you." His smile was well-bred, his deep voice bland, his keen gaze in contrast, that of a connoisseur contemplating his newest prize. "I like your jasmine perfume."

"And you'd like to have sex with me."

"Of course I would. But I won't."

"So obliging and benevolent." Sarcasm in every syllable.

He laughed. "You're a cynic."

"A realist."

"Same thing." He smiled. "Although I know what you mean. I'm a cynic, too."

"Charming as you are," she said with sweet mockery, "this spiriting me away is useless. I'm not going to have sex with you, and you don't really want to talk to me about my family. So maybe I should scream and call out for help from your driver. Would he come to my rescue?"

"You could try."

"What does that mean?"

He shrugged. "No one's ever screamed for help before. I have no idea what Ogilvy would do."

"You arrogant ass."

"Sorry. I may not be *completely* sober. Also, you're a totally new experience for me."

"A woman who says no, you mean."

"Only at first, if I recall," he pleasantly replied.

Maybe it was his insouciance that was most annoying or his unconscious arrogance, or the way he shamelessly assumed no woman could resist him. Which latter fact might also pertain to her but was nevertheless irritating.

Whatever the cause, she came up out of the seat in a swift lunging attack and slapped his smug face. Hard. Instantly mortified, shocked at her childish actions, she dropped back into her seat, flushing in embarrassment.

He took no notice, other than to growl, "Christ, watch it. You almost took out my eye."

A distinct casualness underlay his words, and she wondered at a man who could be so imperturbable under duress. She shouldn't have found it admirable. She certainly shouldn't have remembered how he'd growled last night in the explosive throes of passion, or how he'd groaned deep in his throat as he climaxed.

How his hard muscles flexed under her hands as he

made love to her with virtuoso skill and brought her to screaming orgasm.

Oh God—what was she doing?

She was going straight to hell if she continued this train of thought.

It took her a moment to restrain her wayward passions and a moment more to be able to speak in a normal tone. "I'm so very sorry. Ordinarily, I would never even think of slapping anyone." She exhaled softly. "You provoke me in any number of ways. Admit, what you are doing is not business as usual for most people."

He chose not to further offend her by saying he did as he pleased because he wasn't most people. "You're right. I'm sorry as well. It's been an odd evening. Too many people perhaps," he said, deliberately neglecting specifics like Clarissa and Flora's irritating skirmish and Harry's interference. "I'll make a bargain with you. Come with me to my villa and I promise to play the role of Lancelot if you like—pure of heart and saintly."

"Why should I trust you?"

His lashes drifted lower and he surveyed her with his cool grey gaze. "The scandal sheets aside, I rarely lie." He smiled. "With the exception of the occasional perjury in the heat of passion. Since we have agreed to dispense with passion tonight, the unromantic truth will hold sway."

Why was she suddenly chagrined?

He was offering her what any self-respecting woman would want. Conversation, pleasant company, a strict propriety. Why was she disappointed?

"You mean it?" An ambiguous query like her equivocal state of mind.

"Word of honor," he easily replied, knowing he had qualified his offer with the phrase *if you like*.

She smiled. "A glass of champagne sounds very nice."

Her smile warmed his heart, a shocking revelation he quickly brushed aside. Reverting to type, he pleasantly said, "When the moon comes up over the river, the scene is quite magical." He grinned. "And I'm not prone to whimsy. It's just picturesque I suppose—the gently flowing river, the moonlight filtered through the willows, an all-encompassing peace. Unlike the city."

"I do have to be home before midnight in order to open the store on time."

"Whatever you say," he amiably replied. "And thank you. I appreciate your company." He actually meant it, the difference between Mrs. St. Vincent and Clarissa or Flora profound. It made him wonder if his prodigality would have been better served outside the world of the beau monde.

He certainly couldn't accuse Mrs. St. Vincent of the sameness that characterized all the women of fashion he knew.

CHAPTER 19

FITZ'S VILLA WAS a picturesque sight as the carriage rolled up a slight incline to the entrance. Rosalind admired the elegant facsimile of the Petit Trianon situated on the crest of a hill and wondered what ancestor had been enamored of French architecture. The charming villa was surrounded by an equally charming Capability Brown landscape of specimen trees, verdant lawns, and colorful flowers; glimpses of the Thames were visible in the distance.

As though intrinsic to such a noble display of wealth, a host of servants rushed out to greet them as the carriage came to a stop on the graveled drive.

Fitz casually waved to his staff as he stepped out, then turned to help Rosalind alight. "Are you hungry?" he asked. "I am."

"Perhaps a little," she murmured, distracted by the splendor of her surroundings. Light gleamed from every window, two tall bronze torchieres stood on either side of the wide bank of stairs, the pale limestone of the exterior shimmered in the twilight, the scent of jasmine pungent on the air. "Jasmine—lovely," she said with a smile.

"That's why I like your perfume. It reminds me of Mertenside. I like it here. Come, we'll say hello to the staff and then walk through the house to the river."

He introduced her to his majordomo and in general to the others lined up on the drive. She watched Fitz chat with several of his retainers as they slowly made their way to the house and was surprised at the casualness of his manner. No arrogant peer of the realm here, only a man comfortable with his staff.

As they walked through twin bronze doors, held open by two footmen, Fitz turned to his majordomo, who was waving flunkeys before them to open further doors. "Tell Hector we could use a little something to eat. He needn't go out of his way. Something simple. And champagne, Chandler. The '73."

Rosalind gazed with awe at the rooms they passed through, the decor lifted wholesale from Versailles, although the rococo furniture was oversize, clearly made for a man, while the sumptuous carpets were pure silk and so plush her feet sank into them.

Strangely, the opulent interiors enhanced Fitz's dark masculinity, the stark contrast between gilt and damask, Chinoiserie wallpaper and graceful furniture only making his strength and virility more conspicuous. Just as a splendid animal outrivaled a trivial display of gilded luxury.

Or a powerful lord minimized his environment.

When they'd walked to the end of an enfilade of rooms and reached the terrace doors, Fitz said, "Thank you, Chandler. That will be all." And with a faint bow, he offered his arm to Rosalind.

They walked out into the twilight again, strolled down a shallow flight of marble stairs, and set out across a velvety swath of lawn that sloped down to the river.

"It is magical," Rosalind commented softly, the evening sky still golden on the horizon, the birds making music in the trees, the river slowly flowing by. "The house, the parkland—everything's so lush and green."

"Thank you. Mertenside's my haven from the city."

"Do you come here often?"

"As often as I can. Would you like to sit outside or inside?" He indicated a glass summer house on the river bank.

"Outside. I was inside all day."

"Was the store busy?" he politely asked.

"Not in the afternoon. It was too hot for anyone to be out."

"It has been unseasonably warm even for August," Fitz affably returned, wondering how long it would be before Mrs. St. Vincent would be interested in more than conversation.

Rosalind, in turn, was wondering if she'd again misjudged Groveland. Was he less a rogue than she thought? Was rumor wrong? Could he be a man like any other?

Two bottles of champagne later, Rosalind was thinking of other things. She was wondering in metaphorical terms whether she would allow herself to have her cake and eat it, too. Even though she shouldn't even be thinking about cake.

Fitz took note of the change in her demeanor—with gratitude.

She laughed freely now, teased him on occasion, and answered his questions without caution. Although he was careful to ask only questions she'd find unexceptional.

It was a proverbial cat-and-mouse game, yet at a more subtle level: the question of who played which role wasn't clear.

Not that Fitz could ever be accused of being anyone's prey. But susceptible he certainly was to the lady's outrageous allure.

As for Rosalind, she more demonstrably fell victim to Fitz's noted charm, but then his skills in that regard were legendary.

"You are indeed an attractive rogue," she said some time later, half raising her glass to him. Dinner had been superb, the champagne was like drinking stars, her companion was surely one of the most charming of men; she was content and happy to a degree that had eluded her for a very long time.

"As you know, I find you the most beautiful of women," he said, smiling back. "Would you like more champagne?" Without waiting for an answer, he picked up the bottle, rose from his chair opposite her, topped off her glass, and sat back down.

She was lounging on a large chaise upholstered in brilliant scarlet raw silk, the contrast of color against the saffron of her gown dramatic.

"You could be one of Alexander the Great's ladies from his India campaign in your Grecian gown, lying on that hot red silk," he softly said. "Roxana perhaps instead of Rosalind."

"And you have the look of a swarthy corsair, dressed all in black with your shirt collar open, your feet bare, and your black hair ruffled from the breeze."

"If you like, we could pretend—"

"Or not," she interrupted. Setting her glass on the table beside the chaise, she decided that she'd fought off her desires long enough. The man was God's gift to women and not just physically... well, perhaps especially there, she thought, recalling his stamina of the night past. "At the risk of sounding like the most shallow of women," she said, prettily crinkling her nose, "I find you much too handsome in every respect."

"And?" He knew the rest, but he was polite.

"I was wondering if you'd like to do something other than talk."

"Yes, certainly."

She smiled. "Do you always just sit back and wait, Groveland? I suppose you do."

"I wasn't exactly sure how to play Lancelot," he replied, sportive and teasing.

"I'm not sure I care."

"Ah, in that case..." Having been given license, he

came to his feet, walked the few steps to her chaise, and sat beside her. The lounge chair was big enough for two for a reason, not that he had women to Mertenside often. But occasionally he did.

"Tell me I'm not the thousandth woman you've made love to on this chaise." Even as she spoke she had no idea why it mattered with a man like Groveland. And so she said a second later, "Strike that last comment. It's quite irrelevant."

"You're not the thousandth, or even the hundredth or twentieth. Is that better?"

"No, none of this is better in any way." She made a small moue. "This is all very much a breach of custom for me. But I want the pleasure you bring me." She shrugged. "I expect it's the champagne talking."

He smiled. "Like last night."

She laughed. "Indeed. Give me another last night and I'll be content."

"When do you have to be back?"

"It depends," she said to the insinuation in his query.

"Good." They were in agreement then. "Would you like to go to the house?"

"If it's private here, no. The night is beautiful."

"It's completely private."

She half turned to him on the chaise and softly sighed. "I wish I didn't feel this way. I should go home."

"I don't want you to go home. In fact," he murmured, shifting slightly so he could brush a finger over the brooch on her right shoulder, "I've been thinking of unclasping this ever since I saw you at the National Gallery. And by the way," he said, softly, "you lit up the room."

"How charming you are. I almost believe you."

"Believe me, darling. I haven't been able to get you out of my thoughts."

"Nor I, you, when I should." She grimaced. "You're the enemy."

"No...we're lovers in the moonlight," he whispered. "And I promise to be gentle."

"Right now, I'm not sure that's necessary." Her gaze was amused. "I'm hot, hot, hot—touch me . . . you'll see."

He did then, tracing the swell of one breast partially visible in the deep vee of her gown, his fingers rough against the silk of her skin.

"Yours aren't the hands of a prince of the blood," she said gently, lifting his hand to her mouth and brushing the pads of his fingers over her lips, remembering his touch from the previous night. A tiny frisson raced through her body at the memory. "These are a workman's hands."

"I play polo and ride without gloves, and shoot"—he shrugged—"and do most everything myself."

She smiled. "Just so long as you do this yourself, I'm content."

"Believe me, I wouldn't relinquish this role to God himself."

"How sweet."

"I'm not in the least sweet, darling." Drawing his hand away, he began to shrug out of his jacket.

"So I recall with great fondness," she purred, kicking off her sandals. "Do you want to undo these pins?" She pointed at the brooches.

He grinned. "It's been my dearest wish all evening. I'll be right with you," he added, quickly unbuttoning his waistcoat.

Tantalized and restive, conscious of their mutual impatience, she watched him discard his waistcoat, slip his suspenders off his shoulders, tug the studs from his evening shirt with one jerk, slip the garment over his head, and toss it aside. Drawing in a small breath at the sight of his powerfully muscled torso, she felt the pulsing between her legs shamelessly pay homage to his potent virility. He was lean and taut, bronzed by the sun or dark by nature, honed to the inch by polo perhaps or maybe his boudoir athletics. And her every sexual nerve and receptor responded to his raw maleness with giddy eagerness. Philanderer he might be, the Don Juan stud of London, but he was so immeasurably fine, she was quite willing to overlook his rash prodigality for one more night of pleasure.

Pushing herself upright on the chaise, she clasped her hands in her lap to stop their excessive trembling. And unlike last night, she couldn't blame her long celibacy for her feverish desires. Tonight it was lust pure and simple.

Glancing up from unbuttoning his trousers, he whispered, "Wait for me."

She nodded, unable to speak, clenching her hands more tightly.

Recognizing Mrs. St. Vincent's precipitous arousal, remembering her tendency to impatience, he abruptly dispensed with his undressing and turned to her before it was too late. "Here, darling, I'm here," he murmured, slipping his hand under her skirt, shoving the silk fabric aside with his other hand, briefly surprised she was sans drawers. Quickly dropping the back of the chaise to a horizontal position, he bent to kiss her, his hand sliding between her legs. At her soft moan, he carefully slid one finger into her tight pussy—Christ—really tight pussy, and at her little whimper, stopped.

"No, no . . ." she breathed into his mouth.

"Sorry." He jerked his finger out.

"What are you doing?" A blurted gasp and then she shoved his hand back.

Far be it for him to gauge her pain threshold, he decided, and proceeded to do as she wished. Not that he wasn't handy with his fingers. Not that he didn't feel strangely responsible that the lady's orgasm be gratifying.

But she was slightly swollen. He could feel the difference from last night, although in very short order—he should have known—she shifted into her frenzied mode, her tissue turned moist, succulent, and pliable, and he was able to make progress.

Increasingly heated whimpers echoed in the night. The lady's hair-trigger libido was in fine form and she climaxed before long, screaming in her wild, willful fashion—the sound ringing out over the verdant lawns and moonlit river.

Wiping his finger on his trousers a few moments later, he silently watched her until her eyes slowly opened. "It's always a race with you, isn't it?" he said, grinning.

"I appreciate your benevolence," she whispered. "I couldn't wait."

"I could tell."

"I want *you* next time, though. You're better."

He shook his head. "Maybe we shouldn't tonight. I wouldn't want to hurt you."

"I feel fine—really." She grinned. "Especially now. Please—I want you inside me." Just saying the words sent an anticipatory flutter up her vagina. But then as Sofia had pointed out, he was the gold standard.

Fitz blew out a breath. "It's tempting as hell, darling, but I don't know." He held up one finger. "This is all you can accommodate."

She sat up. "Why don't we try?" Reaching over, she unbuttoned one of his trouser buttons still undone.

He stopped her, his hand hard on hers. "No, let's not." It wasn't as though he'd been abstinent anytime the decade past. He could wait.

"Then let me see that you come another way."

No fool he, he lifted his hand from hers.

"I'm enamored of your lovely cock." Looking up from her unbuttoning, she smiled at him prettily. "If you don't mind."

He grinned. "What do you think I'll say?"

Her brows flickered in facetious reply. "Tell me if you like it later."

"I can tell you right now I will." The thought of her mouth on his cock added inches to his erection.

After she'd opened his trousers, she unbuttoned his silk underwear. As she pulled his rigid upthrust penis away from his stomach, he slowly inhaled, waiting for her to lower her head.

But she didn't. She traced his length with her fingertips,

partially circled it with her fist, brushed the shiny crest with her knuckles, lightly squeezed his testicles. Gently she stroked his engorged length, up and down and over again.

He was breathing hard at this point, growing frustrated and wondering suspiciously why she was toying with him. "If you don't mind," he said tautly, taking her head between his hands, "I need more than that." And cupping her head with one hand, he pressed downward, grasped his cock in his other hand, and brought her mouth on target.

Fighting his hold, she looked up, wide-eyed. "Am I supposed to put this huge thing in my mouth?"

The little vixen *was* toying with him. And fuck if it wasn't working; his cock increased sizeably. "It's no bigger than it was last night," he said, and shoved her head back down.

"Oh yes it is."

But the last of her words were muffled as her lips closed over his cock.

He gasped at the initial contact and then he shut his eyes against the agonizing pleasure as she slowly drew him in, and when his cock bumped the back of her throat, he softly groaned.

He had no idea why her mouth was any different than any other woman's mouth, but it was. Nor did he understand why her tongue licking the flanges of the crest of his cock and gliding down the shaft made him break into a cold sweat, made him think of words like *nirvana* and *everlasting bliss*. Made him consider coming in two seconds like a green adolescent. But he didn't because he knew how good it would feel if he repressed that impulse—a lesson learned long ago—and he let the lady continue.

He couldn't know of course that Rosalind had other plans. Devious, selfish plans, she'd learned yesterday, worked well. Wanting what she wanted, she thought with an inner smile, like Groveland. And she rather thought she'd be successful because his observations about her receptivity aside, she knew her body rather better than he. Or at least since she'd met the darling of every lady in

London she'd come to know her body—and the creamy droplets running down her thighs meant she'd have him.

When the duke's breathing grew labored, when she felt his penis begin to twitch, she quickly lifted her head and said to his astonished gaze, "Don't move," and a second later was straddling his thighs.

He said, "No," but with little conviction this near orgasm.

"Oh yes," she said in her prim schoolmistress voice that under other circumstances might have been grating but now sounded like the "Hallelujah Chorus" to his ears, and before he could take another labored breath, she was sliding down his cock.

Not easily, but so incredibly and exquisitely snugly, he thought his head would explode from the rapturous friction.

He didn't move; he didn't so much as twitch a muscle, not wishing to hurt her—and even more, not wanting her to stop. And when she finally did, when she was impaled well and good on his cock, he decided life couldn't get any better than this.

But she slowly raised herself and settled back down again and life got considerably better. And in the following few minutes as she moved up and down he saw the world in vivid colors previously obscured, heard birdsong with fresh clarity, felt a soul-stirring delirium warm his senses.

He held her gently when she finally climaxed, and only after she raised her head from his shoulder and kissed his cheek, did he lift her away and come himself.

He wondered afterward as he silently wiped himself dry with his shirt whether their adversarial roles in the Monckton Row project somehow accentuated his passions. Whether hostility in one arena turned to violent feeling in another? Because he'd never felt this mad hysteria and impatience, the raging lust as he did with the delectable Mrs. St. Vincent.

When Fitz hadn't spoken for some time, Rosalind quietly said, "Are you angry with me?"

"No, God no," he said, quickly refocusing his attention. "Far from it."

"Oh good. I wouldn't want you to think me a conniving female."

He laughed. "Hardly. You're enchanting."

His urbane reply reminded her of what he was. A virtuoso at this game while she was a tyro. And perhaps in a libertine's world, she'd outstayed her welcome. "I should be getting home," she said, offering him an opportunity to conclude her visit.

"Why don't we go inside? It's cooling off."

"You needn't be polite."

More than cursory politeness after sex wasn't his strong suit, but then nothing about Mrs. St. Vincent fit his normal pattern. "I'm not being polite. I enjoy your company."

"The sex you mean."

"Very well, the sex." He smiled and began buttoning his trousers. "Come inside anyway."

"I'd love to."

"You're a refreshing little puss. No pretense. I like that."

Brushing her skirt back down, she said with a sweet smile, "You know what I like about you."

NEITHER ONE SLEPT much that night. Neither was willing to forego the pleasure. Both considered such chimerical, high-flying sensations fleeting and best savored in the here and now.

She shouldn't want him so.

He shouldn't crave her with such rash disregard for their strategic differences.

But she did and he did and reason took a holiday that summer night at Mertenside. He ordered them a snack long after midnight, his kitchen willingly obliged him, and they ate on the balcony outside his bedroom, lying side by side on a chaise meant for one. He found she giggled and adored

it when he'd never liked women who giggled. And he
further endeared himself to her by reciting wholesale her
favorite poem, Byron's "The Destruction of Sennacherib."

"I'm impressed," she whispered, kissing him afterward.
"That's a very long poem." She wanted to say, *Did you
learn it for a woman?* but didn't so as not to shatter the
affectionate mood.

"My governess liked it," he said, scrupulously refrain-
ing from adding more, the evening and company more
agreeable than any in memory.

Comforted and disburdened of her jealousy, she gently
touched his cheek. "You bring me enormous pleasure, darling Fitz."

"I haven't felt this good since…" He shrugged.

"Since you last came?"

He laughed. "Tart."

"And glad of it."

"Not as much as I, darling. Would you like to try a bed
in another bedroom for variety?"

"I thought you'd never ask…"

When morning came, they repeated the bland courtesies of the previous morning but without the argument this
time. And after a delightful bath and an early breakfast,
Fitz had them driven back into the city. They parted at Bruton Street Books with well-bred politesse. Both were careful not to speak of future meetings, but they were careful
as well, not to rule them out.

It had been a night of memorable pleasure.

CHAPTER 20

Good morning, your Grace."

"Good morning, Mallory. Quite a nice day in the making out there," Fitz cheerfully said as he entered Groveland House. "Bring me coffee in the study." It was too early for his mother to be out of bed; he needn't play host yet.

For a fraction of a second Mallory debated ruining the duke's good mood, the staff protective of the young master—as they called him in private, the term of endearment impervious to the passage of time. The majordomo glanced at the envelope on a silver salver set on a table in the center of the entrance hall and understanding what was required of him, cleared his throat. "Mr. Hutchinson sent a message early this morning, Your Grace." He moved to the table and picked up the envelope. "Hutchinson's man said it was urgent."

They've found something. His pulse rate quickening, Fitz took the envelope held out to him, ripped it open, and pulled out the card enough to read the single line: *The search was productive.* Glancing up, Fitz said, "Send some bacon and toast with the coffee. And tell the duchess

when she wakes that my schedule will be uncertain today."
Shoving the note into his jacket pocket, he set off across
the grand baroque entrance hall transported from Rome by
some long-ago ancestor.

While not yet in full possession of the facts, but knowing that Edward St. Vincent had been involved in illegal activities, Fitz experienced a moment of triumph.
Not that he'd seriously considered failure. With enough
money, one could always find capable people willing
to perform a service. The bromide *The end justifies the
means* was a respected business practice for the indus-
trialists, financiers, and wealthy landowners who ruled
Britannia.

Fitz was no exception; he played the game his way with
his rules. Within the law, of course. But then that's why
Hutchinson was on permanent retainer—to distinguish the
legal nuances. Not that Fitz felt he'd stepped over the line
in regard to Mrs. St. Vincent. She would be handsomely
paid for her property. Very handsomely indeed.

As for his small niggling unease undermining a sense
of total victory, he reminded himself that Rosalind would
soon be a woman of no small wealth. Her life would be
considerably altered for the better because of his purchase.
She could even buy herself some new furniture, and if she
didn't, he would.

By the time he reached his study, he'd rationalized away
all the disquieting issues having to do with pretense and
evasion and dispatched the lot to perdition. Coffee arrived
practically on his heels and in short order, he was enjoying
the morning paper with his breakfast.

As he was reading the latest reports on the civil unrest
in South Africa, Stanley appeared in the doorway. "I apologize for interrupting, Your Grace, but there's a rather...
delicate matter..."

"No need to apologize. Come in," Fitz offered, immune
to delicate matters after all the scandals in his past. He set
aside the paper. "Would you like coffee?"

"No thank you, Your Grace."

"Sit down." Fitz waved him to a chair. "What can I do for you?"

"Ordinarily I wouldn't bother you about the matter, Your Grace, since you instructed me to handle these, er, situations myself. But, the thing is," Stanley went on, sitting on the edge of his chair, "Lady Buckley has been most persistent and... well, that is... I'm at a loss how to deal with her demands."

Fitz grinned. "Can't tell a peeress to go the hell, you mean."

Stanley sighed. "I'm not sure even that would help. She doesn't take no for an answer. Yesterday, she sent three notes, then dispatched her personal maid with a further message in which she threatened to descend on Groveland House herself if you didn't reply. I had to make clear to her maid that you literally were *not* at home; I wasn't simply respecting your privacy. Your mother didn't even know where you'd gone, I said. Lady Buckley's maid finally accepted my explanation." He grimaced. "It was most disturbing."

"I happened to speak to Lady Buckley last night at the Turner show at the National Gallery. I doubt she'll bother you."

The young man's expression brightened. "Perfect, sir. Then I shan't be deluged with her ultimatums today."

Fitz half smiled. "I can't fully guarantee that. I may have left Lady Buckley in a pet. But, look, my dear boy, should Clarissa come to the house, let her in. If I'm home, I'll be happy to see her. And if I'm not, she'll soon realize she's wasting her time."

Stanley pursed his mouth. "It's just that ladies don't as a rule call on gentlemen."

"Clarissa rather overlooks the rules, I'm afraid. Just do your best."

Stanley blew out a breath. "Very well, Your Grace."

"And consider, Stanley, if you can handle Clarissa, it's good training for the machinations of Parliament. After you've worked for me for a time, I'd be happy to sponsor you as an aide to any number of members I know. Mother said you had an interest in government."

"Yes, sir. I do, sir. I'd be most grateful for your sponsorship," the young man said with feeling, clearly overwhelmed by the prospect. "Thank you so much, Your Grace."

"You're perfectly welcome. God knows we could use some intelligent men in government. Do what you can about Clarissa. But I'm relatively indifferent to her tantrums so don't anguish over the situation."

"I shall do my very best, sir."

"I'm sure you will." Fitz smiled. "Is there anything more?"

"No, no, Your Grace." Stanley jumped up. "Thank you for your advice and consideration."

"Anytime, Stanley. We're quite informal at Groveland House, so if you ever have a question about anything, don't hesitate to ask."

Clarissa was going to be a problem, Fitz reflected as Stanley walked out. Not that he hadn't anticipated as much even before taking her to Green Grove. She was spoiled, impetuous, self-centered, and demanding. But she was also a hot little piece, which partially offset her volatile personality. Still, poor Stanley would have his hands full. Fitz glanced at the time, decided he still had leisure to go through his mail, and coming to his feet, walked to his desk. Stanley had stacked everything in neat piles, private correspondence, business documents that required his signature, the daily papers, magazines. Fitz quickly scanned the several notes and invitations Stanley understood required his perusal, even more quickly flipped through the business documents, pushed the papers aside, and sifted through the new periodicals.

If the cover of *Facts and Fantasy* hadn't prominently displayed the title *The Duke's Doxy* in a bold red font, *and* if an image of a scantily clad female with a peach in her hand hadn't appeared beneath the title, Fitz wouldn't have pulled the magazine from the pile and studied the cover with a frown. A frown that deepened as he turned to page ten and began reading the salacious account.

He swore under his breath several times as he read, and once finished, he leaned back in his chair and swore some more. The characters were clearly recognizable at least to him. With luck, not to others. He wasn't concerned with scandal so much as he was infuriated at the lurid level of detail. Bitch. She'd used him. That's why she'd asked so many questions that night. It wasn't naïveté; it was a damned cross-examination!

So much for his unease over forcing Mrs. St. Vincent to sell. She apparently had no compunction about using *him* for profit. Still, hadn't she made it clear from the start that it would be all-out war?

Sex aside—or maybe not. Perhaps sex was just a skirmish of another kind. Whatever it was, he had no intention of relinquishing the field of battle until it was tactically useful. In other words, when he'd had his fill of the lovely Mrs. St. Vincent.

THE BARRISTER WAS all smiles when Fitz walked into his office.

"Good morning, Your Grace. I have excellent news."

"Then we both do," Fitz replied. "Your men apparently found something."

"Indeed. Mrs. St. Vincent was out last evening," Hutchinson explained as Fitz took a seat across from him, "so my men took the opportunity to search her apartment and discovered rather a lot." He smiled broadly. "Enough to justify a raid, Your Grace. More than enough."

Fitz didn't mention he'd been with Rosalind. "Perfect," he said instead, brushing aside the slight prick of conscience that persisted despite his displeasure over her writing. "Should Mrs. St. Vincent be jailed in the course of this raid, see that she is immediately released," he said, the state of England's jails being what they were. "There's no need to have her traumatized."

It might be a little late for that once she's dragged off to jail, thought Hutchinson, but ever the circumspect retainer, he politely said, "I'll attend to it, Your Grace."

"Tell me now," Fitz said, postponing his disclosure until hearing Hutchinson's account. "What exactly did your men find?"

"First, it seems Mrs. St. Vincent sells erotica from a small back room in her shop. Such sales are relatively common, so courts may not take issue, but such sales *do* come within the purview of Britain's obscenity statutes. Of more significance, however, were the several manuscripts found in an armoire and the partially finished manuscript discovered in a desk drawer. There's no question about the erotic content of these stories."

"A partial manuscript? Did it have a title?"

"Something about harems, I believe. It was in a different script than the manuscripts in the armoire." Hutchinson pursed his lips for a moment. "My men concluded it was a woman's hand. Very likely Mrs. St. Vincent's."

"I expect it was."

"You must be referring to your news."

Fitz nodded and pulled the small periodical from his pocket. "This week's edition of *Facts and Fantasy*" he said, sliding it across Hutchinson's desk. "The cover story is an account of my first night with Mrs. St. Vincent." His brows rose. "In considerable detail."

Hutchinson flipped through the magazine before setting it down. "So there's no question the lady is involved in illegal publications."

"None."

"Then your ninety thousand is entirely safe."

"Entirely." He should have felt more satisfaction. Instead, Fitz was discontent, Hutchinson's wretched Gustave Doré engraving of London's teeming masses in a dark, brooding slumscape mirrored the sourness of Fitz's mood. "I suppose since Mrs. St. Vincent appears to be the author of this unfinished manuscript, she's in more difficulty than if only her husband's manuscripts had come to light?"

"Yes, of course. In the latter case, she could plead ignorance. Naturally, that is not the case with her own work. Perhaps you'd first like to apprise her of the facts," Hutchinson offered, recognizing a hesitancy in Groveland he'd not seen before. "Let her know you know, as it were, and if she still doesn't see the advantage of accepting your offer, then the possibility of a raid could be advanced to exert additional pressure. Unless you've changed your mind after, er…" He stopped, about to say *after getting to know Mrs. St. Vincent better.* With the lady under surveillance, Hutchinson knew not only that Rosalind had gone to the National Gallery but also that she'd left with Groveland.

"No, not with ninety thousand at stake."

"I wanted to be sure." Hutchinson should have known better with Groveland's penchant for discarding lovers. "In that case, I'll begin the process required to execute a raid, although these things take time. Any number of bureaucrats are involved, the action is exceedingly rare these days, and that in itself requires genuflection to the right parties."

"How long?"

"Ten days, perhaps a little more."

Fitz nodded. "Get started."

Hutchinson had not won his preeminent position as a barrister by overlooking details. He asked one last time, "Is there a possibility the lady's interests could be, shall we say, reconciled?"

"I doubt it." *Good God, I'll have to bring Hutchinson a less dismal engraving. That one could put you off your feed.* That he'd not noticed the somber print before was testament to his present mood. "On second thought," Fitz murmured, a brooding note in his voice, "let me think about this for a short while. Not that you can't begin the due diligence," he added crisply.

"I understand. With the operational snail's pace of the bureaucracies, it can't hurt to at least begin some initial conversations."

Fitz was relieved to hear Hutchinson speak of a snail's pace, when timing shouldn't have mattered one way or the other. When it wouldn't have in the past. When, in fact, he would have simply given Hutchinson the order to proceed without further thought. "I'll decide soon," Fitz said. "I'll be out of town for a day or so."

"Very well. I'll wait to hear from you."

"I'd prefer that your contacts not mention any names until absolutely necessary. Is that possible?"

"It can be arranged." *Interesting*, thought Hutchinson. *Groveland doesn't want the lady exposed to scandal. At least for the moment.* "I'll tell my sources we'd like the names on the writs to remain anonymous until the papers are served."

Fitz smiled tightly. "Thank you." He exhaled. "That should do it then."

"Yes, indeed."

Fitz came to his feet. "Thank your men for their quick results."

"I will. A pleasant journey, Your Grace."

Fitz looked at him blankly.

"On your travels out of town, Your Grace."

"Ah, yes. Thank you." Fitz smiled politely. "I'll stop by on my return."

"I'll have updates for you by then."

"Excellent." Fitz turned to go and then swung back because he wasn't finished with Mrs. St. Vincent just yet. Business was business; sex was sex. "I have another commission. Could you find a female doctor—someone exceptionally well-qualified—and have her pay a visit to Mrs. St. Vincent? Today preferably. Don't look at me like that. It's all quite innocent. Just make sure she's good."

"If she's a female doctor, she's by definition good," Hutchinson pointed out. "Otherwise she'd never have been admitted to medical school or granted a degree."

"You're right; I stand corrected. If you'd have her call on Mrs. St. Vincent as soon as possible, I'd appreciate it. Naturally, see that she's well paid for her time."

"Consider it done." Apparently Groveland was willing to overlook Mrs. St. Vincent's exposé for the benefits of her company. Hutchinson pulled a sheet of paper toward him, picked up a pen, and began writing.

Moments later, Fitz was standing on the pavement wondering if he *should* escape the city for a time. While his comment had been a spontaneous act of evasion—unnerving thought—distancing himself from Mrs. St. Vincent's potent allure would give him the opportunity to regard her more dispassionately.

She'd gotten under his skin—alarmingly so.

Touched previously impervious nerves.

Incited a degree of sexual yearning he'd never experienced before.

Christ, just thinking of her brought him erect even with her using him for all the world to read.

Quickly moving down the street, he forced himself to think of something less arousing—or maybe something equally arousing but within his ability to control. Clarissa had said her husband was away from the city. Why not pay her a visit, restore his sense of equilibrium as it were—about fucking?

Redress his renegade tailspin into some manic craving.

Reestablish casual sex as an unimpeachable certainty in his life.

Good God, he thought, turning toward Hyde Park, he was in enough of a quandary that he was actually looking forward to having Clarissa storm and rage at him. Temporarily, of course. Then she'd turn sulky and pout, he'd cajole and flatter—he knew how to play the game. Eventually she'd begin to smile, and in due time she'd welcome him into her bed because her husband was old, she wasn't, and her appetite for sex was voracious.

CHAPTER 21

A FREQUENT VISITOR of late when Lord Buckley was away from home, Fitz was welcomed by Eliot, the butler. "Is Lady Buckley in?" Fitz inquired, although he wouldn't have been ushered in if she wasn't.

"The mistress is resting." A code of sorts.

Fitz handed over his gloves and cane. "I'll see myself up." He half turned as he reached the base of the stairs. "Lord Buckley is away?"

"For a fortnight, Your Grace." The duke was generous with his gratuities.

"Thank you. Some champagne when you have time." Then Fitz took the stairs two at a time, goaded by a need to efface restive memory. Clarissa was safe, familiar—like him in her untrammeled approach to amour. And right now, he needed a reliable touchstone to the civility that passed for feeling in the fashionable world.

Reaching the door to her apartments, he walked into the sitting room unannounced. A maid was dusting Clarissa's many bibelots scattered over the tabletops. "Lady Buckley won't be needing you," he politely said.

The young woman blushed, curtsied, darted for the door, only to turn at the last to watch Fitz stroll toward Clarissa's boudoir. A small sigh escaped her; all the ladies on the staff were hoping the duke would take notice of them. He was known for his unrestricted hospitality toward women of all classes. Shutting the door behind her a moment later, she rushed toward the back stairs to share news of the duke's visit with her female coworkers.

Unaware of the burning interest he generated in the female staff, Fitz paused at Clarissa's bedroom door and flexed his fingers. Clarissa was prone to throw things when in a pet.

On alert and prepared, he pressed down on the latch and shoved open the dove grey door.

Clarissa was sitting at her dressing table. Catching sight of him in the mirror, she grabbed a silver-handled brush, spun around, and flung the brush at his head. "Get out you beastly man! Out, out, out!"

Deftly catching the missile, Fitz dropped it on a chair and moved forward, his palms up in appeasement. "I've come to apologize. I shouldn't have left you last night. I had too much to drink."

"No you didn't," Clarissa snapped, tossing her golden curls with a theatrical flourish. "Everyone knows you can drink a battalion under the table. You followed that red-haired tart. Don't say a word. I saw you. Is she your newest hussy?" she sneered.

"No, she's nobody."

"Obviously, she's a nobody," Clarissa said with a contemptuous little sniff. "I've never seen her before." The beau monde was small, cloistered, and exclusive.

Not about to discuss Mrs. St. Vincent when he was in Clarissa's boudoir in order to forget her, pleased to see that her expression had softened, Fitz pulled up a chair and sat. "Tell me what I must do to apologize for my boorishness last night?" His voice drifted lower, turned husky. "I'm quite willing to say or *do* just about anything to earn your favor."

A smile began to form on Clarissa's full lips, her eyes widened in feigned surprise. "Anything at all?" Clarissa whispered, deliberately shifting on the tufted stool so her pink lace dressing gown fell partially open above and below the tie at her waist.

"Just name it, sweetheart," he drawled, taking note of the lush expanse of silken flesh on display. "I've been thinking about you all morning." He lounged back in the gilt rococo chair, confident that detente had been reached.

"What a darling," Clarissa purred. "So you've been thinking of me..."

"Ever since I woke," he lied, surveying her with a roving glance that lingered for a moment on her splendid breasts showcased in the wide gap of her dressing gown. "I shouldn't have walked away so rudely."

"But you did, you bad, bad boy." Holding his gaze, she pursed her lips in a sultry little pout. "And with a little nobody."

"It was business."

Clarissa softly snorted. "Please."

"It was. She owns a bookstore I'm trying to buy." He recognized some minimum explanation was required.

"You and a *bookstore*?" Clarissa's pale brows rose. "You can do better than that."

"It's true. It's near a property I'm developing." *Reveal only what's necessary to allay suspicion—no more.*

Clarissa stared at him for a moment, her gaze assessing. "You actually mean it."

He smiled. "I actually do. Am I forgiven now?"

Her lashes drifted lower. "Perhaps."

He opened his arms in a conciliatory gesture. "I came to make amends, darling. Just tell me what you require as penance."

"Penance?" A mischievous gleam came into her eyes. "What a tantalizing notion."

He laughed. "Will whips be involved?"

"Does it matter?"

"It depends on who's holding the whip."

She smiled. "Barbarian. Must you always be in charge?"

"It's a habit," he drawled.

"And a very nice one come to think of it," she whispered, memories of Fitz's dominant role in bed arousing her senses. With a husband like hers who was not only old but also pale and bloodless after years behind a desk, Fitz's sheer maleness was a potent aphrodisiac. Not that Harold hadn't made piles of money while working behind that desk, for which she was grateful. But money didn't satisfy her sexual cravings. "To be perfectly honest, darling, I have no good reason to take offense about last night. I might have done the same to you. We both are who we are," she said with a candor that surprised even herself. "Thank you for coming to visit me today." She smiled. "For your ears only, darling, but you are a most welcome change from my husband."

And you from Mrs. St. Vincent. "While you're the most delectable woman I know," he smoothly returned.

Rising, she took two steps, dropped into Fitz's lap, and twined her arms around his neck. "I adore your flattery," she whispered, "and your, shall we say, excessive stamina. You make me very happy, and God knows such feelings are rare in our world."

Clarissa had done her duty by her family, marrying a rich man old enough to be her father. That she would indulge herself on occasion was to be expected. Who in the ton wouldn't? But she was also surprisingly frank today. "You're speaking your mind, sweetheart." His gaze was amused as he held her lightly in his arms. "Should I be worried?"

She gave a little twitch of her shoulder. "How long have we known each other? I don't mean as lovers—socially."

He did a quick mental calculation; she was quite a bit younger than he. "Six years."

"I've been married seven years."

A wary look came into his eyes. "Don't say you want a child."

She laughed. "Good God, Fitz, don't flinch like that.

Relax, I don't want a child. Harold already has all those awful children from his first marriage—who think they're going to inherit his fortune," she said with a flicker of her brows. "Not that they'll be penniless, but I'm getting my share."

"Good for you."

"I've earned it."

He didn't doubt she had. Lord Buckley wasn't known for his charming personality. Wales liked him for his millions, and the rest of society tolerated him because of Wales. "You've earned a little holiday from time to time as well."

She giggled and leaning close, kissed his cheek. "What's your excuse, darling? You have no one to command your life."

He grinned. "Perhaps, I just like holidays." And today he truly needed a respite from real life.

She wiggled on his lap, gauging the extent of his readiness. "Hmm, you feel wonderful—as usual, I might add."

He smiled. "The feeling's mutual."

"What do you want to do first?" she whispered, licking his ear.

Fuck until all thoughts of Mrs. St. Vincent are eradicated. "You decide," he said as his erection swelled. "I'm at your disposal."

She leaned back enough to meet his gaze. "I *love* when you let me play the upstairs maid."

He grinned, and instead of saying *You want that again?* he said gruffly, "Have you turned down my bed, Mattie?"

Clapping her palms to her cheeks, her blue eyes wide, Clarissa whispered, "I'm sorry. I completely forgot."

"It seems as though you're going to require additional training, my dear. You need to better learn how to anticipate my needs. A good maid anticipates, Mattie," he sternly said. "How many times have I told you that?"

"I'm sorry, Your Grace, so very sorry. I promise, it won't happen again."

"It better not happen again or I'll have to dismiss you without a character."

"No, no, please…don't be cruel. I'll be ever so good."

"It's not a question of goodness, my dear Mattie; it's competence that's required of a servant. That and knowing how to implicitly follow orders. If I give you one more chance, will you mend your ways?"

"I'll do anything, Your Grace. Just don't dismiss me without a character."

"Very well. Go over and ready the bed for me. And yourself. You know what I require."

A rap on the door interrupted the little drama.

Clarissa was about to shout, "Go away," when Fitz put his finger over her mouth and called out, "Come in."

A flunkey entered carrying a tray with a bottle and glasses. Quickly averting his eyes, he hesitated.

"Set it down anywhere," Fitz said blandly. "And thank you."

When the door quietly shut on the servant, Fitz slapped Clarissa's bottom. "Go. Fix the bed."

She didn't move. "What makes you think you can order champagne in my house?"

"I thought I might pour it in your pussy and lick it up."

She giggled. "In that case, how can I be angry with you?"

"How indeed. Now, are you going to put on your maid's cap and take care of my needs or should I go home?"

"Don't you dare!"

"I really don't think a maid should talk to her master in that fractious tone."

"I'm sorry. I'm sorry."

"That's better. Now move."

While Clarissa scrambled to find her maid's apron and cap in her lingerie semanier, Fitz opened the bottle of champagne and drank down a goodly portion, fortifying himself for the coming drama. Then he rose from the chair and moved to the bed, stopping to pick up the robe Clarissa had discarded on the floor. Stripping the braided-silk tie from the pink lace peignoir, he wrapped it around his fist, leaving enough tail to serve as a whip.

"You're much too slow, Mattie," he grumbled as he approached the bed. "You haven't straightened the sheets."

"It'll be ready directly, Your Grace," Clarissa hastily replied, setting the little lace cap on her curls. Offering him a deferential little curtsey, she dashed toward the bed. "Just one minute more, Your Grace!"

Nude except for a scrap of lace apron tied at her waist, she could have been featured on any of the lewd postcards sold on the streets of London. With her huge breasts, narrow waist, and full hips, there was no question why she'd been able to snare a man of Buckley's wealth, Fitz decided. She was the archetype for fashionable female beauty: bounteous and shapely, a pretty face, and nothing but pleasure on her mind.

"What in the world are you doing?" He unbuttoned his suit coat and shrugged it off. "I swear you haven't learned a thing since last week. You know what's going to happen if you can't perform your duties properly."

"Please, Your Grace—look, I'm making the bed ever so perfect!" Quickly running her palms over the bottom sheet, she was making a hash out of smoothing the linen, household duties not Clarissa's field of accomplishment.

Fitz smiled faintly at her clumsiness. "If you didn't have such a juicy cunt," he drawled, "I'd fire you in a minute. You're fortunate I like a wet little quim like yours, Mattie, or you'd be out on the street. Although, you still might be," he growled, "if you don't improve."

She spun around, her fleshy breasts jiggling with her brisk pirouette. "Please, please, don't fire me, Your Grace. I'll do anything—anything at all!" And she licked her bottom lip like the little tart she was.

"If you're trying to entice me, Mattie, it won't work," he said harshly, scowling appropriately in his role as truculent master. "I want a maid who works, not plays the strumpet. Your attempt at seduction offends me; I am a God-fearing man! Now, bend over," he coldly ordered. "You must be punished for your impertinence."

Clarissa turned and fell facedown over the side of the

bed with lightning speed, her arms spread wide, her lush bottom advantageously positioned.

"I hope you're just being dutiful, Mattie," Fitz acidly remarked. "I hope you're not looking forward to your whipping."

"Oh no, Your Grace!" she cried. "I'm scared to death of my whipping. It's ever so painful, Your Grace, and leaves my poor bottom sore and stinging. I can't hardly sit for a week."

"Perhaps you'll learn your lesson one of these days," Fitz testily said. "You understand, I take no pleasure in whipping you, but your incompetence can't be tolerated. If I allow such behavior to continue, soon my entire staff will be in disarray."

"I know that. I most certainly do," she obsequiously murmured. "I can tell, Your Grace, how much you dislike whipping me."

Her pink bottom was swaying from side to side, her lush sex slick and primed, and Fitz knew if he rammed his cock into her, he'd slide in like a knife through butter. "This is going to hurt me more than it hurts you," he growled. "Now lift your bottom higher so I have a better view of your juicy slit."

"Like this, Your Grace. Is this high enough?" she said soft and breathy, rising on her toes and tilting her derriere upward.

"It'll do for now," he muttered. "And don't forget, if you cry out, I'll stop."

"I won't," she softly panted. "I promise."

Raising his hand high, he brought the braided silk down and whacked her plump, rosy bottom soundly, the force of his blow leaving a red welt on her pale flesh.

Whimpering, she clenched her thighs tightly against the fierce pleasure throbbing through her vagina, trying to ward off an immediate orgasm, wanting the wild, seething thrill to last. She adored this game; it always made her dripping wet, or maybe it was the way Fitz played his part. He was a natural tyrant, sweet man, although she cared less

about his motivations and more about the serial orgasms
he offered her.

Fitz had a rare zest for domination that day, as if physically chastising Clarissa would somehow appease or
indulge his moody discontent. However, despite laboring at his task through several of Clarissa's orgasms, her
flagellation fantasy was unable to sufficiently distract him.
Habitual custom failed to serve as antidote to his discontent. Softly swearing in frustration, he finally dropped the
makeshift whip, unbuttoned his trousers, and resentful and
surly, turned into the malevolent master he'd been playing. Without warning, he buried his cock in Clarissa's ripe
cunt.

She squealed at his sudden, rough entry, but he didn't
hear or didn't care and swiftly pounded his way to orgasm,
jerked out, and came on her back.

"My goodness, darling," she murmured, turning to look
at him over her shoulder, her little maid's cap all eschew.
"That was rather violent."

"I was tired of waiting." He didn't say he was sorry
because he wasn't, nor was he likely to explain the turmoil
in his brain. "Now, get up on the bed, you hot little jade,
and lift up your legs. I'm going to drink some champagne
out of your pussy."

Nothing helped though. No matter how many times he
came, he couldn't forget Mrs. St. Vincent or more to the
point, the incredible sex.

It wasn't like this. This was normal sex, sex without
emotion. Orgasmic sex that never came within calling distance of fervent feeling.

Fuck—as if he was looking for *that*.

HOURS LATER, THEY lay sweaty and exhausted in
the shambles of the bed, Clarissa's head on Fitz's shoulder,
his arm around her.

"Are you going to Margo's country house party next
week?"

"God no. Margo's a bore."

"Oh pooh. Then I don't want to go."

"I heard that Roddy will be there. He's back on business. Without his family. I'm sure he'll be happy to entertain you."

Clarissa sighed. "Sometimes I think I should have married Roddy even if he didn't have much money. He has a lovely tea plantation in India now and tons of servants, and everyone says the climate isn't so ghastly in the highlands."

"Seriously, darling, would you be happy on a tea plantation?"

She ran her fingertip down Fitz's taut stomach. "I think I could be."

"You'd be miles away from everyone, with no society to speak of . . . except for retired military men and government clerks." He gently stroked her back. "And you'd be poor. Why not just roger Roddy on his visits home and enjoy Buckley's wealth."

She sighed again. "I don't know. Sometimes I think I wouldn't mind being poor—except that my family depends on me of course." Another sigh. "Have you ever been in love, Fitz? I mean really in love?"

"Nope."

"Does it bother you that you haven't been?"

When in the past he wouldn't have hesitated a second, he found that the lovely Mrs. St. Vincent had somehow leaped into his mind. But he quickly brushed the image aside and said, "It doesn't bother me at all."

"That's because you're a man. Men don't fall in love like women do."

"Should I send you some pearls or diamonds, or maybe those new opals from Australia?" he interposed, intent on changing the subject.

"Black pearls," Clarissa instantly replied. "Nicer ones than Margo's."

"You pick them out. I'll let Montgomery know you're coming in."

His generosity elicited numerous kisses, which led to other things, and it was another hour before Fitz left Clarissa's bed—and house.

It was all well and good, he thought, spending the day in bed playing make-believe and coming so many times he was drained dry.

What wasn't so fine, he decided, as he strolled away from Lord Buckley's new mansion on Park Lane, was that he'd no more than walked out of Clarissa's boudoir, than he was thinking of Rosalind—again, no matter her guile and artifice.

Fuck.

So much for sex as a blot to memory.

Apparently, it was not a permanent modifier.

What now?

Drink, cards, another woman?

As if in answer, the pungent odor of sex suddenly wafted upward and struck his nostrils.

He grimaced.

Home first, to bathe and change.

CHAPTER 22

WHILE FITZ WAS entertaining himself or Clarissa or both or maybe at the core, neither, Rosalind was shocked by a visit from a doctor.

She wasn't certain whether the woman had waited until the store was deserted or she'd only just walked in. Rosalind had been too busy stocking shelves to notice. But when Dr. Swindell approached her, introduced herself, and explained the reason for her visit, Rosalind turned bright red. "You must be mistaken," she croaked, setting down the books she held. "Are you sure you have the correct address?"

"Forgive me," the slender, middle-aged woman gently replied, familiar with women who were too embarrassed to admit they needed her help. "I didn't realize I wasn't expected. I was asked to call on you."

"By whom?"

"A Mr. Hutchinson. He's a barrister who lives in my neighborhood."

Rosalind bristled at the name, momentarily recalling her first meeting with Groveland's hireling. "Why would he think I need a doctor?"

"Mr. Hutchinson didn't say. Although his note gave the impression that a client of his had asked me to call on you. I'm sorry if I've offended you." Since many women found it difficult to talk about female complaints, Dr. Swindell added, "Might you require medical help of some kind? I specialize in female disorders and naturally, I'm most discreet."

Finally recognizing the common denominator at the mention of female disorders, Rosalind was about to point-blank dismiss the doctor Fitz had hired when she more sensibly realized that she might benefit from the visit. There was no question she'd been in discomfort that first morning after sex with Fitz; she was also ignorant of the long-term consequences of excessive sexual activity. Perhaps it would be wise to take advantage of the doctor's expertise. Rosalind glanced around the store, in the event a customer had walked in.

"I waited until everyone left," the doctor noted, conscious of Rosalind's anxious survey of the shop. "And might I add, I have no interest in moral issues when it comes to health care." She'd been told that Mrs. St. Vincent was a widow; she'd also assumed from Hutchinson's letter that some man was paying the charges. "We live in a new modern era after all. The culture is changing rapidly, social conventions are in flux." She smiled. "Even female doctors are no longer looked upon as curiosities or misfits."

No matter how delicately put, Rosalind understood the message. There were those who would construe her behavior with Groveland as improper. "Thank you for your understanding. However," Rosalind went on with a faint grimace, "you can understand my reluctance to disclose, er, details of a personal nature."

"If it's any consolation, your sense of modesty is common. I see it every day in my practice. But please be frank. I'm sure I can help remedy whatever is troubling you."

Rosalind hesitated. "The fact is," she began, then blew out a small breath, embarrassed to be talking to a stranger about such private matters.

"Please, go on," Dr. Swindell prompted, cool and unruffled.

"Well...you see, lately"—another small sustaining breath—"after having been long celibate, I've engaged in rather a good deal of intercourse. As a result, I experienced a decided tenderness—much improved now," she quickly added.

"Yours is a very ordinary complaint, my dear. Women who haven't previously engaged in sexual relations or those who have become active again after a long hiatus often feel as you do. If I could examine you, however, I could better determine whether some remedy is required."

Rosalind blushed furiously. "I couldn't possibly. Not now. The store is open until six, I'm here alone, and actually I feel quite well again."

The doctor checked a small jeweled timepiece pinned to the lapel of her grey tailored suit. "Since you won't be available for several hours, why don't I leave you some salve. It will alleviate any tenderness. Then, at your convenience, you could come round to my office. I don't anticipate anything of a serious nature, but an examination would allow a proper diagnosis. My office is in my home, so you could make an appointment for any evening." Opening her leather valise, she rummaged through its contents and came up with a small jar. "Apply this to your tender areas as needed. Also, a good hot soak in the tub does wonders," she added with a smile, handing the jar to Rosalind. "Do you have any other complaints?"

Only that a libertine duke has embarrassed me by sending over a complete stranger. At the word *libertine*, Rosalind was suddenly seized by panic. A libertine was by definition promiscuous. Might she have contracted some dreadful disease from Fitz? "Maybe I should make an appointment now," she said.

In her years of practicing medicine, Dr. Swindell had become adept at reading people. She recognized fear when she saw it. "How does tomorrow at seven sound?"

"Tomorrow at seven would be *most* welcome." The

prospect of having to worry about some dire affliction for a protracted period of time would have been torture.

"Let me give you directions." The doctor wrote down her address on a page from a small notepad. "There now." She tore off the sheet and handed it to Rosalind with another warm smile. "Until tomorrow, my dear."

At the doctor's departure, Rosalind was left with an unsettling sense of unease.

Walking back to the counter to dispose of the jar and note, she glanced at the clock. Bloody hell, she had hours yet before she could lock up the store. Much too much time to worry about possible unsavory repercussions from Fitz's prodigal past, she thought, nervously fussing with the papers on the counter before her. *Too much* time to concern herself with potentially alarming diseases. Why hadn't she thought of the risks before she succumbed to his charm? How could she have been so incautious?

Even as she asked herself the questions, she knew why. She'd been tempted like all the women before her—by his dark good looks and flagrant masculinity, by his seductive smile and practiced charm, by the sensational pleasure he dispensed with such facility.

Despite short interruptions by customers that afternoon, the tumult in her brain continued apace—the question of should she or shouldn't she have succumbed, the more fearsome issue of possible medical problems, the continuous steamy memories of Fitz doing what he did best.

She kept her eye on the clock as she wrote up new orders a short time later, willing the hands to move more quickly as a bored child might. Although longing for the six-o'clock hour had nothing to do with boredom and everything to do with escaping the public eye. She needed time alone to deal with her turbulent, conflicted emotions. She needed the quiet of her apartment to put everything into perspective, to remind herself that she'd had a life before Fitz. A busy, contented life.

Hearing the shop door open, she looked up and was

shocked out of her musing. There he was, as if conjured him up from her imagination.

"What are *you* doing here?" she tartly asked, his casual appearance annoying. Particularly when her own feelings were in anarchy.

Fitz quickly checked to see if she was picking up anything heavy to heave at him and was pleased to see nothing but the weightiness of her scowl. "I told myself to stay away, but as you see, I couldn't," he said, opening his arms in a brief gesture of demur. "I was wondering if you'd like to go out for dinner tonight? Anywhere you like." He was offering her carte blanche, knowing full well they would likely meet friends of his. But no more than he'd scrutinized why he'd come here after Clarissa's, he ignored the issue of his friends. It was about casual sex, he told himself, and nothing more. Why shouldn't he treat her like any other lover?

Instead of politely accepting his invitation, Rosalind gave him a hard, gimlet-eyed look. "How could you have a doctor call on me? I might very well have been embarrassed in front of my customers!"

"I doubt it. Hutchinson would have warned her about the need for discretion. Did you like her?"

"Do you actually care?" she shot back, irritated by his cool composure, by his exquisite pale linen suit that cost a fortune, by the fact that he felt no compunction about blatantly interfering in her life. "Admit, the only reason you had her sent over was to make sure nothing curtailed your libertine pleasures. And speaking of libertine"—she jabbed her finger at him—"if you gave me some ghastly disease, so help me God, I'll do you in somehow!"

"Relax," he said smoothly, undeterred by her threats. "I don't have any diseases. Believe me, I'm probably more phobic than you about contracting something that might kill me." His smile flashed, quicksilver and waggish. "Consider, I have much more to lose than you."

She should have taken issue with his comparison, but

she was so relieved, she unintentionally smiled. Not willing to so easily absolve him from his past sins, she hastened to scowl again. "Everything isn't about money, Groveland."

"After our rather intimate relationship, feel free to call me Fitz." He chose not to argue about the seasoned orthodoxy concerning the virtues of wealth. "And if you don't mind, I won't address you as Mrs. St. Vincent unless we're out in public."

"You needn't worry. I shan't be going out in public with you again," she acerbically returned. "Last night at the Turner exhibit was more than enough embarrassment for me."

He bowed with practiced grace. "Please, accept my apologies." Not that he hadn't apologized to her lavishly and unstintingly at Mertenside last night.

"It's a little late for apologies." She wasn't in a reasonable mood. He was much too blasé, too familiar as well with making amends to women and being forgiven. At base, too inexcusably privileged to understand ordinary mortals. His emerald watch fob alone would feed a family for years.

"Come to dinner with me. You set the rules."

Certainly that was capitulation—or suave charm, more like. Nevertheless, perhaps for purely practical reasons, she should consider taking Mrs. Beecham's suggestion and put herself out to please the Duke of Groveland. On the other hand, Mrs. Beecham might be shocked to learn how very far she'd *already* put herself out for him.

Although, that's not what Mrs. Beecham had meant.

And that's not what this was about.

Even with pleasure and practicality in the balance, in the cold light of day reaching a decision wasn't difficult. "Thank you for the invitation, but no." She couldn't afford to be seen with a man of his lascivious reputation. She couldn't afford the scandal. A widow with a small business wasn't allowed a single misstep. The Turner exhibit notwithstanding, of course.

"Then I'll have my chef come over and cook for us."

Fitz suddenly recalled her austere kitchen. "Or why don't I have dinner brought over instead?"

"Why don't I end this conversation," Rosalind said, determined not to be seduced by a man who regarded sex as a form of amusement and herself as a temporary diversion. Someone who would likely forget her name in a fortnight. "I'm too sore in any event—even more so than last night," she lied, intent on discouraging him. She gave him a lowering look. "As a matter of fact"—she picked up the small jar from the counter—"*your* doctor left me some salve for my affliction. So don't bother yourself tonight. I'm hors de combat."

He smiled faintly. "I was just suggesting dinner."

"As I recall, you said something about champagne last night and didn't mean it for a second."

"I certainly did." His tone was bland; censorious women he'd dealt with before. "Can I help it if you changed your mind?"

"I'd appreciate it if you *did* help even if I change my mind," she perversely said.

He grinned at recall of her insatiable appetite for sex. "So I'm supposed to be the sensible one."

"I suppose that's asking too much of a rake," she retorted. "Of course it is," she said, answering her own question. "So I shall be the sensible one tonight. Kindly close the door when you leave."

"Five hundred pounds says I won't make the first advance."

"I'm not betting with you. For one thing, I don't have five hundred."

"I'm just saying I can abstain if you can."

"No, you can't."

"Then take the bet. You'll be richer for it."

"I'm not betting with you. You're totally unscrupulous."

He was more than willing to take the blame for their mutual passions if it would serve his cause. "You're right, forgive me. I'll turn over a new leaf, I promise. I'll be virtue itself."

She looked at him suspiciously. "Why are you doing this?"

He would have liked to think it was for sex, but it didn't look as though sex was on the menu and yet he was still interested. "God knows," he honestly replied. Then he smiled. "Perhaps it's the challenge."

"Here's a challenge for you." Her voice was cool. Everything was a game with Fitz. Curiously, she'd been hoping for an answer based on earnest feelings. Which only proved that she wasn't cut out for the fast life. "Go without something you want for a change."

"Something being you."

"Yes, me in all my fascinating guises," she lightly asserted, taking pleasure in Fitz's mutinous expression. "Consider me the one who got away."

"What if you didn't get away?" A gentle query despite his moody gaze.

"But I already have. I'll be quite alone tonight, although I'm sure you won't lack for female companionship."

A predatory gleam came into his eyes. "What if I already found the female I want?"

"If that was directed at me, I doubt your suit would be persuasive," Rosalind said, overconfident and naive about men who considered themselves exempt from ordinary rules of conduct.

"Surely you could use five hundred pounds." A man's argument, blunt and to the point.

"Of course I could, but unlike the other ladies you dally with, I'm not for sale," she smugly noted.

He was motionless save for a slight arch to his brows. "Everyone's for sale."

"Really? You think so?"

"I know so. The price just varies."

"You're a cold bastard." *But gorgeous in so many ways*, her less righteous persona unhelpfully pointed out.

"And you're one hot little piece," he drawled.

Her smile was dazzling, cheeky, flaunting in its presumption. "But unfortunately not available to a rogue like you."

"You didn't seem to mind a rogue's touch last night or the night before," he smoothly noted.

"Perhaps I've had my fill, no pun intended," she archly replied. "You'll find someone else to warm your bed, I'm sure."

She shouldn't have continued to provoke him.

Those who knew him better wouldn't have been so rash.

In a few quick strides, he circled the end of the counter, pushed her against the wall, pinioned her with his body, and bending his head so their eyes were level, said taut and low, "Don't fuck with me."

"Unhand me this instant," she hissed. "Someone might come in."

"I'll lock the door."

As he turned, Rosalind looked past him and froze. "Oh, God help me, Lady Harcourt's about to come in!"

Fitz glanced at the door and swore.

"Do you know her?" Rosalind breathed, her panicked gaze on the entrance.

"Of course."

"Hide, hide, *please*—get out of sight...her hand's on the door latch!" She could visualize her entire world disappearing beneath a wave of scandal if Lady Harcourt saw them together. She read sermons for amusement and railed against the promiscuity of society.

Responding to her terror, Fitz dropped to the floor. "Get rid of her," he hissed, sitting against the high counter facing her, his legs on either side of her feet, his head conveniently at the juncture of her thighs.

"And if I don't?" She took orders poorly.

"Then maybe I'll come up from under your skirts and wish dear old Adelaide a pleasant afternoon," he threatened, flicking the hem of her skirt in warning.

She shot him a wrathful look. "Monster."

His smile was impudent. "Sorceress."

"Good afternoon, Lady Harcourt," Rosalind sang out in a voice slightly breathless at the last for Fitz had lifted her skirt, slid his hand between her thighs, and easing it between the divided legs of her drawers, rested his fingertips ever so lightly on her cleft.

"Good afternoon, my dear." The elderly woman closed her parasol and set it by the door. "I do hope you have some new sermons from Cardinal Newman."

"Indeed, Lady Harcourt. They're on their usual shelf." Unable to move with her ankle securely in Fitz's grasp, Rosalind prayed Lady Harcourt didn't ask for help.

"Lock the door when she leaves," Fitz whispered.

"I will not."

"Consider, darling, you might prefer not fucking with spectators looking on." He was gently caressing her pouty sex, delicately inspecting the extent of the tenderness she'd alluded to, deftly arousing her passions.

"Fitz, don't," she breathed. "Please...don't." But she swallowed a gasp for he'd slid the tip of his finger inside her the merest fraction and made contact with the bud of her clitoris. Every carnal nerve in her body violently swooned in response and instantly quivered for more.

"There now, you're getting nice and wet," he murmured, his voice softly approving, as if she'd accomplished something praiseworthy. Her clitoris was swelling, his fingers were being drenched, her vagina was pulsing, and her protests notwithstanding, she was definitely receptive.

"Stop, Fitz"—Rosalind slapped his head—"not now. She might see."

If the lovely Mrs. St. Vincent hadn't been squirming and rocking against the deft pressure of his fingers, he might have taken her protests to heart. Glancing up, he whispered, "Hush, darling. You don't want Adelaide to hear you. By the way, you have the most welcoming little quim. I'm getting hard just thinking about trying to get inside."

"Oh God," she softly wailed, attempting to suppress the ripples of pleasure spreading outward from Fitz's silken touch, mortified that she was melting inside when any self-respecting lady regardless of—oh Lord, what was he doing? "Don't, Fitz, for God's sake, don't!"

"I won't if you don't want me to, darling," he whispered, having eased her labia open with his thumb and tucked her skirt hem into her waistband with his other hand. "It's up to you, of course." And leaning forward slightly, he slowly measured the length of her distended clitoris with the tip of his tongue.

Gasping in shocked surprise, she jammed her palms against his head. But the pressure of her hands quickly relaxed as his tongue skimmed the twitching nerves of her clitoris and his long, slender fingers sunk palm deep inside her and stroked her throbbing vagina.

A moment later, sliding her fingers through his dark, ruffled hair, she gave herself up to a wholly new gluttonous pleasure, moving against his mouth, needing to ease the uneasable ache.

He felt her move, felt her clitoris swell, renewed his attention to her clit with single-minded professionalism, bringing her quivering little nub to full-blown, ready-as-could-be tumescence. She was slippery wet, her stimulated flesh moistening his fingers, the sleek fluid trickling down her thighs, and he hoped like hell Adelaide found her damned book of sermons quickly because Mrs. St. Vincent was getting really worked up and she wasn't the patient type. Not that he was either, ergo his impetuous journey here after Clarissa's. It appeared that Mrs. St. Vincent's pussy, for inexplicable reasons, was the current magnet for his cock.

There was no reasonable explanation for his obsession, but then again, none was required.

Consummation alone was his holy grail.

"Mrs. St. Vincent! I don't see the cardinal's books!"

"Just to your...right...Lady Harcourt!" Rosalind called out, her voice faltering with her passions near fever pitch, with Fitz's talented fingers inciting a frantic, shameful desire, with her senses beginning their impassioned, head-strong march to delirium. "Stop...oh God...please," she whimpered.

"Come first." Maybe this was about control; maybe he

needed her to be as necessitous as he. Payment as it were, for his irrational pilgrimage to her store. "Come and I'll stop." He smiled as she shivered and the throbbing tissue surrounding his fingers pulsed and fluttered, as she softly groaned at the soul-stirring rapture. "There . . . that's a good girl. That was a nice little spasm. If you come fast enough, darling," he huskily murmured, "by the time Adelaide finds her book, you'll be able to breathe again."

As if he had but to whisper the prurient, shameless words of encouragement, she suddenly shuddered, gasped, and grabbed the counter as a white-hot flood of rapture rushed through her cunt, jolted her brain, brought her moments later—ravished and flushed—to a white-knuckled standstill. Skittish in her compromised position, she drew in a deep breath, forced herself to a semblance of calm, and smashed Fitz's head with her fist. "Damn your rashness," she hissed.

He looked up, his gaze amused. "You always come so fast I didn't think it was a problem. And admit, you feel much better now."

"Smug bastard," she grumbled.

"Just be a dear and get rid of Adelaide."

"And if I don't?" She felt as though she should resist him, as if her virtue were at stake.

"Then *I'll* get rid of her," he quietly said.

"Don't you dare!"

"You have no idea what I dare," he drawled.

"The dear man has written two new tracts," Lady Harcourt cheerfully exclaimed, holding two books aloft as she walked toward the counter. "Isn't he the most exciting religious mind of our time! Such insights, such profundity. It quite enlivens my life."

"Each to their own," Fitz drolly muttered.

Shooting him a heated warning glance, Rosalind shook down her skirts and said, "Indeed, Lady Harcourt, Cardinal Newman's works are very popular."

"My dear, the heat must be bothering you. You're quite flushed. Perhaps a cool glass of water would do you well."

"I believe I'll take your advice, my lady. The temperature is most vexing."

"You wouldn't want to suffer from heatstroke, my dear. My late, dear husband was brought low by just such an occurrence. He was never quite the same after."

"I'm sorry to hear it. Rest assured, I shall drink a glass of water."

Rosalind quickly wrapped the two small books and handed them over.

"If you'd send a note to the house should more tracts arrive, I'd be most grateful," Lady Harcourt said.

"Indeed, I shall. Enjoy your reading, Lady Harcourt."

WHILE ADELAIDE WILL be grateful to hear of Newman's new work, I'm grateful she finally left," Fitz said, coming to his feet as the door closed on the noblewoman. "This time I'll make sure the door is locked."

Sated and replete, Rosalind was once again capable of clear thinking. "You should go instead." Cooler postcoital reason prevailed, as did varying degrees of self-reproach for her shameless behavior.

Fitz rather thought it was his turn. As for the lady, she climaxed so easily he understood why Edward St. Vincent had written erotica. And that might be another less rational reason why he wasn't about to leave. "I'll be right back," he declared, moving from behind the counter and making for the door.

Directing her testiness at Fitz rather than admit that she'd not only succumbed to his seduction but also had done so with barely a struggle, Rosalind irritably remarked, "Really, Groveland, I wonder how you ever get any women into bed with your despotic manner."

He turned his head at the preposterous comment. She had just climaxed thanks to him, had she not? And pursuing women were a constant in his life. "Maybe you could give me lessons," he drawled. "You seem to have gotten the hang of it." Locking the door, he flipped over the Open sign to Closed.

"Go to hell," she said, his recognition of her eager response exasperating and embarrassing. "Get out of my store."

"Darling, bitch at me later," he pleasantly replied as he returned to the counter. "In all fairness, it's my turn."

"It certainly is no such thing!" Having fallen prey to his deft persuasion only served to harden her resolve. Then again, postorgasmic, purified motives were more easily managed. "For your information," she haughtily announced, "I am a nonconsenting adult."

Her ridiculous protest amazed him, but then he'd not led a conventional life. Perhaps people who conformed to society's rules fought their natural impulses. He inwardly smiled. Until they didn't of course—to whit, her recent climax.

Moving behind the counter where Rosalind stood defiant and watchful, he picked up the jar of salve from the counter and shoved it in his pocket. "If you're still nonconsenting ten minutes from now, I've lost my touch." And having just brought her to orgasm, he was pretty sure he hadn't.

"You could at least ask nicely," she muttered, struggling with the abiding temptation of wanting him when she shouldn't.

He glanced at her flushed cheeks and grinned. "Would you like to fuck, Mrs. St. Vincent, or rather, how much would you like to fuck? There's no question you like it."

She tried to kick him, but he moved too fast.

His lips twitched into a mocking smile. "Save your energy for the main bout, sweetheart. I'm in the mood for a brawl." He had his own reasons for not wanting to be here. His own struggle with compulsion. Holding out his hand, he said, thin-skinned and edgy, "Let's see who wins this match."

She took a step back.

"My darling little bitch," he whispered. In a flash, he lunged and swept her up in his arms. "Now mind your manners." His voice was gruff; it was an order.

No, no, no, she silently cried. She would not respond to his brute behavior. She would not allow her body to turn ravenous at his growled command as if she didn't have an ounce of restraint! She would remember who he was—a disreputable rake—and who she was and how she had everything to lose and nothing to gain by continuing this purely physical relationship!

But no matter that she tried to ignore his hard-muscled body pressed against hers as he took the stairs at a run, or the scent of his cologne in her nostrils, and his stark classic beauty close enough to kiss, her traitorous libido was undeterred. Or more aptly, adamant and frantic, as if her senses recognized the feel, scent, and sight of their perfect mate. With electrifying speed, a hard, steady pulsing began to throb deep inside her, her nipples went taut, her skin flushed in a Darwinian signal of readiness, and her overwilling sex turned ripely moist.

On this particular occasion, she would have preferred being in ignorance of the new landmark studies in the developing field of sexology: Krafft-Ebing's *Psychopathia Sexualis* and Havelock Ellis's *Man and Woman* and *Studies in the Psychology of Sex*. She would have preferred not knowing all the pertinent signals of female receptivity. She might have better girded her loins as it were and repulsed Fitz's advances.

Not that she could seriously forestall him with his physical superiority. And such reflections on his formidable strength and power served only to further excite her already highly charged libido. Her wanton senses shifted their attention to the central instrument of pleasure—his glorious penis at full stretch, perfectly formed, trained to the inch, capable of giving the most exquisite sexual satisfaction. Really, it was impossible to fight her vaulting urges. And considering the delectable reward, perhaps, in the end, absurd. "You win," she said grudgingly, but honest at least. "I wish I could resist you, but I can't."

"Nor can I you," he muttered, reaching the top of the stairs.

"Does this happen often?" she asked, clearly bewildered by her feelings that seemed impervious to scruple or prudence or even a scintilla of reason.

"Never."

"Are you sure?" She was struggling with irrepressible desire when she'd always prided herself on logic.

"Bloody right, I'm sure." He strode into her parlor.

"Because you're stud to all of London," she snapped back, inexplicably jealous of every woman he'd ever know.

"Damn right."

"Don't have me make you do something you don't want to do," she pettishly asserted.

"Believe me, *darling*"—the word more curse than endearment—"you're not making me do anything. Or at least not rationally. I'm pretty much out of control."

"Don't blame me."

"I don't know who else to blame," he growled. Then quicksilver, he made a course correction. "Forgive me. You're quite blameless in all but your prodigious allure. I'm like a moth to the flame," he added with a smile. "So just bear with me." He shoved open her bedroom door with his foot.

She sighed. "We're both operating outside the pale."

"But it's an enchanting land nonetheless."

"Enchanting beyond belief."

He gazed at her for a moment as he stood at the side of her bed, both avarice and wonder in his eyes. "Enchanting in a thousand ways," he softly agreed. Setting her down a moment later, he dropped into a sprawl beside her, his head resting on his hand. "I must take care not to hurt you. Or hurt you anymore." Leaning over, he gently kissed her cheek. "For which I'm vastly sorry." As if recalling something, he pulled the jar from his suit coat pocket. "Although, there's this if you wish."

"I don't need it. I feel extremely well." She suddenly frowned. "Although, you've no doubt dealt with this problem before."

He hesitated for a fraction of a second, debating how

best to answer. The women he played with weren't novices. "Actually, no," he said. "You're the first"—he smiled—"in a variety of ways. All of them good by the way. I expect your fair skin might be the problem," he politely added. "As for me, I'm dark as the ace of spades; my skin is impervious to wear and tear."

"Him, too." Reaching over, she touched the bulge evident beneath the linen of his trousers.

He grinned. "The Black Corsair if you like." He ran a fingertip over the skirt fabric covering her mons. "And you have the sweetest little pussy. We'll have to see if they can play together later."

"How much later?"

He laughed. "Greedy puss."

"I wish I could say no."

There—the proper Mrs. St. Vincent again. But rather than speak his mind, he politely said, "I'm glad you can't."

"Are you?" She shouldn't have asked; it was gauche to ask a man about his feelings. Particularly a man like Fitz who was known far and wide for his disdain of the tender emotions.

"Yes, very much," he softly said. "Because I can't say no either." He looked away for a second before meeting her gaze again. "I lectured myself against coming to see you, and yet here I am"—he grinned—"and bloody glad to be here." His voice dropped low. "I was serious about dinner, too. Come dine with me afterward. My wealth and title insulate me from censure and by extension, you as well. You needn't worry."

She shook her head. "I'm not sure."

"About dinner or the dispensations allowed a duke?"

She grimaced. "About everything."

"At the risk of offending your virtuous sensibilities—" He paused abruptly as she gave him a skeptical look. "I'm speaking in general terms; you must admit you're of a conventional bent, other than your flame-hot passions," he added with a smile. "But back to my point. Life is to be lived, darling. Maybe not as prodigally as I do, but nevertheless lived. How sad it would be to grow old without ever knowing—"

"This bewitchment?"

He nodded, neither willing nor able to define his feelings. He'd avoided sincere emotion too long. Or perhaps having been raised as he was, he had never learned to recognize it. "Are we done talking?" he asked, malelike in his avoidance.

She smiled. "If you like."

He grinned. "You know what I'd like."

"The same thing as I. We are obsessed, or at least I am."

"We both are. I was thinking of taking you home with me and keeping you locked away."

"And I'd go if life allowed. But unfortunately, I have a store to run and a living to make."

"I could take care of that for you."

For a brief moment, silence fell.

Fitz cringed. He shouldn't have even thought it, let alone said it.

Rosalind knew better than to take seriously what was expressed in the heat of passion, although the notion was enchanting. "Thank you, but I prefer my life as it is"—she smiled—"especially when you come calling."

"Speaking of calling—only if you're sure you're well enough—why don't we put some of this salve on my cock and he'll come call on your pussy?"

"It sounds like a lovely experiment. Smell it, too. It's lavender scented."

He grinned. "Then I'll be bringing flowers when I call."

"At the risk of adding to your conceit, you needn't bring anything but yourself and I'm content."

He held out the small jar. "Should I do it or you?"

"Me, me," she playfully said, fluttering her fingers.

"God Almighty," Fitz whispered, "you're the most endearing little bookstore owner I know."

"And you're God's gift to women," she replied with a smile. "But handsome men and carnal pleasures aside,

Fitz, darling, just for the record, I have no intention of selling my store. I want to be perfectly plain about that. Sex is just sex."

"Then, just for the record, I, too, intend to keep pressing my suit." He flickered his brows and grinned. "I'm hoping you'll finally see the light." *And sex is just sex* was his gospel.

"I don't want to talk," she whispered, the subject too contentious. It was better to concentrate on sex and nothing more.

"I never do when I'm with you." He smiled and brushed a fingertip over the soft curves of her mouth, as practical as she about what brought them together. "Now kiss me and make me happy."

It turned out to be a kiss that wasn't about sex.

It was a happy-to-be-together kiss.

There was a certain innocence in their kiss as well, as if they both hadn't had others in their life before. As if the world was fresh and new.

"You can't keep smiling like that when I'm kissing you," Fitz teased. "I'm losing my concentration."

"You should talk," she said, trying not to smile and failing. "I don't know whether to kiss you back or ask you what the joke is."

"No joke, darling. I just never knew sex could be so much fun."

"You're just pleased because you're getting your way."

He always did. But he also knew that having everything didn't bring happiness. "You decide then."

"About what?"

"About anything?"

"Don't be so generous. I might take you up on your offer."

"Please do." Realizing that he was actually willing to give her anything, he quickly stepped back from the brink of such unreserved sentiment and said with a grin, "Would you like the shirt off my back?"

"You read my mind," she playfully replied, as intent

as he on not straying into the realm of earnestness. "The sooner the better."

Even without his current incentive, he could shed his clothes quickly, and in record time he was undressed and helping Rosalind do the same. He was seated on the side of the bed, she was standing between his legs nearly nude now save for her drawers and silk stockings.

"I adore when you wait on me," she purred, her hand on his broad muscled shoulder, her gaze on his bent head as he slid her drawers down her legs. "It's very provocative. It makes me hot, hot, hot."

He glanced up, his grey eyes amused. "Everything makes you hot, sweetheart." Then, grasping her waist, he lifted her off the floor, kicked her drawers aside, and set her down again.

"Everything about *you* makes me hot."

"Better yet," he murmured, rolling one garter and silk stocking down her leg. Looking up a second later, her stocking and garter discarded, he held her gaze for an overlong moment. "Since now you're *my* current addiction."

"Sexual addiction."

He shook his head and began removing her other stocking. "My everything addiction—my eat, sleep, every-waking-minute addiction." His useless detour to Clarissa's a case in point.

She smiled. "How sweet."

"Fuck, yes," he said, but he was smiling too as he dropped the second stocking on the floor. "You fucking up my life is sweet as hell."

"How nice of you to say," Rosalind murmured, sultry and low, his wanting her as much as she wanted him deli-cious and wonderful. And not at the moment open to the threat of logic.

"Just so long as you like the things I *do*," he softly replied, lifting her up and depositing her, seated, on the bed, "we'll get along famously."

"We already do," she said, watching him lie down

beside her, cross his arms under his head, and stretch out in all his powerful, virile glory.

"This should smooth the way even better." He held out the jar of salve.

"I'm not sure I need this."

"Why take a chance? I heard the doctor was very good."

Rosalind was tempted to ask how he knew and who had told him and how much she was involved in that conversation, but this close to his splendid erection that was her *continuing* addiction, she thought better of it and instead, took the jar from him.

He in turn was tempted to ask whether this episode would be featured in chapter two of *The Duke's Doxy* but decided against it for similar reasons.

The scent of lust pervaded the small sunlit bedroom.

Subverting smaller discontents.

Sitting cross-legged beside him, she uncapped the jar, scooped out a small dollop of lavender-scented salve, and said with a gratified smile, "I think he's bigger than usual." Fitz's upthrust erection lay hard against his stomach, stiff and massive, the red crest brushing his navel.

"He's been thinking of you."

"What a sweetheart." Bending low, she brushed the swollen tip with her lips, drew it into her mouth for a fleeting second before sitting up again. "He smells like soap."

"I just had a bath."

Her first thought was to ask why, but she doubted he'd tell her, and in any case she didn't really wish to know why he was bathing in the middle of the afternoon. "How thoughtful of you," she said instead and reached for his penis.

At the slight umbrage in her voice he automatically braced himself, not entirely sure of her mood. But he visibly relaxed as she gently grasped his cock.

She grinned. "Nervous?"

"Not anymore."

"I wouldn't be so foolish when I need this."

"Much obliged," he drawled.

Both highly motivated, they avoided the subtext of their conversation in favor of imminent sexual satisfaction.

Drawing his rigid erection away from his stomach, she held it upright and placed the dollop of salve on the turgid head of his penis. "It looks like you just came," she said, admiring her handiwork.

"Keep it up and I might," he said, a muscle twitching over his high cheekbone. This little game was going to require considerable restraint when he'd been wanting to fuck Mrs. St. Vincent since he dropped her off this morning.

"You have to wait." She drew a portion of the ointment down one side of his penis, her finger gently tracing the thick webbing of dilated veins on her descent.

"Then you have to hurry," he said on a suffocated breath, calling on all his willpower to resist doing what he wanted to do. And it wasn't playing this game.

"So I'm not always the one who wants to rush."

"You just came."

"And you didn't?"

That small fretful tone again. "Not since last night," he lied.

"Then I'll hurry and you wait just a little and," she said, the pique gone from her voice, "we'll see if we like this"—another swift brushing downstroke that gleamed down his erection—"or not."

Very soon—not as soon as he'd have liked, but soon—his penis was glistening with ointment.

"It looks very tempting," she said with a little wistful sigh. "I wish it was eatable."

"Next time I'll bring jam."

"Bring lemon curd. I love it almost as much as I love him," she murmured, sliding her fingertips around the shiny head of his cock.

It was his own fault, he decided, letting her come first. Usually she was famished for sex. Although he also knew with anyone else he could have waited for hours. Not a thought he cared to dwell on. "If you indulge me now, darling, you can name your price." An unprecedented declaration from the Duke of Groveland who had always been able to take his pleasure with a notable insouciance.

"My goodness!"

Her look of feigned surprise was so operatic he burst out laughing, momentarily distracting his thoughts from orgasmic goals. "Don't plan on making a living on the stage, darling."

"And I suggest you refrain from making such outrageous offers. Someone might take advantage of you."

"The offer's still open. You have five seconds. Five, four, three, two—"

"Stay with me tonight."

"Little fool, I would have anyway. Ask for something later." Past waiting, like some randy adolescent, he pushed her onto her back, rolled on top of her, and put his glossy cock into her luscious cunt.

There was something to be said for a frictionless fuck, the ointment adding a new impressionable dimension to the concept of unreserved access. He had to deliberately curb his forward progress in order not to batter her and the head of his cock in the bargain. But once he found his rhythm, the lady quickly accommodated him, and with a familiarity of considerable practice now, they made their way to that blissful elysian of orgasmic delight and sensory bewitchment they'd discovered together.

She didn't know it was as new to him as it was to her.

Nor did he understand she felt the same as he.

For a woman who wrote erotica, he expected a certain libidinous propensity.

While everyone knew, she thought, that Groveland reveled in prodigal sensation.

But rather than discuss nuances of feeling that bordered on fondness and affection, they chose to verify those sensations in more pleasant ways. With a kind of sumptuousness and self-indulgence, with happiness, with gratitude in the end.

CHAPTER 23

THAT SAME AFTERNOON, in the village of Riverston, in a remote corner of Yorkshire, a barrister from London was seated in the cluttered and noisy morning room of Rosalind's parent's. Birds of every size and color chirped and sang from cages, their living presence in contrast to the other miscellany of dead objects from nature in the form of skulls, insects, animal skeletons, and dried flora laying topsy-turvy on shelves and tabletops.

Amidst this repository of nature, Lady Pitt-Riverston and Mr. Symon were having tea and chatting as they awaited the arrival of the Honorable Algernon Pitt-Riverston who had been sent for to lend his expertise to the occasion. Rosalind's mother was by nature warmhearted and agreeable, and soon Mr. Symon was discussing his wife and children as if he and Lady Pitt-Riverston were long lost friends.

"Perhaps you'd like to bring your little ones a bird or two from our menagerie," she cheerfully offered. "Little Benjy and Marcella are the most adorable warblers. They understand perfectly when you talk to them," she added with a smile. "And they know their numbers."

"Thank you for offering," Symon politely replied, wary of birds that knew their numbers or people who said they did—however kind Lady Pitt-Riverston. "But the city is no place for birds. The fog, you know," he said with a grimace. "It's quite insalubrious."

"Indeed," Lady Pitt-Riverston agreed with a little *tsk, tsk.* "We are fortunate to live in the country. Would your children like that little collection of beetles?" She indicated a glass-topped box with rows of colorful beetles pinned to a green velvet ground. "Howard is forever bringing more of them home."

"It's lovely of you to ask, but with the long train ride, I'm afraid they may be damaged in transit."

"More tea, then, Mr. Symon? Another cake perhaps? You could use a little weight on your bones."

"Tea, please. It's excellent."

"A China green, Mr. Symon. Howard's favorite. There now," she said, pouring tea into his cup. "And I'm just going to put another small piece of cake on your plate," she firmly added.

He didn't argue. Having avoided birds and beetles, he could deal with an extra piece of cake. For the next few minutes, it wasn't necessary to do more than nod his head and drink his tea for Lady Pitt-Riverston was explaining at some length how to teach birds their numbers.

Rosalind's father was attending to some experiment and was only fetched once Algernon arrived. He appeared in a workman's smock and slippers, still scribbling in a notebook as he entered the room.

"You must set that aside now, my dear," his wife admonished. "Mr. Symon has important matters to discuss with us."

It took the baron a fraction of a second to respond, but after adding a few more notations, he set the notebook and pencil aside, smiled at those gathered around the tea table, and sat down to join them. "I'm told this has something to do with Rosalind," he said, fixing Symon with his clear blue gaze.

"Mr. Symon represents a client in London, Howard."

"You've come a long way," Lord Pitt-Riverston noted, "when Rosalind could be spoken to directly."

"There is a slight problem, my lord," Symon tactfully replied.

"With your client and my daughter."

"Yes, sir."

"And who might your client be?" The baron had the direct, assessing gaze of a scientist.

"The Duke of Groveland, my lord." Symon went on to explain the situation with the Duke of Groveland's urban development. Their daughter's bookstore was within the tract the duke wished to acquire, and she was the last property owner who had not yet agreed to sell to the duke. He then cited the sum Fitz had offered. "So you see, the duke is very generous. I've come to speak with you today in hopes you might be able to persuade your daughter"—he nodded at Algernon—"and sister to agree to the duke's terms."

"She's refused him?" Algernon sharply queried.

"Many times, I'm afraid." Mr. Symon offered the party a pained smile. "The sum she'd realize from the sale would be more than enough to buy another shop in a different location, as well as leave her with a considerable profit."

"My goodness, twenty thousand!" Lady Pitt-Riverston murmured. She was in charge of household expenses; her husband took no notice of money or more pertinently in their case, the lack of it.

"It's a bloody fortune," Algernon said bluntly. "She's a fool if she doesn't take it."

"Perhaps you could apprise her of your sentiments," Symon diplomatically noted.

"Now, now," the baron interposed. "Rosalind must have her reasons for refusing. She's an intelligent woman. Perhaps there are extenuating circumstances. I'm not sure we should interfere." He and his daughter shared common crusading convictions; he respected the choices she'd made. "Although, I certainly understand it's a large sum, my dear," he said, turning to his wife, not unaware of the sacrifices she made to keep their household solvent. "Perhaps we should at least wait to hear from Rosalind."

"That's ridiculous," Algernon responded. "She obviously doesn't understand the benefits of twenty thousand pounds. It would change her life."

"I think she's quite content," the baron said, understanding his daughter's feelings since fulfillment for him was a simple matter of puttering around his laboratory.

"Your father might be right, dear," Lady Pitt-Riverston said, with a smile for her son. "How can it hurt to wait a bit?"

Understanding his only ally was Algernon, otherwise his business was done, Mr. Symon proposed to have a private conversation with Mrs. St. Vincent's brother. "Thank you kindly for listening to my proposal," the barrister said with a pleasant smile before turning to Algernon. "If you'd care to share a pint with me before my train leaves, Mr. Pitt-Riverston," he said, "I'd be interested in hearing about the local grouse hunting." Rising to his feet, he picked up his hat and bowed to Lady Pitt-Riverston. "Thank you again, ma'am."

"I'd be more than happy to help you," Algernon returned, coming to his feet as well. "Thank you for tea, Mother. Father." He dipped his head. "I'll see you tomorrow."

Mr. Symon would have been willing to wait for the morning train if it meant returning with the commitment Hutchinson wanted. Now to see if the brother had a price or more aptly, the exact amount of that price.

A short time later, he and Algernon were seated at a table in the local village pub. Once their cognacs were served, Symon lifted his glass. "Thank you for keeping me company. Cheers."

Algernon dipped his head, raised his glass, and the men drank down their cognacs.

Pleased to see that his companion was a tippler, Symon signaled for more drinks. "As you may have surmised," he said as they waited for their drinks, "I wanted to discuss something other than grouse hunting."

Algernon smiled faintly. "By all means, please do. I don't hunt in any case so I wouldn't have been of much help in that regard."

"I was hoping you could help me in another way, Mr. Pitt-Riverston. And if you were so inclined, I'm sure the Duke of Groveland would be *most* grateful."

"How grateful?" Algernon had not inherited the philanthropic genes in the family.

"I'm sure you could name your price," the barrister smoothly replied, pleased to find a family member who understood how business was conducted. "Just between us, sir, may I say your sister seems to put no value at all on money. Twenty thousand is an enormous sum." Symon had been one of the many agents sent to make offers to Rosalind.

Algernon snorted. "She's blind to the ways of the world—she sees herself as some ministering angel to the poor," he added with a sneer. "Neither she nor her dilettante of a husband had any appreciation for the solid principles that have made Britain the envy of the world. Industry and professional men drive the engine of commerce. Not poets," he spat, "or free libraries for the poor."

"I couldn't agree more." Symon would have agreed with the devil to get the job done.

"So how might I help you?"

"How much influence do you have with your sister?"

"To be perfectly honest, I'm not sure. But rest assured, I shall exert what pressure I have to make her understand the merits of accepting such a generous offer."

"I'm sure the duke would be willing to offer you a down payment for your immediate assistance, and should you persuade your sister to sell, you need but name your reward."

"Three hundred now." Crisp and clipped.

"Very well." A tidy sum Symon thought; the brother

was greedy. But he took out his wallet and counted out the bills.

"I'll send her a telegram immediately, then follow up with a letter. If she still remains adamant, I'll travel down to London and deal with her face-to-face. I'll make it clear to her that our parents could use financial help and with twenty thousand she could do so. There is filial duty after all; she is not ignorant of the principle. And so I will remind her."

Their drinks came and Symon lifted his. "To a profitable association."

"To our common goal," Algernon added, holding his glass aloft.

The men drank, both pleased with the arrangement.

Algernon was richer by three hundred pounds, equal to a modest annual income for the lesser gentry, and the future held the possibility of real wealth.

The men parted with assurances and smiles, their bargain made.

Symon could report that he'd been partially successful in his assignment. Furthermore, he didn't miss the evening train to London.

CHAPTER 24

FITZ LEFT ROSALIND'S apartment early the next morning. Throughout the day, Rosalind half hoped he'd stop by again, even though she realized the folly in harboring such expectations from a man who viewed women as amusements. At times, relatively tender amusements as he'd indicated last night, but she knew better than to anticipate any permanent interest. Her life had been too challenging to put much store in silver-lining fantasies. And despite Mrs. Beecham's comment about dukes marrying beneath them, she was not about to take complete leave of her senses in that regard.

While Rosalind was reminding herself not to lose sight of reason when it came to Fitz's charming ways—sexual and otherwise—Fitz was doing his very best not to think of Rosalind *at all*. He refused to yield to what he considered uncontrollable urges today. It was a matter of principle.

He actually escorted his mother to a luncheon that day, followed by a short musical recital. Not short enough in his estimation, but then with plenty of brandy he managed to survive the performance without losing his good humor.

In fact, on the carriage ride back to Groveland House, Julia said, "You seem in fine fettle today, darling. Even playing cavalier to me without so much as a grumble." She looked at him with a twinkle in her eye. "To what do I owe this pleasure?"

He was lounging back on the seat opposite her, the carriage top down on the warm afternoon, his gaze half-lidded against the sun. "I haven't seen much of you since you arrived. I thought I'd do my filial duty."

"Why today?"

He laughed. "Don't look at me with such suspicion. You'd think I never accompany you anywhere."

"You don't."

"I do when you ask me." He lifted his brows. "The Turner exhibit, for instance."

"You left me there. Along with Miss Nesbit."

"If you're going to quibble with me," he drawled, amusement in his gaze, "I won't ask you where we're going next."

She looked at him as she had when he was young and trying to keep something from her. "Are you sick, darling? You can tell me."

He rolled his eyes. "No, I'm not sick, Mother. I'm in excellent health."

"You were out all night."

"I'm out most nights."

"That's true," she agreed, experiencing some relief. "I thank you then for your company, although you have to admit, darling, you don't often escort me to luncheon."

"I was just in the mood today."

"If you say so." She wasn't convinced.

"I do." Then he took out a flask from his coat pocket, uncorked it, and drank a long draught.

It must be that woman, Julia thought with a mother's instinct. "I was planning on going to Charlotte's tea next if you're looking for something to do."

He groaned. "Good God, Mother, why do you bother with that self-righteous prude?"

"If you must know, Kemal will be there. Charlotte's husband is in the Ministry of Trade, and he and Kemal are discussing something or other," she said with a dismissive wave of her hand.

"If Kemal's there, you won't need me." Being dutiful had its limits and Charlotte Dalton was his. He couldn't stomach the woman; she thought she could entice him as a suitor by slyly calling attention to her daughter's virginity.

His mother smiled, well aware of Charlotte's crude presumption. "You could just tell Charlotte you can't abide virgins."

"I believe I have in every possible way short of gross discourtesy, Mother. She is completely obtuse and oblivious to the fact that virgins went the way of sailing ships."

"I believe there are still a few."

He offered her a jaundiced look. "If they're very plain." At which point a picture of the splendid Mrs. St. Vincent sprang into his mind in not so subtle contrast. "I'll get off at Brooks's," he abruptly said and swivelling around gave instructions to the driver. "You don't need me with Kemal for company, do you?"

"No, of course not." Julia scrutinized her son, taking note of his sudden discomfort. "If you need anything or if you wish for entertainment tonight, Kemal and I are dining with Derby."

Fitz looked up, his flask halfway to his mouth. "Thank you, but I'll find some entertainment of my own." Raising the flask to his mouth, he drained it.

"Do you have plans to go to Green Grove anytime soon?" Fitz normally went grouse hunting in August or rusticated in the country.

"I'm not sure. What about you?"

"We might drive out next week," Julia said.

"I'll come along if I can," he lied. It wasn't that he disliked Kemal; he just preferred not seeing Kemal play husband to his mother when the man already had four wives. A son's protective impulse perhaps, but there it was.

Despite drinking and gambling at Brooks's in the course

of the following hours, however, his memories of Mrs. St. Vincent persisted. In fact, the more he drank, the more vivid they became. Not a particular surprise. He'd decided to play cicisbeo to his mother in order *not* to spend the day drinking, knowing what it would do to his self-control. He was like a dog with the neighborhood bitch in heat, he thought—driven willy nilly to fuck her. And liquor only made the craving worse.

He didn't stay more than a few hours at Brooks's. He left for Madame Rivera's determined to exhaust himself. If he fucked someone else until he couldn't fuck anymore, he hoped to annihilate his lustful need for the enticing Rosalind.

A petite, pretty blonde was riding Fitz some time later and silently offering up thanks for her good fortune. All the ladies vied for his attention when he called, knowing darling Fitz always gave pleasure in rich full measure. "I'm so glad you're staying," she purred, slowly sliding back down his cock.

After hours of drinking, he was fighting to stave off the compulsion that had brought him here. "I can't think of a better place to spend the night," he murmured.

"Lucky me..." He was the only man she knew who could last til morning.

WHILE FITZ WAS doing his prurient best to forget Rosalind, she was locking up the bookstore before setting off for her appointment with Dr. Swindell. In the course of the day, she'd reconciled herself to the practicalities of serving as the Duke of Groveland's idle entertainment. All the pros, cons, and harsh realities had been neatly compartmentalized and locked away.

If she saw him again, fine. If she didn't, she understood the rules apropos casual liaisons. They were by definition *casual*.

She took a few moments to stop by Mr. Edding's. With the interruptions of late, she wished to let him know she was behind schedule. Not that she would divulge the reasons why—that Fitz had been consuming all her leisure time. But Mr. Edding deserved some warning so he could adjust his publication schedule.

As she walked into his shop, she immediately noticed his apprehension. Thinking perhaps she was jumping to conclusions, she smiled. "Good evening, sir. I came to beg your indulgence. My next manuscript will be delayed I'm afraid."

"You mustn't be seen here," he whispered, although they were quite alone. "I didn't dare send you a message in the event someone was watching, but you must go. Immediately."

The panic in his voice was disturbing. "Watching?" she whispered back.

"I believe I'm under surveillance." He glanced outside with a furtive look. "Someone learned of my publishing activities. The authorities may swoop down on me at any moment. You must go and *don't under any circumstances* come back until you hear from me. Now go!"

No further explanation was required. She knew full well that the obscenity laws viewed Mr. Edding's publishing ventures as criminal.

"Here," he hissed, shoving a packet of stationery at her. "Pretend to take money out of your purse, so it looks as though you came in to purchase some stationery."

She could feel herself beginning to sweat and understood why Edward had never told her of his writing. He was protecting her. Miming a money transaction, she took the package from Mr. Edding and whispered, "I hope you're wrong about this."

She was careful not to look about as she exited the shop, not wishing to appear suspicious. But she found herself glancing in shop windows as she moved through the city, trying to see if someone was trailing her. If she was being followed, however, her pursuers were discreet. She could detect no one giving chase. And by the time she reached Dr. Swindell's, she'd had time to calm the worst of her fears.

Surely no one could implicate her in Mr. Edding's activities. Her name was never on anything she wrote, she was paid in cash, she only rarely entered his shop. Furthermore, if Edward had escaped the law for the length of time required to write fourteen books, surely she was safe, having written only a few serials.

She was surprised to find the doctor's townhouse was not only posh, but in a fashionable neighborhood. But then nothing but the best for Fitz and his minions, she reminded herself. However, she was genuinely shocked at the degree of elegance she saw after being ushered inside by a courteous servant. The entrance hall was decorated with artifacts from Pompeii, including replicas of furniture and Roman wall paintings. The carpet was silk and obviously from Persia if her expertise garnered from books was credible. She had no firsthand knowledge since her family could never afford anything so fine.

The servant who welcomed her escorted her down the hall to the back of the house, waved her into a small examining room, and quietly shut the door behind her.

Two large windows overlooked a manicured garden teeming with late summer roses. A riot of color struck the eye, blossoms tumbling over the garden walls, climbing up trellises, flourishing in neat beds bordered by boxwood hedges. She thought of her own pitiful garden behind her store, where sunlight was limited to a few hours a day and her efforts at growing roses had largely met with failure.

She softly sighed.

Oh, for a gardener of one's own.

And the funds to buy hundreds of roses.

And the wherewithal to take down the buildings on either side of her garden that blocked the sun.

Her reflections gave way as the door opened.

"Good evening, my dear," Dr. Swindell said as she entered the room. "Are you feeling any better?"

"Yes, thank you. The salve was an excellent restorative." *In more ways than one*, she thought, remembering how easily and painlessly Fitz's erection had slid in and out. "You have a most lush garden," she added.

"The roses are *my* restorative. Gardening is my means of relaxation, although I have help as well." She waved to a screen in the corner. "If you like, you can change into a gown. I'll come back in a few minutes."

Rosalind was tempted to say, "I feel fine, don't bother," but understood it might be useful to see that all was well, Fitz's avowals of good health notwithstanding. Still, this was a novel experience for her and she couldn't say she was looking forward to being peered at and probed.

But once she was undressed and the doctor returned, the examination went relatively smoothly. Dr. Swindell put her at ease by chatting of impersonal matters during the exam and by so doing, diverting her attention from the procedure.

"There now," Dr. Swindell said when she was finished, offering her hand to help Rosalind sit up. "Everything looks fine, barring a return of that small inflammation you mentioned. I would caution you to a modicum of prudence in terms of overindulgence—if you wish, of course," she added as Rosalind blushed. "I'm not suggesting it's necessary. You'd know best how you feel. But should you need it, I'll send along some more salve."

"Thank you, that would be useful."

"If you have any questions of any kind, please, ask away. I'm not in the least judgmental."

"Well...that is..." Rosalind hesitated, not in the habit of discussing such things. "Need I...worry about...some dangerous disease?" she finally stammered.

"There's always the risk," the doctor replied, Rosalind's reluctant query common in her practice. "I don't like to promise my patients absolution from such possibilities. Naturally, it depends on one's partner—on their fidelity."

"I understand." Her heart sank. As if *fidelity* was even in Fitz's vocabulary.

"You could use a condom of course—as an added measure of safety. I could give you some if you like and save you the necessity of going to a chemist."

She was politely saying, *You wouldn't have to expose your sexual activity to the world.* "Thank you—a few would be useful," Rosalind murmured.

"A wise choice, my dear. Forethought is excellent insurance against disease. While you dress, I'll make up a small package for you."

As Rosalind dressed, she contemplated how significantly her world had changed in a few short days. Here she was, dressing after a doctor's examination she might never have contemplated before. Not only that, she was bringing home condoms and salve so she might engage in sexual activities with a man she barely knew.

If he even elected to return.

Not a material certainty, Fitz's departure that morning polite but devoid of any promise of future assignations.

On her journey home, that uncertainty looped through her mind, dogging her despite her best efforts to consider more pleasant prospects. But she wanted to see Fitz again—whether it meant ultimate heartache or not. Whether it was sensible or not. Although, clearly *she* wasn't when she coveted a man like Fitz; surely their encounters were akin to that poetic line about ships passing in the night.

She would be wise to keep in mind the fleeting nature of his liaisons. It would be insane to contemplate actually caring for a man of his ilk. She grimaced. Particularly after so few days. *Good God, I am a fool.*

By the time she'd traveled the considerable distance from the doctor's and was nearing home, she'd beaten down most of her rash inclinations and was commending herself on her good sense. She'd reconciled herself to simply enjoying Fitz's company if and when he appeared. Just that—enjoy—and nothing more. *Carpe diem* would be her motto.

If only he hadn't been waiting for her, such well-founded pragmatism might have prevailed.

But he was.

Lounging in all his *jeunesse dorée* glory against her bow window, tall and rangy in a suit of ecru linen, his dark hair shoved behind his ears as if he'd combed it with his fingers, his face so starkly beautiful her breath caught in her throat.

She screamed and began running toward him.

Propriety and prudence be damned.

She didn't get far; he ran faster, and when they met, he swept her up in his arms and kissed her soundly, needing corporeal evidence that she was real and he was no longer bereft.

She finally whispered, "Mfphffp," against his mouth because passersby were stopping to stare.

He raised his head politely but minimally and grinned. "Forgive me, I might be a little drunk."

"I don't care," she whispered, lighthearted, content, happier than she'd ever been in her life. "But we should get off the street."

"I brought you something," he said with a smile, kissing her again without regard for their audience. "You'll like it." He winked. "Guaranteed."

"You think so?" she asked playfully, hugging him as if he were her salvation from the shipwreck of life, not *altogether* concerned with observers when she was beginning to believe in castles in the air.

"I know so. It's a harem present." He didn't even watch her face as he spoke, the gift untainted by malice—for her pleasure alone.

But once they reached her apartment, he sat down on the nearest chair with her on his lap, took her purse and package, set them aside, and simply held her. "It's been quite a long day," he gruffly said, leaving a trail of kisses across her forehead and down her cheek. "Way too long…"

It was amazing, she thought, how happiness filled her to overflowing when Fitz was near—spilling out in a smile she couldn't contain. Even when she should have known better than to care about a man like him. "I missed you," she whispered, enraptured and smitten. "There. I'm like all the other adoring women in your life. And I don't care."

"You're nothing like the others. Not even close." If he

hadn't drunk so much, if he hadn't found Madame Rivera's intolerable for the first time in his life, if he didn't feel as though he'd reached safe haven when he'd never so much as thought of the phrase before, he wouldn't have added with such vehemence, "Thank God you finally came home."

And you were here. "I'm sorry you had to wait."

"Where were you?" Another first—wanting to know where a woman had been, when he normally wanted to know when they were leaving.

"I went to see Dr. Swindell."

"Christ," he muttered, knowing he was responsible. "I knew I should have been more careful last night."

"No, no, everything's fine. I'd made an appointment yesterday, so I kept it, that's all."

He leaned back marginally and scanned her face. "You're sure?"

"Positive."

He exhaled in relief. "I'll be on my best behavior; your present can wait," he added. "It was probably a selfish gesture anyway."

She grinned. "You, selfish?"

"Point taken. On the other hand," he said, smiling in return, "you've been known to make a few selfish demands yourself." His smile widened. "*Give me more* comes to mind."

"Or how about, *Give me my present*?" Curiosity overcame politesse.

"No," he said, shaking his head. "You were at the doctor today because of me. It can wait until you're in the pink of health again."

"I am, for heaven's sake. I'm perfectly fine. I couldn't be better. Just show me. Please . . ."

Since he was here in the first place because he couldn't resist her, he was hardly in the position to deny such an appealing plea. "It's just a toy," he said in dismissal.

"I *love* toys." Had some other woman spoken in that coquettish voice?

With a reluctant sigh and a grimace, he pulled a narrow

shagreen box from his pocket. "This is for later now. I don't want to argue."

It's jewelry, she thought at the sight of the leather box, *a necklace perhaps from the shape*. But as she was beginning to take issue with what she perceived as his customary gift for the women in his life, he flipped open the lid.

"Wherever did you get *that*?" she blurted out, shocked—and intrigued.

"At a jeweler's. It's a Renaissance piece, but don't worry, I was assured that it's been thoroughly cleaned. Apparently, it's a Cellini object d'art."

"Are you serious?"

He grinned. "I generally try not to be, but in this case I am."

"May I touch it?"

"Certainly."

She ran her fingers lightly over the gold engraved dildo, then lifted it from the silk-lined box and studied the amorous images. As she turned the exquisite piece to view all the scenes, the starkly erotic content triggered an immediate and heated response—which was the point no doubt of the portrayals of mythical figures engaged in amorous play. Although Fitz's erection pressing into her bottom also contributed to her expeditious arousal. A charming combination in any event. "Maybe we could try this," she murmured, a distinctly carnal heat warming her senses, melting inside her.

Fitz shook his head. "We should wait."

"This is smaller than you."

"It's metal though—not in the least pliant."

"I hardly think your erection is what you'd call pliant."

"It is in contrast to this. I'm not arguing, darling." He took it from her hand and shoved it in his pocket. "We'll use it some other time."

"Or you could just watch."

He looked at her from under his lashes. "Now you're trying to torment me."

"At least *he's* interested," she said softly, shifting in his lap, his rigid length pronounced.

"Don't be difficult," he growled, steeling himself against his cravings, "when I'm trying to be unselfish."

"I won't blame you," she replied, rubbing against his swelling erection, only the linen of his trousers and her skirt barricade to consummation. "I take full responsibility."

He softly groaned.

"Let me just try this little toy. Please?" She'd take her pleasure where she could as per her carpe diem promise to herself. With Fitz tomorrows were uncertain.

"I'd rather not. I'm content just to hold you." After the misery of his day, he was more than content, or maybe the contrast between Madame Rivera's and Rosalind's parlor was pleasure enough. "Or we could go out to dinner."

"Or I could pout."

He chuckled. "As you like to say to me, you can't always have what you want."

"You're cruel. I had a perfect bill of health. Come, Fitz, give me either the Cellini or you. Consider, you've awakened my feverish desires. You can't just ignore me. Please, please, be a dear…"

There wasn't a man with a heartbeat who could have refused.

And his blood was coursing through more than his heart at the moment.

"I'm doing this against my better judgment," he declared, rising to his feet with her in his arms and moving toward the bedroom.

"I love when you play the gallant," she purred, raining kisses on his face and neck as they moved through the parlor, his benevolence only heightening her affection and desires. "I find it wildly provocative."

He shot her a disgruntled look. "I find everything about you wildly provocative," he grumbled. "And just for the record, I tried to say no." A record in every sense of the word.

"How sweet." She shivered, anticipating the intoxicating obverse of no, her vagina liquid with longing, well ahead of her in eagerness.

"I'm not going to be sweet for long," he growled.

But his *long* was less precipitous than hers for once he deposited her on the bed she said, with a strong hint of her school mistress voice, "Do hurry, Fitz—please!"

It would have been better if his first thought wasn't *Now I know why she wrote erotica.* Or if he wasn't so personally involved, enamored, or stupid that he'd overruled his instincts and habits of a lifetime to come and see her again. Or if she hadn't added in an imperious tone that set his teeth on edge, "Please, don't play the dominating male right now."

He was unfamiliar with women like Mrs. St. Vincent who were completely devoid of flattery and honeyed blandishments. But perhaps that was why she appealed to him, he more sensibly decided, tamping down his temper. There was no point in being disagreeable when she was flame hot and willing.

"Sorry, darling," he smoothly replied, avoiding a contretemps that had nothing to do with her. She was visibly panting; only a fool would take offense at her ready passions.

"I'm sorry, too, really I am," she whispered, aware of the brief flash of anger in his eyes. "I can wait."

But she was shrugging out of her bodice as she spoke, her skirts were rucked up over her thighs, her drawers untied, and he decided perhaps neither of them should wait for long.

Sitting on the edge of her bed, he smiled. "You're an insatiable little puss, but far be it from me to deny you."

"Thank you," she sweetly said, too close to consummation to take a chance of offending him. Dildos aside, his strong body most appealed.

"Such acquiescence, darling."

"I wouldn't want to put you out of humor," she said, slipping her drawers down her legs and tossing them aside.

He grinned. "At this stage."

Her gaze was half-lidded, her hips gently swaying. "Indeed."

"Then lie down, sweetheart, spread your legs, and let me know when you've had enough of Cellini." It was at least smaller.

She immediately complied, one arm free of her blouse, the other not, and lying with her thighs open, flagrantly available, she smiled her temptress smile. "You're such a darling…"

In a way he was for letting her have her way, when he'd thought better of it. But perhaps his French governess had schooled him too well—or rather, schooled him to perfection, his many satisfied lovers would attest—for he agreed to what she wanted. "Stop me if this hurts," he murmured, sliding the smooth metal over her sleek cleft.

She nodded, and took a very small breath as the cool dildo glided over her labia and entered her. How many women had felt the pleasure of this toy in the last three hundred years, she wondered. Were they, too, in illicit affairs? Were they in love or infatuated like she? Was their lover as beautiful? Did they feel this degree of infinite bliss…?

He saw her smile and smiled himself at the half-undressed woman with tousled hair and pinked cheeks who had lured him into her seductive net. And when in the past he would have balked at being caught, instead, he set out to please her.

She whimpered once and he stopped.

Her eyes opened and she looked up at him with a fevered gaze.

"More?"

Her eyes went shut.

Understanding, he exerted a modicum more pressure, and so it went—he carefully monitoring her response, she softly moaning, catching her breath from time to time. At which point, he always stopped until she gave him leave to continue.

But orgasms never took long with the ravenous Mrs.

St. Vincent, her libido on a very short fuse, her orgasmic impetuosity charmingly predictable.

But when she came—more quietly than usual—he glimpsed tears seeping under her lashes and panicked. "Christ, I'm sorry," he whispered, carefully withdrawing the dildo, scrutinizing the gold surface for traces of blood, calling himself every kind of brute for not being more sensible.

Reaching up, Rosalind brushed his lips with her fingers. "Tears of happiness, darling," she whispered, knowing the truth would never do. "I'm not hurt." She was lovesick instead, craving a man she could never have, desperately enamored after a few brief days. Foolish beyond words.

"Honestly?"

"Cross my heart."

"Dammit, that's it," he firmly said, his heart still racing, not sure he could believe her. "We're done. We'll have tea instead."

"No we won't because I want you too much. And if you say no, I'll cry. Really, Fitz, I'll make a scene."

She wasn't smiling. God, he dreaded crying women. On the other hand, he daren't do anything that might harm her. That's what came from becoming attached to a virtuous woman, he decided with an inward sigh. They turned out to be fragile as hell. "I wish you wouldn't cry," he said, testing the waters. "And I also wish you'd wait."

"We could wait until we undress," she offered as if she were actually complying when she was in fact being bloody difficult.

He groaned. "I'm trying to be virtuous—Jesus, don't tempt me. I'm not good at resisting temptation."

"Nor am I. Perfect," she brightly said.

"No it isn't," he grumbled. "We might end up dealing with some goddamn catastrophe." Abruptly coming to his feet, he walked to the window and stared at her blighted garden.

"I'll lock you in." She swung her legs over the side of the bed. "I won't let you go."

He spun around.

"Come back to bed, darling," she coaxed, "and hold me."

He looked at the irresistible woman who drew him back against his better judgment day after day, her half undress more provocative than nudity, her heavy auburn hair framing the stunning beauty of her face. "Just hold you," he replied.

"Yes, yes, that's all," she lied, playing Circe without compunction for the first time in her life. Why shouldn't she seize what happiness she could, when Fitz was no more than a meteor passing through her life?

He approached her slowly, though, not quite trusting her, trusting himself less, and finally stopped, indecisive and restless, beside the bed.

"You're much too nice, Your Grace," she teased, looking up into his grave gaze.

"And you're much too enticing, Mrs. St. Vincent."

"Maybe we could come to some agreement."

"I wish we could."

"I'm sure we can." She slipped off the sleeve still half draped on her arm, shrugged out of her blouse, and began unbuttoning her chemise.

He didn't move, save for his rising erection.

But when she'd slipped off her chemise, exposing her large, resplendent breasts, and began unbuttoning the waistband of her skirt, temptation was too great for a duke who had commanded the world since adolescence. Jerking her to her feet, he shoved her skirt and petticoat down her hips, pushed her back on the bed, and fell on top of her fully dressed and shod, still unbuttoning his trousers.

"Don't say I didn't try," he said through clenched teeth, swiftly guiding the head of his cock to her sex. "And don't fucking say I hurt you." Goaded past the point of civility, he flexed his quads, swung his hips forward, and plunged into her sleek, ripe body.

He wouldn't have had to worry about injuring her, his forward progress unimpeded in the slippery heat of her well-lubricated cunt. Relieved, gratified, mostly lecherous and lustful, he settled into a deft, experienced rhythm sure to please his partner and ultimately himself.

Today, everything about Fitz intensified her frenzied ardor—his restive need, the wildness in his eyes, his smooth, restrained thrust and withdrawal that brought a thin beading of sweat to his forehead, the erotic sensation of him fully clothed under her hands, over her, the titillating friction of his trousers on her thighs. He was as hotheaded as she, as skittish and high strung. As immune to reason.

He'd waited for her to return. She knew the feeling; she'd been waiting for him ever since the first night he made love to her. And now he was offering her pleasure as only he could and she wanted it all—every enchanting measure—until he left her. As he would most certainly, she sadly knew. But not right now.

"You please me, darling Fitz," she whispered, her orgasm fast approaching, passion and tenderness a feverish, heady tumult that warmed her heart and soul.

He looked surprised for a fraction of a second at the winsomeness in her voice, then he raised one brow and smiled. "You're the sunshine of my life," he softly said in return, braced his shoe soles against the foot of the iron bedstead, and pleased her even more.

SLIDING OFF HIS jacket and shoes, Fitz held Rosalind close after their first frantic passions had been appeased, her head on his shoulder, the warmth of her body pressed against his. Advising himself against making more sexual demands, he politely made conversation. "Tell me," he suavely remarked. "How did you like Dr. Swindell?"

"She was very nice." Stretching upward, Rosalind kissed his cheek before resting her head on his shoulder once again. "She's ever so pleasant. By the way, she sent condoms home with me." She sat up and smiled at Fitz. "I was warned to be vigilant against disease."

Not entirely sure whether she was serious, he said, "If you want me to use a condom, I will."

She wrinkled her nose. "At the time, it sounded reasonable, but now I'm not so sure. Am I being incautious?"

"If you're asking whether I'm a threat, I'm not."

"What about"—she reminded herself she was going to be adult about their carpe diem relationship—"others."

He didn't immediately answer because he was tempted to say he was uninterested in other women. But he wasn't quite so irrational. "I'm always careful," he said instead. "If the circumstances warrant, I use a condom. You decide, though. If the doctor thinks you should, we'll use them."

"I'm angry with you when I have no right," she said with a sigh.

"We're both in no man's land, darling. I can't stay away as you know." He shrugged faintly. "I've decided not to think about it."

"I did as well until I saw you waiting for me, and then I went crazy."

He grinned. "We'll go crazy together."

"I must say, you do have the most delicious methodology in that regard." Pleased that she wasn't alone in her lunacy, she dropped back down on his shoulder and tracing a finger along his jaw shadowed with late-day stubble, changed the subject to something less fraught with emotion. "The doctor had the most gorgeous rose garden. It was absolutely stupendous."

"In what way?" He was uninitiated in the merits of stupendous gardens.

"She had every imaginable color rose. They spilled over her garden wall, ran up trellises, covered the entire yard space like a carpet. It looked like a fairy-tale land. She has a gardener, though, which accounts for the garden's pristine condition, and of course, she has the money to buy all those gorgeous roses."

"Would you like some roses?" Jewelry was unacceptable, he'd discovered, although sex toys were well received. But he would have liked to buy her other things. A novel feeling after a lifetime of having his retainers buy gifts for his lovers.

"No, no... I don't have time to take care of a garden in any event. But thank you for asking. It was just so beautiful, that's all... it caught my fancy. And speaking of things catching my fancy," she purred. "I do believe its been at least five minutes since I climaxed."

"Do you think it's wise?" An indication of his affection. He would not in the past have been so altruistic.

"Don't even start again," she said with a delicious pout.

"Very well," Fitz replied, understanding there were times to hold one's ground and times not to. "Let me see to my obligations." Setting her aside, he sat up and began undressing.

"That's better," she lightly said. It would never do to pretend making love was anything more than a game. "And I have orders for you this time."

CHAPTER 25

THEY WERE WAKENED early by a loud rapping on the door.

"I'll go," Rosalind said, not about to let Fitz open the door. Still half-asleep, she stumbled downstairs to find a telegram messenger at her door and instantly went pale. Outside of the business community, telegrams were only used in emergencies—generally for deaths in the family. Her hand was trembling as she took the telegram from the young boy.

After the youth was gone, she stared at the folded sheet, fainthearted. Finally, she shut her eyes, ripped it open, took a deep breath, opened her eyes, and quickly scanned the brief message.

> GROVELAND'S AGENT WAS HERE TO DISCUSS SALE OF
> YOUR STORE WITH MOTHER AND FATHER. TWENTY
> THOUSAND IS A FORTUNE. VERY STRONGLY ADVISE
> YOU ACCEPT OFFER WITHOUT DELAY. ALGERNON.

Her fear turned to anger, and for a moment Rosalind couldn't decide where first to direct her wrath: at Fitz for sending the agent or at her brother for meddling in her life. As usual.

Since Algernon had the advantage of being beyond range, it was left to Fitz to bear the brunt of her displeasure. However, after a night of incredible bliss and given her unquestionable affection for the man who was the source of unalloyed sexual pleasure, she found herself unable to dredge up a suitable rage. After all, only the day before yesterday he'd said again that he intended to do everything he could to buy her property. She certainly couldn't accuse him of guile.

By the time she walked through the store and ascended the stairs, she'd calmed down. If she wanted Algernon's advice, she'd ask for it. As for Fitz's attempt to influence her family, apparently neither her mother or father had been persuaded. A point for her side, she decided.

Entering the bedroom a few moments later, she held the telegram aloft. "No one died I'm happy to say. Instead, my brother sends news of your agent's visit. Apparently, he met with my family and Algernon instructs me to sell to you."

Fitz was lounging on the bed, and as she spoke he closely assessed her tone and expression, neither of which he characterized as lethal. His smile flashed white against his swarthy skin. "A sensible man, your brother."

"I should beat you," she muttered, dropping the telegram on the floor as she moved toward the bed.

His gaze was amused. "Please do."

"Stop, Fitz! I'm *very* angry with you."

"I understand, although if you come a little closer," he murmured, "I know I could make you feel better."

"Damn you," she grumbled, unable to walk away when she should, when anyone with sense would toss him out on his ear. Dropping onto the bed, she slapped away his hands, leaned back against the headboard, and fixed her gaze on him. "No matter what," she said heated and sulky, "sex aside, even wild, explosive sex, I'm *never* selling my store."

"I believe I may have heard that once or twice before,"

he pleasantly said, his hard, lean body all grace and power beside her, his skin dark against the whiteness of the sheets. "Not that your views or mine should interfere in any way with our carnal interests. Come, darling," he gently coaxed, careful not to touch her. "I haven't had near enough of you." A jarring thought after a night of sex, but shockingly true.

"Just so you understand I mean it," Rosalind grumbled, although her body was already opening in spontaneous welcome; he had but to ask and the entire essence of her being was ready to oblige him.

"I understand completely. I really do." He could sense her arousal and felt better, not wishing to be alone in this insanity. "But I also understand," he said, quietly cajoling, "that you and I have some improbable sexual connection that has redefined the perimeters of pleasure. And whatever it is—aberrant or extraordinary—I need it and you and to hell with the rest."

She made a moue, struggling to equate her reckless need with anything at all in her life prior to Fitz. "Are you sure this"—she wiggled her finger between them—"is really wise?"

"Sure as I'm breathing."

"That sure." But she felt a warm glow melt away her misgivings.

"Oh, yes, my darling nymphet. Whatever it is you have, I want, day and night, night and day. I am seriously crazed."

She smiled, her gaze teasing. "I expect you tell all the ladies that."

He snorted. "Naive babe. I am the Sphinx itself to everyone but you." He frowned briefly with his world in total flux, then smiled again because he didn't really give a damn. "Now, come here," he said, his one-track brain on track, "and let me hear you scream again when you climax. I swear my cock doubles in size at the sound." That, too, was unnerving, but not so much that he was willing to forgo the pleasure.

She quickly glanced at the clock.

"There's time," he said. "Although, if you'd let me, I could find some help for your store and you could entertain me without interruptions."

She wrinkled her nose. "Tempting, but I relish my independence."

"I wasn't asking for your independence, just this." He reached out and brushed a fingertip over her silky mons. "Otherwise, stay as independent as you wish."

"As would you, I expect."

His eyes widened for a fleeting second, the notion of curtailing his freedom unimaginable. But he'd not polished his skills in boudoirs around the world without acquiring the necessary gallantries. "Perhaps you can persuade me otherwise," he amiably said.

"How urbane you are, Fitz." She smiled. "But hardly believable."

Not willing to expressly perjure himself, he smoothly replied, "I have something you *can* believe in; I'm ready to fuck you anytime, anywhere, any which way."

"Then we share a common interest," she sweetly returned, knowing better than to persist in a conversation of little value to either of them. "You have another hour to show me your formidable skills, and then I must bathe and dress for the day."

"Are you sure I can't change your mind—that I couldn't interest you in a drive out to Mertenside on this lovely summer day?"

"Now I know what it's like to see the devil with an apple."

"I'd be more than willing to reform if you but asked," he playfully observed.

While she hadn't meant it literally, Fitz was indeed temptation incarnate. And she wondered for a cheerless moment how she would bear it when he left her. Quickly dismissing her melancholy when happiness was within her grasp, she facetiously replied, "Let me write up a list of remedial measures for you to undertake."

He grabbed her then, no longer asking permission,

unwilling to wait a minute longer, doing what he pleased as befitted both his station in life and his expertise in the bedchamber. Rolling onto his back, he effortlessly lifted her, deposited her prone form on top of him, and gently wrapped his arms around her. "There now," he whispered, gazing up at her, "all is right with the world."

She wished for that moment she might arrest the passage of time and preserve forever the look of tenderness in his eyes, the euphoric happiness that infused her soul, the sumptuous sensation of her skin on his as she lay atop him.

How was it that the wanting never went away?

What had happened to her a few short days ago that she no longer had command over her emotions—or her life?

"I should say no to you a thousand times a thousand different ways."

His shoulder lifted in the merest shrug. "Just not now," he said in gentle dissent, unwilling at present to face the brutal cross-purposes of their lives.

"As if I could anyway," she answered with a small sigh.

His smile could have rivaled the sun. "Good. Good," he said again, in relief or perhaps only in pleasure.

Then in a smooth roll, he shifted their positions and as smoothly entered her. He made love to her slowly, slowly, not letting her rush, wanting it to last, as if time were his enemy. And she concurred, understanding after the night past when sex had become something more—something meaningful and pure—that what they shared was rare.

He shouldn't have come in her. He had no idea why he did. He immediately apologized and offered to run to the chemist for a palliative douche.

She should have been outraged. Instead, she calmly said, "Once can't be a very serious problem. Don't worry."

When in the past he would have been not only worried but also uneasy as hell, he just reached for one of the towels that was laying about, and said, "I can wipe you up at least."

"I suppose it is *the least* you can do, darling," she quipped. "Considering the lapse was yours."

"I really am sorry," he softly said.

"I know."

And a small sadness quite separate from their conversation momentarily surfaced.

Experienced at avoiding earnestness, Fitz spoke first, asking if he should run her bath.

She congratulated herself for her poise in responding.

And for the remainder of their time together, both were careful to speak only of banalities. They breakfasted together, then walked downstairs when it was time for the store to open. Fitz kissed her good-by and started to leave, but after only a step or two he came back to the counter and kissed her again before finally walking out of the store.

She watched him until his figure disappeared into the crowds on the pavement.

CHAPTER 26

ON REACHING HOME, Fitz sat with his mother as she breakfasted, acknowledging her attempts at conversation with distracted monosyllabic replies so often, she finally said, "Good heavens, Georgie, it's not the end of life as you know it to actually harbor some feelings for a woman."

He shot her a look of stunned surprise and set down the glass of brandy he was holding.

"Sweetheart," she softly said, "you aren't the first person in the world to be enamored. Nor is it necessarily an evil requiring three brandies at this time of day. Personally, I'd say it's about time."

"You're mistaken."

"As you wish."

"That's exactly what I wish," he curtly said.

"Fine. Would you like another brandy?"

"No. She writes erotica," he gruffly said, looking at his mother from under his lashes. "About me." His mouth twitched into a mocking smile. "Does that change your notion about Mrs. St. Vincent's place in my life?"

"What place is that, darling?" his mother asked, unfazed by Rosalind's writing.

"One that screws up everything."

"Does it have to?"

He sighed. "That unfortunately is the current riddle of the universe."

"Because you're about to ruin her."

"Probably." He rose to his feet. "I'm going north to Craievar for grouse hunting."

"Now?"

"Tomorrow." He ignored Pansy dancing at his feet, yipping for attention. "Do you need anything before I go?"

"Not at all. I'm fine, darling. Do you know when you'll return?"

"No."

He was moving away from the table as he spoke, so she decided against saying what was on her mind. "Are you home for dinner tonight, dear?" she called out.

He raised his hand and waggled his fingers in answer, and a moment later closed the breakfast room door behind him.

"My, my, my," Julia said aloud, picking up Pansy and setting her on her lap. Her little boy was nonplused by a woman. And not just any woman, but a woman who didn't toady to his wealth and title and wrote about his boudoir athletics. Definitely a woman of extraordinary character.

Julia checked the small calendar on the jeweled timepiece pinned to her bodice and smiled. She rather thought Fitz wouldn't be staying in Scotland long.

ALGERNON FOUND FITZ at Brooks's that afternoon, having been directed there by Stanley. In his moodiness, Fitz was seated alone in a corner of the reading room, safe from his friends who never read. A bottle of brandy, half-empty, sat at his elbow, a full glass in his hand, and sunk as he was in peevish, sullen reflection, Rosalind's brother was forced to clear his throat twice before Fitz looked up.

"I'm Pitt-Riverston," Algernon said. "I came down to London to speak with you."

Fitz regarded Rosalind's brother with a shuttered gaze. "May I offer you a brandy?" he said, and after a nod from Algernon, he waved him to a chair and raised his hand for a flunkey.

The men spoke of the weather and train travel until a servant brought a glass, poured Algernon a brandy, topped off Fitz's glass, and left.

"Now, what can I do for you?" Fitz softly asked, the man opposite him bearing no resemblance to Rosalind, looking very much like a country solicitor dressed in his best suit.

Algernon smiled. "I was thinking perhaps I could do something for you."

Ah, Fitz thought. *A man with a price.* "What exactly might that be?"

"Persuade my sister to sell her little bookstore."

Fitz's brows rose faintly. "You have no loyalty to your sister?"

"Rather, Your Grace, I consider family loyalty of greater import. Something, apparently, my sister fails to recognize. As you may know, my parents have little wealth, they're elderly, and I thought I might make it clear to Rosalind that she is now in a position"—he smiled silkily—"because of your generous offer, to alleviate the burdens of poverty for my parents."

"You are unable to do so?" A cool, gentle query.

"Alas, my country practice doesn't allow for such assistance. If only I could, of course, I'd be more than willing to relieve my parents' need."

"You think you might be successful in persuading your sister to change her mind?" Fitz's bland query belied his watchful gaze.

"If not, there are other ways to deal with her, Your Grace. From time to time, I take care of small legal issues for Rosalind. I drafted her husband's will, for instance, helped her with the death duties and such. She doesn't always take notice of what she's signing."

"So you would be willing to circumvent your sister's wishes?" Fitz said with deliberate composure.

"Only for the good of my parents, sir," Algernon suavely returned. "For no other reason. It's not as though Rosalind would suffer unduly. Your agent made it clear that she'd be amply compensated for her property."

"I see." Fitz wondered what he might have done a week ago with such an offer. "Let me think about your proposal," he said after a moment, setting his glass on the table beside his chair. "Leave me your direction. Where are you staying in London?"

Algernon shook his head. "I'm taking the train home today."

"Then I can find you in Yorkshire. In the meantime, let me offer you a small payment for your journey. Will five hundred do for now?" Fitz asked, taking money from his pocket. "My architect is redrawing my project, and once he's finished, I'll discuss this with you again. I appreciate your interest in helping your parents. Very commendable I'm sure." Taking out a large bill, he handed it to Algernon. "The merest down payment, sir. We'll be talking again in the near future. Now then, may I offer you a carriage for the ride to the station?"

His lip was curled in a faint sneer as he watched Rosalind's brother walk from the room. *What a thoroughly unlikeable fellow. A Judas.* He could have bought him for very little. He still might.

Which was the dilemma of course.

Which was why he was sitting in the empty reading room at Brooks's nursing a bottle of brandy, trying to deal with the chaos in his brain. Fuck. This wasn't supposed to have happened. None of it. Not the obstinate Mrs. St. Vincent throwing a wrench into his plans, particularly not her insinuating herself into his life and raising havoc with what had been prior to their meeting a perfectly contented and orderly existence.

He knew what the remedy was; he'd known almost from the first.

Put distance between himself and his craving.

Coming to his feet, he walked from the reading room, then from Brooks's, and swiftly made his way home. There was no need to wait until tomorrow to set off for Scotland.

In short order, Fitz was dressed in country tweeds, and along with Darby was boarding a train to Aberdeen. He was in too deep, thinking of Mrs. St. Vincent too much, going to see her like some love-struck callow youth. He might be headstrong, but he refused to be foolhardy. Not over some woman.

He'd even had Stanley telegraph ahead to insure that his gamekeeper and beaters were in readiness on his arrival. He'd concentrate on grouse hunting and salmon fishing as he'd done every August. *Before her*, the voice inside his head pithily noted.

For a fleeting moment, Fitz had debated taking Clarissa north with him but quickly dismissed the thought. If he was alone with the volatile Clarissa in the isolation of his hunting lodge he'd go out of his mind. In any event, there were local women enough to entertain him—should he be interested. Which choice of phrase stopped him cold. *Should he be interested?*

Bloody hell, since when wasn't he interested in fucking?

He was careful after that to make certain that he had distractions aplenty. He'd had Darby buy every magazine and paper at the station, and once on board, he immediately dispatched himself to the club car. As it turned out, several of his friends were traveling north for hunting, and thus he was able to divert himself enough that he managed to keep thoughts of Rosalind largely at bay.

When he stepped off the train in Aberdeen, he inhaled the cool air off the ocean, and sleepless during the long train ride, found himself looking forward to his bed. Not an immediate possibility with the lengthy drive to his lodge still before him, but in a little more than an hour he'd be snug in his hermitage.

*   *   *

AFTER THE THIRD day of waiting for Fitz to appear, Rosalind resigned herself to the fact that she'd been discarded like so many of his lovers. In that anxious time of expectation and dashed hopes, she'd experienced the full range of emotions: chagrin and humiliation, moping and discontent, even the occasional forlorn tear. But ultimately she'd come to the conclusion that rather than dwell on regret, she'd instead be grateful for the pleasure Fitz had given her, and get on with her life.

Never say she wasn't of a practical bent.

In fact, she'd had a lifetime of challenging experiences to nurture that pragmatism.

She actually slept for the first time that night, reconciled to the realities of Fitz's ephemeral passions and if not precisely content, at least no longer burdened with useless hope.

HAVING REACHED WHAT she felt was a reasonable assessment of her brief and pleasant liaison with Fitz, Rosalind was surprised at the hot wave of jealousy that swept over her when Clarissa walked into her shop two days later. Not that she knew her name; she knew only that the woman had been with Fitz at the Turner exhibit and had flaunted her intimacy with him as a lover would.

The pretty blonde was even more voluptuous at close range, Rosalind peevishly thought, her summer walking dress of rose pique displaying her considerable assets in the form-fitting style currently in fashion. Her breasts were impressive under the tailored bodice, as was her wasp waist and the swelling curve of her hips. She wore a wide-brimmed leghorn straw hat embellished with large cabbage roses and gracefully tipped to one side in order to display her magnificent ear drops of pink diamonds.

Her stylish appearance made Rosalind feel dowdy and graceless in her plain blue skirt and white blouse. She might as well have had a sign on her forehead that proclaimed *Shopkeeper,* she sourly reflected.

Clarissa didn't even bother to pretend she'd come in for a book. She made directly for Rosalind, recognizing her as the woman Fitz had followed out of the Turner exhibit. Coming to a stop before the counter, she placed her fingertips encased in fine white kidskin on the countertop, leaned forward slightly, and said with a distinct scowl, "Where's Fitz? Tell me."

Rosalind was taken aback at the sharpness of her tone *and* her startling demand.

"You needn't look so surprised. I know you're taking him to bed," Clarissa tartly said. What she didn't say was that her maid had spoken to a maid at Groveland House and she'd discovered that the bookstore lady from the Turner exhibit was regarded as Fitz's latest paramour.

That she'd resisted the inclination to view her competition for so long had to do with her tiresome husband's unexpected return to the city on business. She'd been obliged to play the dutiful wife—disgusting role—but he was gone once again and she very much deserved a reward. So she was here for a dual purpose: to see her rival and also find Fitz, the latter far outweighing petty curiosity.

"For heaven's sake, speak up. Tell me where he is this instant." After several days of Harold's unrelenting tyranny, she needed some personal gratification, and who better than Fitz to deliver pleasure?

"I have no idea where he is," Rosalind cooly replied, tamping down her temper with effort. Already feeling deprived with Fitz having decamped, Rosalind was accutely sensitive to the differences between herself and this intruder; the stark contrast between the chic aristocrat's wealthy trappings and her relatively meager ones not only aggravated her but also put her out of humor. "You might want to check his home," she sullenly said.

"I already have, you simpleton," Clarissa snapped. "No one knows where he's gone." Julia had been away from home, not that she would have enlightened Clarissa in any event. As for the servants, they knew better than to divulge the whereabouts of the duke. "Do you expect him tonight? We both know he's been sleeping with you."

Rosalind nervously glanced around, the woman's voice having risen in volume. "I haven't seen him for days," she quickly replied, needing to rid herself of this dangerous interrogator before a customer took notice. This was not the time for false modesty since the woman knew Fitz had been with her. "I have no idea of his whereabouts and I doubt I'll see him again."

"Is that so?" Clarissa's smile was gloating. "I suppose he tired of your common ways," she snidely declared, surveying Rosalind with a contemptuous glance. "Dear Fitz has such a droll sense of adventure, not to mention a libertine's indiscretion. He allays his boredom with women like you," she said with pointed rudeness. "I hope you didn't get your hopes up."

Rosalind swallowed her heated retort. She dared not antagonize this woman, the risk too great with customers near. "I believe you're right. Ultimately, he *was* bored." She even went so far as to look down in feigned mortification.

"I do believe you're toying with me, you little trollop," Clarissa murmured. "If you're not telling me the truth about Fitz's whereabouts, I'll make a scene, you little bitch." Her smile was chill. "Consider your reply carefully, Mrs. St. Vincent. I care nothing for your reputation."

Having been unmasked as an actress, Rosalind was momentarily at a loss. She wished to ask, *How do you know my name?* But more important, she needed this woman gone. "As you apparently know, the duke visited on occasion, but I assure you, he left several days ago without mentioning his plans. I have no idea where he is. And that's the truth."

Clarissa stared at her, her gaze coldly appraising.

Rosalind turned red under the scrutiny. "If it matters," she said, "I have no illusions about my position in the duke's life. We are the merest acquaintances." There, that was the best she could do other than pray for deliverance.

"Hmm…" Clarissa weighed Rosalind's words for a moment. With deceit so prevalent in her life, she recognized dishonesty better than most. "You're right, of course," she finally said. "It's best you have no illusions about Fitz. He's quite out of reach for someone like you." Then without another word, she turned and swept from the store.

Only after Clarissa's carriage pulled away from the curb did Rosalind allow herself a sigh of relief. Disaster had been averted.

And whomever her fashionable visitor had been, the lady wasn't likely to return—rather like Fitz, Rosalind ruefully decided.

NOR DID SHE see him in the following week, her life reverting once again to a familiar routine.

Sofia stopped by to visit, and Rosalind's Saturday night lecture was a smashing success thanks to the strong interest in new job opportunities for females of the laboring class. The lecture offered definitive information on the skills required, suggested various scholarships that were available for training programs, and explained how to apply not only for them but also for college scholarships at schools receptive to women. The enthusiasm of her audience was heartwarming. Rosalind felt as though she was making a small difference in the lives of the working poor.

Her sense of satisfaction was partially mitigated by the lingering sense of loss over Fitz. But she wasn't so foolish as to expect to see him again. She knew better; it would just take time to forget him.

And so Sofia reminded her. Since she was the quintessential person to give advice about leaving lovers behind, Rosalind couldn't discount her counsel. But after the Saturday night lecture, when Sofia suggested, "Let me have Arthur bring along a friend tomorrow. We'll go on a picnic," Rosalind shook her head.

"I wouldn't be very good company."

Sprawled on the sofa as usual, Sofia studied Rosalind

for a moment "How long has it been?" There was no need to elaborate.

"Slightly more than a week—ten days actually."

"You know, darling, he's not apt to come back. It's just his way," her friend added, looking at Rosalind over her wineglass. "He's a selfish man."

"I know." Rosalind smiled faintly. "I'm fine—really. I don't talk about him with anyone but you. And I'm getting better."

"You are. I saw you laugh tonight—more than once."

"The crowd was wonderful, wasn't it—so engaged and interested, asking questions for such a long time. I think we might have helped those three young women apply for college, too."

"Indeed we did," Sofia said with a grin. "You have become our local benefactor, Mrs. St. Vincent of Bruton Street Books."

Rosalind grimaced. "That reminds me—the word *benefactor*," she explained. "My brother sent me another carping letter, reminding me that it was my *duty* to be the benevolent hand of charity for my family."

"What he really means is for him," Sofia grunted out, having met Rosalind's brother.

"Exactly. In fact, Mother has written to say both she and Father are quite content with whatever I decide. They are in no need of money." Rosalind smiled. "Which is very sweet of Mother, who has been stretching Father's meager income for years."

"Then your brother can go to hell," Sofia brusquely said, up-to-date on the state of Algernon's coercive measures.

"I said as much to him in my last letter, although perhaps more diplomatically."

"I'm not so sure diplomacy works with him. You might have to be blunt or he'll never give up. He wants that money."

"Well, he's not getting it."

"Nor is Groveland it seems," Sofia pointed out with a

lift of her brows. "He's not sent over any agents lately, has he?"

"No. I think he understands my position. I was very plain about my feelings on several occasions."

"So at least something good came from your friendship. He has ceased making demands."

"Yes, apparently." *He's ceased making demands of any kind, unfortunately.* "Naturally, I appreciate his kindness and consideration," Rosalind said, complimenting herself for her maturity and practicality. *As if you have a choice*, the unhelpful voice inside her head pointed out.

CHAPTER 27

NOT MORE THAN five hours later, in the dead of night, Rosalind came awake to the sounds of an ax breaking down her door and in due time, learned to her disgust and chagrin that the Duke of Groveland was not in the least kind and considerate.

She barely had time to throw on a dressing robe before her bedchamber was invaded and she was read her arrest warrant by a beefy constable who clearly took pleasure in citing each of the obscenity laws she was accused of violating. It was also plain that he found a woman who wrote erotica repugnant, for he'd look up from time to time as he laboriously read the legal citation and glare at her with contempt.

She unflinchingly met his contempt. The Pitt-Riverston bloodlines preceded the Norman invasion; she could stare down any second-rate functionary.

While the red-faced officer droned on, Edward's manuscripts were being dragged from the armoire by two of the dozen men who had swarmed into her bedroom, and Rosalind suspected this assault was related to Mr. Edding's surveillance. But it wasn't until her unfinished manuscript was plucked from her desk drawer that she experienced alarm. Now *she* was implicated and any possible hope of evasion was gone.

Once the evidence was in the policemen's hands, she was allowed only a brief opportunity to dress. Even more mortifying, two constables remained in her bedroom while she changed behind a screen in the corner. It wasn't until she'd been shoved into a closed police wagon and the door locked behind her, that she had a moment to gather her thoughts.

Or try. Myriad questions raced through her mind: How could she, perhaps along with Mr. Edding, have been exposed? What or whom had first brought him under surveillance? How was the location of Edward's manuscripts known when Mr. Edding had never been in her apartment? The police had gone directly to the armoire.

Was it possible Edward had mentioned the location to Mr. Edding? She doubted it. They didn't appear to be more than acquaintances from what she'd gathered. Had Mr. Edding drawn the attention of the constabulary for some other infraction and she'd simply been dragged in by accident? Had he been arrested tonight as well? Not that the origin or motive behind her arrest particularly mattered now that she was on her way to gaol. Her immediate dilemma was how best to confront the criminal charges against her.

If she had any hope of prevailing against the accusations, the first thing she must do is find a competent barrister *and* the necessary funds for his services. Groveland's offer immediately came to mind of course. There was no other way she could secure the large sum required to defend against a case as serious as hers.

Even as she came to the conclusion that Fitz's offer was her only salvation, a more damning thought insinuated itself into her consciousness. A notion so malevolent, she quickly brushed it aside. But no matter how many times she dismissed the scurrilous idea, her mind refused to be diverted and presently, she was forced to at least entertain the possibility that Fitz might be involved. Because the simple fact was: other than Sofia, no one but Fitz had been in her bedroom since she'd begun writing for Mr. Edding. And clearly, Sofia was not a suspect.

Unwilling to acknowledge Fitz's infamy, she tried to conceive of some other causative link that might have brought the police to her door. She *must* have overlooked some other connection, she insisted, not wishing to admit to something so dastardly. Fitz simply couldn't be so tender and indulgent and then turn on her with such sinister purpose. Unless he was a monster in the Dr. Jekyll and Mr. Hyde vein.

At base though, even should diabolical behavior be involved, Fitz's offer for her store was her only hope. Her parents couldn't help, and while her brother was perhaps slightly more prosperous, he wasn't likely to come to her aid when he wanted her to sell her store anyway. So, Fitz's offer, iniquitous as it might be, was in the way of a last resort.

Not that she didn't desperately long for some reasonable explanation that would exonerate Fitz. *Stupid fool*, she thought with a grimace. Half in love with him, she was willing to forgive him anything. Like all the other women he'd known.

Rosalind's musing was curtailed as the wagon came to a halt at the station house and she was unceremoniously pulled from the wagon and marched to a cell. While Captain Bagley had taken it upon himself to serve the warrant for reasons of personal gain and moral duty, the private warrant also signified an offender of possible gentility— as did the woman's hauteur, he disgruntledly noted. He decided it might be circumspect to separate her from the rabble in the common holding cell.

Rosalind, unaware of her special treatment, took one look around the small wretched cell and decided she'd remain standing until such a time as she was allowed to see a barrister. The stone floor and walls were damp, small puddles evident in low areas of the floor, the single, barred window too high to reach, although a sliver of moonlight dimly illuminated the area. A plank bed with a stained blanket hung from chains on the wall, and a low sink apparently was meant to function as both a toilet and wash basin. She shuddered.

Never one to be fainthearted, however, she gave herself a bracing talking-to, told herself she would seek justice in the morning, and began to pace. Now, how best to secure a barrister, she reflected, trying to organize a plan of action as well as distract herself from her sordid surroundings.

First, she would not become demoralized or tearful over the necessity of selling her store. She'd simply buy another with what money remained after her trial, she briskly decided. That she might be convicted, she'd not even consider. It wasn't as though she hadn't faced serious challenges before in her life. There was no point in bemoaning one's fate. Right now, she needed solutions.

AN HOUR AFTER the cell door closed on Rosalind, Prosper Hutchinson was wakened by his valet.

"A message, sir. I was told to see that you received it immediately."

Under the light of the kerosene lamp in his valet's hand, Hutchinson read the note, crumpled it in his hand, and immediately abandoned his bed. "Don't wake up, dear," he said as his wife turned over and gazed at him with drowsy eyes. "I'll be back by breakfast."

As he swiftly dressed, he asked for details on who'd delivered the note and when. *Damned idiot in Brewster's office, but at least the clerk had the good sense to alert me.* Then he swore roundly, consigning all the incompetents in the bureaucracy to hell. "Sorry, Philip," he muttered, "but this is going to be one helluva mess. Have the carriage brought round."

"I have already, sir." The elderly man spoke with the immutable calm of an experienced retainer. "It's beginning to rain out. You'd best wear your mackintosh," he added holding out the coat.

Five minutes later, swearing under his breath, Prosper was being driven across town to the police station near Bruton Street. A short time later, after accosting the stout, obstinate constable who was captain on the night shift, Prosper's curses were decidedly more forceful.

"I done my duty, sar, and that's that," Captain Bagley said, his mouth and jaw set firmly. He didn't approve of taking the Lord's name in vain. "That female prisoner ain't goin' nowhere."

Hutchinson glared at the heavyset man behind the desk. "Who authorized her arrest, dammit! There were distinct orders to hold the warrant until further notice!"

"It ain't right, sar, to ignore criminal activity, no matter what. The law's the law fer you and me and everyone," the captain stubbornly declared, a pious fanatic against all forms of what he perceived as vice.

"Who's your superior, you imbecile!" Hutchinson shouted. "You had no right to serve that warrant!"

"I don't rightly know that it's any of your business, sar," the constable pugnaciously replied. "I'm in charge here tonight."

"Damn right it's my business, and when I've gotten to the bottom of this fiasco, you'll be out of a job, you cretin!"

"That may be, but I doubt it. Ain't right fer anyone to athwart the law," Captain Bagley muttered belligerently. "The prisoner is guilty as sin," he added with a sneer. "We found all the evidence we need right there in her house— no mistake."

Short of shooting the stupid oaf where he sat, Prosper had no recourse but to return to his carriage and hie himself to the home of one of the judges he knew who owed him a favor.

Even there, he was foiled.

"Once the lady is jailed, she passes into one of Her Majesty's prisons to await trial at Clerkenwell or Central Criminal Court."

"I know that, dammit! I also know she won't stand trial for at least a month."

"I'm sorry, Prosper, but I can't simply override an arrest warrant"—Judge Hillard shot his friend a jaundiced look as they sat in opposing chairs in his study—"that you yourself instituted by the way."

"It was on hold until final approval." Prosper's hands were clenching and unclenching on the leather chair arms. "How the hell it made it's way to Bruton Street Station is an issue I'll deal with later. I want her out—*now*!"

"I wish I could help you, but my hands are tied. And unfortunately, Captain Bagley is known to have a crusading zeal when it comes to enforcing the obscenity laws."

"I want him cashiered," Prosper said coldly, leaning back in his chair and meeting the judge's gaze with an icy stare.

"In due time, my friend. It's certainly not going to happen tonight. If I might be so bold as to ask, why this raging urgency at this ungodly hour? Is the lady a friend of yours?" he slyly inquired. "And more to the point," the judge added with roguish smile, "does she indeed write lewd stories?"

"Judas Priest, William. I have neither the time nor the inclination for adultery or any interest in satisfying your salacious queries. If you must know, the lady is a special friend of an important client."

The judge's gaze narrowed. "How important?"

"Important enough for you to make sure the lady is freed in the morning. I don't care what you have to do, just do it." Prosper smiled thinly. "My client will reward you generously."

"Christ, Prosper, you're asking too much. I'm not sure I can do it. The court views these cases of moral depravity harshly. I can't guarantee her release."

"He's a duke."

"I'll see what I can do."

"Thank you," Prosper crisply replied and rose to his feet. "I'll wait to hear from you."

But he dared not wait to notify the duke, and to that end, he had himself driven to a telegraph office where he sent Groveland the unhappy news. Since Prosper handled his business affairs, Fitz generally left word of his destination on leaving the city.

Early the next morning, at the same time Rosalind was watching a tin plate of unappetizing porridge being slid through a slot at the base of her cell door, Hutchinson's telegram was delivered to Fitz's dressing room where he was being shaved.

For a moment his heart seemed to stop.

"Have a mount saddled," Fitz barked, frightening a servant who was carrying away his breakfast tray with the rough fury in his voice. "Now!" he shouted at the terrified man. "Give me that," he growled, swiping the razor from Darby's grasp and lunging to his feet. "Rosalind's been arrested, damn someone's stupidity." Striding to the mirror, he proceeded to shave himself with rough, quick strokes.

Wiping the lather from his face, he dropped the towel, grabbed the shirt Darby held out, and shoved his arms into the sleeves. "Follow me later. I'll commandeer whatever train's in the station, so you'll have to take the next one." He wrenched his trousers from Darby's grasp and jerked them on. Three minutes later, dressed and booted, he was taking the stairs at a run.

Reaching the drive a few moments later, he leaped into the saddle, waved off the groom, and spurred his mount.

He rode to Aberdeen like a man possessed, using whip and spur, his racer gallantly responding. The Thoroughbred was lathered and winded by the time they reached the station. Tossing the reins and two guineas to a street boy, Fitz shouted directions to his hunting lodge as he ran toward the platforms. Fortunately, the stationmaster knew him, his consequence and fortune, and quickly accommodated his wishes. Conductors were sent through the station, warning travelers of the imminent departure, and short minutes later, the engine pulled out of the station an hour early.

Fitz had much too much time on the journey south to reflect on all that had gone wrong. He was to blame of course. There was no excusing his orders to have an arrest warrant drawn up. Not that it was supposed to have been served without his permission. Yet, regardless the reason for the blunder, it was he who had agreed to the scheme. Calling himself every kind of blackguard and villain, he stared blankly out the train window, the image of Rosalind suffering in some revolting cell looping through his brain, torturing him, consuming him.

What had seemed a perfectly reasonable expedient—good business, in fact—only brief days ago had turned to disaster. Rosalind was in gross danger in the terrifying stew of humanity inhabiting a prison, exposed and defenseless against the scandal ensuing from her arrest as well, at risk of complete ruin.

Thanks to him.

He was in agony, tormented by visions of her vulnerable and alone in the noisome environs of a jail, and in his anguish he no longer questioned what she meant to him. He cared for her in untold ways distinct from lust and passion. In ways so baffling and unorthodox he could neither identify nor put a name to his feelings. Not that he'd admit to something so binding and heartfelt as love. Old habits die hard.

But he couldn't avoid his feelings, whatever they were.

You can run, but you can't hide, he decided with a rueful smile, reflecting on his wretchedly unhappy sojourn in Scotland.

Now, whether he'd be able to repair the damage wrought by this botched affair was another question.

Christ—Rosalind took issue over something as simple as him sending over a doctor. He rather doubted she'd be quick to forgive him after having been thrown in jail.

But do something he must, although he'd not come up

with any useful redress by the time he stepped from the train.

Hutchinson was waiting for him on the platform, the stationmaster in Aberdeen having telegraphed ahead with the duke's arrival time.

"A major fuck-up it seems," Fitz murmured as Hutchinson quickly fell in line beside him. "Is she out?"

"No, I'm sorry to say, Your Grace. It was the most egregious error, and no one seems capable of setting it right."

"We'll take care of it now." Crisp authority in every syllable.

Hutchinson was feeling considerably less assured after having called in a great number of markers today to no avail. "I feel I should warn you, Your Grace. The law courts can be extremely uncompromising when it comes to obscenity cases such as this. I've talked to more than a dozen people today with little result."

"Tell me what's transpired on our drive to the station," Fitz said, lengthening his stride.

Hutchinson started running.

Once they were in the carriage, the barrister explained as best he knew, all that had occurred. First, a clerk's error had mistakenly sent the envelope with the arrest warrant from the judge's chambers to the Bruton Street Station. Second, even though the envelope had been clearly marked *Private; Hold*, Captain Bagley had taken it upon himself to open the superintendent's mail and then took it upon himself to save the world from what he had characterized as *foul smut and depravity*.

"After failing to persuade Captain Bagley to release Mrs. St. Vincent, I attempted to find a judge who could free her from gaol. I spoke to several, Your Grace, but I was told by each that there are strict procedures that can't be altered. A hearing before the court is required."

"Like hell," Fitz muttered. "But thank you for trying, Hutchinson," he added, offering Hutchinson a kindly smile. "Once we reach the station, I'll do the talking."

"As you wish, Your Grace, but I must caution you about

expecting too much. I've been working on this all day with nothing to show for my efforts."

Fitz flashed his barrister a smile. "Don't worry, Hutchinson. All will be well." And as he spoke, an idea leaped into his mind, without reason, quite illogical in fact, but the more he thought about it, he warmed to the notion, damned if he didn't.

Fitz chatted on the remainder of the drive to the police station, his cheerfulness and good humor causing Hutchinson a certain unease. Had the duke taken leave of his senses when faced with the chaos and confusion of the situation? Was he overcompensating somehow for his plans having gone awry? Or was he drunk and not showing it?

But on arriving at the station, Fitz gracefully leaped from the carriage without any sign of stumbling or awkwardness, and Hutchinson was forced to relinquish his drunkenness theory. He wasn't yet willing to discount the other impairments, however.

He was soon dissuaded of the duke's possible derangement, though, for the moment they stood before the superintendent in charge of the station on the day shift, the duke said crisply, "I'm Groveland. I've come for my wife. I believe she was mistakenly arrested last night. If she is released immediately, I won't be inclined to sue."

Then the duke smiled, Hutchinson noted, with the most benign sweetness and added, "I understand perfectly how mistakes can be made."

When the superintendent exhibited a modicum of suspicion and failed to move, Fitz said, "Come, my good man. If you have a wife, surely you understand Lady Groveland must be fit to be tied by now. I shall be obliged to pay handsomely for this mistake, regardless of whose error it was." He smiled faintly. "But the little ladies are worth all the trouble, are they not? Can't live without 'em, although," he said with a wink, "I'd trade the next few hours with you if you know what I mean."

"Yes, sar, the wife does go on a tear at times," the superintendent cautiously replied, weighing the illustriousness of the man standing before him. There were nobles and there were nobles. "The thing is, sar, the lady isn't Lady Groveland, but a Mrs. St. Vincent," he submitted. "Said so right on the warrant it did."

"Yes, I know." Fitz offered the superintendent a long-suffering sigh. "I'm afraid my wife has fallen under the spell of the suffrage movement and uses her maiden name at times. A most curious group of women if you ask me—those suffragettes—forever petitioning Parliament and chaining themselves to fences about town. But Lady Groveland wishes to play the role of a modern woman, so naturally, I'm willing to indulge her—to a point," he gruffly added. "I've financed a small bookstore for her so she may pretend to be a businesswoman. The store is Lady Groveland's version of Marie Antoinette's little hamlet—you recall... where the queen played at being a milkmaid." A lift of his brows. "It all comes down to the need for domestic tranquility, my good man. I'm sure you have occasion to indulge your wife's whims as well. Not that the genders are born to agree, but there it is."

"Mrs. Wilton has taken up tennis, sar, so I do know what you mean. Sweaty business, that. Although, there's another bit of business, sar. A right lot of bawdy books were found in the lady's bedroom."

"Ah, yes... those are mine. Lady Groveland is quite innocent of such matters as naturally a woman should be." Fitz smiled. "She prefers poetry—sunny skies and flower-filled fields... that sort of thing. Like most women, I suppose."

"The books are yours? You'd swear to that?"

"Indeed I would. Feel free to fine me for the infraction; most men indulge in an earthy story from time to time as you no doubt know. Although, I understand that your subordinate took it upon himself to open an envelope marked *Private*. Perhaps it would be best not to have that brought up in court."

Superintendent Wilton flushed, then frowned. "Unfortunately, Captain Bagley's a lay preacher in a fire-and-brimstone street church. He sees sin around every corner. Personally, I'm Church of England—a sensible church that. In charge of the religious holidays and pomp-and-circumstance occasions, otherwise it stays out of your life. And rightly so."

"I couldn't agree more. As a duke, naturally, I have responsibilities in the various parishes on my estates, but my clerics have instructions not to interfere in my villagers' lives."

The superintendent's eyes widened. If this man was a duke, the lady in his jail was a duchess and all hell would break loose if word got out that he'd arrested a duchess. He couldn't afford to be sacked. "Bagley was out of line, Your Grace, no doubt about it. I'll see that Lady Groveland is released immediately." Before word of her arrest leaked out.

"Excellent, thank you. Why don't you get Mrs. Wilton some little trifle," Fitz murmured, pulling a bill from his pocket and placing it on the superintendent's desk. "Purely a charitable contribution," he added with a smile.

The constable's eyes popped on seeing the thousand-pound banknote.

The money, together with the fact that a duke was in fact, if not theory, above the law, and that the woman in jail was Lady Groveland, was more than any underpaid government employee could overlook with impunity. "I'll have Lady Groveland fetched right quick, Your Grace. And may I offer my apologies for the misunderstanding."

"I'll come with you," Fitz said, wanting to personally apprise Rosalind of her new status. He wasn't altogether certain she would agree with his story unless he was there to prompt her.

CHAPTER 28

THE CELL DOOR opened, and Rosalind turned around to find a uniformed policeman with Fitz standing behind him, a finger to his lips.

Her first impulse was to fly at him screaming in rage.

Her second more practical reaction was to quietly wait for events to unfold. Time enough for vengeance. Although Fitz's appearance probably meant that hiring a barrister wouldn't be required—which also meant she could keep her store. *That* in itself qualified as revenge.

Fitz took note of her smug smile and inwardly winced.

Not that he didn't deserve her displeasure, but he wasn't looking forward to the coming row. He had no experience with truckling.

"Lady Groveland, allow me to apologize for the shocking miscarriage of justice," the superintendent said with a stiff bow and a nervous smile. "You have been most grossly served by Captain Bagley. I assure you he will be severely punished for his conduct." Red faced, the superintendent swallowed hard and putting a finger to the brim of his hat, bobbed another awkward bow. "My apologies again, my lady. You're quite free to go."

Rosalind dipped her head with ducal grace. "Your apologies are accepted, sir." She smiled. "It was rather an adventure. And I'm quite unscathed. Hello, my dear," she said, turning a bland gaze on Fitz. "Thank you for arriving so swiftly."

"I would have come sooner had I not been in Scotland shooting. Naturally, I apologize for my tardiness."

"No need. I was indisposed for a very short time."

The superintendent stepped aside so Rosalind could exit the cell, his concern only that the duke and duchess be gone from his station as quickly as possible and more important, that no scandal accrue to him.

Fitz held out his arm as Rosalind entered the corridor.

She looked up and held his gaze for a potent moment before placing her fingers on his forearm. "How was the shooting?"

"It could have been better," he said, moving down the hallway.

"I'm sorry to hear it."

"Not as sorry as I was to hear of your difficulties."

"Pshaw, it was nothing. Don't give it another thought."

Her fingers were digging into his arm, and if looks could kill, he would have been dead. But she carried off her role with aplomb, even while they were in the carriage with Hutchinson. It was only when they deposited the barrister at his home that she turned on Fitz, her eyes flashing with anger.

"Aren't you going to say it wasn't you?" she demanded acidly.

"Would it do any good?"

"Not in the least." Quickly rising, she shifted to the opposite seat where Hutchinson had been sitting and coldly said, "Take me home."

"Just for the record I didn't order the arrest. It was a mistake." He knew better than to offer the most bland demur. He had no real defense in any event.

"But a mistake you had a hand in," she snapped. "You were the one who told them where to find the manuscripts, weren't you?"

"No." A literal if not complete truth.

"You bloody liar," she hissed. "No one else has been in my bedroom."

This wasn't the time to take heart at such news, but nevertheless he did, pleased that he alone had breached the citadel. Equally pleased after his lamentable time in Scotland that she was within reach, regardless her temper. "I'd like to make amends if you'd let me," he quietly said. "You need but tell me what to do."

She stared at him. "You're unbelievable! You think this some mild outrage that can be smoothed over with a bloody apology? You think my arrest is some mere bagatelle that won't cause a ripple in my life, that I can put this humiliation behind me with ease!" Her voice had risen, a flush colored her cheeks. "How *dare* you make light of this!"

"I'm not," he muttered, willing to play the penitent for the wrong done Rosalind. "I understand the delicacy of the situation."

"*Delicacy!* We're not talking about some social gaffe! My door broken down and police swarming into my store is not a *delicate situation*!"

"I understand," he said, submitting with grace. "I'll make it up to you. Tell me what you want."

She glared at him. "How typical. Everyone's for sale, aren't they, you bastard? Maybe in your world they are, but not in mine. Do me a favor," she spat out. "From now on stay away from me and my store."

"What if I don't? Are you going to call the police?" He was struggling to control his temper. Groveling wasn't his strong suit. Nor did women ordinarily scream at him.

"Good Lord, Groveland," Rosalind waspishly said, "surely you have any number of other ladies you can harass. Kindly acquit me of your attentions."

"I don't recall you being particularly discontent with my attentions in the past," he drawled. Scotland had been disagreeable and unsatisfactory from every angle. He hadn't slept much in over a week. And Rosalind's damned arrest hadn't been his fault exclusively or at all, he churlishly decided, since he'd never actually given the order to proceed.

"You'd be surprised what an arrest and a night in a foul jail can do to a sexual relationship," she derisively noted. "You might want to think about excising that little subtlety from your future seductions."

Bitch, he thought, although he couldn't fault her logic. "Look," he softly said, making a conscious effort to reduce the heated rhetoric, "none of this should have happened. I'm sorry it did. And I understand you're angry"—he paused at her indignant snort, counted quickly to ten, then continued in a purposefully mild tone—"but I'm quite willing to do anything to atone for the wrong that's been done you. I won't press you anymore to sell your store. How would that be?" It was a huge concession, a very expensive one.

"Don't do me any bloody favors. For your information, I wouldn't sell to you if I was penniless and starving. Now, I'm done talking," she tartly added. "Take me home."

"And if I don't?" Equally frustrated, unequipped as well to deal with resistance when he'd encountered little to none since assuming the title at seventeen, he reverted to type. "What are you going to do about it?"

"I'll jump from this carriage and walk home. Now give your driver directions or I'll jump."

Reaching out, he smoothly locked both doors, then leaned back in his seat. "Don't tell me what to do."

Her nostrils flared. "This is exactly why we don't suit. I don't take orders either."

"Sometimes you do."

She braced her hands on the seat and lifted her chin in defiance. "I am vastly uninterested in sex with you, you ruthless bastard! If you dare touch me, I'll fight you to my last breath."

Astonished at the bitterness in her voice, he took pause. While he'd never yet been unable to talk his way into a lady's good graces, he'd never had a woman thrown in jail before. He had to admit, it was an extreme event; perhaps different skills were required. "Relax," he calmly said. "I'm not looking for a fight."

"I'm relieved." Sarcasm dripped from every icy syllable.

Reaching up, he rapped on the carriage roof. "Bruton Street Books," he called out.

The remainder of the journey passed in silence.

Seated in the corner, her scowling gaze focused on the scene outside, Rosalind stewed and silently condemned Fitz to the everlasting fires of hell.

Lounging in the opposite corner, Fitz closed his eyes and dozed off.

Damn him, she fumed, even more furious on hearing his soft snores. *Isn't that just like the shameless, arrogant autocrat. Nothing fazes him because he is untouchable. The world bends to his will.*

The world well might, but she never would. *Never, never, never*, she vowed.

As the carriage stopped at her bookstore, Fitz came awake and sliding upright, unlocked the door. "If you need anything, please don't hesitate to call," he offered, all well-mannered grace—as if she'd not spent the previous night in a filthy jail cell because of him, as if they hadn't just quarreled, as if she'd not coldly repudiated his attempts to apologize.

"Don't hold your breath," she snapped.

"As you wish," he murmured, not saying more since the driver had jumped down, opened the door, lowered the step, and was waiting to help her alight.

Rosalind shot him a last irate look, stepped from the carriage, and was immediately overcome by a fresh wave of rage. Her shattered front door had been replaced, the new door the very image of the former, down to the yellow paint and brass hinges. Damn Fitz and his money and minions who jumped to do his bidding. Had the man ever *once* been gainsaid in his entire life?

Apparently not—at least to this point, she huffily reflected, entering her store to find an unknown man behind the counter and the shop bustling with customers.

"Good afternoon, Mrs. St. Vincent," Stanley courteously said in greeting. "Did you enjoy your holiday in the country?"

Biting down her anger, she answered with equal politesse. "Indeed I did. Thank you for taking over in my absence."

"My pleasure, Mrs. St. Vincent. Miss Eastleigh is upstairs waiting for you."

Did nothing fall outside Groveland's purview, she indignantly brooded as she walked through the store. Next thing she knew, her parents would be coming to visit. Or some long lost childhood friend. Damn his interference!

As she walked into her parlor a few moments later, Sofia jumped to her feet. "Thank God you're back. Was it gruesome?"

"Yes, it was. Who's that man downstairs?"

"Groveland's secretary. There're other servants in the back of the store."

"Who summoned you?"

"I didn't ask his name. A solicitor I'd guess from his appearance and manner. Come sit down. You must be exhausted. He said you'd been arrested."

"I'm fine now," Rosalind said, dropping into a chair, profoundly grateful to be home. "Have you been here long?"

"Since morning."

Rosalind held Sofia's gaze. "Who else knows?"

"No one. Workmen were repairing the door when I arrived at seven, the shop was filled with Groveland's flunkeys, and the solicitor who brought me here in his carriage explained I alone had been summoned since we were close friends."

"Christ. Is there anything they don't know?"

"It doesn't seem so. A chef and his helpers brought over food and wine and stocked your larder; some maidservants straightened up the apartment, changed the linens, and took the soiled things away."

"Damn him," Rosalind muttered.

"For what precisely if you don't mind my asking?"

"I was arrested because of him. Because of my store, I suspect, although we weren't precisely on good enough speaking terms for me to ask for details. The police took all Edward's manuscripts from the armoire as well as mine from my desk drawer and no one knew of their location."

"Except Groveland."

"Yes, except him."

"Because he snooped in your bedroom."

Rosalind scowled. "He's utterly ruthless when he wants something."

"Now what?"

Her expression lightened. "Now I keep my store for certain. He won't dare press me after what he did to me."

"How do you know you're safe if he's as ruthless as you say?"

"He tried to apologize—at least at first," Rosalind explained.

"He did? Hardly his style." Sofia had been in company with Groveland at enough art events to be aware of his patrician air of command. Not that he was arrogant; rather, he was unaware of dissent since his wishes were largely unchallenged. Or perhaps always unchallenged.

"I wouldn't know," Rosalind said with a shrug. "Maybe he'll change his mind. Not that I care a whit. I had no intention of selling before, and after my recent experience in jail, I certainly won't now." She pushed herself out of the comfortable chair, suddenly feeling weary to the bone. "I need a bath and some sleep. I didn't dare sit down all night. The place was squalid."

"I'll make you tea and a plate of some of Groveland's chef's delicacies."

"If I wasn't so hungry, I'd spurn his food, but I haven't eaten for a very long time."

"Go, take your bath. I'll stay with you tonight."

"Thank you." Rosalind offered her friend a grateful smile. "I'm exhausted."

After Rosalind bathed, Sofia served her dinner in bed and listened to her postmortem of the frightening events. "He's exactly what I thought he was from the first: a selfish, uncompromising tyrant who simply wants what he wants without regard for anyone else," she bitterly finished. "I shouldn't have been foolish enough to have been taken in by his charm."

"At the risk of resorting to a platitude, all's well that ends well. You're free, you have your store," Sofia pointed out, not for the first time. In the interval before she fell into an exhausted sleep, Rosalind gave voice to the full tumult of her feelings, as if the horrific hours she'd recently survived required exorcizing. And more than once, she raged at Fitz for his role in her vile confinement. Then, as if her psyche was completely without judgment, after she dozed off, she dreamt of him.

Resting in a chair by the bed, Sofia heard Rosalind murmur Fitz's name in her sleep, with fondness and yearning. Not that her wistful longings were likely to prosper, Sofia decided, knowing Groveland's reputation for serial dalliance. But at least there was a possibility that Rosalind would no longer have to defend her store from his covetous ambitions. With luck, Sofia reflected. She wasn't entirely sure Groveland would give up so easily.

CHAPTER 29

FITZ SHOULD HAVE slept that night. Particularly since he'd slept little since leaving London—what was supposed to have been a holiday in Scotland having turned into a period of sleeplessness and drink. He'd hunted very little, indifferent to the sport for the first time in his life. Indifferent to everything for the first time in his life.

And the feeling apparently followed him to London.

Fuck.

Another problem—that had nothing to do with profanity. He found himself uninterested in sex unless Rosalind was involved, that disinterest not only disturbing to his bachelor spirit but also leaving him with considerable free time on his hands. He'd picked up the telephone to call Clarissa at least a dozen times that evening because fucking her was a mindless amusement and he could use both at the moment. But each time he'd stopped just short of making the call and poured himself another drink instead.

Christ, he hadn't been sober since leaving London.

Nor did he break the cycle in the next few hours.

It was nearly two when he walked into Stanley's bedroom and woke him. "I was wondering how your day at the bookstore went," he said to the startled young man he'd shaken awake. "Sorry," he said with a smile, "I can't sleep." As Stanley scrambled out of bed and pulled on his robe, Fitz sat down, took another drink from the bottle he'd brought with him, crossed his legs, and looked as though he was settling in for a lengthy conversation.

"Well, sir," Stanley mumbled, racking his brain for some pertinent facts with which to regale his master, who apparently hadn't slept since he was still dressed, albeit casually sans jacket and tie. "There was a steady stream of customers throughout the day, starting very early in the—"

"What did she look like when she walked in? Did she seem angry? Exhausted, I suppose. What did she say to you?"

Understanding the reason for this late night visit, Stanley took a chair across from Fitz. "Mrs. St. Vincent was very courteous, Your Grace. She asked no questions but replied to my greeting most graciously. She went directly upstairs when I told her Miss Eastleigh was waiting for her."

"She didn't seem angry?"

"No, sir, not at all."

"I thought I heard you up," Julia cheerfully noted as she walked into the room.

"You have excellent hearing, Mother," Fitz drawled, his mother's apartments well away from Stanley's room.

"I couldn't sleep," she pleasantly said, smoothly lying. Fitz had been closemouthed and drinking heavily when she'd come home from her evening's entertainment; she was concerned enough to check on him. "Is Stanley going to help at the bookshop again tomorrow?"

Fitz gave her a sardonic look as she stood in the doorway. "Do you know everything?"

"Really, darling, as if the servants don't talk. I hope Mrs. St. Vincent is none the worse for her unfortunate arrest." She could have been asking after Rosalind's bridge score so bland was her query.

"She's fine," Fitz brusquely replied.

"She looked quite well, Your Grace," Stanley politely interposed, trying to appear undisturbed by his employers' presence at two in the morning. "Her friend Miss Eastleigh said she fell asleep early."

"Excellent. I expect she was exhausted after her ordeal."

"Yes, apparently."

The dowager duchess smiled at her son. "You should do something nice for her, dear."

"I shall, Mother."

"But not jewelry, darling. She's not like the others, as you've already discovered."

He could have asked, *What would you suggest?* since he had no clue, but the last thing he wished to do at the moment was discuss his love life with his mother. "I'll think of something," he crisply said.

A small silence fell.

"I have some business to discuss with Stanley, Mother, if you don't mind," Fitz murmured, raising the bottle to his mouth and drinking a large draught.

A faint frown creased Julia's brow. "You've been drinking a good deal, darling."

"I'll stop tomorrow," he suavely said.

She pursed her lips at his facile and obvious mendacity. "Very well, darling." She nodded at Stanley. "Call for Darby if you need help getting him back to bed. I'll see you at breakfast, dear."

Once his mother was gone, Fitz peppered Stanley with further questions about Rosalind, the store, Sofia—well aware that he was obsessed yet unable to quell the formless turmoil in his mind. And drinking obviously wasn't the answer, if there even *was* an answer after his heated encounter with Rosalind in the carriage.

"I forgot to mention, sir, two of the footmen watered Mrs. St. Vincent's garden in the back. They said it was suffering from the heat."

A full-blown green and flowering prospect appeared in Fitz's mind, the closest thing to an epiphany he'd ever experienced. The weight of the world suddenly lifted from his shoulders. In preparation for bringing this newly revealed truth to fruition, Fitz set the liquor bottle on the floor, turned to Stanley, and smiled.

"What do you know about roses?"

"Very little, sir. That was my mother's domain, along with the gardener, of course."

"I need all the information you can find on rose gardens. First thing tomorrow. I'll talk to our gardeners as well. The roses out back seem to be flourishing. Those are roses, right—in those beds around the fountain?"

"Yes, sir."

"Good. Excellent. I'll let you get some rest now," Fitz said, coming to his feet, a plan quickly forming in his mind. "Thank you for your time."

"You're very welcome, Your Grace."

"You'll check on those roses first thing tomorrow?" he asked, moving toward the door.

"Immediately, sir."

"Perfect. You're a very accomplished young man, Stanley."

"Thank you, sir."

Fitz swung back as he reached the doorway. "I need a sizeable number of roses. Did I say that?"

"No, sir. How many would you like?"

"Enough to fill a small yard. I'm not exactly sure; I'll see that you get the dimensions."

Fitz strolled away, smiling, his spirits much improved. He rather thought he'd found something other than jewelry to warm the lady's heart.

CHAPTER 30

FITZ BUSIED HIMSELF writing two notes on his return to his apartments. The first he addressed to Sofia. He explained he needed her help, described briefly what he had in mind, and enclosed several large bills as a token of his appreciation. Next, he wrote to his architect a rather lengthier message, detailing some changes he required in the development plans for Monckton Row. He sealed both letters, set them on his desk for morning delivery, promptly went to bed, and slept like the proverbial baby.

He woke up at nine thoroughly refreshed, arranged for his messages to be delivered, quickly bathed and dressed, and arrived in the breakfast room well before his mother. In fact, he'd read most of the *Times* and was on his second helping from the array of food on the sideboard when Julia walked in, Pansy trotting at her heels.

Fitz looked up and smiled. "Good morning, Mother. I need some advice on roses."

"Certainly, dear. What would you like to know?" He wasn't drinking, he looked rested, he was dressed, and from the remains of food before him, he'd actually *eaten* something for breakfast. All clearly excellent signs.

"Have you ever had an epiphany?"

"Don't say you've turned religious," his mother responded, wondering if his present repudiation of drink had to do with some strange religious experience.

"No, Mother. Nothing so radical. An idea came to me last night completely without warning. A very good idea, I believe." He smiled. "Something for Rosalind other than jewels you'll be happy to know."

Julia's smile was sunshine bright. "I am indeed, although I knew you'd think of something, darling. She's a most delightful young woman. Unlike so many others you've amused yourself with," she added, sitting down at the table and nodding to have her coffee cup filled by a servant who stood by. "Not that a young man shouldn't take his pleasures, but I must admit, I'd hoped your heart wasn't involved with all the frivolous ladies of your acquaintance."

"Are you disparaging your own kind?" Fitz drolly inquired.

"I beg your pardon? I do believe I take an interest in things other than fashion and gossip. My racing stud is as good as yours, and if I didn't help support our local politicians, you would have to pay for all those elections on your own. Not to mention, my charities are well funded and well run."

"I was only teasing, Mother. You're not frivolous in the least."

"I should hope not. I forgot to mention my support of the suffrage movement. A cause by the way that Mrs. St. Vincent is actively involved in I understand."

Fitz looked up from his kippers. "Who told you that?"

"I forget," Julia airily replied, dropping two sugar lumps into her cup. "Now what's this about roses?" she queried, not wishing to continue a conversation about her monitoring Fitz's activities.

Understanding he was more or less defenseless against his mother's meddling, he decided he might as well put it to good use. "Recently, Rosalind saw a lovely rose garden and was lamenting about the state of her roses, which are a disaster even to my unpracticed eye. Things look rather brown and wilted—no doubt the hot weather is somewhat to blame. But, regardless," Fitz went on, leaning back in his chair, "I thought I'd surprise her with a rose garden—something green and lush and blooming. Bring her faded garden to life as it were and in the process, hopefully put myself back into her good graces."

"How clever you are."

His lashes lowered faintly. "We'll see. She may not like it."

"Of course she will. What woman doesn't like roses? Not one," Julia briskly said, answering her own question. "Now is this a surprise? It must be of course." She smiled. "Women love affectionate surprises as you no doubt know."

"I've noticed," Fitz murmured, smiling back. "I've already asked her friend, Miss Eastleigh, to lure her away from her apartment this evening in order to give us time to plant the garden."

"Capital! This will be such fun, darling. I'll ring up the gardener immediately and begin making plans."

"Stanley is doing some research on roses as well, so stop and see him on your way out. I'll see to the setting up of lights for the workmen. We won't have much time. Three hours at the most."

"Matheson will arrange for the men. And, darling, you can't imagine how many new roses have come on the market lately. Every woman I know has added scads of roses to her garden. I don't know if you've noticed, but your rose garden is rather nice out back."

"I have," he politely lied. "Thank you, your taste is excellent."

"A word of warning, darling; some women have what they call friendship gardens—you know, plants that are mementos of family and friends. So make sure nothing is pulled up that might have that look."

His brow furrowed. "That look? How do you recognize it?"

"Oh, dear, if I didn't have a diplomatic dinner to attend

with Kemal tonight, I'd come and oversee the project. Never fear," she crisply added, "I shall warn Matheson. He's very good, you know." An understatement for the man who managed all the lavish gardens on Fitz's estates. "Don't worry about a thing, darling. You will have your garden."

HIS MOTHER'S ASSURANCE wasn't sufficient to persuade Fitz that his gesture would produce the requisite results. Nor could he fault Rosalind for being angry with him. He had played a rather major role in her imprisonment; that it had all been a misguided blunder did not excuse him.

He was gratified to receive a reply from Sofia shortly after noon, promising to carry out his wishes. He went out to talk to Matheson after that, only to find that the head gardener and his mother were out shopping for roses. But in answer to his questions, another of the gardeners took him around the garden and pointed out a great variety of roses in every imaginable color. And none were in the least wilted, Fitz was pleased to see. Which meant he could indeed deliver on the little patch of Paradise he'd been picturing in his mind. Not that a few little trifles of jewelry might not be advisable. An added token of his affection just in case.

Which thought brought him to a standstill on the steps of the terrace, the essential question: exactly how much affection was involved in this effort of his? That decisive calculation was not yet completely resolved in his mind. He knew he wanted Rosalind more than he'd ever wanted anything, but for how long? he asked himself, not unaware of his past record with women. He must decide before he saw her again. This time, with this woman, he daren't make a mistake he'd live to regret.

Softly swearing, he continued his ascent and entered the house through the library. A few minutes later, he left word of his destination for his mother, and after a quick detour to Grey's, he rode out to Mertenside for the afternoon.

He needed peace and quiet.

He needed to think.

CHAPTER 31

"ARE YOU MAD? Why would I go to a Thompson lecture?"

"Because Dr. Maud Warren is giving the rebuttal," Sofia said, leaning against Rosalind's counter and smiling at her. "Maud's new research disputes all of old Thompson's outdated theories about women's inferiority. It should be exciting; the hall will be packed with women."

"I'm not sure I need that kind of excitement; the police will be there in force." The police presence at events such as this was meant to intimidate.

"We can sit in the back and leave if things get out of control. Say you'll come. Violet and Christina will be there. We should lend them our support."

The two young ladies were just beginning their college careers, having received scholarships at *Girton College, Cambridge*, thanks to Rosalind's training sessions. "If they're going to be there," Rosalind murmured, "perhaps we should go." Her Saturday night lectures *were* about inspiration and change after all.

"We'll come home directly after. I'll have you back by ten at the latest."

"Good. It's been a busy day." Rosalind smiled. "Although, I do adore Maud Warren's poise in the face of ranting, self-righteous men like Thompson. It should be amusing."

"Absolutely. Thompson always begins shouting when his theories are disputed, as if the louder his voice, the more persuasive his argument will be. If nothing else, Thompson's temperamental sideshow will help take your mind off Fitz," Sofia kindly observed, aware of Rosalind's dreams last night, not to mention having heard the full litany of Fitz's transgressions at dinner.

"I'm not sure anything will take my mind off Fitz." Despite every effort to resist, she thought of him constantly. "It's stupid, I know. I'm probably the five hundredth woman who's passed through his life, and none of us has left so much as a ripple on his psyche."

"You never know," Sofia replied, although she was careful not to say more. Fitz wasn't exactly known for his permanent attachments. His note may have been nothing more than a seduction ploy.

"Oh yes, I do," Rosalind firmly said, her pragmatism coming to the fore once again. "I'm not his style if he even has one, which isn't altogether certain since he amuses himself with women of every age, rank, and description. And he's not *my* style by any stretch of the imagination"— she grimaced—"his obvious and impressive charms aside, of course."

"Darling, look, if nothing else, your thoughts will be diverted for a few hours at least." Fitz's impressive charms were too much in demand for her to offer Rosalind any false hope. "And we'll also learn something about Maud's new research. Apparently, female test scores at the universities have been exceeding men's in every discipline."

Rosalind chuckled. "I could have told them that, although it's wonderful that Maud has evidence to document the fact. Have you ever thought about going to university?"

Sofia shook her head. "Not when I'm making so much money with my painting."

"Once my finances are in a better state, I just might apply."

"Good. You spent too many years taking care of Edward. It's about time you thought of yourself." *And if Fitz enters your life again, you'll have someone to pay your university fees.*

"My thoughts exactly." Along with reminding herself to stop her useless brooding about Fitz.

"I'll be here at six. We'll have a quick supper at the tea shop on the corner before we walk to the hall." Crossing her fingers behind the screen of her skirts, Sofia smiled and said, "I don't think you'll be sorry you went."

CHAPTER 32

THE LECTURE WAS by turns irritating, amusing, and inspiring.

Thompson spoke first, offering his conventional lecture on women's role as ordained by God—that of a woman who can sing, dance, draw, walk well into a room, and be the pride of her parents and husband. As a physician and a man of science he also considered it his mission to bring the light of scientific objectivity to the Woman Question. A vast body of research, chiefly of brain weights, head sizes, and facial proportions, *proved*, he asserted, that women were much lower on the evolutionary scale than men and the differences between the sexes could be expected to widen even further as man evolved and specialized. According to Thompson, the more primitive female role concentrated on her animal function of reproduction, and the controlling influence of the ovaries on every aspect of a woman's life, was evident in a full range of diseases from irritability to insanity. He spitefully added that the influence of the ovaries over the mind was particularly on display in woman's artfulness and dissimulation.

After reciting his lengthy list of diseases to which women were prone due to the fact that the Almighty, in creating the female sex, had taken the uterus and built up a woman around it, Thompson concluded that the inequality of the sexes would only increase with the progress of civilization. He urged women to avoid too much reading or mental stimulation or they would risk permanent damage to their reproductive organs and in consequence the grand purpose of their lives: motherhood.

When he finished, he was roundly cheered by his proponents in the audience.

Coming to the podium to a chorus of boos, Maud Warren calmly waited for the catcalls to subside before speaking. She began by suggesting that it might be possible to view doctors' determination to elaborate the nature of woman, the sources of her frailty, and the biological limits of her social role with a touch of cynicism since this newly discovered ill-health among women was scarcely imagined a hundred years ago. The increased attention to women and their ovaries (or at least those of more affluent women) could instead be the result of doctors functioning as businessman. The vague and all-inclusive symptoms supposedly originating in the ovaries had created a very lucrative new field of medicine.

In practice, Maud pointed out, the same doctors who zealously espoused the ills of wealthy, *delicate* women had no time to spare for the poor. Someone had to be well enough to do the work, and working-class women, according to these doctors, were *not* invalids of their ovaries. A very convenient logic, she noted.

The theory of innate female illness predicated on diseased ovaries was skewed to account for class differences with reference to ability to pay, she suggested. Since poor women couldn't pay for medical care, they were miraculously immune from the popular medical and evolutionary opinions.

Maud thoroughly rejected the sickly model of femininity and offered statistics showing how many women were beginning to carve out activist roles for themselves in society. These new women of robust health and independence were entering the universities in great numbers despite various popular manifestos warning that higher education caused women's uteruses to atrophy, induced women to insanity, and precipitously lowered the birth rate among college-trained women. She contrasted the thundering warnings of dire consequences to society by offering evidence of women's significant achievements in colleges and universities, and by so doing, managed to make Thompson apoplectic.

He thundered at her, accusing her of undermining the family and the God-given role of women. He fulminated against the women's movement that was sapping culture of its strength and destroying all those tender qualities of mind and disposition that make women so noble and admired.

When Thompson and his cohorts ceased their shouting, Maud quietly explained that the Woman Question was not in the end up to men to answer. It was a question of what women want and need and how best they can achieve their goals.

Ultimately, it was about equality between the sexes.

As the hall erupted in opposition cheers and jeers, with a wave to Violet and Christina who were enjoying the confrontation, Rosalind and Sofia slipped out into the summer night.

"I prefer not waiting until the police start arresting people," Rosalind explained as they exited the hall. "Although Maud is always so composed. I don't know how she does it. Thompson, in contrast, looks like a lunatic."

"I agree. I wish I could behave with as much maturity. My temper's fierce."

"I'm not sure I'm inclined to admit a failing after Maud's invigorating lecture, but if I were, my temper could be better controlled, too." Rosalind smiled. "Not that I'm in the mood for anything but assertive opinions at the moment. Maud's inspiring."

"For all her achievements—don't forget she has a good marriage, a fine family, and a profession," Sofia observed, concerned Rosalind might be in an overly militant frame of mind to face a possible visitor at home.

"Maud's lucky."

"She works hard to balance her priorities."

"I know, I know—it's not all luck. She's an amazing person."

The night was balmy, the streets still bustling with pedestrians and traffic now that the sultry heat of the day had dissipated.

When they reached the bookshop, Rosalind asked, "Would you like to come up for tea? We can continue singing Maud's praises over a cuppa." She grinned. "That lovely purple tinge on Thompson's face is etched in my memory."

"And mine. The old goat is unbalanced. But it's getting late," Sofia noted. "So thanks for the invitation, but I think I'll go home." She had her instructions. "I might bring over my new hollyhock painting tomorrow and hang it in the gallery, though."

"I'll make room for it in the morning. Speaking of flowers"—Rosalind sniffed the air—"do you smell roses?"

"No," Sofia lied. "You're probably smelling my perfume."

"Ah, no doubt," Rosalind murmured.

"I'll see you tomorrow," Sofia hastily remarked, not wishing to be caught in the middle of Fitz's enterprise. "It won't be too early; Lyla's coming over with my new canvas." After a quick wave, she hurried away.

But the moment Rosalind entered her apartment, the intense scent of roses overwhelmed her. Turning on the light, she took off her straw bonnet and scanned the small parlor. Nothing was amiss. Discarding her hat, she moved through the room, walked into her bedroom, and followed her nose to the open windows, where the sweet fragrance was pungent in the air.

The moon was partially obscured by clouds or the haze that hung over the city in the summer. But even through the dimness and shadow, the contours and shapes in her small

yard and garden looked different. As was the heady scent
of roses and the faint outlines of a *fountain that hadn't
been there when she left*! Along with the sound of *running
water*!

Her heart racing, she dashed back through her apartment, took the stairs at a run, and throwing the back
door open, stood transfixed on the threshold as her backyard was suddenly flooded with light. Hundreds of fairy
lights illuminated the garden, the twinkling bulbs twined
through her small hawthorn tree, strung in graceful loops
on the buildings rimming the garden, corded through
low boxwood borders, offering up a dazzling spectacle of
winding paths, symmetrical parterres, and roses by the
score.

"Do you like it?"

The deep voice came out of the shadows and a moment
later, Fitz emerged from the gloom, his twill trousers and
linen shirt stained and smudged with dirt, the splendor of
his face and form undiminished by the grime, his smile
breathtaking.

"It's very beautiful." *Like you*, she thought, when she
shouldn't think anything of the kind. When she should be
embracing independent womanhood. "You shouldn't have
done it, though." Nor should she allow herself to be captivated by him or his grand gesture.

"I wanted to make amends. And I knew you didn't
like jewelry." He approached her slowly, uncertain of his
reception. Her reply had been decidedly neutral as was her
expression—not a scintilla of a smile graced her face.

"Was Sofia in on your plan?" Snippets of conversation
from the evening suddenly made sense.

"I hope you don't mind," he said to her terse query. "I
wanted to surprise you."

"I'm surprised."

He drew in a small breath, unable to decipher her mood,
the pitch of her tone carefully modulated, minutely cool.
"If you don't like it, I'll change it."

"Because you can do anything you want."

"No, because I want to please you."

"For how long?" Part defiant, part sardonic; she would not be so easily charmed.

"For as long as you wish." Notwithstanding his contemplative afternoon at Mertenside, he'd not known until that very moment he aspired to the concept of forever. "I mean it."

"Until you don't mean it." She softly sighed. "You just want what you want because you can't have it. Before long—I'll give you a week—you'll be appalled at your rash behavior."

He didn't want to argue. He didn't know how to logically or reasonably explain his feelings. He only knew he was vastly content and happy now that she was here with him. "Come, look at the garden," he invited, wanting to avoid a contentious discussion. He held out his hand. "I've learned all the flower names today. Christ, sorry"—he quickly wiped the dirt off his hands on his pant's legs and offered his hand again.

She couldn't help but smile, the image of London's most prodigal rake memorizing flower names and mucking in the dirt an unlikely picture. But vastly endearing. "Then you know more than I do," she replied in a scrupulously bland tone, banishing the word *endearing* from her thoughts. But the moment she placed her hand in his and his fingers gently closed on hers, she was warmed heart and soul.

"At the risk of offending you," he said with a small smile, drawing her down the flagstone path, "I could tell you didn't know much about flowers from the state of your garden. You'll find it much improved."

"I see that, and apparently," she noted, indicating his besmirched clothes with a sweep of her hand, "you did more than supervise."

In the past that would have been his opening to suggest a shared bath, but he was walking on eggshells tonight. "Actually, I learned quite a lot today," he politely said, carefully avoiding anything remotely suggestive of sex.

"Did you know each rose plant needs a banana peel under it for fertilizer?"

"I doubt very many people know that," Rosalind replied with utter sincerity.

"Well, now we both do. Let's sit here." He pointed to a red Chinoiserie garden bench. "You can see most of the garden from this spot and I'll point out the important roses." While she sat and he lounged in his usual way, his long legs stretched out before him, his dusty boots planted on the flagstone, his thigh lightly touching hers, an unwanted shiver raced up her spine.

Gratified to feel her small tremor but not about to jeopardize the occasion by pressing his advantage, Fitz said with well-mannered grace, "If you're interested, I learned in the course of the day and evening that there are what are termed *important* roses. And it's not just to do with rarity or expense. It has to do with duration of flowering, size of the blooms, the intensity of fragrance, the reputation of the hybridizer—Pernet-Ducher in Lyon is the best. That white over there is one of his called Aimée Vibert, and that pink is a bourbon rose called Souvenir de la Malmaison, and the lilac-colored cabbage rose is called Rose de la Reine." He grinned. "Should I go on?"

"You amaze me. I doubt your reputation will survive such humble pursuits," she drolly said, having tamped down her treacherous desires.

"I care nothing for my reputation." She looked like a schoolgirl in her white blouse and green-striped skirt. An enchantress despite her lack of finery.

"But then you never did, I suppose."

"If it bothers you, I'll begin to care," he quietly said.

"You needn't concern yourself with what I wish."

"On the contrary, nothing else matters."

"Fitz, please." He was too close, too beautiful, too destructive to her peace of mind.

He liked that she'd spoken his name so softly; he liked the uncertainty in her tone. He particularly liked that he was with her again no matter the circumstances. This afternoon at Mertenside, he'd discovered that at least. "I'm only happy when I'm with you," he said, husky and low. "I don't know why; I know less why it matters, but it does. I'm sorry in every possible way for what happened to you while I was in Scotland. I want you to take me back." Shocking words from a man who had never asked anything of a woman.

"I can't take you back because I never had you."

"You did." His long lashes drifted fractionally lower. "I didn't know it, but you did."

"If I were so daft and reckless as to agree, I'd only be hurt in the end. You would vanish one day. You know you would."

"I don't think so."

"See." She nodded. "I rest my case."

"I wouldn't leave. Is that better?"

"You're just being accommodating now; you do that well." She smiled wryly. "It's your speciality, darling."

The word *darling* seared itself into his brain, gave him hope. Not that he'd ever had to deal with repudiation before, and for that reason perhaps he chose to be auda-cious. Or maybe love made him say what he'd been loath to say before. "I'd be more than willing to accommodate you for the next fifty years or more if you'd let me," he said, sliding upright on the bench and holding her gaze. "Marry me. I'll make you happy, my word on it."

"Are you drunk?" His proposal was ludicrous.

He shook his head. "I haven't had a drink since yes-terday, and that's a record. We spoiled, self-indulgent debauchees are rarely sober." He smiled. "You called me that the first time we met."

She remembered. "And now you've reformed."

"I believe I have." He grinned. "I aspire to please your every desire. Above all, I want to make you happy." He shrugged faintly. "It's a novel sensation, such high-minded selflessness, but there it is . . . my irresistible compulsion."

"Do self-indulgent debauchees attach any significance to love? Not sex, Fitz, love." She was insane, of course, to ask for so much when he'd promised her marriage. Any other woman would have replied with an unhesitating yes. But after a marriage that had become a casualty of disappointed hopes, she was no longer naive.

"Do *you* love me?" he countered.

She looked away. Too many women had loved him, she jealously thought.

Taking her chin between his thumb and forefinger, he gently turned her head back. "Tell me."

"You didn't answer my question." She would not bestow her heart on a profligate's whim. How could she even contemplate such lunacy?

"I can't live without you," he said, letting his hand drop. "I think of you day and night. I'd keep you in my pocket if I could. And if that's not love, it's something close. You're the world to me." He ran his fingers through his hair, suddenly restive under the unprecedented circumstances. "And I don't say that lightly," he admitted. "You've seriously disrupted my life."

"Maybe it's time someone did." Cautious she might be, but Fitz's sincerity was plain. Was it possible to believe in love again—in a man like Fitz's declaration of love? In the baffling, sometimes fallible and difficult concept?

"You can fix the disorder in my life, though." He grinned, immune to difficulties of any kind if she would agree to be his wife. "Just say yes."

"You're looking way too smug." She doubted any woman had ever said no to him.

He quickly swept his hand over his face. "Better?" But the corners of his mouth were still twitching.

"You can't always have your way," she said half-grudgingly. She'd built an independent life for herself the last few years and Fitz was blowing it apart like a wild force of nature.

"Other than having you say yes, I don't care if I do or not. I'll willingly take orders," he said, shocking himself with his unexpected largesse. Next thing he knew, he'd be writing love poems. "Come, make my mother happy," he quipped, in compensation perhaps for his abnormal compliance. "Marry me."

She gave him a narrowed look. "This isn't about your mother."

"Forgive me. I'll be serious. But for God's sake, say yes and put me out of my misery. If it would help with your decision, let me point out that my architect is redrawing my entire neighborhood project. Your store remains where it is; the buildings on both sides will be lowered slightly to allow more light into your garden. And you can have half of the buildings on the block to do with what you will." He smiled. "I thought you might like to have apartments set up for your poor customers or perhaps a school for the young women you're helping. But you decide and I'll have the papers drawn up."

Suddenly in one fell swoop all her dreams had come true, everything she'd been working for so hard was not only possible but also likely. "It's all overwhelming, Fitz," she whispered, scarcely able to breathe.

"No, darling," he whispered back, taking her hands in his. "You're the one who's overwhelming. Truly, I'm at a loss without you. I can't eat, I can't sleep, I wasn't interested in sex, and until yesterday I'd been drinking myself into an early grave. So when do you want to get married? Tomorrow? Today?" She hadn't formally agreed, but his talent for reading women was functioning again.

"What do you mean you weren't interested in sex?" she asked incredulously, the phrase *not interested in sex* a trumpet blast in her brain.

"You unmanned me, darling. No women looked even remotely interesting. I'll admit it unnerved me at first, but not enough to actually climb in bed with anyone," he casually noted. His libido never in doubt, he'd not been unnerved for long.

"Really," she breathed, his admission the final seal of approval, the ultimate compliment as well.

"Really." He smiled. "I'll expect due compensation for my unusual abstinence."

"Perhaps that can be arranged," she softly said, no longer unsure or in doubt. "Since you happen to be the love of my life."

His brows flickered in playful rejoinder. "I was hoping you'd say that. No, I was desperately hoping you'd say that," he added, not an iota of teasing in his voice this time.

"One more thing—and I apologize for even saying this," Rosalind noted, but not wanting things left unsaid like they'd been with Edward. "I'd like to go to university." Maud's words were still ringing in her ears. Many in the aristocracy viewed higher learning as bourgeoise; she wasn't sure if Fitz was among them.

"Done."

"Just like that?" she whispered.

"I know the provosts at Oxford and Cambridge. I'm a prominent benefactor."

"It's truly frightening, Fitz, being offered so much." She took a small breath against her sudden fear. "What if it all goes away?"

"I'm not Edward," he gently said; he'd read all of Hutchinson's reports. "I promise to love you always. And take care of you."

"What if . . . I don't want . . . to be taken care of?"

He smiled at the new modern woman gazing up at him with tears in her eyes. "Then I won't." He bent his head and gently brushed her lips with his. "Unless there's times you want me to." He kissed her softly. "You tell me when," he whispered.

Her bottom lip trembled. "How about . . . now?"

"I'd love to." His heart was in his eyes. "And that's love, love, not sex, darling. And no one knows the difference better than I. Which reminds me, I brought you some rings," he said, sliding his hand into his trouser pocket. "Don't get upset," he quickly added at the sudden set of her mouth. "They're engagement rings; I was hopeful, not presumptuous. Just hopeful. Here—take your pick." He held open his hand. "Actually, take them all."

She'd never seen such enormous, colored diamonds. There must have been six or eight rings sparkling on his palm. "This is too extravagant for a church mouse," she said with a tremulous smile.

"Nonsense. You're my city mouse now," he added with a grin, sliding a large pink diamond on one of her fingers. "There. Do you like it?"

She took a deep breath and gazed at the ring dwarfing her knuckle. "Who wouldn't?" she whispered.

"How about these then?" He quickly embellished seven more of her fingers with a rainbow of rings.

"I suppose you know this is completely overwhelming." She included the garden with a sweep of her be-ringed hand, the shock to her system considerable after a life of relative penury. "Does anyone ever say no to you?"

Fitz laughed. "You forget, my obstinate little darling, that you've been saying no to me ever since we met."

She smiled, feeling less disadvantaged at his reminder. "And you were captivated."

A teasing light came into his eyes. "That and I wanted to win."

"And now we both have."

"Yes," he softly agreed, knowing full well that only love could have inspired him to change his Monckton Row plans. "So what do you say, my dear Lady Groveland?" he murmured, liking the sound of the designation, liking more that she'd agreed to share her life with him. "Do you think maybe we should start our new life with a bath?"

EPILOGUE

THEY WERE MARRIED by special license the follow-ing day because Fitz wouldn't wait. As it turned out, it was a wise decision since Rosalind discovered she was preg-nant a week later when she threw up on her new husband as they were breakfasting in bed.

He was delighted; she was as well for she hadn't been sure she was capable of having a child after so many years of barrenness in her first marriage.

"It wasn't my fault after all," she cheerfully said a few minutes later, looking over her shoulder at Fitz, who held her between his legs in his very large bathtub.

"Of course it wasn't your fault," he replied, under-standing what she meant but no more willing to mention Edward's name than she. "You're perfect in every way," he added like a besotted husband. "Although you may want to consider putting off your university studies for a time."

"Are you saying I should?" Her voice held the smallest edge.

He grinned. "God no. I wouldn't dare. You and junior or

junioress may go off to university until the day you deliver for all I care."

"And then what?"

"Darling, darling, stop. You're free to do whatever you wish, whenever you wish—short of sleeping with another man, of course. There, I draw the line."

"As I do with you on that same score," she firmly said.

He could have said *I've slept with so many women I've had my fill*, but circumspect, he said instead, "We are agreed. Now then, we should have the dressmaker sent for. You'll be needing new clothes."

And so Fitz unfailingly remained in the months to come, amiable and benevolent in every way to his darling wife. He had, after all, sampled extensively from the smorgasbord of sexual amusements in the past and understood he was most fortunate to have found the love of his life.

As for Rosalind, she too realized that Lady Luck had clearly taken a hand in her meeting Fitz. And having secured her heart's desire, she was truly grateful and blissfully content.

London, January, 1892

Osmond, Baron Lennox, was known for his luck at cards.
Oz would call it skill, but regardless the reason, there was
no doubt he was on a winning streak tonight. A crowd
had slowly gathered round the table as the stakes rose and
Brooks's members, gamesters to the core, were hazard-
ing wagers on how long Elphinstone would last. Viscount
Elphinstone had been losing heavily. While his pére could
afford it, Elphinstone was clearly rankled. He was slumped
in his chair, coatless, disheveled, red-faced, and looking pugnacious—although that may have been due to the
family's propensity to breed true on their bull dog features.

Elphinstone's major opponent at the table was lounging
back in his chair, his dark eyes amused, a half smile on his
handsome face, nonchalance in every lithe contour of his tall,
lean frame. Or rather indifference some might say; Lennox
never seemed to care whether he won or lost.

"It ain't fair, Oz. You always get the good cards," the young
Marquis of Telford groused, staring at his cards with obvious
disgust.

Lennox glanced up. "Lady Luck's been good to me tonight," he murmured, taking a card from his hand and dropping it on the green baize.

"As usual," Elphinstone growled.

A servant approached and bent to whisper in Lennox's ear. The baron nodded without looking up from his cards. "Your turn, Harry. This is my last hand."

"Nell getting tired of waiting?" Harry Green waggishly queried.

Oz's heavy-lidded gaze met his friend's droll glance for a telling moment. "Are you talking to me, Harry?"

The Earl of Ogilvie's youngest son grinned. "Hell no. Slip of the tongue."

"Someday an irate husband is going to have you horsewhipped, Lennox," Elphinstone muttered.

"Only if he's not man enough to call me out," Oz drawled. The viscount's wife was a pretty little hussy; could he help it if she was in hot pursuit?

A sudden hush greeted Oz's soft-spoken challenge.

The eyes of the crowd locked on Elphinstone, each man wondering if he'd respond or more to the point how he'd respond. Lennox was young and wild, his temper as easily provoked as his lust, and while he'd been fucking his way through London the last two years, he'd also had more than his share of duels.

With not so much as a bruise for his exertions.

Elphinstone finally growled something under his breath, his nostrils flaring, his narrowed gaze two pinpricks of anger. Then not inclined to end his life or be maimed, he scanned the breathless crowd. "You won't see blood tonight on my account," he spat. Turning back to Oz, he snarled, "I'll raise you a thousand," recklessly wagering his father's money rather than staking his life.

Held breaths were released and a collective sigh of relief wafted round the table; Elphinstone wouldn't have stood a chance at ten paces. Or even a hundred. Ask Buckley, who'd barely survived his recent ill-advised challenge.

Oz almost felt sorry for Elphinstone, who'd no more meet Oz on the dueling field than he'd satisfy his wife in bed or even know enough to be decent to her. Almost felt sorry. "I'll raise you another thousand," he gently said. The cards he was holding were as near perfect as the law of averages allowed. What the fuck; the ass didn't deserve his pity. "Make that two."

Five minutes later, much richer and in a hurry, he was in the entrance hall and a flunkey was holding out his coat for him. "It's still raining hard out there, sir."

"That's England," Oz said with a smile, sliding his arms into the sleeves and shrugging into his grey overcoat. "More rain than sun." Handing the man a guinea, he turned and strode toward the door. Standing outside under the portico a moment later, he watched the rain pouring down like the heavens had opened up, felt the wind tugging at his coat skirts, surveyed the tree tops tossing in the gusts and was suddenly reminded of Hyderabad during the monsoon season. Christ, he must have drunk more than usual tonight—too much if those old memories were surfacing. Deliberately shaking off the unwanted images, he dashed down the stairs and entered his waiting carriage. "Drive like hell, Sam," he said, dropping into a seat with a smile for his driver who had been taking refuge from the storm inside the conveyance. "I'm late as usual."

"I'll get you there right quick." Sam slipped out the opposite door.

Oz half dozed as the well-sprung carriage careened through the streets of London at a flying pace. His life of late was slightly deficient in sleep. With Nell's husband in Paris, she'd been consuming a good deal of his time. Additionally, he had a shipping business to run, he'd been working at translating a recently purchased rare Urdu manuscript, and of course Brooks's was a constant lure to a man who loved to gamble.

Once Lord Howe returned from Paris next week, Nell would be less persistent in her demands. He smiled faintly. Not that he was complaining. She had a real talent for acrobatics.

As the carriage drew to a halt before a small hotel, newly opened by a gentleman's gentleman who had recently retired with a tidy sum, Lennox came fully awake, shoved open the carriage door, and stepped out into the downpour. "Don't wait, Sam," he shouted, and ran for the entrance.

A doorman threw open the door at his approach, and swiftly crossing the threshold, Oz came to a stop in a small foyer. He smiled at the proprietor behind the counter. "Evening, Fremont. Damn wet out there." He shook the raindrops from his ruffled hair.

"Seasonal weather I'm afraid, sir. Would you like a servant to run you a hot bath or bring up a hot toddy?"

"Maybe later. Which room?"

"Thirteen, sir."

Nell had chosen Blackwood's Hotel in Soho Square for its seclusion, and they'd been coming here with great frequency the past fortnight. Taking the stairs at a run, he rehearsed his apology. He couldn't say the game was too exciting to leave; he'd have to think of another excuse.

Striding down the hallway, he glanced at the passing brass number plates. Arriving at the requisite room, he opened the door and walked in.

"You're late."

A soft, breathy tone, with a touch of impatience. Knowing well what stoked Nell's impatience—the randy tart liked it morning, noon, and night—he answered in a suitably apologetic tone. "Forgive me, darling, but one of my ship captains arrived just as I was leaving the house." Christ, it was dark. Why was just a single wall sconce lit in the far corner? Was Nell in a romantic frame of mind? But then he saw her toss back the covers and pat the bed beside her and rather than question the degree of darkness, he quickly shed his wet coat, his two rings, and stripped off his clothes.

"I like your new perfume," he murmured as he climbed into bed. Dropping back against the pillows, he pulled her close. "Are you cold, darling?" She was wearing a nightgown.

"No."

"In that case, we can dispense with this." Pushing the silk fabric up over her hips with a sweep of his hand, he rolled over her, settled smoothly between her legs, and set out to apologize to Nell in the way she liked best.

A door to the left of the bed suddenly burst open, a gaggle of people trooped in, the bedchamber was suddenly flooded with light and a portly man in the lead pointed at the bed. "There!" he cried. "You are all witnesses to the countess's base and lewd moral turpitude!"

Lennox stared at the woman beneath him. Not red-haired Nell. A blonde. "What the hell is going on," he snarled.

As if in answer, the spokesman declared with an oratorical flourish to the cluster of people crowded round the bed, "If required, you will testify in court as to exactly what you have seen here tonight—to wit . . . a clear-cut case of moral turpitude and venery! Thank you, that will be all," he crisply added, dismissing the motley crew with a wave of his hand.

His eyes like ice, Lennox surveyed the female under him. "I don't believe we've met," he said with soft malevolence. Obviously he'd been gulled for someone's monetary gain.

"Nor need we," the lady coolly replied. "You may go now. Thank you for your cooperation."

Lennox didn't move other than to turn his head toward the only man remaining in the room. "Get the fuck out or I'll shoot you where you stand." He always carried a pistol—a habit from India.

Isolde Perceval, Countess of Wraxell in her own right, nodded at her barrister. Not that he was likely to put his life at risk for her, but should he be considering anything foolish, she rather thought she could deal with this hired actor herself.

As Mr. Malmsey shut the door behind him and quiet prevailed, Isolde gazed up at the very large man pinning her to the bed. "I thought Malmsey explained what was required of you?" she mildly remarked. "But if you'd like an additional payment, kindly get off me, and I'll be happy to fetch my purse and pay you whatever you wish."

Oz's brows rose. "Is this some farce?"

"Far from it. With your cooperation of course. As Mr. Malmsey no doubt pointed out, your silence is required."

Silence about what? Through a minor alcohol-enduced haze, Oz speculated on how he'd landed in this bizarre scenario. "What room number is this?"

"Thirteen."

Then where was Nell? Still waiting somewhere. Merde.

"Don't move," he brusquely said. "I'll be right back." His expression was grim. "If you wish my silence, I suggest you comply."

"There's no need for belligerence. I'm quite willing to accommodate you."

You had to give her credit. The lady wasn't easily rattled, although having organized this performance—with witnesses to boot—bespoke a certain audacity on her part. Sliding off her, he left the bed, slipped on his overcoat, buttoned it, and exiting the room, made his way downstairs to speak to the proprietor.

"A slight problem has arisen, Fremont," he said, with a rueful smile for the man across the counter. "Room thirteen is occupied by an unknown person."

"Oh, dear." The trim, dapper man quickly flipped through the guest ledger and a moment later looked up with a pained expression. "I apologize most profusely, sir. I should have said room twenty-three." His face was beet red. "I most humbly beg your pardon."

"Rest easy, Fremont," Oz replied, good-naturedly. "No great damage has been done. Although, if you'd be so kind as to inform the lady in room twenty-three that I'm unable to meet her tonight, I'd appreciate it. Tell her that a business matter of some importance has delayed me."

"Naturally, sir, as you wish, sir." Relieved he wouldn't meet with the baron's wrath, the proprietor deferentially added, "Would you like me to express your profound regrets to the lady?"

"I would, thank you. And see that she has a carriage waiting for her."

"Yes, sir. Consider it done." Fremont gave no indication that he knew Lennox was nude beneath his coat. The baron was a very generous man, his gratuities commensurate with his fortune. Not to mention, his forgiving nature tonight was a profound relief.

As Oz turned to leave, he swung back. "You don't happen to know the name of the lady in room thirteen?"

"A Mrs. Smith, sir," Fremont answered, one brow lifting at the obvious fraud.

"Ah—I see. Thank you."

Racing back upstairs, Oz slipped through the doorway of room thirteen and shut and locked the door. There she was—right where he'd left her. That she'd not taken the opportunity to run suggested this situation was critical in some way. Interesting . . . as was the lovely lady. Shedding his coat, he walked to the light switch by the connecting door, flicked off the bright overhead fixtures, and moving toward the bed, turned on another wall sconce.

A small apprehension appeared in Isolde's eyes. "What are you doing?" Seated against the headboard, she jerked the covers up to her chin.

He heard himself saying, "Coming to make a bargain with you." While not entirely sure what had motivated his reply, the persuasive influence of a beautiful woman, opportunity, and considerable liquor couldn't be discounted. Not to mention on closer inspection, her charms were even more impressive.

"Kindly do so once you're dressed."

"You're not in a position to give orders," Oz gently noted, thinking he really must have drunk too much tonight since the alarm in the lady's eyes was so perversely satisfying. As though prompted by his thoughts, he glanced around. "Is there any liquor here?"

"No."

But he spied a tray with decanters on a table in the corner and walking over to the table, he poured himself a brandy, returned to the bed, and raised his glass to her. "See, you were mistaken. Would you like some?"

"No, I would not," Isolde crisply replied. "Kindly inform me of this bargain of yours so we may both be on our way."

Since his intentions weren't entirely clear, he climbed back into bed, took a seat beside her, and said, "First tell me why I'm here—because clearly the man Malmsey hired is not." Lifting the glass to his mouth, he drank half the brandy.

Good God, he wasn't the actor! "I have no idea on either score," she tersely said, profoundly troubled by the unsettling turn of events. "If I did, you wouldn't be here annoying me and some anonymous actor would have long since left."

"An actor?" Oz grinned. "Did the poor man know what he was getting into?"

"I'm sure he did. He was well paid for his role."

"Apparently he was," Oz drolly noted, "considering he didn't show up for his performance."

"Obviously, there was some mistake. But," Isolde mockingly added, "since you performed well, all turned out in the end."

"If I agree to accommodate you." The word *perform* was triggering rather explicit images.

"You already have."

"Not completely." This lady along with her story piqued his interest. Or maybe he'd become bored with Nell.

"If it's money you want," she said with a touch of disdain, "just say so and we can stop playing games."

Oz lifted his glass to her. "I haven't even begun playing, countess," he silkily murmured.

"I find your innuendo shameless and irritating," Isolde snapped, bristling with indignation. The man was equally shameless in his nudity; he didn't even attempt to cover himself.

"Now, now," Oz murmured, fascinated by her willful personality, "there's no reason we can't be friends. Where are you from?" He hadn't seen her before, and if she was indeed a countess, he would have met her—and more to the point, wouldn't have forgotten so splendid a woman. She had the face of an enchantress—sensual blue eyes dark with storm clouds, a fine straight nose, soft cherry red lips that fairly begged to be kissed, and a stubborn little chin that was infinitely fascinating to a man who knew far too many willing females. A glorious halo of pale hair framed her features, and even with their brief bodily contact, her voluptuousness was conspicuous.

"I have no intention of being your friend, nor need you know where I'm from." She must extricate herself from this unexpected and potentially disastrous predicament—and quickly. Her plans didn't include someone who might talk out of turn. Everything depended on a nameless lover who couldn't be found and cross-examined.

"Then perhaps," Oz drawled, "I should tell Mr. Malmsey that I don't choose to cooperate with this scheme, and if he persists, I'll sue him for every penny he has."

"You're the one who barged in," she argued, reminding herself that he'd eventually name his price; everyone did.

"And you were the one who said I was late." His lazy smile was full of grace. "Surely I'd have been remiss to keep a lady waiting."

"How very smooth you are. But impertinent, sir."

"While you're quite beautiful," he softly countered. "Although, I expect you already know that. Tell me, is this little drama perpetrated to give your husband cause for divorce? If so, I don't understand why your lover's willing to expose you to all the prurient interest and scandal on your own. Where's the scoundrel's backbone?"

"So you would assume responsibility if your lover was exposed in court?"

"Certainly. Any honorable man would."

"Why then would an honorable man toy with another man's wife?"

Oz's dark brows shot up. " You can't be serious. Or perhaps you live in a cave. Although, if you do," he cheekily murmured, surveying the portion of her nightgown visible above the covers, "you have a fashionable modiste in there with you. That's quality silk you're wearing." Anyone in the India trade knew silk.

"Who are you?" she asked, curious about a man acquainted with grades of silk.

Perhaps she did live in a cave; he was well known for a variety of reasons, some of them actually acceptable. "You tell me first."

She watched him drain the rest of his drink, wondered why she wasn't more alarmed, and wondered as well where he came from with his deeply bronzed skin. "Are you drunk?" Would he remember any of this? How much should she divulge? And how honorable would he be if she related her tale?

He hesitated a fraction of a second. "I'm probably not completely sober."

"Are you dangerous?"

He shot her a look. "To you? Hardly."

"I'm relieved," she sardonically murmured.

He smiled. "I'm relieved you're relieved. Now tell me your name."

"Isolde Perceval."

"From where—the ends of the earth? I haven't seen you in society."

"I avoid society."

"Obviously." He dipped his head. "Osmond Lennox. Pleased to make your acquaintance, ma'am."

"Now that the courtesies have been observed," she sardonically noted, "be so kind as to tell me what you want, so we may end this charade and go our separate ways."

"You."

Her eyes flared wide. "You can't be serious."

"I am." There, certainty—his plans no longer moot— although wealthy noblemen were as a rule unrestrained in their whims. "Think of it as recompense," he said with a small smile, "for the shock to my system. When your witnesses barged in, I thought someone was seeking vengeance for my many sins. Or was about to horsewhip me."

She knew very well what horsewhipping implied, but only interested in extricating herself from this critical impasse, she said, "Well, no one was seeking revenge. You're quite unharmed. And what you ask is naturally impossible."

"Surely you can't claim to be a virgin."

"I hardly think that's an issue I should be discussing with a stranger."

"We're not complete strangers," he drawled, knowing if she'd been a virgin, she would have been quick to say so. Also, a divorce case with witnesses was about adultery. She couldn't possibly be a virgin. "If you prefer not discussing your chastity, explain how you plan to use your obviously hired witnesses?"

She chewed on her bottom lip.

"While you're deciding on your reply, excuse me while I get myself another drink. It's been a very weird night"—he grinned—"at least so far."

She watched him walk away when she shouldn't—when

she should avert her eyes from the sight of a nude man. Or so society would have it. Not that she'd ever been overly concerned with the shibboleths of society. And truth be told, he was quite beautiful in face and form—with an unmistakable brute virility beneath his charming manner. He'd threatened to shoot poor Malmsey and seemed quite capable of doing so. She'd have to pay her barrister an extra premium for that fearsome threat.

As he returned to the bed with his refilled glass, Oz was pleased to see that the lady was no longer clutching the bedclothes to her bosom. He was equally pleased she didn't seem squeamish about a nude man in her bed—another good sign. "Now," he pleasantly began, taking his place beside her once again, "I think I deserve some minimum explanation." He held her gaze for a moment. "Particularly if this goes to court and I happen to be involved."

"It shouldn't go to court."

"Shouldn't or won't?"

She made a small moue. Frederick had threatened a breach of promise suit among other extortion demands.

"That's what I thought. So is this about your marriage?"

"No."

He shot her a sharp look. "No?"

"I'm not married."

"But you were." She'd been designated a countess by the barrister.

"No."

He softly sighed. "I'm not leaving until I know what's going on, so you might as well tell me. I can stay here as long as Fremont keeps bringing up liquor."

"You know the proprietor?"

"Yes, Mrs. Smith," he sardonically replied.

"He shouldn't have disclosed that."

"I pay him well."

"For his silence about your assignations."

He nodded.

"So you're a Lothario," she said with distaste.

"No, I'm a man. Now what's going on."

His voice had taken on an edge, while talk of him staying

here for days was disconcerting not to mention worrisome for any number of reasons. "Very well, if you must know—"

"I do," he brusquely interposed.

"Then I'll tell you. I'm a countess in my own right, but as you know, in situations such as mine, I simply hold the title as steward for the next male in line to inherit. In my case, a cousin has decided he doesn't wish to wait—I might outlive him you see—and he intends to marry me or use any number of other tactics to gain access to my funds."

"What of a marriage settlement?" They were written to protect family fortunes.

"First, I loathe my cousin and wouldn't marry him if he was the last man on the face of the earth. Secondly, Frederick's pursuit has been persistent and very determined since his gambling losses have mounted. I expect there'd be coercion involved with a marriage settlement. He's completely unscrupulous."

"Have you no one to protect you?"

"Naturally, I could hire guards, but I'm hoping it won't come to that. My plan"—she smiled—"in which you recently participated, is to so completely ruin my reputation so that even Frederick will be forestalled, at least in his marriage plans. The rest Malmsey can handle in court." Her voice took on a derisive tone. "I doubt he'd be personally moved by this scandal, but fortunately for me he has a domineering mother who prides herself on virtue and decorum."

"In the scramble for a fortune, people have been known to overlook even the most egregious scandals," Oz drily noted. "How can you be sure your scheme will serve?" He really meant how can you be so naive?

"I can't of course. Not completely. Yet you've not met Lady Compton."

"Actually, I've had the misfortune," he replied with a grimace. "My condolences on your prospective mother-in-law."

"Bite your tongue," she retorted. "If all goes well, I shan't be saddled with her or her despicable son. My little drama, as you call it, will be published in all the scandal sheets tomorrow—without naming my partner of course, only myself. You are quite safe you see. Now, if you wish payment, I'd be more than happy to pay you. Money," she quickly added.

"I don't need money." As heir to the largest banking fortune in India, he could buy a good share of the world if he wished. And he retracted his naive assessment. The scandal sheets could ruin a person. Although, someone with large gambling debts might overlook even that degree of infamy.

She shifted slightly under his gaze. "Surely you wouldn't take advantage of a woman."

"I doubt I'd have to."

Her brows arched into perfect half-moons. "Is that usually effective?"

He smiled. "Always."

"Such arrogance." She glanced at his crotch. "And yet—I see no visible signs of your interest."

"I was raised in India."

"And?" More arched brows and a decidedly jaundiced look.

"And I'm capable of controlling my, er, impulses." He grinned. "Although, if you'd like to see interest"—he swept his hand downward—"observe."

The transformation was not only instant but profound, and wide-eyed, she took in the provocative sight.

"Is that better?" he said velvet soft. "Interest-wise?"

She slowly wrenched her gaze from the display, his enormous erection stretching from crotch to navel, his blood pulsing wildly through the tracery of tumescent veins standing out in high relief on his resplendent length. "You're definitely a flashy fellow," she said, meeting his amused gaze, fully aware as well of the soft pulsing beginning to flutter through her vagina. "Still, I think I'll restrain myself."

"At least keep me company for a short while." His voice was well-mannered, his gaze amicable. "Thanks to you, I seem to have missed my assignation. Surely, that's not too much to ask." He recognized the look of longing in a woman's eyes. He knew as well that her taut nipples pressing through the silk of her gown had something to do with his erection and her desires—restrained as they might be. Temporary as they might be if he had his way. "Would you like a drink? Fremont set out a nice assortment of liquor."

The smallest of hesitations.

"Why not," she said, thinking to humor him and better gain her ends.

"Then I'll be right back, ma'am"—he glanced at her over his shoulder as he slipped off the bed—"correction . . . miss." He casually strolled away as if he wasn't nude and blatantly aroused, she wasn't a stranger, and they'd be sharing nothing more than a game of whist when he returned. "You have a choice," he offered, standing at the liquor tray a moment later. "Sherry, cognac, brandy, or hock."

"Cognac. Just a little."

"How are you getting home?" he asked, as he poured her drink. "Could I drive you somewhere?"

"No, thank you," she replied, trying not to stare at his enormous erection. "I believe Malmsey is waiting for me."

He nodded toward the door through which the surprise party had entered. "Waiting in there?" He preferred not being monitored.

She shook her head. "Downstairs."

Good. "So does Malmsey know Fremont as well?" he queried, moving back to the bed.

"I'm not sure. He might."

At least he does now. Fortunately, Fremont was the soul of discretion; Lady Perceval's intrigue was safe. Not that it should matter to him one way or the other, yet she shouldn't have to suffer the unwanted machinations of her cousin. Nor should she be required to resort to such drastic measures to retain control of her title and wealth. "Would you like me to call out Compton?" he abruptly asked, handing her a glass. "I could see that he never bothers you again." While dueling was illegal, it was still privately practiced.

The casual certainty in his voice gave her pause and, quite inappropriately, pleasure as well. "While I appreciate the offer," she more prudently replied, "I don't think it would serve."

"It would serve perfectly. He'd be dead—not a great loss if you ask me, the man cheats at cards. Your reputation would remain unscathed and"—he grinned as he settled back on the bed and rested against the pillows—"you might be inclined to thank me in some agreeable way."

She laughed. "I admit there's a certain appeal to your plan, but, no, I couldn't be party to something so crass." If he could urbanely disregard his erection, she should be able to as well.

"As if his wanting to marry you for your money isn't crass."

She smiled. "So blood-thirsty, Lennox. Is it your Indian upbringing?"

"Hell no. Dueling is a European foolishness wrapped up in a mantle of honor. In India if you want someone murdered, you hire assassins or a poisoner and have the job quietly done." He shrugged dismissively. "It's different here."

"My goodness. You quite alarm me."

"No I don't. Not unless by alarm you mean something else entirely."

"Such as?"

"Your nipples," he said, nodding at her breasts; he didn't mention her veiled glances at his erection. "They've been signaling your aspirations for some time now."

"Aspirations don't necessarily equate with actions."

His lashes lowered faintly. "In our case, why not? We're alone. I'm thoroughly aroused as you can see," he politely said, as if she hadn't noticed several times already. "I can tell that you're not exactly indifferent to me. What's the point in denying ourselves?"

"So blunt, Lennox," she sardonically observed. "No sonnets or odes to charm a lady?"

"'Ah Love! Could you and I with Fate conspire. To grasp this sorry scheme of things entire. Would not we shatter it to bits. And then remold it to our heart's desire.' I could also recite it in the original Persian if you like." He smiled. "Is that better now? Or would you like more verses to entice you?"

"I'm not sure I wish to be enticed."

"Why not? Making love is one of life's great pleasures."

"Or sorrows."

He could have asked, but he didn't want to know. Even

while he understood the merits of asking in terms of facilitating a seduction, he didn't. There was something about her, an intrepid heroine willing to stand up for her rights no matter the consequences, that reminded him of things he'd rather forget. Right and wrong had nothing to do with the reality of the world, he'd discovered. You could be moral to the core and right as rain, and no one cared.

He had his own sorrows when it came to love.

All he wanted tonight was sex.

And if not with Nell, Lady Perceval would do.